About

USA Today bestsellin[g] ... lively, sexy stories for b... Medical Romance lines... child, Sarah dreamed of... took a few interesting det... ...way, she is now living that dream. With her writing career, she has successfully combined business with pleasure and she firmly believes that reading romance is one of the most satisfying and fat-free escapist pleasures available.

Carol Marinelli recently filled in a form where she was asked for her job title and was thrilled, after all these years, to be able to put down her answer as 'writer'. Then it asked what Carol did for relaxation. After chewing her pen for a moment Carol put down the truth—'writing'. The third question asked—'What are your hobbies?' Well, not wanting to look obsessed or, worse still, boring, she crossed the fingers on her free hand and answered 'swimming and tennis'. But, given that the chlorine in the pool does terrible things to her highlights, and the closest she's got to a tennis racket in the last couple of years is watching the Australian Open, I'm sure you can guess the real answer.

Scarlet Wilson wrote her first story aged eight and has never stopped. Her family have fond memories of *Shirley and the Magic Purse*, with its army of mice, all with names beginning with the letter 'M'. An avid reader, Scarlet started with every Enid Blyton book, moved on to the *Chalet School* series and many years later found Mills & Boon.

She trained and worked as a nurse and health visitor, and currently works in public health. For her, finding Mills & Boon Medical Romances was a match made in heaven. She is delighted to find herself among the authors she has read for many years.

Scarlet lives on the West Coast of Scotland with her fiancé and their two sons.

Hot Single Docs
COLLECTION

July 2018

August 2018

September 2018

October 2018

November 2018

December 2018

January 2019

February 2019

Hot Single Docs: Waiting For You

SARAH MORGAN

CAROL MARINELLI

SCARLET WILSON

MILLS & BOON

Published in Great Britain 2018
by Mills & Boon, an imprint of HarperCollins*Publishers*
1 London Bridge Street, London, SE1 9GF

HOT SINGLE DOCS: WAITING FOR YOU © 2018 Harlequin Books S.A.

St. Piran's: Prince on the Children's Ward © 2012 Harlequin Books S.A
Special thanks and acknowledgement are given to Sarah Morgan for her contribution to the *St. Piran's Hospital* series.

200 Harley Street: Surgeon in a Tux © 2014 Harlequin Books S.A
Special thanks and acknowledgement are given to Carol Marinelli for her contribution to the 200 Harley Street series.

200 Harley Street: Girl from the Red Carpet © 2014 Harlequin Books S.A.
Special thanks and acknowledgement are given to Scarlet Wilson for her contribution to the 200 Harley Street series.

ISBN: 978-0-263-26832-4

09-1218

MIX
Paper from
responsible sources

FSC
www.fsc.org
FSC™ C007454

This book is produced from independently certified FSC™ paper to ensure responsible forest management.

For more information visit: www.harpercollins.co.uk/green

Printed and bound in Spain by CPI, Barcelona

ST. PIRAN'S:
PRINCE ON THE
CHILDREN'S WARD

SARAH MORGAN

CHAPTER ONE

TASHA rehearsed her speech as she walked through the busy emergency department towards the on-call room. Inside she was panicking, but she was determined not to let that show.

Hello, dear darling brother, I know you're not expecting me, but I thought I'd just drop in and see how you're doing. No, she couldn't say that. He'd know instantly that something was wrong.

You're looking gorgeous today. No, way too creepy, and anyway they usually exchanged insults so he'd definitely know something was up.

Josh, of all my brothers, you've always been my favourite. No. She didn't have favourites.

You're the best doctor in the world and I've always admired you. That one just might work. Her brother certainly was an excellent doctor. He'd been her inspiration. And her rock. When their father had walked out, leaving his four children and his fragile, exhausted wife, it had been Josh, the eldest, who had taken charge. Wild, handsome Josh, whose own marriage was now in a terrible state.

But at least he'd had the courage to get married, Tasha thought gloomily. She couldn't ever imagine herself doing anything that brave.

Was it because of their parents, she wondered, that all the O'Haras were so bad at relationships?

Since her last relationship disaster, she'd given up and concentrated on her career. A career couldn't break your heart—or so she'd thought until a few weeks ago.

Now she knew differently.

Terror gripped her

She'd messed everything up.

Hating the feeling of vulnerability, Tasha stopped outside the door. Fiercely independent, it stuck in her throat that she needed to ask her brother for help, but she swallowed her pride and knocked. She needed someone else's perspective on what had happened and the one person whose judgement she trusted was her older brother.

Seconds later the door was jerked open and Josh stood there, buttoning up his shirt. His hair was dishevelled and he was badly in need of a shave. Clearly he'd had a night with no sleep but what really caught her attention was the stupid grin on his face. A grin that faded the instant he saw her.

'Tasha?' Astonishment was replaced by shock and he cast a fleeting glance over his shoulder before pushing her back into the corridor and closing the door firmly behind him. 'What are you doing here?'

'What sort of greeting is that?' Badly in need of a hug, Tasha heard her voice thicken and the bruises of the last month ached and throbbed inside her. 'I'm your little sister. You're supposed to be pleased to see me.'

'I am, of course, but—Tash, it's seven-thirty in the morning.' Josh let out a breath and rubbed his hand over his face to wake himself up. His free hand. The one that wasn't holding the doorhandle tightly. 'I wasn't expecting— You took me by surprise, that's all. How did you know where I was?'

'I asked one of the nurses. Someone said they thought you were in the on-call room. What's wrong with you? You look ruffled.' It was the first time she'd seen her cool, confident brother anything other than immaculate. Tasha looked from him to the door that he was holding tightly shut. 'Did I wake you?'

'No. I— Yes, but it doesn't matter.'

'Busy night?'

'Sort of.' His gaze darted to the corridor and back to her. 'What are you *doing* here, Tasha?'

Because she was watching his face, she saw the fevered expression in her brother's eyes and the way the flush spread across his cheekbones. The signs pointed to one thing...

He had a woman in the room.

But why be so secretive about the whole thing? His marriage to Rebecca was over—there was no reason why he shouldn't have a relationship. Surely he wasn't embarrassed about her knowing he had a sex life? It was no secret that women found her brother irresistible.

Still, it was a relief to find an explanation for his weird behaviour and she was about to tease him unmercifully when she remembered that she couldn't afford to antagonise him.

Instead, she gave him a playful punch on the arm. 'I thought I'd just drop in and see you.'

'Before breakfast?'

'I'm an early riser.'

'You mean you're in trouble.' His dry tone reminded her that her brother knew her too well.

Tasha thought about everything that had happened over the last month. *Had she done the wrong thing?* 'Not trouble exactly,' she hedged. 'I just thought it was a long time since we'd had a good chat. Is there somewhere we can talk?' She glanced at the on-call room but he jerked his head towards the corridor.

'My office. Let's go.'

Feeling like a schoolgirl on detention, Tasha slunk after him through the department, aware of the curious stares of the staff. The main area was packed with patients, including a young girl lying on a trolley, holding her mother's hand. Noticing that the child was struggling to breathe, Tasha moved instinctively towards her just as a doctor swept up in a white coat. With a murmur of apology, Tasha moved to one side, reminding herself that this wasn't her patient. Or even her hospital. She didn't work here, did she?

She didn't work anywhere.

Her stomach lurched. Had she been impulsive and hasty? *Stupid?*

It was all very well having principles, but was there a point where you should just swallow them?

Trapped by sudden panic, she paused. The conversation drifted towards her. 'Her hay fever has suddenly made her asthma worse,' the mother was telling the young doctor. 'Her breathing has been terrible and her eyes and face are all puffy.'

Tasha gave the child a sympathetic smile, wishing she was the one taking the history and searching for the problem. The fact that her hands ached to reach for a stethoscope simply renewed her feeling that she might have done the wrong thing.

Medicine, she thought. She loved medicine. It was part of her. Not working in a hospital made her feel like a plant dragged up by its roots and thrown aside. Without her little patients to care for, she was wilting.

Biting her tongue to stop herself intervening, she followed her brother down the corridor but something about the child nagged at her brain. Puffy eyes. Hay fever? Frustrated with herself for not being able to switch off, she quickened her pace. It wasn't her business. This wasn't even her department. And anyway, what did she know? She was feeling so battered and bruised by the events of the past few weeks she didn't trust herself to pass opinion on anything, not even the adverse effects of a high pollen count. Feeling really dejected, she followed her brother into his office.

It was stacked with books and medical journals. In one corner was a desk with a computer and an overflowing tray of paper. Tasha noticed that the photograph of Rebecca had gone and she felt a stab of guilt that she hadn't asked how he was. Was she was turning into one of those awful people who only thought about themselves? 'How are you doing? How are things with Rebecca?'

'Cordial. Our separation is probably the first thing we've ever agreed on. It's all in the hands of the lawyers. Sit down.' Josh shifted a pile of medical journals from the chair to the floor but Tasha didn't feel like sitting down. She was filled with restless energy. The stability of her brother's life contrasted heavily with the instability of her own. She'd been sailing along nicely through life and now she'd capsized her boat and she had no idea where the tide was going to take her.

The lump in her throat came from nowhere and she swallowed hard.

Damn.

Not now.

As the only girl in a family of four older brothers, she'd learned that if you cried, you never heard the last of it.

Fighting the emotion, she walked to the window and opened it. 'I love Cornwall.' She closed her eyes and breathed deeply. 'I've lived in so many places since I became a doctor and yet this is still home. I can smell the sea. I can't wait to pick up my surfboard. I've been trapped in a city for too long.' The plaintive shriek of a seagull made her open her eyes and for a moment the memories threatened to choke her.

Home.

'So, what brings you banging on my door at this unearthly hour—what have you done?' Josh sounded distracted. 'Please tell me you haven't killed a patient.'

'No!' Outrage was sharp and hot, slicing through the last of her composure. 'Far from it. I *saved* a patient. Two patients, actually.' Tasha clenched her fists, horrified to realise just how badly she needed someone else to tell her she'd done the right thing. *That she hadn't blown her career on a childish whim.* 'I had an incident—sort of. You know when you just have a feeling about a patient? Perhaps you haven't actually had test results back from the lab, but sometimes you don't need tests to tell you what you already know. Well, I had one of my feelings—a really strong feeling. I know it wasn't exactly the way to go about things, but—'

'Tasha, I'm too tired to wade through hours of female waffle. Just tell me what you've done. Facts.'

'I'm not waffling. Medicine isn't always black and white. You should know that.' Tasha's voice was fierce as she told him about the twins, the decisions she'd made and the drug she'd used.

Josh listened and questioned her. 'You didn't wait for the results of the blood cultures? And if it wasn't on the hospital-approved formulary—'

'They had it in stock for a different indication. You remember I went to the conference of the American Academy of Pediatrics last year? I told you about it when we met for supper that night. The data is *so* strong, Josh. We should be using it in Britain, but it's all money, money, money—'

'Welcome to the reality of health-care provision.'

'The drug is at least fifty per cent more effective than the one I was supposed to use.'

'And three hundred per cent more expensive.'

'Because it's good,' Tasha snapped, 'and research of that quality comes at a price.'

'Don't lecture me on the economics of drug development.'

'Then don't lecture me on wanting to do the best for my patients. Those babies would have died, Josh! If I'd waited for the results or used a different drug, they would have died.' In her head she saw their tiny bodies as they lay with the life draining out of them. She heard their mother's heartbreaking sobs and saw the father, white faced and stoical, trying to be a rock while his world fell apart. And she saw herself, facing the most difficult decision of her professional life. 'They lived.' She felt wrung out. Exhausted. But telling her brother had somehow made everything clearer. Whatever happened to her, whatever the future held, it had been worth the price. She didn't need anyone else to tell her that.

'The drug worked?'

'Like magic.' The scientist in her woke up and excitement fizzed through her veins. 'It could transform the management of neonatal sepsis.'

'Have you written it up for one of the journals?'

'I'm going to. I just need to find the time.' And now she had time, she thought gloomily. Oodles of it.

'But the hospital authorities didn't approve and now you're in trouble?'

'I didn't exactly follow protocol, that's true, but I'd do the same thing again in the same circumstances. Unfortunately, my boss didn't agree.' Tasha turned her head and stared out of the window. 'Which is why I resigned.' Saying the word made her heart plummet. It sounded so—final.

'You did what?' Josh sounded appalled. 'Please tell me you're kidding.'

'No. I resigned on principle.' The anger rose, as fresh and raw as it had been on that morning when she'd faced her boss after two nights without sleep. 'I said to him, *What sort of department are you running when your budget comes before a baby's life?*'

'And no doubt you went on to tell him what sort of department he was running. Tactful, Tasha.' Josh rubbed his hand over his jaw. 'So you questioned his professional judgement and dented his ego.'

'A man of his position shouldn't need to have his ego protected. He shouldn't be that pathetic.'

'Did you tell him that as well?'

'I told him the truth.'

Josh winced. 'So…I'm assuming, given that he was the sort of guy to protect his ego, that he didn't take it well?'

'He's the sort of person who would stand and watch someone drown if health and safety hadn't approved a procedure for saving them. He said the manufacturer did not present a sufficiently robust economic analysis.' Tasha felt the emotion rush down on her and forced herself to breathe. 'So then I asked him if he was going to be the one who told the parents they'd lost both their babies because some idiot in a suit sitting behind his desk had crunched the numbers and didn't think their children's lives were worth the money.'

Josh closed his eyes briefly. 'Tasha—'

'Sorry.' The lump in her throat was back and this time it wasn't going anywhere. 'I *know* I should have been unemotional about the whole thing but I just can't be. Honestly, I'm steaming mad.'

'You don't say? Are you about to cry on me?'

'No, absolutely not.'

'The only time I've ever seen you cry was when Cheapskate died.'

They shared a look. Cheapskate had been the dog their mother had bought after their father had walked out. Tasha remembered hugging his warm body and feeling his tail thumping against her leg. She remembered thinking, *Don't ever leave me,* and then being devastated when he'd done just that.

'He was a great dog.'

'He was a lunatic.' But Josh's eyes were gentle. 'Tell me about those babies you saved. Are they still doing well?'

'Discharged home. You should have seen it, Josh. You know what it's like, trying to calculate these paediatric doses—they never have trial data in the right age of child, but this...' She smiled, the doctor in her triumphant. 'It's why I trained. To push boundaries. To save a life.'

'And you saved two.'

'And lost my job.'

'You shouldn't have resigned.'

It was a question she'd asked herself over and over again. 'I couldn't work with the man a moment longer. He was the sort who thought women should be nurses, not doctors.

Basically he's a—a—' She bit off the word and Josh gave a faint smile.

'I get the picture. Has it occurred to you that you might be too idealistic, Tasha?'

'No. Not too idealistic.' The conviction came from deep inside her. 'Isn't that why we're doctors? So that we can push things forward? If we all did what doctors have always done and no more, we wouldn't have progress.'

'There are systems—'

'And what if those systems are wrong? I can't work for someone like that. Sooner or later I would have had to inject him with something seriously toxic…' Tasha gave a cheeky smile '…but first I would, of course, have made sure it was approved by the formulary committee.'

'You're incorrigible.'

'No, I'm a doctor. I can accept that there are some patients I can't help. What I *can't* accept is that there are some patients I'm not allowed to help because someone has decided the treatment is too expensive! I mean, who decides what's important?' Tasha paced across his office, her head swirling with the same arguments that had tormented her for weeks. 'I told him that if the chief executive took a pay cut we'd be able to easily fund this drug for the few babies likely to need it.'

'I'm beginning to see why you felt the need to resign.'

'Well, what would you have done?'

'I have no idea.' Her brother spread his hands. 'It's impossible to say if you're not in that situation. Why didn't you wait for the blood cultures? Or use the first-line choice?'

'Because the twins were getting sicker by the minute and I felt that time was crucial. If we'd waited for that one drug, only for it to fail… My instincts were shrieking at me, Josh. And even while I was running tests, my consultant was telling me it wasn't sepsis and that the twins were suffering from something non-specific caused by the stress of delivery.' And she'd spun it around in her head, over and over again, looking for answers. 'Sometimes you see a patient and you're going through the usual and it all seems fine, except you know it isn't fine because something in here…' she tapped her head '…something in here is sending you warnings loud and clear.'

'You can't practise medicine based on emotion.'

'I'm not talking about emotion. I'm talking about instinct. I tell you, Josh, I *know* when a child isn't well. Don't ask me how.' She held up her hand to silence him. 'I just know. And I was right with the twins. But apparently that didn't matter to Mr Tick-All-The-Boxes Consultant. He has to play things by the book and if the book is wrong, tough. Which is a lame way to practise medicine.'

'And no doubt you told him that, too?'

'Of course. By the time he'd had all his evidence, he would have had two dead bodies. And he was angry with me because I saved their lives. He could have had a lawsuit on his hands, but did he thank me?' The injustice of it was like a sharp knife in her side, digging, twisting. 'Haven't you ever used instinct when you treat a patient?'

'If by instinct you mean clinical judgement, then, yes, of course, but, Tasha—'

'Wait a minute.' Tasha interrupted him, her brain working and her eyes wide. 'That little girl—'

'What little girl?'

'The one waiting to be seen in the main area. I heard the mother say that hay fever was making her asthma worse, but her eyelids were swollen and her face was puffy. I thought at the time that something wasn't right—just didn't seem like allergy to me—and—'

'That little girl is not your patient, Tasha.'

'She was wheezing.'

'As she would if she had asthma.'

'As she would if she had left-sided venous congestion. I knew there was something about her that bothered me.' Tasha picked up his phone and thrust it at him. 'Call the doctor in charge of her, Josh. Tell her to do the tests. Maybe she will anyway, but maybe she won't. In my opinion, that child has an underlying heart condition. Undiagnosed congenital anomaly? She needs an ECG and an echo.'

'Tasha—'

'Just do it, Josh. Please. If I'm wrong, I'll give up and get a job in a garden centre.'

With a sigh, Josh picked up his phone and called the doctor responsible for seeing the child.

While he talked, Tasha stood staring out of the window, wishing she didn't always get so upset about everything. Why couldn't she be emotionally detached, like so many of her colleagues? Why couldn't she just switch off and do the job?

'She's going to do a full examination, although she thinks it's asthma and allergy combined. We'll see. And now you need to relax.' Josh's voice was soft. 'You're in a state, Tasha.'

'I'm fine.' It was a lie. She'd desperately wanted a hug but was afraid that if someone touched her she'd start crying and never stop. 'But I do find myself with a lot of free time on my hands. I thought…' She hesitated, *hating* having to crawl to her brother. 'You're important. Can you pull a few strings here? Get me a job? The paediatric department has a good reputation.'

'Tasha—'

'Paediatrics is my life. My career. I'm good, Josh. I'm good at what I do.'

'I'm not debating that, but—'

'Yes, you are. You're worrying I'll mess things up for you here.'

'That isn't true.' Josh stood up and walked over to her. 'Calm down, will you? You're totally stressed out. Maybe what you need is a break from hospitals for a while.'

'What I need is a *job*. I love working with kids. I love being a doctor. And then there's the practical side. I was living in a hospital flat so now I'm homeless as well as jobless.'

Tasha felt as though she had an enormous mountain to climb. 'Resigning seemed like the only option at the time. Now I realise why more people don't resign on principle. It's too expensive.'

'I can't pull strings to get you a job at the hospital, Tasha. Not at the moment. We've spent a fortune opening a new paediatric burns unit. There's a head-count freeze.'

'Oh.' Her stomach swooped and fell as another door slammed shut in her face. 'No worries. I'll sort something out.' She tried to subdue the niggling worry that her last consultant wouldn't give her a decent reference. 'Sorry, I shouldn't have asked you. I shouldn't have just shown up here.' *The list of things she shouldn't have done was growing.*

'I'm glad you did. It's been too long since I saw you. All you've done for the past three years is work. Since things ended with Hugo, in fact.'

Hugo? Shrinking, Tasha wondered why her brother had chosen that particular moment to bring up her disastrous love life. Could the day get any worse? 'I love my work.' *Why was he looking at her like that?* 'What's wrong with loving my work?'

'No need to get defensive. Maybe it's time to take a break. Rediscover a social life.'

'Social life? What's that?'

'It's part of work-life balance. You were going to get married once.'

The reminder scraped like sandpaper over sensitive skin. 'A moment of madness.' Tasha spoke through her teeth. 'Do you mind if we don't talk about it? Just thinking about Hugo makes me want to put my fist through something and at the moment I can't afford to pay for the damage. Anyway, you're a fine one to talk. You're a total workaholic.' *But he'd spent the night with a woman.*

Tasha wondered if he'd confide in her, but Josh was flicking through some papers on his desk.

'How flexible are you?'

'I can touch my toes and do a back flip.' Her joke earned her an ironic glance.

'The job,' he drawled. 'How would you feel about a break from paediatrics?'

'I love paediatrics, but...' But she was desperate. She needed something. Not just for the money but to stop herself thinking and going slowly mad. She needed to be active. 'What do you have in mind?'

'I happen to know a man in desperate need of twenty-four-hour nursing care for the next month or so. He's asked me to sort something out for him.'

Tasha instinctively recoiled. 'You want me to give bed baths to some dirty old man who's going to pinch my bottom?' She frowned at the laughter in her brother's eyes. 'What's so funny about that? You have a sick sense of humour.'

'What if I tell you the guy in question happens to be seriously rich.'

'Who cares?' Tasha thrust her hands into the back pockets of her jeans, wondering what Josh was finding so funny. Her brother was clearly enjoying a joke at her expense and she felt a flash of irritation that he could laugh when she was in such a mess. 'What's the relevance of his financial status? You think I'll nurse him, he'll fall in love and marry me, then I'll kill him off and inherit his millions? When you suggested a job change, I didn't realise you were talking about a sugar daddy.'

'He's too young to be your sugar daddy.'

'And I'm not interested in marriage. I'm a cold-hearted career-woman, remember? I'm dedicating my life to my patients. So far my longest and most successful relationship has been with my stethoscope.'

'This guy isn't interested in marriage either, so you'll make a good pair. Strictly speaking, he should be in hospital for at least another week but he's creating hell so they're happy to discharge him providing he arranges professional help. He needs someone medical to deliver quality care at home and he's willing to pay premium rates.' He named a figure that made Tasha's jaw drop.

'He obviously has more money than sense. What's the catch?'

'The catch is that he's an athletic, super-fit guy who isn't used to being stuck in bed. As a result his temper is somewhat volatile and he's terrifying everyone who comes within a metre of him. But I'm sure you'll cope with that. I'm guessing it will take you about—oh—five minutes before you point out his shortcomings.'

'As jobs go it doesn't sound appealing...' But it was a job. And it was just for a couple of weeks. 'I suppose it would give me something to do while I look for a more progressive paediatric department. A place where the patient takes priority over paperwork and protocol.' Tasha frowned as she weighed up the pros and cons. 'So basically I have to help Mr Grumpy Guy with his physio, say *There, there* when he's cranky, feed him antibiotics and check he's not weight bearing. Anything else I need to know? Like his name?'

Josh smiled. 'His name, little sister, is Alessandro Cavalieri.'

Tasha felt the strength drain from her legs. Her heart pounded with a rhythm that would have concerned her had she not been too busy staring at her brother. 'Alessandro? *The* Alessandro?'

'The very same. His Royal Highness.'

She hadn't thought it was possible for the whole body to blush. Suddenly she was a teenager again and sobbing her heart out. 'The answer is no.' The words stumbled out of her mouth, disjointed, shaky. 'No! And don't look at me like that.'

'I thought you'd jump at the chance. You were crazy about him. He was all you ever talked about—Alessandro, Alessandro, Alessandro.' Josh mimicked her tone and Tasha felt the flush of mortification spread from her neck to her ears.

'I was seventeen,' she snapped. 'It may have escaped your notice but I've grown up since then.' But not enough. Not enough to be cool and detached. Not Alessandro. *No, no, no.* The humiliation crawled over her skin.

'I know you've grown up. That's why I'm offering you the job. If you still felt the same way you felt about him back then, you wouldn't be safe.' Josh's eyes teased her. 'Oh, boy, were you dangerous. Teenage hormones on legs. You threw yourself at him. Being royalty, he travelled everywhere with an armed guard but the person he really needed protection from was you. Every time he turned round, there you were in another minuscule bikini. I seem to remember he told you to come back when you'd grown a chest.'

Tasha relived humiliation and discovered it was no better the second time around. Dying inside, she folded her arms and gave her brother a mocking smile. 'Laugh it up, why don't you?'

'My little sister and the prince. You used to scribble his name all over your school books. I particularly liked the *Princess Tasha* you carved on the apple tree in the garden, although the heart was a weird shape.' Josh was clearly enjoying himself hugely and Tasha tapped her foot on the floor, irritated on the outside and squirming on the inside as she remembered those horrible, hideous months.

She'd been a little girl with very big dreams. And when those dreams had burst… 'Have you quite finished?'

'For now. Good job you were a late developer or he might have taken you up on your offer. Alessandro has always had a wicked reputation with women.'

And her brother clearly had no idea just how well deserved that reputation was, Tasha thought desperately, trying to block out images she just couldn't face.

Josh was still smiling. 'Anyway, he's been nagging me to find him someone to nurse him but it's been a nightmare because of the security clearance. And I have to be careful who I give him because if they're pretty he'll seduce them.

It's unbelievably complicated. You have no idea how much red tape we're trying to cut through. If we wait for the palace to approve someone, the guy will be in hospital for at least six months and that can't happen because the press are disrupting the place.'

'Why is security a problem?'

'He's the crown prince. Don't you watch the news? His older brother was killed in an accident. All very tragic.' Josh rummaged through the papers on his desk and pulled out a newspaper. 'Here. Your teenage crush is now officially Europe's most eligible bachelor.'

Tasha snatched the newspaper from him. Her head was filled with unsettling images of Alessandro playing in the garden with her brothers. *Alessandro stripped to the waist, a sheen of sweat on his bronzed chest as he kicked a ball into the goal with lethal accuracy.* 'I read about his brother. It was completely awful.' She tried to imagine bad boy Alessandro as Crown Prince. Nothing about the way he'd treated her had been princely. 'He was the black sheep of the family.'

'Alessandro always had a difficult relationship with his parents but he was close to his brother. It's been hard for him. And he's now heir to a throne he doesn't really want. He prefers his freedom.'

Freedom to break hearts all over the world. 'I can't imagine Alessandro in a position of responsibility.' And that was the attraction. Restless, edgy, a danger-seeker. The devil in him had drawn her.

'He wasn't given any choice. It's a matter of succession. He's the heir, whether he likes it or not. So what do you think? I'd say it's the perfect job for you.' Josh was looking pleased with himself. 'You idolised him.'

'I did not idolise him. And the last thing I want to do is act as nurse to Alessandro Cavalieri,' she snapped. 'He's arrogant, full of himself...' *Super-bright, scorching hot and sexy as hell.*

He'd—and she'd—

Oh, God.

Feeling the blood rush into her cheeks, Tasha turned to look out of the window. She couldn't face him.

Sexual awareness shot through her, as unexpected as it was unwelcome. The man wasn't even in the room, she thought angrily, so why did she feel hot all over?

It was just her memory playing tricks.

What you found sexy at seventeen just made you angry at twenty-eight.

This was the man who had destroyed her dreams. He could have treated her kindly and let her down gently, but instead he'd been brutal. Cruel.

She should thank him, Tasha thought numbly. He'd screwed up her confidence and her relationships with men, but he'd done wonders for her career. When she'd finally emerged from under the rubble of her fantasies she'd given up on relationships and focused on her studies. Instead of parties, she'd spent her evenings with books. And her family hadn't questioned it. Her brothers had just been relieved that wild Tasha had finally settled down to study. They had no idea what had happened that night.

Thank goodness.

Josh would have killed him.

Her brother was idly flicking through correspondence, apparently unaware of her trauma. 'He was pretty arrogant, I suppose…' Josh signed a letter. 'But that was hardly surprising. When we were at university, women couldn't leave him alone.'

Tasha stood stiff as a board. 'Really?'

'You were crazy about him.' Josh dropped the letter in his in tray. 'Are you embarrassed to face him again?'

'No! Of course not! I just—have better things to do with my time, that's all. I'm a paediatrician. I need a job in paediatrics. I need to think of my CV.'

'Because it's just that it occurred to me that you did flirt with him a lot.'

I want it to be you, Alessandro. I want you to be the first.

Tasha felt as though she'd been plunged head first into a furnace. 'I was a teenage girl. I flirted with everyone.' Why was she reacting like this when it had happened almost ten years ago? *Get over it, Tasha.*

But humiliation wasn't so easily forgotten. Neither was Alessandro, which was crazy because she probably wouldn't even find him attractive any more. It had just been the whole prince thing and her impressionable, romantic teenage brain.

She knew better now.

Tasha leaned against the wall, forcing herself to breathe slowly. *Unfinished business*, she thought. He'd walked away and left her wounded. She'd never had the opportunity to defend herself, to tell him how much he'd hurt her.

Anger flashed through her, sharp and bright.

There was no way she could nurse him through a broken ankle. She was more likely to break the other one for him.

Tasha opened her mouth to turn her brother down and then a thought flitted into her brain. Shocked, she shook her head. *No. She couldn't do that.* It would be juvenile. Shallow. It would be…

Fun?

Satisfying?

It would teach him a lesson.

'This nursing job…' Her lips moved and she heard herself speaking. 'Does it involve moving in with him?'

'Yes, of course. He needs someone there day and night for a month or so. Maybe a bit longer.'

Day and night.

That was plenty of time to drive a man out of his mind. *To make him sorry.*

She'd show him that he no longer had any effect on her and at the same time she'd finally purge him from her mind. The spectacular man in her head was the product of a teenage fantasy. Living with the reality would cure her of that once and for all. And it would give her a chance to restore her dignity.

Josh put his pen down slowly. 'You're thinking about it? A moment ago you were telling me he was arrogant and full of himself.'

'He was young. He's probably changed.' She didn't believe it for a minute. A man like Alessandro would never change. Looks, wealth and influence were welded together. 'It would be great to see him again. I'd like to help him.' Tasha tapped her foot on the floor as she considered the various forms that 'help' could take.

'You're sure you won't find it awkward? You were crazy about him.'

'Awkward? Gosh, no.' She told herself that whatever awkwardness she was going to feel would be eclipsed by his. And she'd be so dignified and mature about the whole thing, that would make him feel even worse. The plan grew in her head. 'I have to warn you, I'm not much of a nurse, Josh. I'm good with kids but moaning adults with man-flu drive me up the wall. I just want to tell them to pull themselves together.'

'It isn't man-flu. His ankle shattered and so far he's been back to Theatre four times. On top of that he has a couple of broken ribs and countless bruises.'

'So you're saying he's pretty much helpless?'

Better and better...

'Completely helpless. That's why it's important that we find the right person. He doesn't want to find himself trapped with someone who doesn't understand him.'

'Right. Well, that's good because I do understand him.' *She understood him perfectly.* He was a rich, handsome playboy who treated women like flashy accessories. His idea of permanency was two dates.

'It's important that whoever looks after him knows what he needs.'

Tasha looked sympathetic. 'I know *exactly* what he needs.'

A wake-up call. A lesson in how to treat women properly. He was used to fawning women treating him with deference. And she needed to finally prove to herself that Alessandro Cavalieri was well and truly in her past. 'I'm very good at persuading patients to take their medicine, so I think I'm just the woman for the job.'

'I'm sure you are. You have good instincts and you're not scared of him. The staff here are intimidated by his status and afraid to tell him what he needs to do. He's walking all over them.'

'That can't be good for his broken ankle,' Tasha said lightly. 'Don't worry. I won't let him walk over me.' *Not this time.* This time she was going to be the one doing the walking.

She looked down at her trainers and wished she was wearing heels.

Josh was watching her. 'You're not going to fall for him again, are you?'

Tasha's laugh was genuine. 'Absolutely no chance of that.' She wasn't that stupid, was she? 'The only thing on my mind is my next job.'

'OK. Good—so you'll do it? Nag him about his physio and make sure he doesn't sneak women into his bed when he's supposed to be resting? Take care of him? That's great. Why don't you pop and see him right now? He's in a private room. I can give you directions.'

Right now?

Tasha's smile faltered. Her heart trebled its rhythm. No, not right now. She'd just lost her job. Well, not exactly *lost* it as such—she'd thrown it away. The last thing she needed was to heap on the humiliation. Facing Alessandro took serious preparation. She needed to get her head together. She needed to look her best.

Aware that Josh was looking at her, Tasha breathed slowly and tried to slow her pulse rate. If she said no, her brother would ask questions. And the longer she waited, the more the anticipation would eat into her. And the advantage of doing it right away was that Alessandro wasn't forewarned. He wasn't expecting to see her.

Tasha strolled to the mirror in the corner of the office and stared at her reflection. Green eyes stared back at her. Green eyes that showed lack of sleep and stress. Doctor's eyes.

Apart from the shadows and the obvious exhaustion, she didn't look that bad, did she?

Mouth too big, she thought. Freckles. Dark hair that twisted and curled over her shoulders. All wrong. As a teenager, she'd been horribly conscious of her gypsy looks. She'd envied the girls with sleek blonde hair and china-blue eyes.

Insecurity crawled through her belly and she glared at her reflection, refusing to allow herself to think like that. At least she had a brain, which was more than could be said for most of Alessandro's women.

But there was no doubt that there was work to be done before she faced her past. Alessandro Cavalieri spent his time with the most beautiful women in the world. Facing him with confidence required more than an emergency repair job, but it would have to do.

With a sense of purpose, Tasha pulled her make-up case out of her bag.

'Poor Alessandro.' She darkened her lashes and added blusher to her cheeks. Not much. Just enough to help the 'natural' look. 'He must be going crazy, stuck in bed. You're right. What he needs is personal attention.'

And she was going to give him personal attention.

By the time she'd finished with him, a shattered ankle was going to be the least of his worries.

She was going to make him writhe with guilt for crushing her dreams so brutally. It was time he realised that women had feelings.

Josh was watching her in bemusement. 'Why are you putting on make-up?'

'Because I care how I look and because I want to look

professional.' Staring into her bag, she selected a subtle gloss lipstick. 'Last time we met, I was a teenager. That's how he's going to remember me. I need to look like an adult—like someone capable of taking care of him.'

'You look very happy all of a sudden for someone who has just lost their job. A few moments ago I thought you were going to cry.'

'Me? Cry? Don't be ridiculous. Don't worry, Josh. I'll take good care of your friend.' Tasha tugged at the clip and her hair tumbled long and loose around her shoulders. Smiling to herself, she gave her head a shake. 'I'll take *extremely* good care of him.'

Alessandro Cavalieri had taken her fragile teenage heart and ground it under his feet.

Payback time, she thought as she added the high-shine gloss to her lips.

It was going to be her pleasure to give him exactly what he deserved.

And maybe, just maybe, once he'd given her a big, fat grovelling apology, she'd be able to put the whole episode behind her.

CHAPTER TWO

'YOUR Highness, you *can't* use your phone in the hospital.'

Alessandro turned frustrated dark eyes onto the nervous nurse, his temper reaching combustion point. 'Then get me out of hospital,' he said silkily, and watched as she bit her lip nervously.

'I'm really sorry but I don't have the authority to do that. You have an infection, Your Highness, and—'

'Stop calling me Your Highness.' The snap of the words was accompanied by a rush of guilt. *She was just a kid.* It wasn't her fault that he wanted the rank and title about as much as he wanted a badly smashed ankle and bruised ribs. 'I apologise,' he growled. 'Being stuck in here hasn't done much for my mood. I'm used to being active.' And lying in bed gave him too much time to think about things he spent his life trying to forget.

The darkness licked at the edges of his mind threatening to engulf him. With a huge effort of will, he pushed it back.

Not now.

The nurse stood rigid, clearly overawed by her royal patient. 'The Chief Executive of the hospital called while you were with the consultant and asked me to tell you that he's increased security so that there's no repeat of yesterday's fiasco—he apologised profusely, Your Highness. We have no idea how that journalist managed to climb up the drainpipe to your room.' She all but curtseyed but this time Alessandro kept his temper on a tight leash. It was obvious that she wasn't going to be able to behave naturally with him, and he'd encountered that all too often in his life to be surprised. No one behaved naturally with him. Everyone had an agenda.

'I'm used to journalists climbing drainpipes and crawling through the windows. It's a fact of life.' He reached for a glass of water, gritting his teeth against the agonising pain that shot through his body.

'Let me help you, sir.'

'I can manage.' Alessandro growled the words just as his shaking hand deposited most of the water over his chest. He switched to Italian, his native tongue, and swore long and fluently while the flustered nurse quietly removed the glass from his white fingers, refilled it and handed it to him.

She stared at his T-shirt, now clinging to his chest. 'Do you want me to—?'

'No. I'm fine.'

Dragging her eyes away from his muscles, the girl swallowed. 'Your senior adviser called, sir. He wanted you to call him urgently.'

Alessandro leaned his head back against the pillow and suppressed the urge to laugh out loud. That was the one good thing about this mess—his advisers were climbing the walls. The wicked side of him revelled in the chaos his accident had caused. 'I can't call him,' he drawled. 'You've just told me I'm not allowed to use my phone.'

'There's a phone by your bed, sir—Your Highness.'

For God's sake— 'You can call me Alessandro. And I think we've both just established that I can't reach anything that's by my bed.'

'There were a few other calls, Your Highness.' She gave him a nervous glance. 'Five journalists and four—er—women. None of them left their names. And Her Highness Princess Eleanor called when you were in the bathroom. She said not to bother calling her back but she left you a message.'

'Which was?'

'She saw on the news that the hospital is besieged by journalists and she asked that you be discreet about what you say to them.'

Alessandro gave a humourless smile.

The dull ache inside him turned into a dark black hole that threatened to suck him down.

So his mother had finally called.

Not when his accident had been announced as a newsflash and no one had known his condition. Not out of concern when he'd been rushed into Theatre for emergency surgery. Not to ask how he was or send love. No, his mother had called because she was worried about his image. Or rather she was worried about *her* image.

You have to think about how you present yourself, Alessandro. It affects all of us.

Wiping the cold, disapproving tone from his head, Alessandro sought distraction. The nurse was pretty, he realised, and he hadn't even noticed. Which said a great deal about his current state of mind. He had a wicked impulse to drag her to the window and kiss her senseless in front of the crowd of hopeful photographers.

But that wouldn't be fair on the girl.

Or on Miranda.

Thinking of Miranda was enough to kill his mood.

He was going to have to make a decision. They couldn't go on like this any longer. It wasn't fair on either of them.

'I don't suppose I can bribe you to smuggle me out of here?' He tried to look as non-threatening as possible. 'I own a home up the coast. Incredible views from the master bedroom.'

The nurse flushed scarlet and her eyes met his. He saw the excitement there and the way her lips parted as she caught her breath. Unfortunately he could also read her mind, which was busy spinning dreams ending with 'nurse marries Prince'.

Thinking of his parents' dutiful, entirely loveless marriage, he felt suddenly cold.

He had no idea why marriage was the ultimate goal for so many people. To him it seemed like the road to hell. He'd rather be trampled by a whole herd of horses than commit to one woman for the rest of his life. Especially a woman whose only interest in him was the fact he had royal blood.

'You understand that this is a purely indecent proposal.' He shifted his leg, but it did nothing to ease the pain. 'My house has amazing sea views from every room and a hot tub on the deck. You can scrub my back and give me a private physio session.'

'This is Cornwall.' A crisp female voice came from the doorway. 'If she uses the hot tub in April, she'll catch pneumonia. Hello, Alessandro. You look as though you're in a filthy mood. Hope I'm not supposed to bow or curtsey.'

It was a voice he hadn't heard for more than a decade, but the recognition was immediate and powerful. His body tightened in a reaction so basic, so elemental that he was relieved that he was confined to bed, with all the privacy that afforded. Temptation, he thought, wasn't something a man easily forgot. And Natasha O'Hara had been temptation on legs. A girl, desperate to become a woman. At seventeen, she'd tried everything to get him to notice her.

And he'd noticed.

Oh, yes, he'd noticed.

Remembering, Alessandro felt his muscles tighten. Sweat dampened his brow. He wasn't sure whether the pain in his chest was due to fractured ribs or guilt.

He'd treated her badly.

She strolled into the room with a confidence that told him the awkward teenager was long gone. There was no sign of the stiff formality that everyone else displayed around him. She didn't blush, call him 'Your Highness', or look as though she was about to bow and scrape at his feet. Her gaze was direct and challenging and he would have laughed with relief if it hadn't been for the uncomfortable feeling deep inside him. Tasha had always shown guts and intelligence. If someone had told her to bow or curtsey, her response would have been to ask why. One of the reasons he'd loved spending time with her was because she'd treated him as a normal human being.

And in return he'd broken her heart.

He shifted uncomfortably in the bed, but the guilt stayed with him.

Was she the sort of woman who bore grudges? Not for a moment did he think she would have forgotten that summer any more than he had.

'Are you going to pretend you don't recognise me?' Her tone was light and friendly and if she was bearing a grudge there was no sign of it.

Alessandro relaxed slightly. Maybe the guilt was misplaced. She'd been very young, he reasoned. He'd probably barely featured on her adolescent landscape. Everything healed quickly in childhood—broken bones and broken hearts.

Still watching him, she paused beside the bed. Her top was a vivid scarlet and she wore it tucked into skinny jeans, her dark hair tumbling down her back in snaky black curls. She looked like a cross between a gypsy and a flamenco dancer and Alessandro felt his mouth dry and his body harden in an all-male reaction.

The wild child had grown up.

'You've spilt water on your T-shirt.' She eyed his damp chest and he felt something stir inside him.

'It isn't easy manoeuvring with a broken ankle and two broken ribs.'

'Poor Alessandro.' Her voice poured over him like honey, soft and sympathetic. 'So that's why you're so cranky. It must be awful to feel so helpless.'

Pain gnawed at his temper, fraying his control. He'd kept his mind off the pain by thinking of ways to get himself out of the hospital, but her presence disturbed his focus. And the way she was looking at him felt wrong. He would have expected her to be angry with him or, if not angry, then at least a little shy? Or maybe embarrassed. After all, he'd— Alessandro moved awkwardly and pain rocketed through him. 'What are you doing here?' He ruthlessly ignored the pain. 'Josh mentioned that you worked at a hospital miles away.'

'Not any more. I'm...' she paused and then smiled '...in between jobs.'

Their eyes met and held and Alessandro wondered what the hell he'd done to deserve this extra punishment. 'You're looking good, Natasha.' *Too good,* he thought, noticing in that single reluctant glance that her body had fulfilled its teenage promise. As a girl, she'd been teenage temptation. As a woman, Natasha O'Hara was a vision of glorious curves that made a man think of nothing but wild sex. And thinking of wild sex made him ache in the only place that wasn't already aching, so he looked away from those smooth arms, tried to block out the image of those slender limbs and told himself that the last glossy mouth he'd kissed had led to nothing but trouble.

'Thanks, Nurse...er...' She squinted at the name badge. 'Carpenter. You've taken enough abuse from this patient for one day. I'll take it from here.'

Nurse Carpenter's face fell. 'But I've just come on duty and His Highness needs—'

'I know exactly what His Highness needs.' The words were a polite but firm dismissal and Alessandro tried to remember whether she'd had that air of command as a teenager. No, definitely not. She'd been full of wide-eyed, barely repressed excitement and optimism. 'Hopeless romantic' hadn't begun to describe her.

The nurse gave Alessandro a final wistful look and melted away.

Tasha closed the door firmly, leaving the two of them

enclosed in the private room. 'Yes, Your Highness, no, Your Highness—it must drive you crazy. Or do you like your women servile?'

She was such a contrast to all the other people he'd come into contact with since he'd crashed into the mud on the polo field that Alessandro found himself laughing for the first time in weeks. 'Definitely not servile.'

'Good, because if I have to call you Your Highness every two minutes, this is never going to work.'

Alessandro watched as she strolled across the room. Something about the way she was looking at him made him uneasy. Or maybe it was just the guilt, he thought. It was definitely there, shimmering underneath the surface. 'What are you talking about?'

'You have to stop eating the nurses for breakfast, Alessandro. They're all terrified of you.'

'I'm a pussy cat.'

Her mouth flickered. 'Right.'

'Maybe I'm a little cranky, but I'm not good at lying in bed, doing nothing.'

'Then you'd better get used to it.' Her gaze was frank and direct. 'I looked at your X-rays. You won't be walking on that ankle for a while. You've made a mess of your bones.'

'Not me. The horse.' But it had been his fault and the knowledge gnawed at him. He'd been distracted. To take his mind off that, he studied her closely. *Was she taller or was it the way she held herself?* There was a confidence about her that hadn't been there a decade before. A knowledge of herself as a woman. It showed itself in the way her hips swayed when she walked and the hint of cleavage revealed by the neck of her casual top. Trapped and immobile, unaccustomed to feeling helpless in any situation, Alessandro set his teeth and tried to think cold thoughts. 'What are you doing here, Tasha?' He hadn't seen her since that night—the night when he'd left her sobbing, her make-up streaked over her beautiful face.

He pushed the memory aside, trying to lose it in the darkness of everything else he was trying to forget.

'Rumour is you're looking for a nurse so you can escape from this place.'

'In this case rumour is correct.' But he was starting to wonder whether being trapped at home with a star-struck nurse who called him Your Highness every two minutes might not be just as irritating as being in hospital.

'I can't imagine who would want the job. As temperaments go, yours is pretty volatile.'

'Once I'm out of here my temper will be just fine. Josh promised to find me a nurse by the end of the day. Do you know if he's had any luck?'

'Depends on your definition of luck.' She picked up the phone that he'd slung on the bedcover. 'You shouldn't be using this in the hospital. It's breaking the rules.'

'So I've been told. Trouble is, I've never been much good with rules.'

Her beautiful mouth flickered into a tiny smile of mutual understanding. 'That's one thing we have in common, then. But while you're in here, you have to behave.'

'Discharge me and I'll behave. So—has he found me a nurse?'

'Not a nurse, exactly.'

'What's that supposed to mean? I have to have someone who knows what they're talking about. And preferably someone who doesn't call me Your Highness at the end of every sentence.' He needed to get out of here before lying here trapped with his own thoughts drove him crazy. He needed distraction.

Tasha lifted her head. Her gaze connected with his. '*I* know what I'm talking about. And I have no intention of calling you Your Highness.'

'You?' Alessandro felt shock thud through his gut. 'You're a children's doctor.' She was also someone he'd carefully avoided for over a decade.

'I'm a doctor. My speciality just happens to be children. But I have all the skills necessary to assist your rehabilitation. I can nag you to do your exercises, throw away the junk food and make sure you take lots of healing early nights—' humour lightened her voice '—on your own. I've never been anyone's nurse before but I'm a quick study.'

His mouth felt dry but he was in too much pain to try and reach for his glass again. 'You're offering to nurse me?'

'We're old friends, Alessandro. It's the least I can do.' Her smile was warm and genuine, so why did he feel so uneasy?

Something didn't feel right.

He decided that this was one of those occasions that merited the direct approach. 'You and I, we didn't exactly part on good terms.'

'No. You were a complete bastard,' she said frankly, 'but that was a long time ago. I was at an impressionable age. Do you honestly think I'm still bothered about something that happened almost ten years ago? That would be ridiculous, don't you think?'

Would it?

He looked at her for a long moment, his eyes searching out the true sentiment behind the lightly spoken words. 'Tasha—'

She leaned towards him, mockery in her gaze. 'I was seventeen years old. I had no taste, and I was overwhelmed by the fact that you were a prince. And now we've got that out of the way, can we just forget it? No girl should be made to feel embarrassed about the foolish crushes she had as a teenager. So what do you say, Alessandro? Am I hired?'

Josh opened the front door of his house, his mood swerving between elation and guilt.

He tried to push the guilt back where it belonged.

His marriage to Rebecca was over. She was the one who had called time on their relationship and moved out. They'd wanted different things. Right through their relationship, they'd wanted different things.

As he hung up his jacket Megan's fragrance engulfed him, wrapping him in memories.

Maybe he'd moved on a bit quickly, but he was human, and when it came to Megan…

Just thinking about her lifted his mood, and he closed the front door, relieved that Tasha had refused his invitation to come home with him. He needed time to think, but already his mind was racing ahead, thinking of the future. He wanted Megan here, with him, all the time. He wanted to laugh with her over a meal, he wanted to sleep with her and wake up with her. They were adults, weren't they? He was past the age of wanting to creep around like a teenager. Snatched moments in the on-call room would never be enough for him. He knew what he wanted now.

He wanted Megan. In his life. For ever.

Energised by a certainty he'd never felt before, Josh checked his phone, hoping to find a message from her, but there was nothing and he was surprised by the strength of the disappointment that thudded through him.

Had she gone back to sleep after he'd received the call that his sister was in the department? He imagined her still lying there, in sheets tangled from the heat of their loving, dreaming about what they'd shared.

Was she planning even as he was planning?

Pondering that question, he threw his keys on the table, feeling lighter than he had in months. Smiling slightly, he retrieved the post from the floor and strolled into the kitchen, lured by the promise of strong coffee.

'Hello, Josh.' Rebecca sat there, her beautiful face pale, her eyes sharp with accusation.

Reality slapped his dreams in the face.

Josh felt the lightness evaporate and a sick dread that he couldn't identify settled around him like a dark cloak. 'What are you doing here?'

'I'm your wife, Josh.' Her tone was brittle. 'This is still my home.'

Guilt churned inside him. It was hard to remember they'd ever been close. Hard to remember that once they'd chosen each other.

'Where were you last night?'

He bit back the urge to tell her to mind her own business. 'At the hospital. It's where I work.'

'But you weren't working, were you? And don't bother lying to me because I phoned the hospital to ask where you were.' She gave a thin smile. 'Consultant's wife's privileges. No one knew where you were, but they did know you weren't on duty.'

Josh felt as though the walls of the house were closing in on him. Moments ago his future had seemed so clear. Now all he saw was murky black. 'Rebecca—'

'Am I supposed to be grateful that you didn't have sex with her in our bed?' Her fury snapped chunks out of the fragile remains of their relationship. 'Who is she, Josh? And don't bother denying there's someone else because I can see it in your eyes.'

It wasn't just in his eyes. It was in his heart. It was all through him and it gave him strength to do the right thing. *To fight.*

Josh straightened his shoulders. 'There is someone. You and I—our relationship is over, Rebecca. We've agreed that, and—'

'I'm pregnant.'

The silence in the room was absolute. It was as if the words had stopped time but he knew it wasn't the case because the hands of the kitchen clock were still moving.

Pregnant. A baby.

Josh felt strangely detached. The words floated through his numb brain but didn't settle. Pregnant. It was as if he was outside himself, looking in. And then reality punched him in the gut. Denial burst to the surface, driven by a desperate need to hold onto the dream. 'No.' The word was dragged from deep inside him. 'You can't be. That isn't possible.'

'Why? Because it isn't convenient for you? Because it isn't what you want?' Her voice rose. 'I've got news for you, Josh. Babies don't always come along at the most convenient moment in your life.'

He knew that. Just hours ago Megan had finally confirmed that the baby she'd lost so traumatically eight years earlier had been his—a cruel epilogue to the night both of them had spent in hell. His decision to save Megan's life all those years before had cost her a child. Their child. The knowledge intensified a guilt and pain that had never left him.

When he and Rebecca had split, his first thought had been, *Thank goodness we didn't have kids.*

And now...

'You know I don't want children.'

Rebecca's laugh was devoid of humour. 'Maybe you should have thought about that before you had sex with me.' There was a coarseness to her declaration that made him feel like scrubbing his skin.

'That was a mistake.' Josh stood still, the ache in his heart more painful than anything physical that she could inflict on him. Now, with some distance, he couldn't imagine why they'd had sex again. What had driven him back into her bed? His brain tried to drag out details from that night but all he remembered was her, urging him on... 'Did you do it on purpose?' Blind with pain, he shot the words at her, wanting the truth even though he knew it wouldn't change the facts. The colour in her cheeks answered his question and he swallowed down the bitter taste of contempt. 'You chose to bring a child into a dead, loveless marriage?'

'You chose to have sex with me,' she said acidly. 'So it's not completely dead, is it? Or maybe you've conveniently forgotten that night.'

No, he hadn't forgotten. The memory sat in his gut, the regret hard and undigested. Of all the mistakes he'd made in

his life, that was the biggest. If he could rewind the clock...
'You were taking the Pill.'

'I'm pregnant, Josh. Nothing either of us does or says is going to change that. So before you get too deeply embedded in this exciting new relationship of yours, we need to think what we're going to do. You're going to be a father.'

CHAPTER THREE

As IDEAS went, this had been one of her worst.

Tense and on edge, Tasha paced around Alessandro's stunning, contemporary clifftop home, wishing she'd never agreed to the plan. But refusing would have invited awkward questions from Josh. And anyway, she hadn't thought for a moment that she'd feel anything for Alessandro except mild contempt.

She'd planned to wash the boy out of her hair—she'd forgotten that the boy was now a man. A man who oozed sex appeal and natural authority even when badly injured. From the moment she'd walked into his private room and seen him watching the nurse through those slanting, slightly mocking eyes she'd known she was in trouble.

The nerves jumped in her stomach and she realised how long it had been since she'd been around a man who had that effect on her. The few relationships she had, she was careful to keep light and casual. She preferred it that way.

Her usual confidence deserting her, Tasha kept her back to him and focused her attention on the house. The place was incredible. Built on one level, floor-to-ceiling glass wrapped itself around the house, giving uninterrupted views over the beach from every angle of the living room. Deep soft sofas in ocean colours grouped around a large blue-and-white-striped rug and there were touches of the sea everywhere. Elegant pieces of driftwood. An old anchor. And then there were the paintings and the books.

Tasha glanced in envy at the bookshelves and wished she had a free month to read her way through the collection while lying on one of those squashy sofas and occasionally looking at the view. Somehow the place managed to be stylish and contemporary while maintaining a cosy, intimate feel.

'How on earth did you find this place?'

'I knew where I wanted to live. When this house came up, someone tipped me off.'

Knowing how much property cost in this part of the world, Tasha gave a wry smile. 'I dread to think how much you paid.'

'The real problem was planning permission. The original house was structurally unsound and we had to persuade them that this would enhance the landscape.'

Tasha glanced up at the double height living room, awash with light. 'Your architect was clever.'

The view alone would have fetched millions. Outside, a wide deck curved around the house, a glass balustrade offering some protection while ensuring that not a single element of the outdoors was lost. The home shrieked style and sophistication. And then there were the gadgets...

It was a contemporary palace, she thought, *fit for a play-boy prince.*

The evidence of wealth was everywhere and the high-tech security meant there was no forgetting the identity of her patient. From the moment the electronic gates had opened onto the long winding drive that led up to the clifftop house, she'd been aware of the security cameras. And then there was the team of highly trained security staff who worked shifts protecting the prince.

Tasha risked a glance at him and thought to herself that he didn't look like a man who needed anyone's protection. From the dark stubble on his jaw to the dangerous gleam of his eyes, he was more pirate than prince.

It occurred to her that she'd only ever met him in her world. Never in his. She'd never thought of him like this, with protection officers on twenty-four-hour rotation.

At seventeen she'd been in awe of the fact that he was actually a prince, but she'd never thought about what that really meant. To her, the word 'prince' made her think of fairy-tales. Of chivalry, bravery and honour. To a little girl whose father had walked out, those qualities had seemed like riches. She still remembered her reaction when Josh had told her his university friend was coming to stay. Her mouth had dropped open and she'd said those words that afterwards she'd regretted for years. '*A real, live prince?*' From that moment onwards she'd been doomed to a lifetime of teasing by her older brothers, but at the time she hadn't even cared. Meeting a prince had been the ultimate romantic experience for a teenager just discovering boys. Her brain had taken up permanent residence in dreamland. Right from the day he'd stepped out of his armoured car, the sun gleaming off his glossy dark hair, she'd carried on dreaming. At twenty, Alessandro Cavalieri had been insanely handsome, but what had really drawn her had been his charm. Used to being on the receiving end of nothing but verbal abuse from her brothers and their friends, his charisma had been fascinating and compelling. Instead of treating her as a tomboy, he'd treated her as a woman. She'd never stood a chance.

She'd dreamed her way through countless lessons, concocting scenarios where Alessandro ignored all the beautiful girls who threw themselves at him because he couldn't look at anyone but her. The reality had been so far removed from the fantasy that the inevitable crash between the two had been catastrophic.

Reminding herself of that fact settled the nerves in her stomach. True, he was even more spectacular to look at now, but she was no longer a dreamy, romantic teenager. Neither was she interested in a relationship with a man whose only commitment was to his own ego. She was past the age when a handsome face was the only thing she noticed.

Relieved to have rationalised the situation, Tasha started to relax. 'The view of the beach is good. The surfing here is some of the best in Cornwall and it's never busy because of the rocks. You have to know what you're doing.'

'Josh told me you all used to spend hours surfing here when you were kids.'

'It used to drive our mother out of her mind with worry.' She rested her head against the glass. 'It's been so long since I surfed.'

'That surprises me. I can't imagine you working in a city.'

'That's where the job was.' *Was*. Tasha felt a ripple of panic but masked it quickly. 'Anyway, it feels good to be home. Familiar.'

'There's a private path from the terrace that leads straight down onto the beach. It's the reason I bought this property. You can surf from the front door. Did you bring your wet-suit?'

'Of course.' Tasha thought about the suitcases in her car. She was like a snail, she thought, carrying her world around on her back. And what was she doing, talking surfing with him? The point of this wasn't to be intimate or cosy. Deciding that it was never too soon to start inflicting a little extra pain, she gave a sympathetic smile. 'Shame you can't join me.'

'Thanks for the reminder.' The irritation in Alessandro's voice confirmed that her arrow had found its target.

'At least I'll be able to get out there and surf, and I'll give you a report,' Tasha said kindly, feeling a flash of satisfaction as she saw his jaw tighten. *Oh, boy, are you going to suffer*. She was about to twist the knife again when he shifted position and she saw pain flicker in his eyes. His naturally olive skin was several shades paler than usual and she could see the strain in his face. The physician in her at war with the woman, Tasha strolled over to him. 'Moving you from the hospital to here must have been a painful experience.'

'It was fine.'

He hadn't uttered a word of complaint but she knew that he must have been in agonising pain. 'I'll try and help you find a comfortable position.'

'I'm perfectly comfortable. And I don't need your help.'

'That's why you're paying me, remember? To help you. You need a nurse to look after you.'

'I needed a nurse because they wouldn't discharge me from hospital without one. Not for any other reason.' Jaw clenched, Alessandro manoeuvred himself onto the sofa, the pain involved leaving him white-faced. The muscles of his shoulders bunched as he took his weight on the crutches. 'I don't need to be looked after.'

Tasha found herself looking at those muscles. Pumped up. Sleek and hard. She frowned. *So what?* It took more than muscles to make a real man. 'So if you don't need to be looked after, what am I expected to do? File my nails?'

'You can do whatever you like. Read a book. Watch TV. Surf—although if that's how you spend your day, I'd rather you didn't tell me about it.' He dropped the crutches onto the floor with a clatter that said as much about his mood as the black frown on his face. 'Do whatever you like. Consider it an all-expenses-paid holiday.'

But she wouldn't choose to take a holiday with him, would she?

Ten years had done nothing but add to his physical attractions, she thought irritably. It was all very well reminding herself that looks didn't count, but everything about him was unapologetically masculine and being alone with him made her feel jittery. Which was ridiculous, she told herself, given that he could barely walk. He was hardly going to leap on her, was he? Anyway, he'd made it clear years before that he didn't find her attractive.

Reminded of the 'flat-chested' comment by her brother,

it was all she could do to stop herself thrusting her chest forward. 'Now that I'm here, you might as well at least let me fetch you a drink.'

'Thanks. A drink would be good.' The tension in his voice reflected the pain he was fighting. 'Whisky is in the cupboard in the kitchen and you'll find glasses on the top shelf. Join me. We'll have drinks on the terrace if I can get myself there.'

Drinks on the terrace?

Tasha felt a flash of alarm. No way. Lounging on the deck, watching the sun go down over golden sand was far too intimate a scenario. That wasn't what she had in mind at all. This was about inflicting pain, not taking pleasure. Not that she thought she was in any danger of falling for him again, but as a scientist reviewing the evidence she had to concede that it had happened before.

'A drink sounds like a good idea, but forget the terrace. You only just sat down, and if you keep moving you'll just make the pain worse.' Whisky, she thought, laced with arsenic or something equally poisonous. Or maybe just whisky along with the powerful painkiller and antibiotics he'd been prescribed. It would knock him unconscious and then she wouldn't need to worry about falling for his dangerous charm.

Not that he seemed charming right now. Pain had made him irritable and moody and he leaned his head back against the sofa, jaw clenched, eyes closed. 'I'll have it straight. No water. No ice.'

In other words, nothing to dilute the effects of the alcohol.

Tasha walked into the kitchen, knowing that every movement she made was being followed by those fierce black eyes. She remembered him telling her that his ancestors had been warriors, descendents of the Romans who had once colonised the Mediterranean island of San Savarre that was his home. It was all too easy to imagine Alessandro Cavalieri in warrior mode.

Irritated with herself, shrugging off those thoughts, she opened cupboards until she found whisky. Closing her hand around the bottle, she hesitated. It would be really bad for him to drink with the tablets, but Alessandro didn't seem to care. Clearly he was seeking oblivion. He'd drink whisky and to hell with the consequences. In fact, he'd probably enjoy the experience of alcohol and painkillers. Tasha put the bottle back. She wasn't here to do what he wanted. She wasn't here to make his life comfortable. It was already comfortable enough.

She glanced around her. The kitchen was like something from an upmarket show home. Light poured through a glass atrium and reflected off shiny black granite work surfaces. It was smooth and streamlined, designed for practicality as well as show.

'I could almost want to cook in a place like this,' Tasha muttered, yanking open the door of the tall American fridge and staring at the contents. 'Nothing but champagne and beer—typical man. What about food?' Exploring the lower shelves, she found some mouldy cheese and a dead lettuce, which she removed and dropped in the bin. 'Good job I went to the supermarket.'

While the ambulance crew had been preparing Alessandro for the transfer home, she'd taken herself into St Piran on a shopping trip for provisions. She'd spent several hours carefully selecting items to help her with her plan, thinking carefully about what would help her cause. Abandoning the idea of using anything from his fridge, she reached for her bag of supplies and pulled out a packet of herbal tea.

Perfect.

She'd yet to meet a man who enjoyed herbal tea.

Humming happily, Tasha boiled water and found two mugs.

Carrying the tea back to the living area, she put the tray down on the low glass table and waited expectantly.

The wait was worth it. His reaction was everything she'd hoped for.

Alessandro stared in disbelief at the pale yellow liquid steaming in the mugs. 'What the hell is that?'

'Herbal tea,' Tasha said earnestly. She groped around for something convincing to say about it. 'It will be good for you. It boosts the immune system and works as a—as a—as an internal cleanser.' As a highly trained clinician, she couldn't believe she was spouting such unscientific nonsense and she braced herself for Alessandro to burst out laughing and demand she show him the data to support her claims, but he didn't. Instead he glowered at her, his eyes narrowing to two dangerous slits.

'Is this a joke? This is your idea of taking care of me?'

'Absolutely. I'm doing what's good for you.'

'Whisky would be good for me.'

Tasha made an attempt at a timid smile. Given that she'd never done 'timid' before in her life, she was reasonably pleased with the result. 'Don't be angry,' she coaxed. 'I remembered afterwards that the whisky won't go well with painkillers and antibiotics so I went for tea instead. I'm supposed to be looking after your health, remember? That's why I'm here. Try it. It's delicious. Caffeine-free and *so* healthy.'

His gaze slid from her eyes to the contents of the mug. 'It looks like something that's come straight from the drains.'

'Really? I find it delicious.' To prove her point, Tasha took an enormous gulp of hers and just about managed not to spit it out. *Utterly vile.* 'Mmm. Are you sure I can't tempt you?'

'Is that a serious question?' The dangerous gleam in his eyes was a reminder to Tasha not to underestimate him. He wasn't tame. And he wasn't a pussy cat. He was a man who was used to controlling everyone and everything around him.

And it was clear to her now that he really didn't want

anyone there. He'd only agreed to it to facilitate his early discharge.

She gave a faint smile. That was good, wasn't it? She didn't want him to want her here. That was the whole point. She was here to make his life difficult and uncomfortable while proving to herself that his charm had just been the creation of her hormonal teenage brain. So far she was doing well.

Apart from that initial jolt she'd felt when she'd first seen him lounging in the hospital bed, she had herself well under control.

She ignored the tiny voice inside herself that warned her she was playing with fire—that however dangerous he'd been as a boy, the threat was magnified now he was a man.

Handing him a glass of water, she kept up the sympathy. 'Take your antibiotics and painkillers now and then you can have another lot before you go to bed.' Unable to switch off the doctor inside her, she frowned at his leg. 'You should keep that elevated. Wait a minute...' She grabbed three cushions from one of the sofas and carefully repositioned his leg. Although she was gentle, she knew the pain had to be agonising, but Alessandro didn't murmur and she felt a flash of grudging respect. At least he wasn't a wimp or a whiner. 'How does that feel?'

'As if a horse trampled on it?' His dry humour bought a smile to her lips but she killed it instantly, unsettled by the ease with which the smile had come. She didn't want to find him amusing any more than she wanted to find him attractive. And then her eyes met his and the desire to smile faded instantly.

Sexual tension punched through her, stealing her breath and clouding her mind. The power of it shook her.

'Take your tablets,' she croaked. She wanted to look away but there was something about those sexy dark eyes that wouldn't allow it.

How long they would have stayed like that she didn't know because the phone suddenly buzzed, breaking the spell.

'Leave it,' he said roughly, but Tasha was relieved and grateful for anything that gave her an excuse to turn her back on him. She felt dizzy. Light-headed—as if she were floating.

'It could be someone important.' Her hand shook slightly as she picked up the phone. *Note to self,* she thought. *Don't look at the guy unless you have to.* 'Hello?'

A woman's voice came down the phone, smooth and sultry.

The dizziness faded in an instant and Tasha thrust the phone at him, plummeting back to earth with a bump. 'It's for you. Someone called Analisa. She doesn't sound too happy.' *And that made two of them.* Clearing the tray, Tasha stomped back into the kitchen.

What the hell was she playing at? Staring at a guy like some sort of dreamy teenager!

Scowling, she tipped the herbal tea down the sink.

If she'd needed reminding what Alessandro was like, it was that phone call.

She didn't understand the language, but it was obvious that Alessandro wasn't spending time placating the woman. Judging from his bored tone, it wasn't going to bother him if Analisa or whatever her name was didn't phone back.

And that, Tasha thought angrily, summed up Alessandro Cavalieri. He didn't care how many women he hurt. Flirt today, dump tomorrow.

She took her time in the kitchen and by the time she strolled back into the living room, Alessandro was no longer on the phone. 'Did you take those tablets?'

'Yes. They would have gone down more easily with whisky.'

'You're going to need a clear head to handle all those women who keep calling you.'

'Are you jealous?'

'Oh, please!' Tasha moved the crutches out of the way before he tripped and did more damage. 'Don't flatter yourself. Fortunately for both of us, I've grown out of the girl-meets-prince fantasy.'

'Good, because girl-meets-prince has never done anything for me. It's all fake.' His tone was irascible and suddenly she wished she'd stayed in the kitchen.

The house was huge, and yet suddenly it seemed small.

It was all too intimate, too—*terrifying?*

'You're very bad-tempered. That's probably because you're hungry. If you're sure I can't tempt you with some of my lovely, delicious tea, I'll go and make us some supper instead.'

'You'd better phone for a take-away because there isn't anything in the fridge.'

'Actually, there was, but most of it looked ready for a post mortem so I threw it away. The only thing within use-by date in your fridge is the champagne, and last time I looked that wasn't listed as one of the five major food groups.' Ignoring the empty space on the sofa next to him, she sprawled in one of the chairs, curling her legs underneath her. 'I gather you don't cook.'

'I have a chef, but while I've been in hospital I gave him time off.'

A chef? 'Yes, well, next time tell him to clean the dead bodies out of the fridge before he leaves. Lucky for you I had the foresight to pick up some food on the way so we're not going to starve.'

'I don't expect you to cook. That isn't why you're here.' His face was paper white and she could see that the slightest movement caused him agony. 'Anyway, I'm not hungry.'

'If you don't eat, you won't recover. Why do you have a chef?'

'I'm a useless cook. And I'm usually too busy to cook. I eat out a lot.'

With women like the sultry Analisa. 'Well, that's not a problem. It will be my pleasure to make you delicious treats.' Generally she hated cooking, but Tasha decided not to share that with him. She'd already decided what she was cooking him for dinner. 'In fact, why don't I get started? You ought to have an early night.'

'I'm not big on early nights.' Those dark eyes found hers. 'Unless there's a reason.'

'A broken ankle and bruised ribs are a reason.' Rejecting the chemistry, Tasha uncurled her legs and stood up. 'The body heals better when it's rested.'

'So you're good in the kitchen?'

'I'm good in every room, Alessandro.' Leaving him to dwell on that comment, Tasha walked back to the kitchen and closed the door firmly behind her.

The irony didn't escape her. Normally she avoided the kitchen. Here, it felt like a refuge from Alessandro.

Trying not to think about him, she emptied her bags over the shiny black work surface and picked up a small bag of extra-hot chillies.

Stir-fry, she thought, *with a kick.*

She couldn't kick him herself, but this should do the job for her.

But as she chopped and sliced she discovered that it was impossible not to think about him. And thinking made her wonder about the dark clouds she saw in his eyes. She'd been a doctor long enough to recognise when someone was suffering. And she didn't think the dark emotions swirling around him had anything to do with the accident.

Might have caused the accident, though, she mused, slicing onion with surgical precision.

Minutes later she had noodles cooking in boiling water and she was stir-frying a generous quantity of garlic, red chilli and ginger. Making a guess at the timing, Tasha gamely tipped in vegetables and juicy prawns and finally added the noodles.

As it sizzled, she turned to the other pan and stirred the contents. It looked identical except for one ingredient—it lacked the copious amounts of red chilli.

Just don't mix them up, she reminded herself as she plated the meal, adding a touch of garnish to make the dish extra appetising.

Pleased with the result, she walked through to the light, airy living room. The sun had dipped below the horizon and the evening was cool. Alessandro lay sprawled on the low sofa where she'd left him, staring with brooding concentration at the waves crashing onto the shore.

'The first time I surfed here I was twenty. Josh brought me.'

And she'd followed them. Egged on by her best friend from school, they'd hidden, giggling, behind the rocks, watching as her brother and his sexy friend stripped down to board shorts.

Tasha put the plates down on the table with a clatter. 'I would have thought a playboy with a private jet and your surfing skills would have chosen North Beach, Hawaii, or Jeffreys Bay in South Africa.'

'I love Cornwall. Staying with your family was one of the happiest times of my life.'

The words pushed her control off centre and Tasha felt her stomach lurch. It had been the happiest time of her life, too. Which had made the abrupt ending even harder. 'Our home wasn't exactly big—it must have felt like a shoebox to you after palace life.'

'It felt like a proper home. And I envied the way you could all just get on with your lives without having to think about crowds and security.'

As a teenager she'd thought it was impossibly glamorous having security guards, but now she could see that it might be an inconvenience, especially for an active, athletic guy like Alessandro.

'I guess Cornwall is a pretty low-profile place.'

'It's not bad. Fortunately this house isn't too accessible. How often do you surf?'

'Me?' Tasha handed him cutlery. 'Not as often as I'd like

to because I generally work long hours. Normally, that's the way I like it. I'm a career girl. But now that I'm looking after you…' she shrugged '…I intend to make up for lost time.'

'So if you're a career girl, how come you're not working right now?'

Unwittingly he'd tapped into her deepest fears. That she might not be able to find another job. *That her altercation with her last boss might have blown her reputation to smithereens.*

Tasha opened her mouth and closed it again, unsettled by the sudden desire to confide. She stifled it, knowing that confiding was the first step towards intimacy. And she didn't want intimacy with this man. 'I'm in between jobs. I've cooked a stir-fry. I hope that's all right with you.'

'Looks delicious.' He picked up a fork. 'I can imagine you as a children's doctor.'

'I'll take that as a compliment. Do you want to try and eat at the table?'

'No, this is fine. You're right that moving around hurts. I think the journey to the bedroom will be enough of a challenge for one evening.'

As he shifted position, her eyes were drawn to his body.

No man had a right to be so good looking, Tasha thought as she registered the strength in those wide shoulders. It should have been enough that he was a prince. And rich. Looking like a sex god as well was just too many gifts for one person.

She might have been irritated if it hadn't been for the fact he was about to eat her food. And that was going to be a real test of manhood.

Hiding a smile, Tasha turned her attention back to her own plate. 'I love your kitchen. The design is fantastic. A whole different experience for me. Dinner for me is usually a cardboard sandwich from the hospital cafeteria at three in the morning.'

'It didn't look anything like this when I bought it. The

rooms were small and the whole place was pretty dark. I worked with an excellent architect and we knocked down almost every wall, put in the skylights...' He glanced up at the roof of the double-height sitting room. 'We decided it was worth gutting the place because it had such potential. We opened it up, let the light flow in. This is delicious, by the way. You're a good cook.'

Delicious? *He thought it was delicious?*

Tasha stared at him in disbelief. 'You like it?'

'After two weeks of hospital food?' He twisted noodles around his fork with skill and precision. 'This is heaven.'

He had to be kidding. It had to be a double bluff. Unless...

Tasha stared down at her own plate. Had she mixed them up?

Cautiously, she took a mouthful, waiting for her mouth to explode into flames from the chilli, but the flavours in her food were subtle and she knew instantly she didn't have the wrong plate. Which meant he clearly had a mouth lined with asbestos.

'Is there any more?' Alessandro speared the last prawn. 'You don't seem to be eating yours.'

'I am. And there isn't any more.' She hadn't thought for a moment he'd eat what she'd served him. Clearly his mouth was as tough as the rest of him.

Feeling aggravated, Tasha finished her food. 'Why did you fall anyway? Was the horse too difficult for you?'

He accepted the slight with a flicker of a smile. 'The horse wasn't difficult. I lost concentration for a moment, but that was long enough for the guy on the opposite team to bring us down. My ankle took most of the weight. My ribs took the rest.' He leaned back against the sofa, his eyes closed.

She wondered why he'd lost concentration.

'You were trapped under the horse? Ouch. So no physical activity for the rest of the summer?'

His eyes opened and he studied her from underneath lush, dark lashes. 'Depends what you mean by physical activity.'

Staring into those dangerous dark eyes, her mouth dried. 'I meant polo and surfing.' Tasha felt the heat slowly spread through her body and wished she'd never mentioned physical activity. Even injured, the man was deadly. 'You look tired. Do you want me to call your security team to help you from the sofa to the bed?'

'No. I have the crutches and I can manage.'

'Independent, aren't you?'

'You could say that.'

Torn between wanting to see him suffer and not wanting him to exacerbate his injuries, Tasha tilted her head. 'The crutches won't be much use while your ribs are so bruised. We might need to think of other options.'

'This is fine.' Shifting to the edge of the sofa, Alessandro picked up the crutches and stood up, taking his weight on his good leg.

Tasha flinched.

That had to hurt.

'Alessandro—'

'I can do it. Just give me space.' There was a stubbornness in his tone. A grim determination to succeed despite the agonising pain. Reluctantly impressed, Tasha stood there, careful not to touch him and distinctly unsettled by how much she wanted to do just that.

'Look, I could call one of those burly security guards—'

'It would help if you could check the route to my bedroom is clear. So far I haven't mastered doing this with obstacles.' His face was chalk-white as he slowly eased his way forward. 'I'll just use the bathroom on the way so that I don't have to make two journeys.'

Tasha watched as the muscles in his powerful shoulders flexed and knew that every movement had to be causing him agony. 'I think you need help.'

He cast her a look that told her he'd be long dead before

he'd accept help from anyone. A crooked smile flickered at the corners of his mouth. 'You're offering to assist me in the bathroom? Now, that could be interesting.'

Trying to work out how the atmosphere had shifted to intimate, Tasha felt her face turn scarlet. 'I just don't see how you're going to manage to do what you have to do without help.'

His eyes lingered on hers for a long moment. Mockery mingled with something else that she didn't even want to put a name to. 'You want to come and watch how it's done, *tesoro*?'

He'd called her that at seventeen and her heart rushed forward, doubling its rhythm. '*Don't* speak Italian.'

'Why not?'

'Because…' Her mouth was dry. 'Because I don't speak it and it's rude to talk a language someone doesn't understand.'

'It's my native tongue.'

'I know. But you're fluent in English so that's no excuse.' She scowled at him. 'I just don't want you falling and fracturing more bones. I'm not sure my patience with this whole nursing thing is going to last that long, so you'd better heal quickly.'

He shifted the position of the crutch. His knuckles were white where they gripped the handles. 'I won't lock the door. If I find myself in trouble, I'll shout and you can come to my rescue. But not on a white charger. I've had enough of horses for one week.'

Pinned to the spot by that dark, sexy gaze, Tasha felt as if she were the one who had eaten the chilli. Her entire body was caught in a fiery rush of heat and suddenly she didn't feel like the one in control. 'Fine,' she croaked, 'leave the door unlocked. Good idea.'

Feeling the heat in her face, she moved through to his bedroom and cleared the suitcase off the bed. His bed was enormous and faced out towards the sea.

How many hearts had he broken in that bed?

Trying to push aside disturbing images of Alessandro's strong body tangled with a slender female frame, Tasha ripped the duvet back so that he could get into the bed and wondered why on earth she'd volunteered for this job. Why had she ever thought she could make his life difficult? The herbal tea had been moderately irritating but the chilli hadn't even registered on his taste buds, and all her digs about surfing hadn't had much impact either.

And now she was stuck here with a man who made her think things she didn't want to think. It had always been like that, she remembered crossly, even as a teenager. When Alessandro had walked into the room there had never been any confusion. She'd known she was a woman.

If she really wanted him to suffer then she needed to do something drastic.

What was a man like Alessandro likely to be missing more than anything?

Tasha gave a slow smile as she thought about the other items in her shopping bags.

Time for Plan B.

The pain in his ribs was excruciating. Even small movements resulted in blinding agony, as if a burning-hot poker was being forced into his chest.

But at least it distracted him from the parts of his life he was trying to forget.

Taking advantage of the privacy of the bathroom, Alessandro gave in to the pain.

He balanced himself against the washbasin and reached for a glass. To add to the pain in his ribs and his ankle, his mouth felt as though someone had started a bonfire. Chilli, he thought, gulping down water. When he'd taken the first mouthful of food he'd thought she must have made a mistake but then he'd seen her eating hers happily. Clearly she liked her food hot. Not wanting to offend her, he'd forced his down, eating it as quickly as possible. If she walked out, he'd be back in hospital and there was no way he was going back to hospital. So he'd forced himself to eat with enthusiasm the food she'd prepared.

He drank deeply, wondering how long it took nerve-endings to recover. There wasn't a single part of his body that wasn't burning.

Frustrated by his own weakness, accustomed to being at the peak of physical fitness, Alessandro used the bathroom and then clenched his jaw against the pain and hobbled back towards the bedroom, trying in vain to find some way of distributing his weight so that the movement didn't exacerbate his injuries.

Tasha had turned back the duvet and smoothed the sheets.

Never before had his bed looked so inviting, but the short distance from the door felt like running a marathon. It didn't help that she was watching him, those cool eyes steady on his face.

'Aren't you taking your nursing duties a little too seriously?' He wished she'd turn away so that he could give in to the pain. 'You're off duty once I go to bed.'

'I'd better help you undress.'

Was she serious? Marvelling at the discovery that extreme pain didn't seem to interfere with sexual arousal, Alessandro gritted his teeth. For his own sanity he knew he didn't dare let her touch him. 'I'll manage.'

'How? At least let me help you change your shirt for pyjamas.'

'I don't own pyjamas.'

'I thought you might say that, so I bought you some when I was out shopping.' Pleased with herself, she picked up a bag and produced a pair of pyjamas.

Distracted from the ache in his loins by the flash of vivid colour, Alessandro blinked. *'Pink?'*

'It was the only colour they had.' Her expression was

anxious. 'Oh, dear. Are you one of those guys who believes wearing pink makes them less masculine? Sorry. I hadn't thought of that. Only I know some guys wear pink shirts these days and I thought these might be OK...'

Was she winding him up? His swift glance at her face suggested nothing but concern. Wondering just how far he was going to have to go not to offend her, Alessandro reminded himself that without her he'd be back in hospital.

Her generosity was the reason he'd be sleeping in his own bed tonight.

All he had to do was keep his hands off her. Which shouldn't be that hard, surely, given that every movement was agony.

'I don't have a problem with pink.' He eyed the pyjamas in disbelief, wondering which idiot had thought there was a market for such a vile creation. 'But I don't think they'll fit over the cast.'

'Leave that to me.' Beaming at him, she picked up a pair of scissors and cut a slit down one of the legs. 'There. Simple.'

Reflecting on the fact that the wretched garment now looked more like a dress than trousers, Alessandro manoeuvred himself onto the bed and let the crutches fall to the floor. Pain lanced his side and he sat still, breathing slowly, hoping it would pass. The helplessness was driving him mad.

'I'll help you take off your shirt.' Tasha sat next to him on the bed and gently eased off his shirt. As she exposed his chest, the breath hissed through her teeth. 'I've never seen bruises like those, Alessandro. How are you still walking around?' Her tone altered dramatically. Light and flirty gave way to crisp concern.

'I'm fine. To be honest, walking isn't any more painful than breathing.' He was taken aback by the change in her. The girl had gone and in her place was a doctor. A concerned doctor. Her fingers gently traced the bruises and when he glanced at her face he saw that her expression was serious.

'Does this hurt?'

'No.'

She gave him an impatient look. 'Honest answers only, please. A man wearing pink is allowed to express his true emotions even if the resulting language is colourful.'

'All right. It hurts like crazy and I want to punch something?'

'And when I do this?' She pressed lower down and Alessandro swore long and fluently.

'OK.' She didn't blink. 'Now I know you're telling the truth.'

The pain was a blinding, agonising flash. Once again he had that sick dread that the doctors might have missed something. Something that was going to keep him bedridden for longer than a fractured ankle and a few broken ribs. 'Are you trying to kill me?' He spoke through his teeth and she straightened, her hair sliding over her shoulders.

'Actually, no. I'm checking you over. I don't like the look of those bruises. Just sit still. I'm going to check your breath sounds.'

'I've already been examined by about a hundred doctors. They kept wheeling in yet another expert to give an opinion.'

'Sorry, but the only opinion I trust is my own.' She disappeared and reappeared a moment later with a stethoscope in her hand. 'Good job I packed this in my box of tricks, although I haven't listened to an adult's chest for quite a while.'

'If that's supposed to fill me with confidence, it doesn't.' It was a lie. Strangely enough, he was relieved to have her opinion. He remembered Josh telling him that Tasha had astonishing instincts to go with her sharp brain. He had no doubt that she was a skilled doctor. Unfortunately that didn't make things any easier and he sat still while she touched the bruising, trying not to think about how her fingers felt on his skin. 'Do you have to prod me?'

'I'm checking there's no underlying trauma. Those bruises are very impressive. Must hurt a lot.'

Alessandro spoke through his teeth. 'Not at all.' As if the pain wasn't enough, he also had the extra hit of sexual arousal. As she tilted her head, her hair slid forward and brushed against his arm. He tried to move backwards but every movement felt as though he were being slammed into a wall.

'Bones have a lot of nerve-endings,' she murmured. 'That's why it's painful.'

'Thanks for the explanation.'

'Generally, when someone breaks a bone, the treatment is to immobilise it. We can put your ankle in a cast to protect it. Unfortunately we can't do the same thing for your ribs.' Tasha put the stethoscope in her ears. 'Every time you breathe, you hurt yourself again.'

'Can't they strap my chest or something?'

'No. Now stop talking while I listen.' She narrowed her eyes and moved the stethoscope on his chest. Her hair whispered across his arm. 'Breathe in for me.'

Alessandro did and almost passed out. Pain skewered him and darkness flickered around the edges of his vision, muting the lust.

Her eyes locked on his. 'Breathe in and out through your mouth.'

Was she trying to torture him?

But when she finally removed the stethoscope from her ears, her expression was serious. 'Your breath sounds are fine, but I'm going to keep an eye on you. To answer your question, they actually did used to strap chests in the old days, but not any more. It impedes movement and stops you breathing deeply—you can't shift the secretions in your lungs and you can end up with a vile infection. Then you're back in hospital on yet more antibiotics.'

The word 'hospital' was enough to make him ride the pain and breathe deeply. 'I get the message.'

'Don't worry—a young, fit guy like you can cope with a couple of broken ribs and heal quickly. It's older patients who suffer.' Digging her hand into her pocket, she pulled out her phone. 'I'm just going to call your doctor. I want to add in a drug.'

'I'm already swallowing the contents of a pharmacy.'

'I want to give you a non-steroidal alongside your pain-killers. I don't know why he didn't give you that. You don't suffer from stomach problems, do you?'

'I've never suffered from anything,' Alessandro growled, 'until a horse fell on me.' Watching Tasha talk on the phone, he found his eyes lingering on the curve of her cheek and the thickness of her eyelashes. She was brisk and professional, giving her opinion bluntly and firmly to a man at least twice her age. Impressive, he thought. And he could imagine her working with children. As a teenager, she'd had an irrepressible sense of fun. Remembering some of the tricks she'd played on her brothers, he allowed himself a faint smile.

'OK, so that's done.' She slid the phone back into her pocket. 'In the morning I'm going to pick you up some extra tablets. I think it will help and so do the guys at the hospital. They should have thought of it, but sometimes it takes a woman to get these things right. Now, then—pyjamas.'

'I can dress without your help.' Alessandro, who had never felt awkward with a woman in his life before, suddenly felt awkward. She was behaving as if they had no history. As if—

Tasha picked up the pink pyjamas and dangled them in front of him, her expression bored.

'I've seen it all before, Alessandro. I'm a doctor.'

'You haven't seen m—' He was about to say that she hadn't seen his body before, but then he remembered that she had. And he'd seen hers. *All of hers.*

And he didn't want to mention that. If she was going to act as if nothing had happened, so was he.

He looked at her cautiously, but her face revealed nothing but professional concern.

'I want to examine the rest of you. Lie back for me.' Her expression serious, her hands moved down his body, sliding and pressing. 'Does this hurt?'

'Everything hurts.' Feeling her cool fingers on his abdomen, Alessandro sucked in a breath. How low did she intend to go?

Lust slammed through him and Alessandro grabbed the duvet and pulled it higher, ignoring the avalanche of pain that rained down on him. 'I'm fine. I can manage. Go to bed. You must be tired.' He wished she'd step back a bit. Her scent was playing havoc with his libido and this close he could see the smoothness of her skin. *How the hell could a guy be aroused when his broken ribs were virtually impaling his lungs*? 'Goodnight, Tasha. Thanks for all your help.'

'If the pain changes, let me know.'

The pain had changed. Suddenly it was all concentrated below his waist and it had nothing to do with being trampled by a four-legged animal. 'Get some sleep.'

'Don't hesitate to wake me up if you need to.' She walked briskly across the room to close the blinds.

'Leave them—I prefer to keep the doors open.'

'You won't be able to sleep.'

He didn't tell her that he rarely slept. 'I'll be fine. I like the fresh air.'

'Well, if you change your mind, just shout out.' Her hips swayed as she walked from window to door. She held a stethoscope in her hand but she walked like a seductress. 'I hope you have a really good night's sleep. I've chosen the bedroom right across the hall and I'll leave the door open so I'll hear you if you shout.'

Great. There were three guest bedrooms, the other two at the far end of the house. Couldn't she have chosen one of those?

After she left, Alessandro spent a frustrating and agonising fifteen minutes removing his shorts. Exhausted, he didn't bother replacing them with the pyjamas. Instead he flopped back against the pillows, drained of energy.

He lay without moving until a noise from across the corridor made him look up.

Tasha was walking across the guest room towards the *en suite* bathroom, undressing as she walked. First she pulled off the scarlet jumper and dropped it in a heap. Her full breasts pushed against a silken wisp of a bra. When her hands moved to the snap of her jeans, Alessandro wanted to groan out a request that she stop, but he couldn't make a sound and the jeans went the way of the jumper and this time the lace was so brief it was almost irrelevant.

His muscles tensed, sending spasms of pain shooting down his bruised body.

Finding it impossible to breathe, Alessandro wondered if one of his broken ribs had suddenly punctured his lung. There was no air in the room. He was suffocating. He lifted his hand to undo his collar and then remembered that he was naked.

As he watched, she stretched upwards to clip her hair on top of her head, the movement accentuating her lean, flat stomach and her long, slim legs. He felt like a voyeur at an erotic floor show. Clearly she'd forgotten that she had both doors open. Either that or she was just assuming he was asleep.

If he called out, he'd embarrass her, and he couldn't look away because his head refused to move.

Telling himself that any moment now she was going to lock the bathroom door, Alessandro kept watching. And he was still watching when she turned her back to him, unfastened her bra and stepped out of her knickers.

CHAPTER FOUR

MEGAN'S hand shook as she opened the door that led to the neonatal intensive care unit.

All day she'd been in a daze of happiness. A daze of happiness that nothing could blunt—not even the knowledge that technically she'd slept with a married man.

Married, but not together, she told herself, wondering why the fact that Josh and Rebecca were almost divorced didn't make her feel any better.

Her head was in a spin and she'd found it almost impossible to concentrate.

She'd thought of nothing else all day, ever since that knock on the door that had sent Josh springing from the bed before they'd had the opportunity to talk about what they'd shared. She had no idea who had been at the door, but whoever it was had been important enough to make sure that Josh didn't return.

Megan had waited for twenty minutes then dressed quickly and exited the on-call room quietly. Her heart had been working double time all the way back to the paediatric ward but she was fairly confident that no one had seen her.

She'd spent the rest of her day stopping herself from checking her phone every two minutes to see if Josh had called. It was like being a teenager all over again.

The extended silence made her jittery and sent her imagination into overdrive.

Was he embarrassed? Did he regret what they'd done?

Reminding herself that Josh was a senior doctor whose working day was ridiculously intense and demanding, she tried to rationalise the fact that he hadn't called. She told herself that it wasn't surprising that he didn't want to publicise their relationship. They were colleagues after all, and affairs between colleagues could so easily become messy.

Having convinced herself that she wasn't likely to see him that day, it came as a shock to see Josh sitting at the computer at the nurses' station.

Megan felt a tiny thrill of excitement bloom inside her.

He wasn't avoiding her. He was here, on her ward.

Her heart pounded against her chest and she was relieved that the other staff appeared to be occupied elsewhere.

Just for this first encounter she wanted to be alone with him. She didn't want to share the memories of the night with anyone but Josh.

Remembering the look he'd given her just before he'd left the on-call room, she gave a little smile and her stomach fluttered with anticipation.

'Hello, Josh.'

'Ah, Megan, I'm glad you're here. We had an emergency delivery in the department. Thirty-four-weeker.' He turned to her, his tone crisp and professional. 'Showing signs of respiratory distress, so we've transferred him to you.'

There was nothing intimate in his gaze—nothing to hint that they'd spent the night together.

Taken aback, Megan glanced behind her but there was no one within earshot.

The baby was ill, she reasoned, and he was an exceptional doctor. Josh would never put his personal life before the well-being of a patient.

Slowly, she put her bag on the floor, controlling her disappointment. 'Was it a normal delivery?'

As he told her, she found herself looking at his hands and the dark hairs dusting his forearms. Those same hands had touched her. Everywhere. *Held her.* It had been genuine, she had no doubt about that. She still remembered the look in his eyes as he'd driven her wild.

That knowledge gave her confidence. 'Josh—'

'I need to get back.' He rose quickly to his feet, interrupting her before she could finish her sentence. 'You might want to spend some time with the mother. She's very upset. The whole thing took about twenty minutes from start to finish. Precipitate doesn't begin to describe it.'

It was a verbal dismissal but it may as well have been a physical slap for the pain it caused.

'Of course.' Megan pushed the words through stiff lips and stood frozen to the spot as he walked past her, careful not to touch. He was as cold as he'd been eight years before. It was as if their night together hadn't happened.

She wanted to say something. She wanted to grab his arm and demand to know what was going on in his head. She wanted to know why he was hurting her like this.

But his face was a frozen mask and her pride kept her hands by her sides as she let him walk away.

Tasha took her time strolling towards the shower.

He was watching her. She could almost feel the heat of his eyes on her back.

Get a load of that, she thought happily as she stepped into the shower. Flat-chested? *I don't think so.*

From the moment she'd decided to do her striptease, her heart had been hammering. First she'd checked he was awake through the crack in the door, then she'd choreographed her walk across the room to ensure that he witnessed every move.

After that all she'd had to do was not give in to temptation and look round. She'd done everything in her power to push up his blood pressure. What she hadn't done was ask herself why she would want to.

Until now.

Muttering to herself, she turned the shower to cold.

Ten years hadn't done anything to make him less attractive. Unfortunately. In fact, he'd filled out in places where it counted. His shoulders were wider, his chest stronger and his arms thickened with muscle. Less of the boy and more of the man. Too much more of the man.

Despite the cold water, her body felt scorching hot again and she wondered why on earth she'd agreed to this.

Another one of her stupid ideas.

She'd thought her feelings for him had been no more than a childish crush. She'd thought the pain he'd caused would have inoculated her against his lethal charm. She'd thought she was immune. If you'd been infected with something once, you shouldn't catch it again, should you?

So why the explosion of chemistry?

Tasha gave a groan of frustration and turned off the shower.

Her brother was right. She needed to get out more.

Wrapping herself in a huge towel, she opened the bathroom door and risked a glance towards his bedroom. It was in darkness. The feeling of superiority drained out of her. If he'd been watching her, he wasn't now. He wasn't lying there tortured with unfulfilled desire after seeing her in her underwear.

He was asleep.

Which said it all. You couldn't torment a man who didn't even bother looking.

Feeling cross and hot and all sorts of things she didn't want to feel, Tasha flopped onto the bed and rolled onto her stomach, burying her face in the pillow. It wasn't supposed to be this way. She was supposed to have taken one look at him and wondered what she'd seen in him. She wasn't supposed to be having the thoughts she was having now. Why couldn't he be a total wimp like all the other men she met on a daily basis? Her last relationship had floundered after less than a week when the doctor in question had taken to his bed with a dose of man-flu. Tasha, who had endless patience with sick children, had been exasperated by his dying-duck impression but she'd dutifully made hot drinks, dished out tablets and made sympathetic noises until finally calling a halt, reasoning that there was no future in a relationship where one of the partners wanted to strangle the other.

Why couldn't Alessandro provoke the same feelings of irritation?

Why didn't she want to strangle him?

'Ugh.' Blocking out images of his broad shoulders, she burrowed under the pillow. The man had to be in agony. The bruises on his chest were the worst she'd ever seen. But had he uttered a murmur of complaint? No. In fact, he'd been so stoical about the whole thing it had been a struggle to persuade him to take painkillers. She wanted him to be a wimp, but he was anything but. And as for the chilli…

Clearly he liked his food hot.

Tasha thumped the pillow angrily and rolled onto her back. So he was tough. So what? That just proved the man had no nerve-endings and she already knew that. A man with the slightest sensitivity wouldn't have treated her the way Alessandro had treated her.

Had she seen a flicker of remorse?

Had he apologised?

No. And she hadn't exactly progressed in her plan to make him suffer. In fact, so far her plan had totally failed to get off the ground.

Wishing she hadn't wasted her limited finances on sexy underwear, Tasha rolled onto her back and stared at the ceiling.

So far she'd failed spectacularly to make him feel remotely guilty for the way he'd treated her, but she couldn't very well back out now without exposing herself to relentless questioning and teasing by her insensitive brother. Which meant she was stuck here.

She lay in the dark, unable to sleep, wondering how

someone with a chest that bruised had somehow managed to get himself to and from the bathroom without help. It hadn't just been the physical strength that had impressed her, it was the mental strength. Somehow he'd pushed through the pain.

He didn't just look like a warrior, he had warrior mentality.

There was a hardness to him that hadn't been there ten years before. He wasn't the same person.

And neither was she.

Tasha was pondering on that when a loud crash echoed around the house.

She was out of bed in a flash, her mind already working through various scenarios. If he'd fallen out of bed, it could have seriously aggravated his injuries. They'd need an ambulance. Paramedics... 'Alessandro?' Sprinting into his bedroom, she saw a lamp lying on the floor where he'd knocked it off the bedside table. On the wall in front of him a football match was being played out on the wide-screen TV and he was watching avidly, his hand locked around the remote control.

'Tash, you're standing in front of the screen!'

'You're watching sport?' Her heart was hammering and she felt weak at the knees. 'You frighten the life out of me and then all you can say is "You're standing in front of the screen"?' Incredulous, she rescued the lamp and waited for her heartbeat to reach a normal level. 'I thought you'd fallen out of bed. I thought you'd broken the rest of your ribs and your skull to go with it.'

'I knocked the lamp off when I was reaching for the remote control.'

'It's two in the morning. What is it with men and the remote control?'

'I wanted to watch sport. I couldn't sleep.'

Him too?

Only she'd been lying there thinking about him while he'd

been thinking about football. The knowledge scraped at her nerves and strengthened her resolve. 'Is it the pain?' Tasha straightened the lamp. 'I thought you'd fallen.' And she'd been terrified of what a fall could do to his broken ribs. Not that she cared, she told herself quickly, but she didn't want to be stuck here nursing him any longer than she had to be.

'It isn't pain. Go back to bed, Tasha. I'm sorry I disturbed you.' He didn't shift his gaze from the screen, watching unblinking as the crowd roared its approval. He was a typical man, obsessed with sport, just like her three brothers. She could walk across the room naked and he wouldn't look up because some feat of sporting prowess was being enacted on the giant plasma screen.

Why had she bothered buying expensive lingerie to drive him wild? she thought crossly. She may as well have worn her ancient Mickey Mouse T-shirt.

The glass doors were still open onto the terrace and a cool breeze wafted into the room. 'Shall I close these now?' She walked across the room. 'You must be freezing.'

'I like the cold air.' Something in his tone made her look at him closely and it was only because she was trained to notice subtle clues that she realised he wasn't actually watching the game. True, his eyes were fixed on the screen, but they were blank. Empty.

And suddenly she knew that the football was an excuse.

Tasha switched on the other lamp and for a fleeting second saw the expression on his face. The humour was gone and in its place was exhaustion and pain. She hesitated and then sat down on the chair, hating herself for not just being able to walk away. It wasn't that she cared, she told herself quickly. It was because he was in pain. She'd never been any good at watching someone in pain. 'You look rough.'

'Go to bed, Tasha.' It was a dismissal she chose to ignore.

She wondered whether he was thinking about his injury or the loss of his brother.

'Things always seem worse at night,' she said casually. 'I see it on the ward with both the kids and the parents. There's something about being in the dark. It makes you think too much.' And she knew that sometimes it helped to talk to pass the time. She'd spent hours keeping frightened kids company at night, playing cards, chatting quietly while the rest of the ward slept. 'What were you doing back in Cornwall anyway? I imagined you in some gilded palace, doing prince-like things.'

'You imagined me?' His head turned and she wanted to bite her tongue. Suddenly she was staring into those dark eyes and everything inside her melted, just as it had when she was a teenager.

'Just a figure of speech. You're the crown prince.' Suddenly she felt awkward, and she wondered why she found it so much easier to talk to children than adults. 'I was sorry to hear about your brother. That must have been very hard for all of you.'

'It's life.' His voice was hard and she floundered, wondering how it was possible to want to comfort and run at the same time. 'What are you doing here, Tasha? Why did you really volunteer to look after me?'

Her heart jumped in her chest. So he wasn't just brave, he was as sharp as a blade.

It wouldn't do to forget that.

'I wanted to help.'

'Really?' The bleak, cold look in his eyes had been replaced by smouldering sexuality that made it impossible to breathe or think. Time was suspended. In the background the crowd roared its approval at some amazing feat of sportsmanship but neither of them looked towards the screen. They were looking at each other, the chemistry a magnetic force between them, drawing them together.

And then he turned his head and closed his eyes. 'Go to bed, Tasha.'

Embarrassment drove her to her feet. Another minute and

she would have kissed that mouth. She would have leaned forward and—

Oh, God.

'Right. Yes. Good. Well—try not to knock over any more lamps.' She fled to the door, wondering what it was about this man that affected her so badly.

She was a career-woman. She was dedicating her life to her little patients. The only thing she was interested in was getting another job as fast as possible.

This time when she walked into her bedroom she closed the door firmly behind her.

The dark rage inside him mingled with frustration. The inactivity was driving him crazy. Almost as crazy as living with Tasha. Even when she wasn't there, she was there. He smelt her perfume, spied a pair of feminine shoes discarded next to a chair.

And now she was surfing. Alessandro watched from the terrace as she carved into the wave, graceful and perfectly balanced. It was like watching a dancer. Some bolder tourists had chosen to visit the beach to take lessons on the soft sand and then try the bigger surf created by the rocks. They huddled in groups, learning to stand on the board, learning to balance, practising the 'pop-up'. Then they ventured into the water and spent the time falling off their boards in the shallows.

Tasha had none of those problems.

Watching her was sheer poetry. He turned away from the window, envying her the opportunity to push herself physically. Before the accident he would have been out there with her. Or maybe not *with* her, exactly. He frowned, not sure how he felt about having her there. She was the reason he was home, and those new painkillers had certainly taken the edge off the agony. But other parts of him weren't faring so well. The inactivity was driving him mad.

As were the phone calls from Miranda.

She wanted to visit.

But he wasn't ready to see her.

Wasn't ready to make the decision everyone wanted him to make.

Driven by a burning desire to recover as fast as possible, he hauled himself to the bed and started the exercises the physio had shown him.

He worked without rest, channelling all his anger and frustration into each movement, pushing himself hard.

By the time Tasha arrived back in the apartment, he was in agony. Still in her wetsuit, her feet bare, she stood and looked at him.

'Did you take your painkillers before you started?'

It cost him to speak. 'No.'

'That's what I thought. Let me tell you something about pain—once it comes back, it's harder to manage. The trick is to head it off before it returns. You should have waited for me. I was going to do the physio with you.' Dropping her towel and her bag on the floor, she walked over to him. Her hair lay in a damp rope over her shoulder and she smelt of the sea. 'The surf is fantastic.'

Her enthusiasm and sheer vitality sprinkled salt into his wounds. 'I saw you. You took a risk with that last wave.'

'I don't think you're in a position to lecture me about risk given that you lay down under a horse.' She glanced down at his ankle. 'How's that feeling?'

'It's fine, thanks.' Speaking required energy he didn't possess and she gave him a knowing smile.

'Fine? Yeah, I bet. Why don't you sit down and I'll check you over.'

Despite the agony, his entire body heated and he reflected on the fact that having Tasha as his private nurse was the worst torture anyone could have invented. 'You already checked me over.' *And he'd had a sleepless night as a result.*

'Sorry, but while I'm in charge, I'll check you whenever I feel it's necessary.' Cool and calm, she faced him down.

'You're my responsibility. No one dies on my shift, got that?'

'I have no intention of dying.'

'You might, if you carry on being uncooperative.' Her smile managed to be both threatening and sweet as she gestured to the bed. 'Lie down.'

It was an awkward manoeuvre. 'When will they take this damn thing off?'

'That cast is holding your joints in the right position while they heal. When the surgeon is happy that your bones are healing, they'll remove it. Usually about six to eight weeks. So that gives you at least another month. Better get used to it.'

'And once it's removed?'

'Intensive physio—hydrotherapy—'

'Hydrotherapy?'

'Basically exercising in the water.' Gently, she pushed him back against the stack of pillows. 'Good for strengthening muscle without stressing bone and joint.'

Alessandro lay on the bed and tried to ignore the pain licking through his body. He wondered if she planned to change out of the black stretchy wetsuit before she examined him. She looked like Catwoman. 'I just want to be fit.'

'You will be, but it's going to take time.' Tasha reached behind her and unzipped the back of her wetsuit slightly. 'If you're worried that you'll never be fit again, don't be. I've seen your X-rays and I've talked to your surgeon. There's no reason why you won't be back to normal in a few months providing you're sensible. If you do the wrong thing now—if you push it when you should be resting—you'll just do damage. You need to take it steadily and do as you're told.'

Relief mingled with humiliation that she'd read him so easily. 'I'm not good at doing as I'm told.'

If he were, then he'd have bowed to pressure and married.

'I know, but if you want to be fully fit again, that's what

you're going to have to do.' Tasha dropped her hands from the zip. 'I need to get out of this gear and take a shower. Then I'll give you a massage to try and relax those muscles of yours. Don't move until I come back.'

'Shower.' Alessandro closed his eyes, not daring to think about the word 'massage'. 'Now you're torturing me.'

She paused, her hand on the doorhandle, a frown in her eyes. 'You could take a shower if you wanted to.'

He gave a sardonic smile and gestured to his cast. 'Oh, yeah—easy as anything.'

'Not easy, but possible. We just have to cover it in plastic to protect it.'

There was a long, pulsing silence. 'You're offering to help me in the shower?'

'That's why I'm here.'

Alessandro wondered if he was the only one feeling warm. Suddenly he wished he hadn't suggested it. Nurse, he told himself. She was offering as a nurse, not anything else. 'I was joking. I can manage.'

'Well, you can't shower on your own, no matter how macho you are.' Her voice was mild. 'But if you don't want a shower, that's fine. I don't want to push you if you're shy.'

Shy?

It had nothing to do with being shy and everything to do with the fact that she was standing in front of him wearing a form-fitting black wetsuit.

'Yeah.' His voice was a hoarse croak. 'That's right. I'm shy. So we'll give the shower a miss for now.'

As she strolled away from him he took comfort in the fact that at least there was one part of his body that appeared to be working normally.

By the end of two weeks, Tasha had reached screaming pitch.

As plans went, this one had backfired big time.

The tension that had been there on the first day seemed to grow with each passing minute.

If revenge was supposed to be pleasurable then she was definitely doing something wrong because she was in agony. The only one suffering was her.

Instead of giving her the opportunity to be aloof and distant, she was being sucked deeper and deeper into his life. His lack of mobility inevitably meant that she did everything from physio to answering the phone.

Even as she had that thought, the phone rang again and Tasha rolled her eyes and answered it, wondering which of Alessandro's many female friends it would be this time.

A brisk voice informed her that the Princess Eleanor wished to speak to her son, but before Tasha could hand over the phone a cool, cultured voice came down the line.

'Are you his nurse?'

Tasha frowned. 'Well, no, actually, I'm a—'

'Never mind. I'm better off not knowing.' In a cold, unemotional tone she demanded to speak to her son and Tasha passed the phone over without question, feeling defensive and irritated and about as small as a bacterium.

Just what was his mother implying?

She'd been expecting to be asked for a clinical update on progress, but clearly his mother didn't consider her worth speaking to.

Angry with herself for caring, Tasha busied herself tidying up and tried not to listen to the conversation, but it was impossible not to pick up the tension between the two of them, even though the conversation was conducted in Italian.

Alessandro replied to what appeared to be a barrage of questions in a similar clipped, perfunctory tone and afterwards he flung the phone down onto the sofa, picked up the crutches and struggled onto the terrace. The loud thump of the sticks told her everything she needed to know about his mood.

Startled by the lack of affection between mother and son,

Tasha stared at his rigid shoulders for a while and then followed him outside. Was she supposed to say something or pretend it hadn't happened? This wasn't her business, was it? And she wasn't supposed to care...

Torn, she stood awkwardly. 'Can I get you anything?'

'No. Thanks.' He kept his gaze fixed on the surfers in the bay. 'Not unless you can conjure up a new, fit body. I need to heal instantly so that I can get back to my life.'

A life he clearly hated.

'I know it feels frustrating, but if you rush things you'll just do more damage.' She tried to put herself in his mother's shoes. Alessandro was her only surviving son. To hear about his accident must have given her a shock. Perhaps it was anxiety that had put that chill in her tone. 'Your mother must be worried.'

'She's worried I'm not doing my duty. Apparently while I'm "lounging" here, enjoying myself with pretty nurses in attendance—that's you, by the way...' he threw her a mocking smile '...my image is suffering.'

So that explained Princess Eleanor's frigid tone on the phone. She'd assumed there was something going on between the 'nurse' and her son. Irritated rather than embarrassed, Tasha glanced at the bruises visible through the open neck of his polo shirt. 'Does she know how badly you were hurt?'

'Yes. Josh called her while I was in Theatre the first time.'

'And?'

'And she said it was no more than I deserved for indulging in high-risk sports. My accident is badly timed. I had fifty official engagements scheduled over the next month, including opening the annual May ball at the palace.'

'Oh. Well, perhaps she's worried that—'

'Tasha, she isn't worried.' He cut through her platitudes, his dark eyes hard and cold. 'My mother only worries about two things—duty and responsibility. My love of polo was bad enough. Having injured myself, I've committed the cardinal sin of making life very inconvenient for her.'

'You're her son and I'm sure that—'

'Let's get one thing straight.' Alessandro shifted his position so that he was facing her. 'As far as my mother is concerned, the wrong son died. It's because of me that Antonio is no longer Crown Prince. I can't bring him back so I'm expected to fill his shoes...' He hesitated and then muttered something under his breath. 'In every way.'

Tasha frowned. *In every way.* What did he mean by that? 'It wasn't your fault. Why are you blaming yourself?'

He turned away abruptly and Tasha felt the tension flowing from him. Darkness surrounded him like a force field and suddenly she knew that the change in him, the hardness, was all to do with the death of his brother.

Her insides softened. 'Do you want to talk about it?'

'No.'

'But—'

'Not everything can be healed by good nursing, Natasha.' The bitterness sliced through her own defences and she stretched out her hand and touched his arm.

'Is that why she rang? To tell you you've made her life difficult?' Anger glowed inside her and suddenly Tasha wished she hadn't passed him the phone.

She should have screened the call.

'She rang to order me to see my advisers, who apparently have a plan for, and I quote, "pulling something positive" out of this disastrous mess I've made.' A cynical smile tilted his mouth. 'Apparently an injured prince may appeal to a certain age group, so she thinks there may be some mileage in media interviews. So that's my contribution to society—providing entertainment for bored housewives.'

'Next time I'm going to tell her you're asleep and can't be disturbed.' Part of her wondered why she felt the urge to rush to his defence and clearly he was asking himself the same question because he stared at her for a long moment.

The hardness left his eyes and he lifted a hand and touched her face. The attraction flickered between them, live and dangerous.

Tasha tried to speak, tried to move, but her body seemed to have shut down and Alessandro gave a low groan, slid his hand behind her head and brought her mouth down on his in a hungry, explosive kiss.

Heat burst through her. Last time she'd kissed him it had been a childish experiment, a desperate desire to grow up fast. There was nothing experimental about this kiss. It was hot and sexual and the explosion of desire gripped her so fiercely that she moaned against his seeking mouth and dug her fingers in the front of his shirt.

It was only as she felt him flinch that she realised how much she must be hurting him. The backs of her fingers were pressed against his bruised chest and she'd leaned into him, instinctively drawing herself closer to his hard body. *Closer to heartbreak.*

'Damn you—no.' Angry with herself, and even more angry with him, she pulled back quickly. 'I didn't want you to do that. I came out here to give you sympathy and support.'

'I don't want sympathy or support. I want you.' He spoke with the assurance and conviction of someone who'd never been turned down by a woman in his life, and she started to shake.

'Don't start that, Alessandro.' She virtually spat the words. 'Don't start all that smooth talk, seduction thing—I'm not interested.'

'Tasha—'

'Age may have given you wider shoulders and longer legs but it obviously hasn't given you a conscience. Do you honestly think I'd put myself through that a second time? Do you think I'm that much of a masochist?' Her voice rose and she saw his dark brows rise in astonishment. 'I'm not interested, Alessandro. I don't want you to kiss me, I don't want you to touch me—' She broke off, aware that her voice was shaking as much as the rest of her. And he was looking at her as if she'd gone mad. *Oh, God, she was overreacting.* She should have laughed it off. Or said she didn't feel anything. Or… Her hands raised, she backed away. 'Coming here was *such* a mistake. I should have said no when Josh asked me. I should have…' She breathed deeply, struggling for control. 'I should have said no.'

'Tasha, wait a minute.' He reached for her but she slapped his hand away and he was forced to grab the rail to regain his balance.

It was a measure of her dedication as a doctor that she made sure he was stable before she walked away.

'Touch me again and I'll break your other leg.' She turned and stalked out off the terrace, her heart crashing against her ribs and terror in her heart.

CHAPTER FIVE

TASHA sat on the bed, her knees drawn up against her chest like a child protecting herself. Her heart was pounding with reaction to the adrenaline surging around her body. The doctor in her recognised the physiological process.

Fight or flight.

The kiss licked like fire through her body, as if that one single touch had set in motion something that couldn't be stopped. She rubbed her hands down her legs, trying to kill the sensations that engulfed her. Why had she let him do that? *Why?*

It wasn't as if she was short on self-discipline. She could say no to chocolate, she'd never been drunk in her life and she'd worked relentlessly to achieve the highest grades possible in her exams. So why couldn't she apply that same single-minded focus to staying detached from Alessandro?

Furious with herself, Tasha thumped her fist on the mattress.

There was something about him that just drew her in. She felt out of her control and that part of it infuriated her more than anything.

Impulse was her greatest fault, she thought savagely. She was a scientist, wasn't she? Impulse shouldn't be part of her make-up, and yet she couldn't seem to stop herself acting on her instincts. First she'd resigned from a job she loved and now she was getting herself involved with the last man in the world any woman in her right mind would get involved with.

So what was she supposed to do next?

She couldn't carry on nursing him, could she? She didn't trust herself.

She was going to have to leave.

She was going to have to make some excuse and—

The door slammed open with a violence that sent it crashing into the wall. Alessandro stood there, his eyes dark as a storm, one hand against the doorframe to balance himself. 'What the hell is going on, Tash? If you feel like that, why did you agree to help me?'

'Get out!' She wasn't ready to face him. *Didn't trust herself to keep him at a distance.*

'I'm not going anywhere. Not until we've had an honest conversation.'

'Honest? What do you know about honest?' It was a struggle to keep her voice even. 'One minute you—you—make a woman feel as though she's the only female alive in the world and then the next minute you—'

'The next minute I…?'

'Just forget it. I don't know why we're even talking about this. *I don't want to talk about this.*'

'We're talking about it because it's obviously on your mind. And it seems to have been on your mind for a long time.' He hobbled into the room, his jaw clenched against the pain, his muscles pumped up and hard. 'That first day in the hospital, I asked you if the past was going to be a problem and you said—'

'I know what I said.' Her voice rose. 'I don't need you to repeat it.'

His gaze was steady on hers. 'If you hate me that much, why did you agree to help me?'

'I don't hate you. I don't have any feelings for you whatsoever.' She threw out the words, knowing them to be untrue. But she badly wanted them to be true. She badly wanted to have no feelings for him. In fact, it was essential for her emotional well-being that she had no feelings for him.

'Which brings me back to the same question—why did you agree to help me?'

'Because I'd messed up my job and I was at a loose end. Because I wanted to prove that you didn't mean anything to me any more, and...' she breathed deeply '...I wanted to see if you were sorry.'

He looked at her for a long moment and then his eyes narrowed and he gave a humourless laugh. 'Ah. Now I understand. You thought you'd punish me, is that it? The strip show was for my benefit. All the "look at me" surfing sessions were designed to make me suffer. All of it was designed to make me suffer. What we shared wasn't water under the bridge. You weren't indifferent. You were getting revenge.'

'It wasn't revenge.' Tasha felt her face grow scarlet as she defended herself. 'I wanted to prove to myself that you were nothing more than a childish crush. The way I felt about you back then was— Actually, I don't even want to think about it. It's just too embarrassing. And, yes, I was angry with you. You behaved like a complete and utter bastard.'

'I know.'

'And then you—' His words penetrated her brain and she broke off and stared at him. 'What did you say?'

'I said I know. I know I treated you horribly.'

'Y-You do?' Stunned by his blunt admission, she stared at him. 'You knew that?'

'Of course. That's why I was so surprised when you waltzed blithely into my hospital room and offered to help me out. Frankly, I was expecting a black eye from you, not assistance.' He watched her cautiously. 'Clearly I was right to be suspicious of your motives.'

'But—' Anger shot through her. 'If you knew you'd behaved horribly, why didn't you ever say anything? You could at least have said sorry.'

'That would have defeated the purpose.'

'The purpose?' Tasha stared at him blankly. 'I don't get it.'

'The purpose was to make you hate me,' he said gently. 'If I'd apologised, it wouldn't have worked, would it?'

'You—you *wanted* me to hate you? Why?'

He gave a crooked smile. 'Because every time I walked into a room you looked at me as though I was the only person there. Because you thought you were in love with me. You were crazy about me, and—'

'All right, all right.' She held up her hand like a stop sign. 'Can this get any more embarrassing? Enough! I know exactly how I behaved. There's no need to rub it in.'

'I was going to say, "and I was crazy about you".' He spoke the words so softly she wondered if she'd misheard.

'You—'

'I'd never been with anyone who behaved as normally around me as you did.'

'I hero-worshiped you.'

'I know, and that was sweet, but the best part was that you were such fun. You were so unselfconscious. The first time I visited you kept trying to remember to call me Your Highness and then you just gave up and called me Sandro, and you were the first person who had ever done that. And you were so beautiful…' He shifted position awkwardly, unconsciously trying to ease the pain. 'Too beautiful. Josh introduced you as his kid sister but it didn't take me long to realise you weren't a kid. Especially when you wore those bikinis.'

Tasha watched him, her heart thumping. 'I wanted you to notice me.'

The corners of his mouth flickered. 'I noticed you.'

'And then there was the ballgown.'

'I wondered when we were going to talk about that. That night at the ball—' his eyes glittered '—I couldn't believe Josh had agreed to take you. The only way I'd kept my distance was because I kept telling myself you were a kid. And

Josh kept telling me you were a kid. And then suddenly you were standing there in this scarlet dress that made you look like a sex goddess—'

'You remember what I was wearing?'

'And suddenly telling myself that you were a kid didn't seem to be working.' His eyes were very dark. 'It didn't help that you were so wildly determined to lose your virginity that night. To me.'

Mortified at the memory of how brazen she'd been, Tasha covered her face with her hands. 'Do we have to talk about this? Isn't there just a nice deep hole I can jump into?'

'I wanted you, too.'

'Oh, sure.' Still cringing, she shook her head. 'Which is why you kissed me senseless and…' *He'd touched her,* she remembered. *Everywhere.* The memory sent fiery heat streaking through her. 'And then you walked away.'

'And why do you think I walked away, Tash?'

His intimate use of her name made her heart thud. 'Because you discovered I was flat-chested? Because I had no idea what I was doing?' His skill had left her trembling and boneless whereas she'd fumbled awkwardly, unsure of herself and of him.

'I stopped because it was the right thing to do, and that is probably the only time in my life I've done the right thing, so you should be grateful, not angry,' he confessed in a raw tone. 'I didn't know if you were a child or a woman. Damn it, I went into your bedroom to give you a message one day and your bed was covered in stuffed toys! One minute you were doing your homework, the next you were wearing a tight red dress designed to drive a man out of his mind. I wanted—well, never mind what I wanted. But I knew I had to do something drastic. That night of the ball I'd promised myself I was going to behave like a real prince. I was going to dance with you and not do anything else. But then we went out to the garden to get some fresh air and the next minute—'

'You don't need to spell it out.'

'Believe me, walking away without looking back was the hardest thing I've ever had to do. And for what it's worth, I'm sorry I hurt you, but at the time I couldn't see any other way. I wanted you to hate me.'

'You could have just told me you weren't interested.'

'I was interested. There was a chemistry between us I'd never experienced before. It was crazy, and—' He broke off. 'You were seventeen. Apart from anything else, it was barely legal.'

A warm glow burned low in her stomach. *He'd wanted her, too.* Tasha wrapped her arms around herself. 'Plenty of people have sex at seventeen.'

'You had your head in the clouds and your eyes on the stars. You were still more of a child than a woman and I had no idea how to handle someone like you. The women I mixed with were usually my age or older—heiresses, society princesses who'd been fed cynicism and experience with baby milk. You were different.'

'And it didn't occur to you to have that conversation with me?' Tasha swung her legs off the bed and stalked over to him, her eyes boring into his. 'I had a brain, Sandro. And a mind of my own.'

'I did the decent thing.'

'*Decent?* You broke my heart, Sandro. You…' She spread her hands, appalled. 'What the hell is decent about making a girl feel totally rubbish about herself? Please tell me that.'

'I didn't make you feel rubbish. I saved you from making a big mistake.'

'*Saved* me? Do you think you could have "saved" me before you ripped off my red dress?' Her face was scarlet at the memory. *The humiliation.* 'Then when I was totally vulnerable and ready to trust you with anything and everything, you suddenly backed away and told me to come back when I'd grown a chest. But that wasn't the worst of it. The worst of it wasn't struggling to get my ballgown back on so that a bunch of strangers didn't see me naked—and you broke the zip, by the way, so I never actually managed to get it back on—the worst was when you walked away from me straight into the arms of a tall, skinny blonde. When you kissed her I thought I was going to die.' It was good to remind herself what had happened, she thought grimly. Good to remind herself why she wasn't going to be seduced by the chemistry again.

'Tasha—'

'You knew I was watching, didn't you? At the time I assumed you didn't know I was still there, but now I see you did it for my benefit. You *wanted* me to see you kiss her.'

There was a stillness about him. A hardness about his eyes that she hadn't seen before. 'I've told you—I wanted you to hate me and forget about me. You were a kid.'

'Did I feel like a kid when you stripped me naked?'

'What do you think would have happened if I'd taken you that night?' His tone savage, he took her chin in his fingers and lifted her face to his. 'Think.'

'We would have made love,' she whispered. 'You would have been the first.'

His fingers tightened on her face. For a moment they stared at each other, sharing the memories through that single look. 'I would have broken your heart.'

The air dragged through her lungs and each beat of her heart felt painful. 'You did that anyway. But I should be grateful. Because of you I buried myself in my books. I gave up on men.'

'That's not what I heard.' His eyes were fixed on hers, his breathing heavy. 'Josh told me you were engaged once—'

Great. More humiliation. 'That didn't work out.' Trying not to think about the fact he'd obviously discussed her with Josh, Tasha pulled away from him. 'I'm not great with relationships. I'm the first to admit it.'

'That makes two of us.'

'You have endless relationships. I read about them all the time in the paper.'

'Those aren't relationships.'

'Right.'

'For what it's worth, I'm sorry I hurt you, Tash. I should have handled it a different way.' He adjusted his balance. 'Forgive me?'

'No! I don't forgive you.'

He was standing close to her. 'There's always been something between us and it hasn't gone away.'

'I'm older and wiser now.'

'You're still the same Tasha,' he breathed. 'Feisty, emotional, warm, giving—'

'Be quiet. I don't trust you when you're nice.'

'I'm always nice, *tesoro*.' His soft, velvety voice wrapped itself around her senses and she felt her willpower crumble.

'I'm still really angry with you,' she choked. 'I'm always going to be angry with you.'

'Even if I say sorry? *Mi dispiace.*'

She felt the warmth of his hand against her head and the heat of his body close to hers. He was a breath away from kissing her again and her eyes closed.

'No, Alessandro—please don't…' There was a tense silence and all she could hear was the sound of her own breathing. 'I mean it—I don't want you to touch me.'

For a moment she thought he was going to ignore her and then she felt his hand drop and he moved away. 'All right.' His voice was hoarse. 'I won't touch you until you ask me to.'

Disappointment mingled with relief, and the confusion of it infuriated her.

It wasn't logical to be disappointed when she was the one who'd asked him to move away.

'That will be never.' Tasha opened her eyes and looked at

him, feeling as though the whole centre of her balance had shifted. 'I'd better find you another nurse.'

'Why? Last time I looked my leg was still in a cast and my ribs were still bruised.'

'I don't think I can do this,' she said desperately. 'I thought it would be easy, but it isn't. We're— You're...'

He was still standing close to her. The warmth of him, the scent of him, wound itself around her insides and sent anticipation skittering through her.

She swayed towards him and then she saw the dangerous burn of heat in his dark eyes and remembered how long it had taken her to recover last time she'd fallen for this man.

She was hopeless at relationships, wasn't she? She didn't want one. She had a career she loved. And she had to concentrate on sorting out the mess she'd made of her professional life.

'You hurt me, Alessandro.' Tasha forced the words past her lips. 'I have more self-respect than to let you do it again. I'll stay and look after you because I gave my word, but it's not going to be any more than that.'

'We thought maybe a carefully placed interview with a celebrity magazine, Your Highness, focusing on your hopes for the future...'

As his advisers droned on, Alessandro stared out of the window towards the waves. It was early morning and there was only one surfer in the waves.

Tasha. She was out there again, enjoying the swell beneath her board and the spray on her face.

Seeking distraction...

It had been three days since their conversation and she'd kept their interaction on a strictly professional level, but that didn't alter the tension that added an edge to the atmosphere whenever they were in a room together.

'Your Highness?'

Alessandro dragged his gaze from contemplation of the surfer. 'Sorry?'

His advisers exchanged glances. 'We were suggesting ways in which you could potentially raise your profile even though you're…' one of them cleared his throat and looked at Alessandro's leg '…incapacitated.'

'Featuring in a celebrity magazine?' Alessandro didn't bother to conceal his contempt for the idea. 'I don't think so.'

'It would be—'

'Shallow and useless,' Alessandro snapped. 'I don't want to be portrayed as some royal layabout. I run a successful multimillion-dollar business.' Or he had until his brother's death. Now a select team ran it in his place and he was only involved in the major decisions.

'The important thing is that the people want to see *you*, Your Highness. They want to know their prince. They'll pay an enormous sum for the interview.' His chief adviser named a figure that made Alessandro shake his head in disbelief.

'They'll pay that much to take pictures of me lying on the sofa with my leg in plaster? The world has gone mad.'

'The money would be given to your favourite charity, Your Highness, and that would be excellent publicity.'

'And both contrived and manipulative.' Alessandro felt bitter distaste for the workings of the media. 'If they have that kind of money to throw around then let them just donate it to the charity in the first place. Cut out the middle man.'

'Her Highness, the Princess Eleanor wants—'

'I know what my mother wants.' His tone cold, Alessandro stared at the thick file they'd brought with them. 'What do you have there?'

'We've outlined proposals for various ways of supporting charity and generally raising your profile in these…' the man's hands trembled slightly as he pushed the file across the table '…difficult and limiting circumstances. The ideas have been approved by the palace. The one that Her Highness particularly wanted us to draw your attention to is—' He broke off, a sheen of sweat on his brow.

'Is?' Alessandro's silken prompt made the man flinch.

'Is the suggestion that you announce your engagement, sir.'

It was like being caught in an avalanche. The cold slammed into him, suffocating him and chilling him right to the bone.

When he didn't speak, the man cleared his throat. 'It's been a while, Your Highness, and everyone assumes—'

'I know what everyone assumes.' Alessandro barely recognised his own voice. He leaned back against the sofa, suddenly exhausted. 'Leave the file. I'll read it and tell you what I intend to do.'

'Yes, Your Highness.'

They left and Alessandro stayed where he was. The file remained unopened.

The thought of allowing sycophantic journalists and photographers into his private life made him cold inside. But the thing that made him coldest of all was the prospect of announcing his engagement. The last thing he wanted was marriage. Given the choice he would have stayed single rather than risk the sort of relationship his parents had. But he didn't have the choice, did he? It was up to him to produce the next generation to rule the Mediterranean island of San Savarre. It didn't matter whether he liked it or not.

Filling his brother's shoes.

He needed to talk to Miranda. He needed to *see* Miranda. But instead of seeing Miranda's sleek blonde hair and elegant clothes, he saw Tasha putting chilli in his food, undaunted by royal protocol. *Hope I'm not supposed to bow or curtsey.*

Tasha, walking away from him.

Since their heated, tense exchange they had hardly seen each other and Alessandro knew that she was staying out in the surf as long as possible to avoid him.

Telling himself that it was probably a good thing,

Alessandro hobbled through to the bedroom and turned on the television in the hope of distraction.

By the time she arrived back from her session in the waves, he'd pulled himself together and he focused hard on the screen as she whirled through the apartment like a tornado, singing to herself as if nothing had happened between them.

Alessandro watched her steadily. *She was putting on an act.*

'Hi, there, hopalong!' she called to him as she stripped off the jacket she'd put on over her wetsuit and walked jauntily towards her bedroom. 'Surf's up today and this time I'm not saying that to make you want to thump me.'

'Tasha—'

'Need to get out of my wet things!'

He had to admire her performance. If he hadn't known better he would have said she was indifferent. But he knew she was far from indifferent. Watching her breeze through the house, he wondered how long she was going to keep up the pretence that nothing was happening between them. 'When I finally get this damn plaster off my leg, I'll join you.' They were going through the motions. Talking about surfing, even though that wasn't the topic uppermost in their thoughts.

He heard the soft hiss of water as she turned on the shower and immediately he started thinking about Tasha naked. And thinking about Tasha naked—

Cursing softly, he picked up the remote control and flicked on the sports channel.

'How did your meeting go?' She was standing in the doorway, wearing a T-shirt and a pair of shorts. Her hair was still wet from the shower and her feet bare. 'What do they want you to do?'

Get married.

'The usual stuff. Palace promotion. I'm afraid I'm not very good at being told what to do. I've always been a bit of a rebel

that way. Antonio was the dutiful one. He was the Good Son.'
He felt the bed give as she sat down next to him.

'You must miss him terribly. I know you were close.' Her
voice was soft and for the time being she seemed to have
abandoned her act. 'I can't begin to imagine how I'd cope if
I lost a brother.'

'We both had our roles. I was the bad boy. Even as kids
it was the same. It never occurred to me I'd have to play his
role. The truth is, I'm not good at it. No matter how much my
parents would like me to be, I'm not my brother.' Alessandro
wondered why he was telling her this. He never talked about
it. Not to anyone.

But talking to Tasha had always been easy. She had a way
of making a person spill the contents of their minds.

'No, you're not your brother. You're you, an individual.'
She hesitated. 'I suppose you have to find a way to do it that
suits you. A way you're OK with. I mean, Josh and I are both
doctors but we're not the same. We don't approach things the
same way. He's very analytical whereas I'm more emotional.
But I don't think either one of us is better or worse than the
other. We're just different.'

'The problem is, my parents don't want different. If they
could have chosen, I would have been the one who died in
that car.'

'Don't say that.' She sounded shocked and then her forehead creased into a tiny frown. 'The other night when we
were talking—you said it was your fault…'

Had he said that to her? 'Forget it.'

'But—'

'If you want to help me, you can fetch that big fat file from
the table in the living room.' Alessandro gave a humourless
laugh. 'I have to go through it and pick out which duties I'm
up to performing. I need to kiss some babies in public.'

And he needed to finally announce his engagement.

'Kiss babies? Sounds like a recipe for disease transmission
to me. I'll warn infection control. Now, lie back and let me

take a look at your ribs to see how quickly you're healing. It will give me some idea of what you're capable of doing. It's no good opening a hospital and then finding yourself as a patient.'

Remembering what had happened the last time she'd touched him, Alessandro's eyes narrowed warily. 'No need. I'm fine.'

'I'm the one who's going to tell you if you're fine.' She pushed him back with the palm of her hand. 'And wipe that look off your face. I'm in doctor mode. I don't think about sex when I'm in doctor mode. And, anyway, I told you I'm not interested.' Ignoring his protests, she unbuttoned his shirt with brisk fingers. The fact that there was nothing lover-like about her expression did nothing to lessen his libido.

'What about the patient?' Alessandro gritted his teeth. 'What if the patient starts thinking about sex?'

'That would be seriously perverted. After all, I'm hurting you. The bruising is better.' Frowning, she trailed her fingers lightly over his chest. 'Does this hurt?'

'It depends which part of me you're asking about.'

'Don't be disgusting. This is why I chose to be a children's doctor.' But her voice was mild as she slid her fingers up to his shoulders and pressed. 'Does this hurt?'

'If I say yes, will you stop?'

'It obviously doesn't hurt as much as before because you're not doing that clenched-teeth thing. I think you're definitely on the mend.'

'Good, then can we—?'

'I just want to listen to your breath sounds.' She'd left her stethoscope on the table by his bed and as she reached for it her hair tumbled forward, brushing over his arm. 'I'm just going to—'

'So am I.' Driven past the point of control, Alessandro cupped her face in his hands and brought her mouth down on his. Her lips opened under his and he tasted shock mingled with sweetness. For a moment he thought she was going to pull away, but as his tongue slid against hers he felt her moan and tighten her grip on his shoulders. There was a delicious inevitability to the kiss that simply added to the excitement. It was the culmination of the tension and anticipation that had been building between them since the morning she'd walked into his hospital room.

Apparently forgetting all her protests about not wanting him to touch her, Tasha ripped at his shirt, hesitating as he gave a grunt of pain when her fingers made contact with bruised flesh. 'Sorry...' She panted the word against his mouth and pulled back but he grabbed her, his fingers hard on her arms.

'Don't stop. For God's sake, don't stop,' he groaned, his mind at war with his senses. 'Do you want to stop? You didn't want to do this—'

'Changed my mind—' Their mouths clashed, the kiss exciting and erotic, and he rolled her onto her back and then swore fluently as pain overtook him.

'This is—'

'A challenge. I have a better idea.' Desperate, she pushed him back gently and straddled him, her hair falling forward, brushing his bare chest. Her eyes were like dark, dangerous pools. 'I'm the one in charge. If I hurt you, tell me.'

'I think that's supposed to be my line.' Alessandro pulled her head down to his and took her mouth with explicit intent, tasting sweetness and a desperation that matched his.

'God, you're beautiful.' He groaned the words against her lips. 'How did I keep my hands off you all those years ago?'

'You didn't.' Frantic, she tore at his clothes and he tore at hers until only flimsy underwear separated them.

Panting, breathless, they kissed like two crazy people. They were so wrapped up in each other that they were oblivious to anything but the heat they were creating. Which was why they didn't hear the sound in the distance.

'Tasha? Alessandro? Anyone there?' Josh's voice came

from the living room of the house and Tasha froze as if she'd been shot. Her eyes flew open and she dragged her mouth from the seductive pressure of his.

'Ohmigod!'

'Oops.' Hiding his frustration, Alessandro gave her a crooked smile and stroked her hair back from her face. 'It's your brother. That's not great timing. You might want to put your clothes on, *tesoro*. I don't want him to see you naked.'

CHAPTER SIX

'THIS is *all* your fault! I told you not to kiss me.' Tasha yanked her top back over her head and freed her hair. 'Stay there. You're not safe to be around. I was in doctor mode. How the hell did we end up naked?'

'Because the chemistry doesn't go away just because you're clutching a stethoscope. I want you, Tasha. Make no mistake about that.' His smooth, possessive declaration stopped her breathing. For an injured man he was far too threatening.

'I...' confused, she tumbled off the bed, grabbing her clothes. Glancing briefly at him, she collided with dark, burning eyes and felt her insides melt. 'No.' It was both a plea and a protest. 'Just—no.'

She'd promised herself that she wasn't going to do this. That she wasn't going to fall under his spell again.

She was a career-woman. She had a five-year plan and it didn't include falling for a wicked, sexy prince. She'd had herself under control. She'd been doing really well.

Until he'd kissed her...

'Damn you, Sandro. I need to get dressed before he comes looking for us.' Her face burning, Tasha grabbed the rest of her clothes, desperately conscious of those coal-black eyes following her every move. The heat was still in the room, simmering between them like a blast from the sun.

If he was bothered by the fact that her brother was in his house, he didn't show it. But Alessandro wasn't the sort to run from anything, she knew that. In fact, that was part of the problem. He had too much of the devil in him.

And that devil had drawn her just as it had when she was a teenager.

In her haste to drag on her clothes, Tasha couldn't untangle her jeans and they were halfway up her legs when her brother tapped on the door and opened it.

Tasha gave a whimper of horror. She didn't know which was worse—her brother seeing her semi-naked, or her brother seeing her semi-naked with Alessandro.

'Hey, you guys—I thought I'd drop by and see if you've killed each other yet...' His voice faded as he saw them and for a moment Tasha stared like a rabbit at oncoming headlights.

Oh, dear...

'Hi, Josh.' Hands shaking, she finally managed to zip her jeans. She felt as mortified as she had when Josh had caught her kissing the captain of the football team when she was sixteen. 'We weren't expecting you.' She tried to sound casual, as if dressing in Alessandro's room was an everyday occurrence. With any luck Josh would decide to turn a blind eye.

But one look at the flat, disapproving line of her brother's mouth told her this wasn't going to be her lucky day.

'What the hell are you doing?' Josh's voice was tight and the shock in his eyes turned dark as approaching storm clouds as he turned his gaze on Alessandro, who stared right back at him.

'Seducing your sister. If you have a problem with that, take it out on me, not her.'

'You—' Josh was across the room in a flash and Tasha hastily planted herself in front of Alessandro.

'No!' Her legs were shaking and she was mortified at being caught kissing, but most of all she was mortified that she'd been kissing Alessandro in the first place.

That definitely hadn't been part of the master plan.

'Josh, calm down! It's nothing to get into a sweat over.'
Actually, it was, but the sweating was going to have to wait
for another time because at the moment her brother looked
dangerous and she felt a twinge of real fear.

'Calm down? *Calm down?*' Josh closed his hands over her
arms and moved her bodily to one side, his voice thick with
anger as he confronted his friend. 'I arrange for my sister to
nurse you and this is how you repay me?'

Tasha bristled. 'Excuse me! I do have a mind of my own,
you know. You might have been the one who suggested it,
but—'

'Shut up, Tasha.' Josh growled the words. 'This isn't your
business.'

Alessandro shifted his leg. 'It certainly isn't yours, my
friend.'

He should have looked vulnerable, but he didn't. In fact,
somehow he managed to look physically intimidating, even
with broken bones and bruised ribs, Tasha thought absently. She wondered whether his natural air of command was
something to do with being royalty or whether it was just the
man.

Warrior Prince.

Josh was red in the face. 'It has everything to do with me.
She's my sister!'

Tasha opened her mouth to protest again and realised that
neither man was taking any notice of her.

Their eyes were fixed on each other in full combat mode.
Alessandro stared Josh straight in the eye, the challenge bla-
tant. 'And this time she's way above the age of consent. I
repeat—it has nothing to do with you.'

This time? Tasha frowned at that remark but she didn't
have time to dwell on it because the two men were squaring
up for a fight.

Josh stepped forward, his expression ugly, his hands
clenched. 'And that's all it takes for you, is it? She's old
enough so that makes it OK? Well, I've got news for you,

Alessandro, it doesn't make it OK. And she's leaving here right now.' Without turning his head, Josh pointed his finger at the door. 'Pack your bags, Tasha.'

Tasha raised her eyebrows, assuming he was joking. When she realised he wasn't, she put her hands on her hips and threw her head back. 'I will *not* pack my bags! Are you deranged? Listen to you!' Her own temper spilled over. 'I'm not six years old, Josh. I'm a grown woman, and if I want to kiss a man, I'll kiss him and I don't have to ask your permission first.' She vented her anger on Josh, even though she knew deep down that most of it should be directed at herself.

She'd been stupid, stupid, stupid…

'You're my sister.' His tone was raw and angry. 'Don't argue with me. Go and pack. This is between Allesandro and I.'

'Oh, for God's sake, will you listen to yourself? "*This is between Allessandro and I,*"' Tasha mimicked his tone. 'What are you going to do, Josh? Challenge him to a duel? Pistols at dawn? This is the twenty-first century. Get over yourself.'

'This isn't your business, Natasha.'

'Well, *excuse* me—' she emphasised each word '—but I was the one naked with him, not you. I think that makes it my business, not yours.'

Josh gave a low growl. 'You were *naked* with him?'

Yes, and she had no idea how it had happened. Clearly at some point during the burn of chemistry, her brain had disconnected itself from her body. But she didn't want to think about that right now. 'So what if I was? *What is your problem?* You do not just barge in here and tell me what to do. Do I ask you what's happening in your love life? Do I lecture you or ask you who you got naked with last night? When I saw you coming out of that on-call room a couple of weeks ago, having had a night of hot sex, did I demand to know who was in the room with you?'

Alessandro raised an eyebrow. 'Hey, Josh, you had a night of hot sex? Good man.'

'Shut up!' Brother and sister spoke simultaneously and Tasha stabbed Josh in the chest with her finger.

'I wanted to ask who she was, but I didn't because I respect your privacy and your ability to make your own decisions. I understand that you're an adult. If you want to have a one-night stand in the on-call room, that's up to you.'

There was a tense, frozen silence.

Josh's face had turned from scarlet to grey. 'It wasn't a one-night stand. And this isn't about me, it's about you.'

'Precisely.' Tasha folded her arms and pursed her lips. 'Which makes it my business, not yours. If I want to sleep with a man, I'll sleep with him. I don't need your permission.'

Josh's shoulders sagged and suddenly he looked exhausted. 'Fine.' His voice was brittle. 'You're right, of course. I apologise.'

Startled by the sudden change in him, Tasha frowned. One minute he was yelling at her and the next he looked as though his brain was on another planet. 'So—when I need a knight in shining armour, I'll text you.'

Alessandro started to laugh. 'I hate to break it to you, Josh, but I think your baby sister is all grown up and slaying her own dragons.'

Josh was still looking at Tasha. A tiny muscle flickered in his cheek and he shook his head slightly, as if trying to focus. 'Just as long as you know he will break your heart,' he said shakily. 'You'll fall in love, because that's what you do, and he'll smash you to pieces. I don't want that for you. I don't want you loving someone you can't be with. I wouldn't wish that on anyone.' There was an anguished note to his tone that killed Tasha's anger like water on flame.

Instinct told her there was more to her brother's words than a throw-away comment.

I don't want you loving someone you can't be with.

Suddenly she knew that his explosion of emotion was

driven by something deeper than her own indiscretion. Something much more personal.

'Josh…' Her voice faltered. 'I—'

'I'm just telling you to be careful, that's all.' Cutting her dead, he blanked the emotion and walked to the door. 'I'll leave the two of you alone. I'm sorry I interrupted. And who am I to give advice on relationships? It's a subject I know nothing about.'

His departure was more painful than his arrival.

Tasha felt her heart clench. Her brother was suffering and she sensed that his anguish went much deeper than concern about her.

Was this about the woman in the on-call room?

'Wait!' Tasha sprinted after him. 'Don't just walk off—for crying out loud, Josh, will you *wait*?'

He kept walking, talking over his shoulder as he strode through Alessandro's double-height living room. 'I need breakfast. I've been working all night. I have to get back to the hospital.'

'I'll make you breakfast.' Catching up with him, she caught his arm. 'The kitchen here is like a spaceship and I can do amazing things with eggs. Please.'

'I need to be on my own.' He shook her off and she saw the emptiness in his eyes as he detached from her. 'I'm sorry I disturbed you.'

Tasha felt a flash of exasperation but this time it was fuelled by real concern for her brother. 'It wasn't like that, Josh—honestly, it was nothing.' She didn't know what it was and she hadn't had time to work it out, but at the moment her priority was Josh. 'I want you to stay. I haven't seen you properly since I arrived. Let's chat. Catch up.'

'Sit down, Josh.' Alessandro's slightly accented drawl came from behind them. Tasha realised that while she and Josh had been arguing Alessandro had hauled himself from the bed and was now gripping the doorframe. His shirt—*the shirt she'd ripped*—hung loose around his body, exposing his bronzed muscled chest. 'I'm going mad trapped in this place. I need male conversation.'

Tasha gave a faint smile. 'Men don't have conversations. They just exchange sporting results.' But she was relieved that Alessandro had added his voice to hers.

Josh looked undecided and the look he gave Alessandro was cold. 'I should go—'

'There's a wealth of difference between what one should do and what one chooses to do,' Alessandro drawled. 'Sit down. Your sister isn't a bad cook, providing you keep her away from chilli.'

Tasha opened her mouth and closed it again. This wasn't the time to give him a lecture on the emancipation of women.

Josh relaxed slightly. 'Are you going to promise not to touch my sister again?'

'No.' Alessandro's tone was calm and he lifted his hand as Josh's eyes flared. 'But I promise to stop if she asks me to. Fair enough?'

Josh's mouth was a tight line. 'I don't think—'

'Hello? I'm over here!' Exasperated, Tasha waved at both of them. 'You don't need to talk about me as if I don't exist. In fact, you don't need to talk about me at all. Let's just drop the whole subject.' She was relieved to see her brother sprawl on the deep leather sofa.

As he ran his hand over his face she realised that he hadn't slept in a long time.

The sunlight pouring through the floor-to-ceiling windows simply accentuated the shadows under his eyes and the pallor of his skin. Why had it taken her so long to notice how awful he looked?

Because she'd been too busy getting her clothes on.

'So…' She sank down on the sofa next to him and curled her legs underneath her. 'You look wrecked.'

'Thanks.'

'Have you been working nights or something?' Even

as she asked the question, she dismissed it. Josh never had any trouble coping with work volume, so it couldn't be that. Which meant it must be a woman. But the split with Rebecca had been mutual…

Using a process of elimination, she mentally ticked off the options and decided that it had to be something to do with the woman he'd had in the on-call room.

She'd thought at the time that he was behaving oddly.

Suddenly she wished she could send Alessandro into the kitchen so that she could question her brother in private.

'So how's the leg?' His expression slightly less black, Josh looked at his oldest friend. 'Are you healing?'

'Yes, but not fast enough.' Alessandro limped over to the other sofa and sat down. He'd mastered the art of keeping his movements as smooth as possible to reduce jarring. 'I'm hoping this cast will be off soon, then I can get back to normal duties.'

'Palace giving you a hard time?'

'They are not amused,' Alessandro said lightly, a sardonic smile on his face. 'I'm supposed to be earning my keep, not "lounging" around here.'

'You can't do much with your leg like that.' Josh's gaze flickered to Tasha. 'Except mess with my sister.'

'Let's not go there again.' Alessandro leaned back against the sofa. His shirt flopped open, revealing smooth bronzed skin and well-defined muscle. Feeling suddenly dizzy, Tasha was about to tell him to button it up when she realised that he couldn't because she'd ripped the buttons.

Concern for her brother mingled with the realisation that the chemistry between her and Alessandro was as powerful as ever.

So much for the childish crush theory. So much for proving to him that she was indifferent.

Satisfied that they weren't going to kill each other, Tasha used the excuse of breakfast to escape to the kitchen.

Behind the safety of the closed door, she took refuge in

mindless cooking to keep her mind off Alessandro. She didn't want to think about Alessandro. She wanted to know what was wrong with Josh.

People said women were complicated, but at least women usually talked about their problems. Frustrated and grumpy, she chopped fruit into a bowl and then remembered she was feeding men and fried a stack of bacon.

Walking back into the living room with a heaped tray, she found the two men deep in conversation about sport. The earlier argument might never have happened.

They were lifelong friends, of course, and the bond showed as they talked easily, barely acknowledging Tasha as she deposited the tray on the table.

'Hello? Earth to Neanderthals,' she said cheerfully. 'I've cooked it, but I draw the line at actually forking the food into your mouths. That bit you can manage yourselves if you really concentrate.'

'Thanks, Tasha.' Josh sat forward and helped himself to bacon. 'I can't be long. They're holding a prince-and-princess party on the children's ward this afternoon and I promised to dress up as a prince. Which means I have a pile of work to get finished this morning.'

Tasha felt her insides tighten at the mention of the children's ward. She missed it dreadfully.

Being with Alessandro had distracted her slightly from her life, but now reality was back with full force. What if she couldn't find another job? What if she'd messed everything up for good?

Oblivious to her anxieties, Alessandro was laughing at Josh. 'You trained for all those years to pretend to be a prince?'

'It isn't funny. I should have said no.'

'So why didn't you?'

He hesitated. 'Because a friend asked me. There are some kids who have been on the unit for ages—they're bored and need some distraction.' Josh bit into his sandwich. 'Someone came up with the idea of having a prince-and-princess tea party so that they can dress up. Tiaras—that sort of thing. Because I'm not officially working today, I'm supposed to arrive halfway through dressed as Prince Charming.'

Tasha slid her hands round her mug of tea. 'You're kidding.'

'I did Father Christmas last year.' Josh wiped his fingers on a napkin. 'What's the difference?'

'Is that a serious question?' Alessandro was still laughing. 'One is fat and wears a red coat. The other is suave and capable of slaying dragons.'

Tasha sat with the mug halfway to her mouth, watching the way Alessandro's eyes shone and his cheeks creased when he laughed.

He was the sexiest man she'd ever met.

It was just as well Josh couldn't read her mind.

'No dragons at our tea party. This bacon is good, Tasha. I can't remember when you last cooked for me. Usually you glare at me and tell me it's not women's work. Are you all right?' Josh frowned at his sister. 'Why are you staring at Alessandro?'

'I'm keeping an eye on his colour,' she said smoothly. 'If he does too much, he gets tired.'

'He didn't look that tired when I arrived.' His tone dry, Josh helped himself to more bacon. 'He looked as though he had all his faculties. He won't need you for much longer.'

Tasha wondered if her brother was having another dig. 'I'll stay until he's able to cope without help.'

'Have you applied for any jobs?'

Tasha leaned forward and stacked the plates. 'Not yet.'

'Why not?'

'Because I don't know what I'd say in the interview about why I left my last job. I'm worried everyone is going to think I'm a troublemaker.' Tasha rescued the ketchup before it could tumble onto the floor. 'I miss medicine. I miss the kids. I miss being part of a unit. I miss—all of it. I'm a doctor. I want patients.' Aware that Alessandro was no longer smiling, she suddenly wished she hadn't said anything. 'Sorry, it's just that I had this great career plan and then—*poof*—I managed to blow the whole thing. Well done, Tasha.' She knew that her light tone hadn't fooled them. 'Anyway, I don't know why we're talking about me. I already have a job for the time being. Preventing Alessandro from trying to run before he can walk.'

'I can tell you're a paediatric doctor. You're treating me like a kid.'

He wasn't a kid at all. He was a grown man and she was horribly aware of every bronzed, handsome inch of him. She'd thought her anger would keep her safe, but her anger had vanished. She'd thought her feelings were all from the past. But the explosion of passion that had erupted between them had nothing to do with the past and everything to do with the present.

Fear flashed through her. If she let him, he'd hurt her again. Just as he had the first time. And she wasn't going to let a man do that to her…

The sooner she found herself a paediatric job, the better.

'You shouldn't feel insecure. You're a good doctor, Tasha.' Josh stole the last piece of bacon. 'Remember that little girl you saw on the unit that day you came to my office to tell me you'd resigned? Turned out you were right. It wasn't hay fever. She had a congenital heart defect.'

Alessandro looked bemused. 'I didn't think Tasha worked on your unit.'

'She doesn't. But she walked past this girl and saw something that none of my doctors had seen.' Josh gave a smile. 'She's very intuitive, my baby sister.'

Snapping out of her dream, Tasha stared at him. 'The girl had a congenital heart defect? You're sure?'

'She's already seen the cardiologist. You probably saved her life.'

'Oh.' She felt an ache of sympathy for the child and the

mother. 'I wish it had just been hay fever. Poor little thing.' Suddenly she missed her job even more. She wanted to be the one looking after the child, supporting her and helping her through a difficult time. She could make a difference, she knew she could.

'This prince-and-princess party…' Alessandro eased his leg into a more comfortable position. 'That must be something I can help with.'

Josh glanced at him with a frown. 'You?'

'You should be saving lives, not dressing up as a prince. I don't have your medical skills, but I can do the prince bit.' His tone was loaded with irony. 'I've never dressed up in a cloak or worn a crown, but if it would help the kids I can do it. Provided someone keeps the paparazzi at a distance. I'm doing it for the children, not the press.'

'Why keep them at a distance?' Tasha jumped to her feet. 'It's a brilliant idea. Your mother wants some good publicity—what better than the prince visiting the children's ward? You can autograph stuff for them. They can have pictures taken with you. They'd love that. I'll come with you.' Better to be on the children's ward as a visitor than not be there at all, she reasoned.

'How far from the car to the ward? I can't walk that far on this damn leg of mine.'

Tasha opened her mouth to suggest a wheelchair but took one look at the set of his jaw and closed her mouth again. Alessandro would drag himself across the ground by his fingernails before he'd agree to use a wheelchair.

'It's a great idea. We can drop you right outside. And Tasha can come with you.' Josh nodded. 'I'll have a word with the staff and let them know you're coming.'

'I've been thinking about a job in NICU. Is there someone there I could talk to?'

Alessandro frowned. 'What's NICU?'

'Neonatal intensive care unit.' Josh shifted in his chair. 'Talk to Megan Phillips.'

Tasha noticed that her brother's tone had altered and wondered if it had anything to do with Megan. Glancing up, she met Alessandro's steady dark gaze. Clearly he was thinking the same thing. He smiled and that slow, sexy smile connected straight to her insides. Her stomach swooped and plunged, the chemistry between them as electrifying and terrifying as ever. Staring into his mahogany eyes, she opened her mouth to speak but he spoke first.

'You've got me through the worst bit. Thanks to you, they let me out of that hospital. I can manage now. If you want to leave, leave.'

He was giving her a choice. And she knew it wasn't just about caring for him.

He was making her decide whether to leave or not.

Both men were looking at her expectantly and Tasha swallowed. She didn't know how she was going to answer until the words left her mouth.

'I'm not in the habit of letting people down. I'll stay until you're fully mobile, just as I promised.' It was easy to convince herself that that was the reason she was staying. 'But I do need to be looking for a full-time job. I thought I'd explore NICU—except that I'm not sure I'll get a reference.'

'You will. I made a few phone calls this week.' Josh leaned back against the sofa. 'Turns out you had a lot of support at the unit. Questions are being asked. People are enraged that you were allowed to resign.'

'Really? Why didn't you say so before?' Tasha brightened. 'Enraged? Oh, I'm so pleased.'

Alessandro lifted an eyebrow. 'You want people to be enraged?'

'I want them to care that I've gone, yes. I'm human enough to want that. And I'm human enough to need to be told I did the right thing—that others would have done the same. I would love an apology from him,' she sniffed, 'but I doubt I'll get that.'

'You won't. They guy's an idiot. Forget about him.'

Josh leaned forward. 'So, about the prince-and-princess party...'

Energised by the knowledge that people were supporting her, Tasha reached for her handbag. 'Leave that to me. I'm going to pay a visit to the dressing-up shop in St Piran. Alessandro and I will see you back at the hospital.'

He'd given her the opportunity to leave and yet she'd chosen to stay.

Alessandro watched Tasha as she gathered bags and put them in the car. Her coat was buttoned from neck to hem and he wondered why she was wearing a long coat when it wasn't cold.

'I've bought tiaras and all sorts of props that should be useful.' She slid his crutches into the boot. 'Be careful as you get in. Sit down, then I'll move your legs.'

She gently moved his leg into the car and helped him with his seat belt. 'Is that comfortable?'

It was agony, but even agony wasn't enough to dampen his response to her.

'Alessandro?' She lifted her eyes to his face and chemistry immediately flickered between them. Flushing, she drew back sharply. 'Right. Well, if you're not too uncomfortable then we'll get going.'

'Tasha, listen—'

'The kids are waiting.' The car door slammed and Alessandro winced as pain rocked through his leg. Fine. So they'd go through the day pretending they hadn't stripped each other half-naked.

'Did you agree to stay with me just to annoy your brother?' He watched her as she slid into the driver's seat. 'If you want to take a job at the hospital, you should take it. I can manage.'

'I promised to look after you until you're out of the cast and that's what I'm going to do. And, anyway, I don't really want to work in the same hospital as Josh. You've seen what he's like. He'll be banging on my door, questioning every decision I make. We'd drive each other crazy.' She drove fast and Alessandro found himself clenching his teeth.

'Do you know these roads well?'

'Yes.'

'Good, because if there are any surprises behind that blind bend, you're about to smack into it head first.'

She shifted gears smoothly. 'Do I make you nervous? Big, tough guy like you?'

An image of tangled metal lodged itself in his head. 'I'm not a good passenger.' He didn't elaborate but she immediately trod on the brakes.

'Sorry,' she muttered. 'I didn't think.'

Her sensitivity surprised him, although it shouldn't have. She'd always been sensitive, hadn't she? *Too sensitive.*

He braced himself for her to question him about the accident that had killed his brother but instead she smoothly changed the subject.

'Did you notice anything strange about Josh?'

'Strange in what way?'

'You didn't think he was tense and on edge?'

'He'd just caught his sister naked with a man.' He watched as the colour bloomed in her cheeks. 'That was reason enough for him to be tense.'

'Yes, but it wasn't that. It was something else. Something personal. Did you see his face when he made that little speech about loving someone you couldn't be with?'

'He's worried about you.'

'I'm not sixteen years old.' This time her gear change was vicious. 'Why do men always think a woman has to be in love? This is the twenty-first century. I don't want love. The most important thing to me is my career. And, anyway, a woman can have sex without being in love.' The words spilled out of her and he watched her steadily, wondering why he wasn't convinced.

'We didn't have sex, Tasha.'

The gears crunched again. 'I'm well aware of that. All I'm saying is that if we *had* had sex then it wouldn't have had anything to do with being in love, and I can't imagine why you'd even think that. Women can have sex like a man. Without emotional involvement. I don't want emotional involvement.'

'Right.' Alessandro tried to imagine Tasha doing anything without emotional involvement, and failed. Her emotions were involved in everything, from cooking chilli to handling her stethoscope. 'So, if that's the case, why are you worried about what Josh said?'

'There's something wrong with him. He's been acting really strangely since I caught him in the on-call room that day I came to see you...' Without breaking the conversation she flicked the indicator and turned into the hospital car park. 'And I know he had someone in the room with him, but he was hiding the fact. He didn't want me to know. But when I saw him, he looked all lit up inside. As if something special had happened. There was an energy about him that I haven't seen for years.'

'So maybe he's found someone. What's wrong with that?'

'Nothing. But today he didn't look like that. He looked exhausted.' She pulled into a parking space and gnawed at her lower lip with her teeth. 'He looked awful, Sandro.'

'He works hard.'

'I know, but he always has. Josh has endless reserves when it comes to work. It's something else. Something to do with a woman, I'm sure of it.'

Looking at her troubled expression, Alessandro wondered why it was that women had to analyse everything in such depth. 'Maybe he's met someone and she's married.'

'Josh would never have an affair with a married woman.'

'He was married himself. Still is, isn't he?'

'His relationship with Rebecca has been dead for ages.'

Alessandro felt the cold trickle down his spine. 'That's what marriage does to people.'

'Do you really believe that?'

'How many happy marriages have you seen?'

She hesitated. 'Just because we haven't seen them, it doesn't mean they don't exist.'

'Does it matter? I thought you said you could have sex without emotional involvement.'

'I can. But that doesn't mean I don't believe that happy marriages don't exist.' She snapped her seat belt and Alessandro watched her for a moment.

'If you're worried about Josh, why don't you just ask him what's wrong, instead of subjecting yourself to all this guesswork?'

'I've tried—obliquely. But he dodges it. And then this morning...' she retrieved her bag '...he just seemed really stressed about something.'

'He'd just seen you naked with me,' Alessandro drawled. He knew from past experience that was sufficient reason to stress Josh. 'In case you hadn't worked it out, your brothers are very possessive of you. Particularly Josh.'

'Maybe we should invite him round for supper so that we can chat properly. I could cook something.'

'Something with chilli?'

She grinned wickedly. 'I don't know how you ate that.'

'The eating it was fine. It was putting out the fire afterwards that was the problem.' Alessandro eased his leg out of the car, clenching his jaw against the pain as Tasha lifted the bags out of the boot.

As he straightened up she slung a cloak around his shoulders.

'All hail, Prince Alessandro. Welcome to the Kingdom of Sick Child.' She curtseyed deep and he stared down at the velvet cloak in wry amusement.

'What on earth is this?'

''Tis your finest clothing, sire. Otherwise known as

prince's-cape-from-dressing-up-shop.' She stood up. 'Don't you dare refuse to wear it—took me ages to track it down. There's a cute crown to go with it. They threw it in free.' As she rummaged in the bag, Alessandro glanced around the car park to check that there were no photographers.

'There is no way am I wearing a velvet cloak and a plastic crown to walk across the car park.'

'Not even for sick children? They might be watching from the window.' She batted her eyelashes but Alessandro didn't flinch.

'If they're watching from the window, they can't be that sick.'

'I just want you to make an entrance.' As she spoke she slid off her coat and Alessandro almost swallowed his tongue as he saw what she was wearing.

'What—?'

'How do you do, Your Highness? I'm the Princess Tasha.' She beamed at him and gave a quick twirl. The shimmery pink dress swirled and floated around her slender frame. Still smiling, she reached into the bag and pulled out a tiara. Ducking down to look in the wing mirror, Tasha slid it into her hair and adjusted it. 'Just need to fit the crown jewels. There. Perfect. How do I look?'

Alessandro ran his tongue over his lips, grateful for the cloak.

When he didn't reply, she frowned at him. 'Do I look like a princess?'

'No.' His voice came out as a hoarse croak. 'At least, you don't look anything like the ones I've met.' And he'd met a few. *Too many.*

Her face fell and she took another sneaky look in the mirror. 'I thought I looked cute.'

'You do look cute. But princesses don't generally look cute. In my experience they're usually hard and cynical.' He gave a crooked smile. 'Comes from having contact with too many wicked princes, I guess.'

'See? *That's* why I'd never want to be a princess. If I can't be the fantasy version, I'm not interested.'

He loved her energy and her sense of fun.

He loved the fact that she treated him the same way she treated everyone else.

Alessandro dragged his eyes away from the twist of hair that had come loose from the tiara and decided that the sooner she went back to work as a doctor, the better for his sanity.

He wondered what would have happened if Josh hadn't arrived in the house when he had. *Would either of them have stopped?*

'Let's go. I don't want to stand around wearing a velvet cloak and a crown for longer than I have to. If the press sees me, I'm never going to live this one down.'

'You'll be accused of being typecast,' Tasha said cheerfully, dropping the car keys into a silky pink bag and waiting while he balanced himself. 'Do you want a hand?'

'No, I've got it.' Leaning on the crutches, Alessandro struggled into the hospital and onto the children's ward.

Balloons were tied in huge clusters and a red 'carpet'—a long piece of scarlet fabric—stretched along the corridor to a brightly painted playroom.

'Welcome, Your Highness.' A nurse in a long flowing dress swept a deep curtsey and Alessandro was about to say something flippant when he saw a little girl in a wheelchair, watching him with tears in her eyes.

Disconcerted, he watched her cautiously.

Great. He'd been here less than five seconds and already he'd made someone cry. Suddenly he wished he hadn't interfered. He should have let Josh do it.

Tasha reached for his arm but he shrugged her off and limped across to the child. He'd volunteered for this so he was going to do it. Without help.

'Hey, there—that's a very pretty dress you're wearing.'

Her face turned the colour of a tomato. 'Are you a real live prince?'

'I am.'

'Is that a real crown?'

Alessandro remembered that Tasha had said you should always be honest with children so he shook his head. 'No, it's plastic. Fake. The police get jumpy if I walk around Cornwall wearing a real crown.' Seeing her face fall, he searched his brain for inspiration. 'But I do have a real one. At home.' Leaning forward, he whispered in her ear. 'If you ever visit my country, I'll give you a private tour of the state jewel collection.'

'You will?' Her eyes went huge. 'Do you have alarms and guard dogs and stuff?'

'All of that. And bodyguards.' Seeing how thin she was, Alessandro felt his heart twist. Suddenly he felt guilty moaning about breaking his ankle. Yes, he was bruised and broken but he was basically fit and healthy, whereas this child… 'How long have you been in hospital?'

'This time? Three weeks.'

'There have been other times?'

'I come in a lot. Sometimes my blood goes wrong.' Her tone was matter-of-fact and she reached out and stroked his cloak. 'The other kids thought it would be an actor or one of the doctors dressed up. You know, like Father Christmas. They always say it's Father Christmas but really it's just a fat man in a beard. They're not going to believe you're a real prince. Do you have proof?'

Caught off guard, Alessandro glanced at Tasha. 'Do I have proof?'

'Absolutely. I brought the proof with me and I have it right here.' Throwing the little girl a dazzling smile, Tasha reached into the bag on her shoulder and pulled out a scrapbook. 'Have a look at this. Here's Prince Alessandro at a royal function at the palace… And he…' she pointed '…he's opening a hospital. Just look at those crowds!' It seemed she'd thought of everything, and as she turned the pages for the child, Alessandro stared at the pictures of himself at various royal events.

Something shifted inside him. Somehow he'd managed to hide his feelings in front of the cameras.

'Wow. Everyone wants to take your picture. Is this your horse?' The little girl pointed to a photograph of him playing polo, and Alessandro nodded.

'He's my favourite horse. His name is Achilles.'

'Do you wear a cloak when you ride him, like Prince Charming?'

'Er—no. I wear pretty standard stuff—breeches and boots.' He gave an apologetic smile and she beamed and took his hand.

'What happened to your leg?'

'I fell off my horse.'

'Ouch.' She peered at the cast. 'You need people to write on that. It's very clean. You need messages and pictures and stuff.'

'You're right, I do.'

'I can help you with that. Can I wheel my chair down the red carpet with you?'

Alessandro looked at the flimsy strip of red fabric and wondered if it would survive. 'Sure. Let's give it a go.'

Who would ever have thought he was so good with children?

Tasha watched as Alessandro handed another little girl a pen so that she could draw a pony on his cast.

Here, in the relative privacy of the children's ward, she saw a different side of him. He was patient, natural, amusing and, most of all, interested.

She'd expected him to try and keep the encounter as short as possible. Instead, he'd settled down amongst the children in the playroom and seemed intent on giving them as much time as they wanted.

'It was generous of him to dress up and play the part.'

Tasha turned to see a young doctor watching her.

The woman smiled. 'I'm Dr Phillips. Megan Phillips.'

Tasha dragged her eyes from Alessandro and stood up quickly, hand outstretched. 'Hi. I'm Tasha O'Hara.'

'Yes, I know. You're Josh's sister.' Something in the way she said it drew Tasha's full attention.

'Josh mentioned you.' She noticed the other woman tense slightly. 'I told him I'd love to talk to you about working in NICU.'

'Oh—right.' Visibly flustered, Megan gave a brief smile. 'Well, I love it.' She went on to detail the pros and cons and Tasha stared at the other doctor, noticing the dark shadows under her eyes. *Shadows uncannily similar to the ones under Josh's eyes.*

With a woman's intuition, Tasha sensed that Megan and her brother were a great deal more than just colleagues. She wondered whether the beautiful, fragile-looking doctor was the woman causing Josh stress.

'Well—it's great to meet you, Megan. Thanks for the inside info.' She decided to do some digging. 'So, how long have you known Josh?'

'A while. We first met at university.' Megan avoided eye contact. 'Not that we hung out together or anything. Josh was Mr Cool—but you know that, being his sister.'

Tasha certainly knew Josh had broken a lot of hearts. She wondered whether Megan's had been one of them.

'If you were at university with Josh, then you must know Alessandro, too.'

Megan gave a brief nod of her head. 'I knew him by sight, that's all, because he was part of Josh's group. I didn't exactly move in their circle. I certainly didn't know he had such a way with children.' The insistent sound of a bleep had both women reaching into their pockets.

Tasha spread her hands in apology. 'It's you, not me—I can't get used to the fact I don't carry one any more.' And it felt strange, being in a hospital and not working.

'I'd better answer this—I slipped off the unit so that I could catch you.' Megan checked the number. 'I expect we'll bump into each other again soon. Maybe we could grab a coffee or something.'

'Yes. I'd like that.' Tasha watched the other woman hurry away from the ward and made up her mind that they were definitely going to meet again. There was something about Megan's pallor that tugged at her heartstrings.

She looked like someone who needed a friend.

Tasha turned back to Alessandro, to find him being swarmed over by children.

Remembering the bruising on his ribs, Tasha strolled over and gently lifted one over-eager toddler onto the cushions. 'Don't climb on the prince. You might damage him and then he won't be able to slay dragons.'

'She doesn't weigh anything.' His tone gruff, Alessandro rescued a little girl in a fairy costume who was about to tumble onto the floor. 'Who were you talking to? She looked familiar.'

'That's because you were all at university together.'

'Really?'

'That's Megan Phillips. Do you remember her?'

'Not the name, but I know the face from somewhere. Can't think where. I met a lot of people at university. Are you going to draw on my plaster?' Gently, he lowered the child onto the cushions and handed her a pink crayon. 'Go ahead.'

Tasha frowned. 'She knew you.'

'Without meaning to sound conceited, a lot of people know me.' He shifted his leg to give the children better access to his cast. 'It doesn't mean I know them.'

In other words, women always flocked to get close to him because of who he was.

'She knew straight away that I was Josh's sister,' Tasha mused, 'which means she must know Josh pretty well. I can't imagine he exactly spends his time waltzing around the hospital talking about me.'

'They work together. They probably chatted in the hospital restaurant over a stale chicken sandwich.'

'Prince Alessandro?' A small girl with her hair in bunches and wearing thick glasses squinted up at him. 'It's time for our story. Will you read it?'

Tasha watched as Alessandro smiled and scooped the child onto his lap.

He was a natural. And he possessed exactly the right combination of strength and warmth.

Strength.

Meeting his eyes, she stared at him for a long moment, wondering what would have happened had Josh not arrived when he had.

She and Alessandro would finally have slept together.

Tasha swallowed. She didn't know whether to feel regret or relief.

CHAPTER SEVEN

'REALLY, we should have invited the press. It would have been a perfect photo call. Even your mother would have approved.' Tasha kept her tone light but underneath she was shaken up. His gentleness with the children didn't fit with the image she had of him as an arrogant playboy.

'If I'd invited the press then I would have been accused of being manipulative.' Alessandro hobbled through to the kitchen, propped himself on one crutch and grabbed a cold beer from the fridge. 'I don't want to be in the newspapers at the expense of some poor family who is going through hell. Neither do I want an innocent child's private trauma broadcast to the world. I don't subscribe to the school of thought that we should all know everything about everyone.' He slammed the fridge door shut, snapped the top of the bottle and drank while Tasha stared at him in amazement.

'What's got into you?'

He lowered the bottle slowly. 'How do you do it?' His tone was savage. 'How do you go there day after day and work with those poor kids? Doesn't it break you apart, seeing them sick?'

She was stunned by the emotion in his voice. 'Yes, sometimes. It isn't always easy, but it's almost always rewarding. And the reason I go in there and work with those kids is because most of the time I make a difference. I'm not saying I can cure them all—' her own voice shook slightly '—but I do everything I can to make a horrid experience better. Some doctors think it's just about throwing the right treatment at a child, but they're wrong. *How* you treat the child is almost as important. Say the wrong thing and suddenly they're twice as scared and anxious.'

Alessandro drained his beer and thumped the empty bottle down on the shiny surface. 'I'm never complaining about my ankle again.'

'Actually, you haven't complained. Not once. Even when you've been in agony,' she muttered. 'You're brave.'

'Brave?' He gave a humourless laugh. 'Brave is that little girl who is never going to walk, or that boy who's on his tenth operation. They humble you, don't they? I mean…' he licked his lips '…we adults moan about the slightest thing. We moan about the weather, our workload, our family, but those kids—they're stuck in bed when they should be out playing with their friends and not even thinking about the way their bodies work, but they don't complain. They're smiling and getting on with it. That sweet little girl without the two front teeth—'

'Hattie?'

'Yeah—the one waiting for a transplant. Do you know that her mum travels two hundred miles to be with her—then she drives home when little Hattie's asleep so that she can spend some time with her two teenagers?' He dragged his hand through his hair and shook his head in disbelief. 'Then drives back again before Hattie wakes up in the morning. Can you imagine living like that?'

'Exhausting. Mentally and physically. Which is, I presume, why you offered her the use of your helicopter.' The generosity of the gesture still shocked her. 'I saw her mother crying and assumed she'd had bad news or something. Then she told me you'd promised to ferry her backwards and forwards until Hattie is discharged. She was completely overcome.'

'It was nothing.' He dismissed his contribution with a

frown. 'It will give my pilot something to do. Do you come across cases like that often?'

'When parents have to travel a long way? Yes. Especially in a rural area like this. And St Piran's is a specialist unit so I expect they take kids from a wide distance.'

Alessandro let out a long breath. 'How long until she gets her transplant?'

'I think they're exploring live donor. Her mother was telling me that a cousin might be a match. In the meantime she needs the dialysis to stay healthy.'

'She seemed so small and fragile.'

'Yes, well, that's probably because the kidneys play a role in the metabolism of growth hormone—chronic kidney disease can limit physical growth.' Tasha helped herself to an apple from the fruit bowl. 'Not that I know anything about Hattie's particular case, of course. I'm just talking generally.'

'If I throw money at it, can I make it go away?' His rough question brought a lump to her throat.

He cared.

'No. But you've already made it easier. She has her mum with her until she goes to sleep. That's a really big deal when you're eight.'

'You're wasted here, looking after me.' He leaned his hips against the counter, his expression serious. 'You should get out there and use that training of yours.'

'Are you trying to get rid of me?'

'No, but I could see how skilled you were with those kids and I know that's what you should be doing. Have you lost your confidence? Is that what's going on here? This whole thing with that idiot you used to work for—has it shaken you up?'

Startled, she felt her breath catch. 'Maybe,' she croaked. 'Just a little.' It was better to tell herself that than believe that she was there because of him. 'I'm still afraid no one will want me. But I've started looking. There just aren't that many speciality doctor posts around right now.'

'What's your dream? Ultimately you want to be a consultant?'

'That's why I worked my butt off in medical school.'

'What about marriage?' His voice was gruff. 'Family? Kids? When you were seventeen that was what you wanted. You wanted the whole fairy-tale. What happened?'

'I grew up. The whole fairy-tale thing bombed.' She gave a careless shrug. 'Anyway, I always thought Cinderella should have picked up her own shoe instead of expecting someone else to pick it up after her. And who in their right mind is going to marry a man she met when she was asleep? If I'd been asleep for a hundred years, I'd want to get out there and party, not walk down the aisle with a stranger.' Tasha bit into the apple, horribly conscious of him. Even with broken ribs and his leg in a cast he was indecently sexy.

'Tell me about Hugo.'

She choked on the apple. 'How do you know about Hugo?' Looking at his face, she scowled and threw the apple into the bin uneaten. 'Josh, presumably.'

'What happened?'

'I don't know.' Irritated, embarrassed, she shrugged. 'The usual. I fell for a guy. He wasn't serious. Only that time I learned my lesson.'

'Which was?'

'A girl has to be in charge of her own happy-ever-after. And it doesn't always have to include a man. I discovered that having a career can be every bit as exciting as sex.'

There was a tense silence.

'If you believe that, maybe you've never had really good sex.'

Her heart doubled its rhythm. 'Or maybe I just have a really great career.'

'Maybe you do. But shouldn't it be possible to have both?'

'Maybe. But there are plenty of broken marriages in my business. Just look at Josh and Rebecca.'

'I don't want to talk about Josh.'

She felt his gaze right through her body. 'I think I'll just—'

'No.' Somehow he crossed the kitchen before she could move towards the door. 'Don't run off. Not this time.'

Tasha backed herself into the kitchen counter. 'Look, whatever you're going to say, I'm not—'

'I was going to say that you're beautiful.'

The words stole her breath. 'Oh. Well, in that case—'

'You were beautiful at seventeen but you were a child then…' His voice was husky. 'Now you're a woman.'

But she felt like a teenager, with her heart pounding and her breathing shallow. 'Sandro—'

'I want you, Tasha.' The words were thickened with emotion. 'But it's your choice. I'm not in a position to throw you over my shoulder and influence your decision. You can walk out of that door, or you can walk into my bedroom.'

Oh, dear God…

Slowly, her eyes lifted to his and her heart tumbled as she met the intimacy of his gaze. His eyes were dark pools of desire. And serious. There was no humour there. No mockery. He was an adult, making an adult decision, and he was asking her to do the same thing. She could walk away. *She could say this wasn't what she wanted.* Or she could…

'On second thoughts, forget the bedroom.' His mouth came down on hers and he kissed her. Desire punched hard and deep and Tasha slid her hands over his shoulders, feeling male muscle flex under her fingers as his mouth plundered hers with erotic purpose.

Dizzy, she remembered that Alessandro had always known how to kiss. It was obvious that the intervening years had done nothing but polish his performance.

Engulfed by sexual excitement, she felt his hand slide to

her bottom, pulling her hard against him, and she tumbled blindly into a well of sensation.

Somehow—and afterwards she couldn't even remember how they'd done it—they made it to the bedroom, still kissing, and Tasha found herself on the bed, staring up into Alessandro's burning eyes.

'Do you know how long I've wanted to do this?'

'About as long as I've wanted you to do it.' There was no pretence between them. No shyness or coyness. And the sheer honesty of it took her breath away.

For a brief, intimate moment he looked down at her, and then he lowered his head and took her mouth again, tasting her, exploring her intimately. And she kissed him back with the same fevered hunger, taking everything he offered and more.

His hands made short work of her shirt and she felt the last two buttons ping onto the floor as he finally lost patience.

'I'll buy you another.'

'Don't bother.' Tasha matched his desperation, tearing at his shirt the way she had only that morning when Josh had interrupted them. It was choreographed madness as they stripped each other.

Naked, they rolled together and Alessandro gave a grunt of pain as her elbow encountered his bruised ribs.

'Sorry.' She braced herself on her hands, murmuring against his mouth. 'I'm really sorry. Just lie still and don't move. I'll do it all.' Before he could protest, she kissed her way down his body, her mouth infinitely gentle as she explored his bruises and moved lower.

This time his groan had nothing to do with pain. 'Tasha…'

She felt his hands slide into her hair but she didn't stop and then heard the change in his breathing as she explored him intimately.

Her intention had been to drive him wild but in the end she

couldn't wait, and she slid up his body and straddled him, her hair tumbling forward onto his chest. 'Am I hurting you?'

'Yes—' his reply was thickened '—but not in the way you mean.' His hands gripped her hips and he shifted her over him, taking control despite her superior position.

Wildly excited, Tasha was about to move when he moaned something against her mouth.

'What?' She dragged her mouth from his and tried to focus on him. 'Sorry?'

'Condom.' He reached out a hand towards the drawer by the bed and she realised that the thought of contraception hadn't crossed her mind. 'We should—'

'Yeah.' *She was a doctor, for goodness' sake.* And it hadn't even crossed her mind. Fumbling in the drawer, she grabbed protection and then they were kissing again, hands and mouths frantic as they feasted on each other.

His hand was between her legs and Tasha felt the skilled stroke of his fingers as he drove her higher and higher.

'Sandro…' She panted his name—heard the growl of frustration deep in his throat, and then he was inside her and the sheer size and heat of him punched the breath from her body.

She came immediately, the explosion so intense and violent that she dug her fingers hard into his shoulders, holding on as everything collapsed around her. Dimly, through the burning fever of blind lust, she knew she should apologise for hurting him, but his hands were on her and he took her hard, each powerful thrust sending her spiralling up towards the peak she'd just left.

This time when she hit, she took him with her and she sobbed his name as he drove into her hard, bringing ecstasy tumbling down on both of them.

He lay on his back with his eyes closed, drained of energy. 'If I'd known it was going to be that good, I would have done it years ago and risked being beaten to a pulp by your brother.'

'So you're basically admitting you're a wimp.' She lay sprawled next to him, one leg across his. Her fingers trailed over his abdomen. 'You have an incredible body, have I told you that?'

'As a matter of interest, which bit excites you the most? My broken ribs or the leg that's in plaster?'

'All of it. I love a vulnerable man.' Smiling, she pressed her lips to his chest. 'You're helpless.'

He captured both her wrists in one of his hands and anchored her hands above her head. 'Not that helpless, *tesoro*.' He rolled, ignoring the protest of his injured ribs. 'Do you know how long I've waited to get you naked?'

'About as long as I've waited for you to get me naked.' She stared up at him, her gaze mirroring the desire he felt. 'If I'd known you were that good at sex, I wouldn't have wasted the last couple of weeks tucking you into that bed on your own.'

'So we need to make up for lost time.' He lowered his mouth to hers, thinking that he'd never been with a woman who made him want to smile and ravish her at the same time.

'When the physio told you to take more exercise, I don't think this is what she had in mind.' With a smooth movement, she wrapped her legs around him and Alessandro hesitated, his hand locked in that glorious, tumbling hair.

'You do know I'm rubbish at relationships, don't you?'

'Me too.' She dragged his head down towards hers. 'Which is why we're going to make the most of this one while it lasts. Now shut up and kiss me.'

'Two skinny lattes, both with a double shot, please.' Tasha stifled a yawn as she dug her purse out of her bag and paid for the coffee. Glancing at her watch, she realised she'd had less than two hours of sleep the previous night.

'Any pastries with that?' The girl placed the coffee on the tray and Tasha looked longingly at the croissants and muffins, wondering whether carbs would wake her up or put her to sleep. Her brain too fuzzy to make a decision, she glanced over her shoulder towards Megan, who had bagged the only empty sofa in the coffee shop. 'Croissant or muffin?'

'Neither.' Megan recoiled and patted her flat stomach, but Tasha ignored her.

'I've got to have something or I'll pass out. I'll get a croissant and we can share.'

She wondered what Alessandro was doing. Was he still with his advisers? *Was he thinking about her?*

'You look absolutely exhausted.' Megan's gaze was concerned as Tasha set the tray down and sank onto the sofa next to her. 'Aren't you sleeping?'

Tasha picked up the knife and sliced the croissant in two. 'Er—not that much.'

'Is Alessandro a demanding patient?'

Demanding? Tasha lifted her coffee and hoped her blush didn't give her away. Yes, he was demanding, and over the last two weeks he had driven her almost mad with his demands, but not in the way that Megan clearly meant. 'I'm just worried about the future. Don't know what to do about my job.' She told Megan the story, surprised by how easy it was to talk to her.

'Tasha, your job prospects are good.' Megan picked up her coffee. 'Between you and me, everyone knows that consultant you worked for is an idiot. Everyone is probably cheering you on.'

'Well, it would be nice to be cheered on from within a job.' Tasha nibbled her croissant. 'Still, at least Josh found me temporary employment. He's not bad, as brothers go.'

'He's an amazing doctor.' Megan spoke with real warmth and Tasha watched her over the rim of her cup, noticing the pink streaks on Megan's cheeks. Her brain slotted together the clues. She remembered Josh's reaction when he'd mentioned Megan's name and the way Megan's face had lit up when she'd talked about Josh on the ward.

'So…' Tasha kept her voice casual '…you know all my secrets. Tell me something about you. Are you married?'

It was the simplest explanation for her brother's behaviour. Why else would he be holding back?

'No.' Megan picked up her spoon. 'Not married. You know how it is with this job. It's hell on relationships.'

'That's true enough.' So if Megan wasn't married, what was the problem? Maybe Megan wasn't interested. 'Personally? I wouldn't have a relationship with another doctor. All those dinners in the bin.'

'I'd be fine with it. In fact, I think it makes it easier if you're both doctors—you both understand the issues.'

'Josh is terrible at remembering social engagements when he's working.'

'That's the person he is,' Megan breathed. 'He focuses on what's important.' She looked up and her eyes shone. 'He's a brilliant doctor.'

Knowing that she was looking at a woman in love, Tasha felt a flash of delight, quickly followed by exasperation.

Josh and Megan were in love. No doubt about it. So why hadn't they got it together?

Was her brother letting his toxic relationship with Rebecca influence his future?

In which case she needed to give him a sisterly prod.

'I can't believe you've been back to the ward every day since the pirate party.' Josh refilled his wine glass as the setting sun sent a rosy glow over the living room. 'When you volunteered to help out with the prince-and-princess party I expected you to be there under sufferance for two hours and then leave, not go back for three weeks running!'

'Alessandro has appointed himself chief wish-fulfiller.' Tasha pushed the casserole towards her brother, careful not to look at Alessandro. She didn't dare look in case they gave themselves away. And she wasn't ready to tell Josh yet. He'd overreact and worry about her. He'd want to know what it all meant—where it was going. And the truth was, it wasn't going anywhere.

The relationship was intense and physical, but she wasn't fooling herself that it was anything other than great sex.

'I never knew you were this domesticated.' Josh filled his plate a second time.

'Took me ages to make it so you might as well eat it. Today our prince arranged for some football player or other to come and spend some time with one of the boys. I have no idea who he was but he had a fit body. The nurses were as interested as little Toby.'

'Which football player?'

Alessandro mentioned a name that had Josh's eyebrows lifting in disbelief.

'You're kidding. How on earth did you persuade him to come?'

'He just picked up the phone,' Tasha said dryly. 'Alessandro is nothing if not persuasive. All those years of being in command, I suppose.'

Lounging in his chair at the far end of the table, Alessandro gave a dismissive shrug. 'I knew he was in the UK. It was nothing for him to spend a few hours with a sick child and it meant a lot to Toby. The little guy has been to hell and back lately.'

And Alessandro had been there every step of the way, giving whatever support he could.

Tasha felt her heart twist as she remembered the look on Toby's face as his hero had strode onto the ward holding a football signed by all the members of the England team. 'How do you know all these footballers, anyway?'

'I know a lot of people.'

'Top athletes always know each other.' Josh cleared his plate. 'That was great, thanks.'

Top athletes? *Was Alessandro a top athlete?*

She knew he played polo, but as it wasn't a game she knew anything about, she had no way of knowing whether he was any good or not. Somewhere in the recesses of her mind she had a vague recollection of Josh once telling her that Alessandro could be the best if he put his mind to it, but at the time she hadn't really paid much attention.

As the two men talked about sport, Tasha thought about the time they had spent together this past month. Alessandro had proved a real hit on the children's ward and had spent hours with the children, talking to them and finding out what they enjoyed most and what their dreams were. Then he'd proceeded to try and make each and every dream come true.

'Megan Phillips thinks he's a hero.' Dropping the name casually into the conversation, Tasha poured herself a glass of water. 'He distracted a child for her yesterday while she took bloods.'

Josh's expression altered. 'You've met Megan?'

'Well, of course. She popped down to the unit on that first day to chat to me and we've got together since then. We went for a coffee together a week ago. She's lovely. The sort of woman you're instantly friends with, even though you've only just met each other.'

Josh put his fork down slowly. 'You went for a coffee? You chatted?'

'Er…yes. Generally when we women go for a coffee we don't sit in silence. Neither do we discuss sporting results.' Tasha gave the two of them a meaningful smile. 'Women know how to talk properly.'

Her brother was very still. 'What, exactly, did you talk about "properly"?'

'Oh, this and that. I don't remember the specifics.' She kept her answer intentionally vague, but the look on her brother's face confirmed what she'd suspected from the moment she'd met Megan Phillips—that there was something going on between Josh and the beautiful paediatrician. 'She really likes you.'

Alessandro sucked in a breath. 'Of course. *That's* where I know her from! It's been driving me mad.' He sat forward and thumped his glass down on the table, a triumphant gleam in his eyes. 'Megan was the one you spent the night with at that party when we were at university! New Year's Eve—that's it! We were celebrating because you were the new hotshot of the emergency department and my team had just won a trophy. You spent the night flirting with this gorgeous girl in a red dress.'

Tasha held her breath.

A tense silence settled across the room. 'I flirted with a lot of women. I don't remember.'

Alessandro smiled, man to man. 'You mean you don't want to remember. Your ego took a real bashing that night. Normally all you had to do was stand there and fight them off, but she wasn't interested. You had to work really hard for once in your life. It warmed my heart to see it.'

Tasha closed her eyes briefly. Why did men do this? Why was their form of communication either ribbing each other or punching each other?

Josh was still. 'I'm surprised you can remember, given that you had your hands full with that blonde from Radiography.'

Wishing she'd never prompted this conversation, Tasha pushed her plate away.

'You were Mr Cool, who was never going to succumb to a woman.' Alessandro was still laughing. 'And then the next morning you looked dazed—Megan Phillips got to you in a way no woman had ever got to you before. And it scared the hell out of you. I saw her around for a few months and then she just vanished. And you couldn't find her. It was a mystery.'

'There was no mystery.' Josh stood up abruptly. 'Nice dinner, Tash. I need to go.'

'Wait.' Alessandro sounded puzzled. 'You look like hell. And she looks like hell, too. You've obviously got something serious going on. So why aren't you doing something about it?'

Josh arched an eyebrow. 'You're giving me advice on relationships?'

'I just don't see the problem.'

'No. You don't.'

'I'm the first to admit I'm rubbish at relationships. That's because I've never felt anything for a woman, whereas *you*—' he emphasised the word '—obviously really care for Megan, so just give in to it! Accept that it's over for you and get on with it.'

'Well, you're such a romantic pair,' Tasha pushed the words past her dry lips, wondering why Alessandro's frank admission that he'd never felt anything for a woman should make her feel this sick. She knew that, didn't she? *So why did hearing him say it hurt so much?* 'I can't imagine why an intelligent woman like Megan would look twice at either of you.' She stacked the plates noisily and then caught sight of her brother's white face and paused. Anxiety shot through her. *She'd never seen Josh like this.* And Josh was her priority right now. 'Alessandro's right, though,' she said gently. 'Why not just finally give in and admit how you feel about Megan? What's wrong with that?'

Alessandro leaned back in his chair. 'Yes, go on. Admit that Mr Cool has fallen hard. Why not?'

Josh curled his fingers over the back of the chair, his jaw clenched, his face an unhealthy grey colour. 'Because my wife is pregnant.' He looked at them then, his eyes blank and soulless. 'That's why not.'

CHAPTER EIGHT

ALESSANDRO woke suddenly and glanced at the clock. Four-thirty a.m.

Outside it was still dark and rain was lashing the windows.

Turning onto his side, he saw that he was on his own in the bed. And then he saw Tasha standing on the balcony, apparently oblivious to the weather as she stared across the beach.

With a frown, Alessandro eased himself out of bed and limped across to her. For the first time in weeks the movement didn't leave him in agony.

He was healing.

Soon the cast should be off and he could begin intensive physio. He'd no longer need a nurse, which was just as well because he knew that Tasha had short-listed at least three jobs and she'd told him that she intended to get her applications off shortly.

And he had some big decisions to make.

'What are you doing out here?' Screwing up his face against the rain, he realised that she was wearing nothing but one of his shirts. 'It isn't exactly Mediterranean weather. Your climate sucks.'

She shrugged him off. 'Go back to bed, Alessandro.'

Hearing the ice in her tone, Alessandro stilled. Underneath

the soaked shirt, her shoulders were stiff. 'Are you going to tell me what's wrong?'

For a moment he thought she wasn't going to answer and then she turned sharply, her hair swinging around her shoulders, her eyes fierce. 'Why the hell are we doing this? I mean—*what* are we doing?'

The question was so unexpected that for a moment he didn't answer.

Programmed to recognise trouble when he saw it, Alessandro chose to keep it light. 'Standing on a draughty balcony in a howling wind and a thunderous rainstorm. We'll probably catch pneumonia. I suggest you come back inside while there's still a chance we'll live.'

'I don't want to go back inside.' She turned away from him. 'Just go back to bed, Alessandro.'

The storm of emotion he sensed in her was greater than the one swirling around them.

'Tell me why you're upset.'

'Why would you even care? You've never felt anything for a woman in your life, remember?' She threw the remark back at him and he flinched.

'That was just banter with your brother.'

'No, it wasn't. It was the truth. You never *have* felt anything for a woman in your life. Why do men do that?' She reached up and pushed her sodden hair out of her eyes. 'I mean, what is so cool about staying single and not committing?'

Alessandro stilled. 'You tell me. You're single. And I haven't seen you making a commitment.'

Her eyes flew to his and then she turned away. 'Just ignore me. I don't know what's wrong—it's just this thing that's happening between Josh and Megan.'

He knew a lie when he heard one.

Josh had been right, Alessandro thought grimly, when he'd said that his sister wasn't capable of not becoming emotionally involved.

Gently, he closed his hands over her shoulders and turned her to face him. 'Tash, look at me.'

She glared at him fiercely and tried to pull out of his grip. 'Just go back to bed. I'll be fine.'

'We're going to talk about this.'

'No, we're not.'

'At least tell me if this is about us or Josh?'

'I'm worried about him.' She was rigid and tense and then the next moment she leaned against him and buried her face in his chest. 'I've never seen him like this. He's so big and tough. Nothing bothers him. There's nothing he can't handle. But tonight he looked really…defeated.'

Alessandro hesitated and then stroked his hand over her head. 'You're right that he's big and tough. He'll handle it.'

'The truth is, I don't think he's ever really been in love before. But with Megan—it's real, Sandro. He really loves her. And she really loves him. Did you see his face when he told us Rebecca is pregnant? What a mess. What a complete and utter mess. When two people love each other that much, they should be together, no matter what the obstacles.'

He wondered if she realised what she was saying.

Feeling cold, Alessandro folded his arms around her and held her close, ignoring the rain that trickled down the back of his neck. Through the thin fabric of his shirt, her body felt warm and soft. And vulnerable.

She might talk blithely about sex without commitment, but she wanted love to exist.

She wanted it badly.

He gave a shiver.

He'd kidded himself that their relationship could be superficial. That both of them could walk away. But Tasha didn't do superficial, did she? Whatever she said to the contrary, she wanted the whole fairy-tale, just as she had as an idealistic teenager. Maybe she didn't even realise it herself, but it was perfectly obvious to him.

'Don't worry about Josh. He'll sort it out.'

'How can he? The woman he's about to divorce is having his child and there's no way Josh would *ever* leave his child. Never. Not after what happened to us as kids.' She lifted her hands to her face and he realised that the raindrops were mingling with her tears.

'Don't cry.' For some reason her tears disturbed him more than the realisation that she hadn't changed. Tasha wasn't a crier. 'Damn it, Tash—don't cry.'

'Sorry.' Her voice was thickened as she scrubbed at her face with her hand, 'I'm really sorry, but I love my brother and I hate to see him in this situation. He should be with Megan but I know Josh will never divorce Rebecca now she's pregnant. And she knows that.' She sniffed. 'That's why she did it. I know Josh is to blame too, but why would any woman want to have a baby with a man who doesn't love her? And quite honestly I don't think she loves him either. She just likes the idea of being married to a doctor. I just don't get it.'

Cold spread through his body as he thought of his own parents. 'A loveless marriage isn't exactly a rare occurrence, *tesoro*. People marry for many different reasons.'

Like political convenience.

'But what about the child? When Dad left…' her breathing was jerky '…I thought it was all my fault. I assumed I'd done something. Parents splitting up, parents who don't want to be together—it's the pits. I know Josh will love that child, I know he will. But if he doesn't love Rebecca and she doesn't love him…' She looked up at him, her eyes swimming with anxiety. 'That can't be good, can it? My parents split up and look how screwed up I am. And yours stayed together and you're screwed up, too.'

Alessandro gave a humourless laugh. 'Thanks.'

'All right, maybe you're not screwed up exactly, but you don't let yourself get close to a woman, which is sort of the same thing.'

'You and I have been pretty close lately.'

'Physically,' she mumbled. 'And we were thrown together

by circumstances. I don't want to talk about us. I want to talk about Josh. I want to wave a magic wand.'

Alessandro smoothed her hair away from her face. 'Josh has to work this out, *tesoro*. You can't do it for him.'

'I want him to be with Megan.' Her voice was desperate. 'You say they met all those years ago and it was special— think of all the time they've already wasted. They should be together for ever.'

For ever.

The words chilled him to the bone more effectively than either the wind or the rain. Alessandro took her hand. 'Let's go back inside.'

Tasha stood under the shower, waiting for the hot needles of water to warm her numb skin. She hadn't realised how cold she'd become, standing on the terrace while the rain sheeted down. She was freezing.

And, as if that wasn't bad enough, she'd made a total fool of herself.

All that talk of love and happy-ever-afters. It was a wonder Alessandro hadn't freaked out and tossed her off the balcony.

She needed to redeem herself fast. Salvage her pride before it ended up in a disorderly heap like last time.

Turning off the shower, she wrapped herself in a warm towel and walked through to the bedroom.

Crossing her legs on the bed, she switched on her laptop, intending to continue her search for jobs. But the moment the search engine appeared on the screen, she found herself typing in '*Prince Alessandro of San Savarre*'.

Glancing quickly towards the door, she checked that Alessandro was still occupied making hot drinks in the kitchen, then clicked the search button.

'Great,' she muttered. 'Over six million results. What on earth is he doing with you, Tasha?'

But the answer to that was all too obvious. He was enjoying

convenient sex while he was trapped in Cornwall. Soon he'd be back to his old life, playing polo and presiding over state occasions.

She ignored all the references to his role as Crown Prince and instead clicked on a result that said 'Sporting Legend'.

As she read, she realised how little she knew him.

He was a top polo player. One of the best in the world, with the potential to be *the* best in the world.

Tasha scrolled down the other results.

The Prince of Polo.

Alessandro the Great.

As she scanned the articles, the same words were repeated over and over again—'exceptional', 'the best', 'generous'. No wonder his injuries had been so frustrating for him. He was an athlete at the top of his game.

Absently, she scrolled down and clicked on another article hinting at trouble at the palace—the Princess, his mother, had expressed her disapproval at her son's sporting endeavours and insisted that he spend more time at home on royal duties.

Frowning, she clicked on an image of him accepting a cup for his team. He looked bronzed and handsome, his eyes burning with the fire of achievement.

Everyone was in agreement that the wild prince of San Savarre had astonishing talent.

Talent that he wasn't allowed to use.

Clicking again, she stared at a picture of him at a charity ball, dressed in a black dinner jacket with a tall, slender blonde on his arm. This time the caption read, *'Prince or Playboy? Will Alessandro of San Savarre ever settle down?'*

Her stomach ached.

They looked perfect together.

Regal. The only thing that spoilt the picture was the expression on Alessandro's face. There was no missing the adoration in the woman's eyes but he looked bored and desperate, as if he'd rather be anywhere else.

I've never felt anything for a woman in my life.

Tasha stared at the image on the screen and then glanced at the name of the woman.

Miranda.

She relaxed slightly. Wasn't Miranda the woman who had been engaged to his brother?

Tasha cursed herself for even caring. She knew only too well what a heartbreaker he was, didn't she? No woman held his attention for more than five minutes. It probably didn't help that he'd been fed a diet of female adoration from his cradle.

He wanted her now, but she didn't fool herself that he would want her once the cast was off his leg and they were no longer trapped together in this small, safe world they'd created.

Panic rushed through her.

She wasn't going to do that again. She wasn't going to jeopardise her career for a relationship.

Still fiddling, she followed another link and saw images of a car wreck.

Apart from his tension in her car the other day, his feelings about the accident were something he didn't reveal. And yet it had changed everything for him.

According to the report, his brother had been alone in the car the night of the crash.

Tasha was still puzzling over that when she heard his footsteps. Quickly she exited the site and deleted the search history. No way did she want him knowing she was looking him up. That would be beyond embarrassing and she'd already embarrassed herself enough with all that talk of love and soul mates.

'I made hot chocolate. I thought you needed warming up.' Alessandro hobbled up to her. 'Are you job-hunting again? I thought you already had interviews lined up.'

'I was just playing around. Thanks for the chocolate. How did you make it with one hand?'

'I can do a lot of things with one hand. Want me to show you?'

'Not right now.' Shaken by a flare of sexual awareness, she flipped the laptop shut and put it on the bed. 'I need to have a serious think about jobs. After all, you have your appointment at the hospital tomorrow and it's very likely that they'll take that cast off. You'll be fully mobile again soon. I need to find myself a job.'

'So you're still Tasha the career girl, then.'

'Absolutely. What else?'

'Out there on the balcony you seemed to be extolling the virtues of love and family.'

'Ugh—for goodness' sake, Alessandro, I'd had a drink! Several drinks, actually. I always get morose after a glass or two of wine.' She put her laptop on the floor and finished her hot chocolate. 'And anyway I was talking about love for Josh, not love for me.'

'Right.' The way he was looking at her said that he didn't believe her and she decided to shift the focus of the conversation.

'Can I ask you something?'

'Sure.'

'Why do you think your mother blames you for the accident? You weren't even in the car that night.'

He put his mug down slowly and for a moment she thought he wasn't going to answer. 'I should have been.' His tone was bitter. 'I should have been the one driving.'

'Why?'

'Because he'd been drinking.'

Tasha put her mug down slowly, realising that those words had great significance. 'You were there?'

'We were both at a fundraising ball. I told him that he was too drunk to drive but he didn't listen.' Alessandro's expression was bleak. 'Antonio never listened, but that probably wasn't all his fault. My brother was treated as the golden boy from the moment he was born. He was used to issuing commands, not receiving them.'

'So he ignored you. Why wasn't he being driven in a fancy bulletproof limo?'

'Because he wanted to visit a woman. And she wasn't the woman he was planning to marry.'

'And he was supposed to marry Miranda, right?'

A tension rippled through his powerful frame and Alessandro sent her a strange look. Tasha was still trying to interpret that look when he turned away.

'I should have stopped him. Taken the keys. Knocked him unconscious. Something.'

'Hold on a minute.' Tasha frowned for a moment and then sat down next to him. 'If he hadn't been sneaking off, or if he hadn't been drunk—are you saying that's why your mother blames you? Because you didn't stop him driving when he was drunk?'

'She's right to blame me.'

'No, sorry, but she isn't. Antonio made his own decisions and it sounds as if they were all bad ones.' Tasha was outraged. 'You can't be blamed for what he did.'

Alessandro lifted his head and looked at her, a faint smile playing around his mouth. 'Beautiful Tasha—one minute you're as gentle as a kitten and the next you're a tiger.'

'I just hate injustice, and if she's blaming you then that's unjust.' She sighed and took his hand. 'When someone dies, people look for someone to blame. It's part of the grieving process. They want an explanation—a reason. I see it all the time at the hospital. That doesn't mean anyone *is* to blame. And you're not, you know you're not.'

'Do I?'

Her hand tightened on his. 'Yes, you do. It's also normal to feel guilt. And that's what's happening to you. But lay out the facts, Sandro. Take away the emotion. Are you really to blame?'

There was a long silence and his hand closed over hers. 'Perhaps not.'

'Definitely not.'

'Tasha—about what you said on the balcony...'

'I was waffling. Take no notice of anything I say when I'm upset. And you're right—this is one thing Josh has to sort out by himself.' She deliberately chose to focus her attention on her brother's relationship rather than theirs. 'We should get some sleep. I'm surfing in the morning and you have that magazine interview.'

A faint frown touched his brows. 'You don't have to leave the house just because I have an interview.'

'Easier if they don't know about us.' Tasha slid into bed and flipped off the light. 'I'll go down to the beach as soon as it's light.'

'Tasha—'

'What?'

'I haven't told anyone about that before.'

She pulled up the covers. 'It wasn't your fault, Sandro. You weren't responsible. He was an adult and he made his own decision. You know it's true.'

He hauled her close. 'My ribs are healing.'

All of him was healing. Soon he wouldn't need her any more.

Once his cast was off and his mobility increased, he'd be able to cope alone.

She'd go back to paediatrics.

Back to her career.

And she was fine with that.

Absolutely fine.

'How does it feel?'

Alessandro moved his leg cautiously, aware that Tasha was watching him closely.

The answer was that it felt strange without the cast. It also felt strange to think that soon she'd be moving out. 'I feel surprisingly good considering I've had it in plaster for so long. The surgeon says that the bones are healing well but they want me to use the swimming pool as much as possible to build the muscle back up.'

And then he'd be returning home to San Savarre. No more delaying tactics.

It was time to face his future.

Distracted by that bleak prospect, it took him a few moments to realise that Tasha had asked him a question and was waiting for the answer. 'Sorry—I missed that. What did you say?'

'I asked if they're arranging for a physio to come to the house.'

'I told them I had you.'

Her gaze turned from concerned to exasperated. 'Sandro, I'm not a physio—'

'But you're a bright girl and you can talk to the physio. She'll do a session with us and then you can take it from there.' It was unsettling to acknowledge that his real reason for not accepting more help was that he didn't want anyone intruding on the little cocoon they'd created.

'Pool running is good.' Tasha whipped a notebook out of her bag and made a few notes. 'You wear a buoyancy aid and move through the water—I'll see if I can borrow the equipment.'

'You see what I mean? I don't need a bunch of different people traipsing through the house when I have you.'

She lifted her eyes from the notebook. 'So you're officially mending.'

'Apparently.'

Their eyes met and he knew what she was thinking because he was thinking the same thing. That this was the end.

They were both moving on.

As someone who did 'moving on' better than most,

Alessandro waited for the rush of relief that inevitably followed the demise of a relationship.

It didn't come.

'They're pleased with the rate of healing.' He maintained the conversation, even though his mind was elsewhere.

'So—that's that, then. You're not going to need a nurse for much longer.'

A nurse? No. He didn't need a nurse.

But that didn't mean—

Making a decision, Alessandro took a deep breath. 'There's something I need to say to you.'

'It's perfect timing.' Her smile was dazzling and she interrupted before he could say what he wanted to say. 'I have an interview on Friday. The job looks really interesting and apparently it's a very progressive department so they might even be able to cope with me.'

The news that she had an interview landed like a thud in his stomach. 'Tasha—'

'How honest do you think I should be about why I left my last job? My natural instinct is to tell the truth, but I have to admit that my natural instinct sometimes gets me into trouble— Oh!' Her flow of speech was cut off as Alessandro crushed his mouth down on hers.

Her lips were warm and sweet and what had begun as a silencing exercise fast turned into a sensual feast. 'God, you taste fantastic.'

'Sandro...' She moaned his name and slid her arms around his neck. As the kiss heated up Alessandro found it hard to remember what he'd wanted to say.

'Wait.' He dragged his mouth from hers, trying to focus through the burn of raw lust that heated his body. 'We have to talk.' He felt the tension ripple through her and wondered why she would react like that when she didn't even know what he was going to ask.

'No, we don't. You don't need to say anything.' Eyes closed, she muttered the words against his mouth. 'We always knew this was just for now. You're moving on. I'm moving on. No worries—although I have to admit I'm going to miss the sex…'

Alessandro pulled his mouth from hers. Her words should have brought him nothing but relief. Instead, tension spread across his shoulders. 'I'm not ready to move on. That's what I'm trying to tell you.'

Her eyes opened slowly. 'You're not?'

'No.'

He stroked his thumbs over her cheeks, thinking that she had the most beautiful eyes he'd ever seen. 'At the weekend I have a high-profile wedding to attend. The Earl of Cornwall's daughter.'

'Is this in an official capacity?'

'Yes. And I want you to come.'

She stared at him for a long moment. 'Me?'

'Yes.'

'You want *me* to come?'

Alessandro stared at her in exasperation. 'Why are you repeating everything? Yes, I want you to come. What's so strange about that? We've spent the past six weeks together.'

'Oh—yes.' She cleared her throat and glanced around self-consciously, apparently only now realising that they could easily be overheard. 'So you're taking me for my medical abilities?'

'No. I'm taking you because I want to take you. I can't stand the formality of these occasions. I particularly hate weddings. I'd love your company.'

'But if it's an official appearance, shouldn't you be taking a princess with blonde hair and a haughty expression?'

'I'm taking you.'

Her eyes were wary. 'Am I expected to call you Your Highness in public?'

'No.'

'Are you going to be mobbed by adoring women?'

'It's a wedding,' he drawled, 'so hopefully not.'

She bit her lip and tilted her head to one side. 'So what would I have to wear?'

Alessandro smiled. If they'd reached the point where she was asking what to wear, it meant that she was definitely coming. 'It will be dressy. It's being held in a castle. Wear something glamorous.'

'A wedding in a castle?' Tasha pursed her lips but couldn't hold back the twinkle in her eyes. 'Sounds pretty downmarket. Might be boring.'

'It *will* be boring.' He sighed. 'All weddings are boring, so kill that shine in your eyes right now.'

'Are they madly in love? How did they meet? Was it romantic?'

'Tasha—'

'Sorry. Just asking. Good. Fine. Boring old wedding.' She gave a tiny shrug. 'I'll find something boring to wear, then.'

'I can't believe he's taking you to the Earl of Cornwall's wedding.' Megan gave a disbelieving laugh. 'That's…huge.'

'I'm the one who's huge compared to all those breedy aristocrats.' Tasha stared down at herself in dismay. 'Can I lose a stone by Saturday?'

'You don't need to lose a stone. You look fantastic.' Excited, Megan hugged her. 'I'm so pleased for you. I know how much you like him.'

'I hear a "but" in your tone.' Tasha extracted herself. 'You think he's going to hurt me.'

'No.' Megan bit her lip. 'But any man as rich and gorgeous as him is bound to attract non-stop female attention. And he does have a reputation.'

'It's someone else's wedding, not ours,' Tasha said blithely, 'so his reputation isn't an issue.' Not for anything would she admit how she felt about him. Not even to Megan, who had become a real friend over the past few weeks.

The only subject they never discussed was Josh. Whenever her brother's name was mentioned, Megan instantly changed the subject.

'Well, he certainly isn't hiding you away. Every time I open a newspaper I see another article about that wedding. It's very high profile and by taking you he's making a statement about your relationship.'

Tasha felt her heart bump against her ribs. 'You think he's making a statement?'

'Of course. You've been living in this little cocoon together, but now he's taking you out in public.'

'As his nurse.'

'Nurses don't usually wear glamorous dresses and have sex with their patients.'

Tasha choked. 'When I first met you, I thought you were dignified and delicate.'

'I'm practical,' Megan said dryly, grabbing Tasha by the arm. 'Come on. We're supposed to be finding you something to wear.' Without giving her the chance to argue, Megan dragged her towards St Piran's most exclusive boutique.

'You have to be kidding. I can't afford this place.' Tasha dug her heels in like a horse. 'I don't have a job, remember?' She'd told Megan everything that had happened at her last hospital and had been relieved when the other doctor had stoutly declared that she would have done the same thing in the same situation.

'Isn't he paying?' Megan paused in front of the heavy glass doors. 'Tasha, he's a prince. He's loaded and he's the one who invited you to this wedding. If he expects you to dress up in something glamorous and photogenic, he should pay.'

'He wanted to pay. I refused.'

'He offered to buy you an outfit and you refused? Are you mad?'

'No, I'm independent.' Tasha scowled at her. 'Do you know how many women fling themselves at him? Loads. And most of them just do it because he's a prince and rich and—well, you know. I don't want him ever to think our relationship has anything to do with who he is.'

Megan stared at her for a long moment. 'Tasha, he *is* a prince. You can't get away from that.'

'No, he's a man,' Tasha said firmly. 'These last few weeks—it's been so normal. He's just a regular guy. Well, maybe not a regular guy exactly because he's super good looking and devilishly charming and most of the regular guys I meet are complete no-hopers. But he doesn't act like a prince. To me he's just Sandro.'

Megan looked as though she wanted to say something else but in the end gave a brief smile and shook her head. 'Yes. Of course. I'm the last person to give advice to anyone on anything of a romantic nature.' It was the closest she'd ever come to admitting that her relationship with Josh was a disaster.

Tasha didn't even know if Megan was aware of Rebecca's pregnancy and she felt torn, knowing something about her brother that she couldn't share with her friend.

But she decided that it wasn't her place to say anything.

It was up to Josh to deal with it the way he believed was best.

Megan was smiling at her. 'I can completely understand why you want to buy your own dress and be independent. So let's do it.' Without giving Tasha a chance to argue, she pushed open the doors that led into the boutique, leaving Tasha no option but to follow.

Deciding that Megan wasn't as fragile as she looked, Tasha slunk in after her. 'I hate this sort of shop—they always look at you as though you have no right to be here.'

Megan lifted her head and smiled at the frosty-faced assistant. 'My friend is going to the wedding of the Earl of Cornwall's daughter. She needs something special. The photographs will be everywhere so it's a super opportunity to publicise the boutique.' She drew breath. 'Which is why you're going to give us a generous discount.'

Tasha cringed, but the sales assistant hurried over, as did her colleague.

'You are in absolutely the right place. We have several things that would be *perfect* for you.'

'Excellent.' Megan smiled. 'Let's get started. Tasha, go and take off those jeans.'

CHAPTER NINE

'So THE Earl of Cornwall's daughter obviously doesn't believe in keeping a low profile.' Tasha blinked as another flashbulb exploded in her face. 'Whatever happened to quiet, intimate weddings?'

'Arabella describes herself as a socialite. She believes she has a duty to be seen.'

'Except that everyone here seems to want to see *you*.' Tasha flinched as a photographer leaned forward over the barriers and pointed his camera towards her. 'Whoa—unless you're airbrushing, that's too close. Please pull back to the next county. Remind me why I didn't specialise in plastic surgery rather than paediatrics?' She kept her tone light, but it was impossible not to feel self-conscious surrounded by an endless stream of beautiful women who seemed completely at home in front of the cameras. It was also impossible not to be aware that the crowd was chanting Alessandro's name.

'Is this why you were invited?' Hating herself for feeling daunted by the crowds, Tasha moved closer to his side. 'Does having you here get her more publicity?'

'Yes.'

'Don't you hate that?'

'Being the star attraction?' A sardonic smile touched his mouth. 'Of course not. Much more entertaining than being on the polo field.'

'Don't be sarcastic. This is exciting.' She slipped her hand

into his and he looked down at her, his eyes glittering dark
and dangerous.

'You look beautiful. If I throw you over my shoulder and
take you behind the nearest large bush, what do you think
will happen?'

Her stomach tumbled. 'I'll black your eye and the press
will get some interesting photos. Forget it, Sandro. I'm all
dressed up. I want to stay dressed up for a while at least. I
want to enjoy the party.'

'Dr O'Hara—can you look this way? Can you tell us who
your dress is by?' a photographer shouted across to them and
Tasha froze.

'How do they know my name?'

'Arabella will have provided them with a guest list.'

'They want to know who my dress is by.'

He lifted his broad shoulders in a dismissive gesture. 'So
tell them.'

Tasha leaned closer to him. 'I would if I knew,' she muttered. 'You're going to have to look in the back and see if
there's a label or something.'

Alessandro looked at her in astonishment and then started
to laugh. 'You don't know who designed your dress? Why
did you buy it?'

'Because it's pretty and it looks nice on me. Why else?'
Tasha glared at him, affronted. 'And I don't see what's so
funny about that. Why are you laughing?'

'Because you, Dr O'Hara, are an original.' Cupping her
face in his hands, he kissed her slowly and deliberately, ignoring the multiple flashes that lit the sky like a firework
display. 'That's tomorrow's picture.'

'What? The back of my head? Now you've smudged my
make-up,' Tasha grumbled, but her heart was racing as she
saw the look in his eyes. Behind the flare of desire there was
something else. Warmth. Intimacy. *Love?* 'I have a feeling
that kiss is going to stimulate interest in more than the designer of my dress.'

'I have a feeling you could be right.'

Remembering the chill in his mother's voice, Tasha shivered. 'Are people going to mind that you've brought me?'

He took her hand in a firm grip. 'I don't care what other people think. Come and meet the bride.'

The day passed in a haze. Tasha was introduced to what felt like a million people, but the only person she was aware of was Alessandro, who didn't leave her side. Whenever anyone called him for a photograph, he hauled her with him, as if they were surgically attached. He acted as if they were a couple.

Something shifted inside her.

Hope sprang through her natural defences.

If their relationship were just about sex, she wouldn't be here, would she? He wouldn't be holding her hand in full view of the wedding guests and smiling down at her with warmth in his eyes.

By choosing to bring her he was making a public declaration about their relationship.

Feeling ridiculously happy, Tasha floated through the ceremony and the speeches, barely hearing a word. Instead her brain was racing forward and she conjured a picture of herself in a wedding dress.

Princess Tasha.

In a dream, she greeted the guests eager to be introduced to her, but her real focus was Alessandro, who looked spectacularly handsome in an Italian suit.

By late evening she'd grown so used to the sound of helicopters arriving and taking off that she barely glanced up when another arrived. It wasn't until she saw the change in body language of the guests that she looked over her shoulder to see who was attracting such attention.

Spying more suited security men, she glanced at Alessandro. 'Someone important?'

'You could say that,' he drawled. 'It's my mother.'

Tasha stilled as she watched the elegant woman move

across the perfectly manicured lawn, flanked by security guards. 'Did you know she was coming?'

'Yes.' His tone was flat and Tasha stared at him in exasperation.

'And you didn't think it was worth mentioning?' Suddenly she felt grubby and self-conscious. 'If I'd known… I don't think your mother exactly approves of me—'

'Who I choose to spend time with is none of her business.' Still holding her hand tightly, he stepped forward as Princess Eleanor approached him. 'Mother.'

Mother.

Tasha winced. It was so formal.

'Alessandro.'

Still holding Tasha's hand firmly, Alessandro drew her forward. 'I'd like to introduce you to—'

'We'll talk indoors.' His mother's tone was colder than the champagne and she turned to the bride, who was almost swooning with delight that she had royalty in attendance at her wedding. 'Arabella. You look beautiful. Alessandro, I want to talk to you. Alone.'

'I want to talk to you, too. But Tasha comes with me.'

Without sparing Tasha a glance, his mother transferred her chilly gaze from his face to his leg. 'Do you still need a nurse?'

'She isn't here in her capacity as nurse.'

'I know why she's here, Alessandro. I'm not stupid. And neither is Miranda.' The woman spoke in a low voice that couldn't be heard by anyone around them, the gentle smile on her face giving no hints to the observer that the situation was anything but completely harmonious. 'And your little plan has worked, so there's no need to overplay your hand. Now, let's go inside so that we can work on damage limitation. Natasha, I'd like you to come too. I think it's best if you hear what I have to say.'

Tasha threw a bemused look at Alessandro but he was staring at his mother. His face might have been carved from marble. 'I agree. We'll go inside.' Without waiting for her agreement, he strode towards the wing of the castle that had been allocated for the use of guests.

'Ow—you're hurting me.' Tasha twisted her hand in his and he released his grip slightly.

'Sorry.'

'Look, maybe you should have this conversation with your mother without me there.'

'You need to be there.'

'Yes, she does.' They entered a wood-panelled library and two security men closed the doors so that they were alone. Princess Eleanor delicately removed her silk gloves. 'Natasha, isn't it? And you're his nurse.'

'Actually I'm a—'

'It doesn't matter. Did he tell you why he invited you here today?'

Tasha frowned, thinking that it was an obvious question. 'He needed to take someone to the wedding. This sort of event isn't much fun on your own.'

'Indeed.' The older woman's smile was chilly. 'But Alessandro doesn't attend these events to have "fun".' She spoke the word as if it were a disease. 'He attends because that's his job—to be seen. He's here to represent San Savarre. And the person by his side should also be representing San Savarre—'

'Tasha is my guest.' Alessandro interrupted in a cold, hard voice that made Tasha look towards him in astonishment. She'd never heard him use that tone before. He sounded... *regal*? Very much the one in charge. 'Unless you want me to walk out of that door and not look back, do *not* insult my guest. Tasha, would you give us a few moments, please? I've decided I do need to talk to my mother on my own.'

'Sure. No problem.' Feeling about as welcome as a virus in an operating theatre, Tasha made a rapid exit. The two stony-faced security men were standing guard outside the door and she slid past them and made her way to the ladies' room, hoping to avoid the inevitable gossip and speculation.

What did Alessandro need to discuss on his own?

And why was his mother looking so disapproving?

She was about to replenish her lipstick when she heard female laughter outside the door. Anxious to avoid everyone, Tasha slipped into one of the cubicles and locked the door.

'I mean, he's utterly gorgeous,' a female voice said, 'so you can hardly blame him for not wanting to settle down.'

'He is gorgeous, but an utter bastard. Fancy bringing another girl to the wedding of the year.'

'You have to feel sorry for her. He's just using her to send his ex-girlfriend a message.'

Tasha opened her mouth. She wanted to alert them to the fact that she was there so that they'd stop talking, but no sound came out.

'It's a double blow to Miranda. First she loses Antonio and now Alessandro. I mean, he hasn't even ditched her for someone royal. Or even someone well connected. That girl he's with is just ordinary—like you or me.'

'Not like you or me.' Her friend gave a catty laugh. 'She didn't even know who designed her dress.'

'That's probably because it's the first time she's ever worn a designer dress.'

'And it will be the last. I'm sure he only brought her here to make a very public point to his mother. Judging from the bodyguards outside the library, they're having the conversation right now. What wouldn't I give to be a fly on the wall? Can I borrow your lip gloss? I left mine at that nightclub last weekend.'

'Do you think she knows that he was supposed to be marrying Miranda?'

Tasha frowned. No, that wasn't right. Miranda had been his brother's fiancée.

'Little Miss Ordinary? Shouldn't think so. If she doesn't

know her dress designer, she's hardly going to be up on palace politics, is she?'

'I thought it was common knowledge that everyone is waiting for an official announcement of the engagement between Alessandro and Miranda.' There was a pause. 'Does this shade look too red on me?'

'No, it's perfect. I heard she's been looking after him.'

'Oh, well, the poor thing is in for a rude awakening when she discovers what he's like. Still, this will probably still be the most exciting thing that ever happens in her life. She's just a nurse.'

Alessandro and Miranda?

Alessandro and Miranda?

Shaking all over, Tasha exited the cubicle. 'Actually, I'm a doctor,' she said, her voice robotic, 'but some of my best friends are nurses, so I'd be grateful if you didn't talk about them as if they're second-class citizens. Next time you fall off your horse, it may be one of them saving your life. And, just for the record, that shade is definitely too red for you. It's very ageing.' Without pausing, she swept out of the room, grateful that whoever had designed her dress had given her sufficient fabric with which to make a dignified exit.

He was supposed to be marrying Miranda. His brother's fiancée.

The tears lodged in a lump at the back of her throat, she continued to walk even when she heard Princess Eleanor calling her name.

'Natasha.'

Tasha thought about pretending she hadn't heard, but then turned, her expression blank. 'I'm just leaving, Your Highness.'

'I need to tell you a few things about Alessandro.'

'Actually, no, you don't. I'm the one who needs to tell you a few things about Alessandro.' As the last thread of her control snapped, Tasha's temper bubbled over. 'Do you know that he doesn't sleep at night because he blames himself for his brother's death? Do you know that he believes that you would have preferred him to be killed? He's living with that, and you're not doing anything to stop it.'

Shocked, the woman stared at her. 'Do you know to whom you're speaking?'

'Yes.' Tasha's lips tightened. 'I'm speaking to a woman who hasn't called her son once in the past six weeks except to nag him about official duties.'

'I have a responsibility towards my country.'

'You also have a responsibility towards your son.'

The other woman straightened her shoulders. 'You seem very concerned about Alessandro's well-being.'

'I'm a doctor,' Tasha said smoothly. 'I'm trained to deal with the physical and the psychological. And, by the way, that child playing over by the tree looks as though she has measles. You might want to remove her from all those people because she'll be infectious. Excuse me. I'm leaving now.' Wondering whether she was about to be arrested for insubordination, Tasha turned away, continuing her walk towards the exit.

Damn and double damn.

Her heart was hammering, her palms were damp and her hands were shaking.

She'd lost her temper again.

Wasn't she ever going to learn?

'Tasha! Tash!'

Hearing Alessandro's voice behind her, she quickened her pace. The last thing she wanted was to speak to him.

When a strong male hand closed over her shoulder, she shook him off. 'Let go of me.' Furious, she whirled around and faced him. 'You are an utter bastard and I hate you. I hope your bloody horse falls on your other leg and breaks it.'

He stared at her, stunned. 'You're upset about the way my mother spoke to you and I don't blame you, but—'

'I'm not upset with your mother. I'm upset with you for not

telling me the truth.' Steaming mad, Tasha turned on him, eyes blazing. 'Why the hell didn't you mention Miranda to me? I knew she was engaged to your brother. Why didn't you mention that you'd taken over that role, too?'

His expression altered instantly and she suddenly felt like sobbing.

Instead, she punched him in his bruised ribs. 'Damn you, Sandro. I wanted you to deny it. I—I hate you.'

'You don't understand—'

'I understand perfectly. You were laid up in Cornwall so you thought you'd have some fun. And that's fine, because I had fun too. But you didn't need to bring me here and use me to send some message to your girlfriend.' Her voice rose but she didn't care. 'You used me. If you wanted me to come to this wedding so that you could send your girlfriend some sort of message, you at least should have had the decency to tell me.'

A muscle flickered in his jaw. 'That isn't what I was doing.'

'Don't lie to me, Alessandro. I want to go home and I want to go home now.' Before she made even more of a fool of herself in public.

'Before you go, my mother would very much like to talk to you again. If you still want to go after that, I'll take you myself.'

'I don't want you to take me yourself. I'm perfectly capable of driving.' Snapping the words out, Tasha dragged her shoulder out of his grip. 'And I don't need to talk to your mother. Everything that needs to be said has been said.'

Suddenly she felt herself crumbling. 'Why did you bring me? It was cruel, Alessandro. Really cruel.'

He stood in perfect stillness. 'I wanted to see whether you would enjoy yourself.'

'Enjoy being mocked? Enjoy being ridiculed? I'm not that much of a masochist.' Her voice felt thick as she struggled to push the words past the tears. 'So now we've established that you should have brought someone else, I'd like to leave.'

Seeing a pack of journalists approach, Alessandro snapped his fingers and a sleek black car appeared from nowhere. 'Take Dr O'Hara back to my house. We'll talk later. In private. There are things I want to say to you.'

'Nothing I want to hear.' Tasha climbed into the back of the car, stumbling over the hem of her dress. The moment the car pulled away, she leaned forward and gave the driver a different address.

She had no intention of going back to Alessandro's house ever again.

It was over.

Josh rapped on the door of Megan's cottage. It had been weeks since he'd slept properly. Not since the morning he'd arrived home to find Rebecca waiting in the kitchen.

He'd been thinking about nothing but this moment—*trying to find another way.*

But there was only one way.

A seagull shrieked overhead and he could smell the sea. Normally he would have breathed deeply and enjoyed his surroundings, but there was nothing normal about today.

When Megan opened the door it took all his self-control not to drag her into his arms for one last time. 'Hi. I should have called, I know, but—'

'Come in.' She stood back and he saw hope flicker in her eyes.

It made it all the harder to step over the threshold because he knew he was going to kill that hope dead for ever.

Once before she'd trusted him with her heart and he'd broken it.

He was about to do the same again.

Blissfully unaware of what was coming, Megan walked in front of him to the kitchen. The house overlooked the beautiful sweep of Penhally Bay. He knew she'd had countless offers from developers. He also knew she'd never accept any of them. The house had been her grandmother's and for Megan the emotional ties were as powerful as the lure of the idyllic surroundings.

'Can I get you something to drink?'

'Just water. Thanks.'

'Water?' She gave a hesitant laugh. 'Josh the party animal drinking water?'

He ran his hand over the back of his neck, thinking of all the times he'd broken bad news to patients. It never came easily, but somehow he managed it. Because this was personal, it was almost impossible to form the words. 'We have to talk.'

'I agree.' Calm, she lifted a jug from the fridge and poured a glass of filtered water.

Josh watched as the water sloshed onto the side and then suddenly realised she wasn't as calm as she pretended to be.

'Do you want lemon? Ice?'

'For God's sake, Megan—' He prised the jug out of her hand even as he brought his mouth down on hers. He felt her gasp of shock and then she was kissing him back, her fingers curling tight into the front of his shirt as if she was afraid he was going to vanish.

It was crazy, insane, stupid, but he couldn't stop himself. His hands were buried in her hair and he was kissing her with a desperation that went bone deep. 'I love you.' He groaned the words against her mouth, 'I love you, sweetheart.'

'Oh, Josh…' Her voice broke and she made a sound somewhere between a sob and a laugh. 'I—'

'I love you so much, which is why this is the hardest thing I've ever had to do.' With supreme difficulty, he drew back, forcing himself to do what had to be done. 'That night we spent together was incredible—'

'I know that, Josh.' Her voice was whisper-soft. 'I know, and—'

'No.' This time his voice was harsh, and he stepped back from her because he knew that if she stopped him now he'd never be able to say what needed to be said. 'You have to listen. You have to let me speak.'

Her eyes were startled. 'All right. Speak.'

'That night was so special. You have no idea.' He raked his fingers through his hair. 'When I left you that morning you were all I could think about.'

A tiny frown touched her forehead and she gave a bemused shake of her head. 'Josh, what on earth is wrong? You're making me nervous, I—I don't understand. Why shouldn't you love me? Why shouldn't I love you? I know it's been a bumpy road getting here, but—'

'I can't be in love with you.' He clenched his jaw as he saw her flinch.

'But—'

'Rebecca is pregnant.' His tone was raw and the words burned his chest. 'She's having a child.'

Megan stood very still. Behind them sunshine poured through the window but neither of them noticed. 'But…that's good, surely? It means she's moved on. She has another relationship.' Her voice faltered. 'Josh? Why are you looking at me like that? What's wrong?'

He couldn't remember ever crying. When his father had walked out he hadn't cried. Even that night Megan had been brought into A and E and he'd failed to save their baby, he hadn't managed to cry. But this time, for some reason, the obstruction in his throat was an immovable object.

'Megan…' He couldn't form the words. It was the hardest thing he'd ever had to say. *The hardest thing he'd ever had to do.* 'It's my child. Rebecca is having my baby.' He watched as the hope in her eyes turned dull. Watched as love drained away, leaving nothing but pools of pain.

'But—if that's true then it means…' Tears glistened in her eyes and she gave a sharp gasp and backed away from him. 'You told me the marriage was over. You told me—'

'It was.'

'But you were still having sex with her?' Her voice rose and she wrapped her arms around herself in a gesture of self-protection. 'We clearly have a very different idea about what constitutes "over". Oh, my God.' Agitated, she paced to the far side of the room and pressed her hands to her mouth. 'I would never have slept with you that night if I'd thought you were still together.'

'We weren't together.' Josh walked over to her but she whirled round, her eyes fierce.

'Don't touch me!' She backed away, the sob lodged in her throat. 'How *could* you? *How could you do that?* You were sleeping with me and your wife at the same time?'

'No!'

'She's pregnant, Josh.'

'It was just one night, weeks before you and I…' He sucked in a breath and spread his hands. 'I can't even explain it—'

'I suggest you don't even try.' The chill in her voice was agonising to hear.

'It was a mistake. Megan, she did it on purpose. She wanted a baby. This was her way of keeping us together.'

'You told me the marriage was over. You told me it was mutual.' The tears slid down her cheeks. 'But you had sex with her, Josh.' She was crying openly now. *'You had sex with her.'*

The memory brought a bitter taste to his mouth. 'It was just once.'

'Is that supposed to make it OK? Because I can assure you it doesn't. It's not OK, Josh.' She scrubbed the tears from her cheeks with her hand and the frantic attempt to hide her distress was more disturbing than any accusation she could fling at him. 'You say you love me and then you tell me this? How do you think that makes me feel?'

Josh closed his eyes. 'Megan—'

'She can give you the one thing I can't give you.' Her voice cracked and she lifted her head to look at him, resignation in her eyes. 'She can give you a child and I can't compete with that.'

'I love you, Megan. And I'm telling you that because I don't want there to be any misunderstanding about what happened here. I truly love you, but no child of mine will grow up as I did, without a father. I won't do that. I have to make this work. For the child's sake.'

'Yes. Of course you do.' Her lips were stiff and her voice was a flat monotone. 'You're going to make it work, I know you will. You'll be a very happy family, you, Rebecca and the baby. If you don't mind, I'd like you to leave now.'

Josh opened his mouth to fight that request and then realised that she was holding herself together with difficulty. And so was he.

With one last look at her trembling frame, he turned and strode out of her cottage.

A happy family?

Not in this lifetime.

CHAPTER TEN

FURIOUSLY angry, Tasha stormed out of the car. It was dark, and the familiar smells and sounds of Penhally Bay should have soothed her throbbing head. Instead she just wanted to punch someone.

Remembering her manners, she leaned back into the car and thanked the driver.

'You've been brilliant,' she muttered, 'and thank you for taking me to the house to collect my stuff. Sorry about the ranting and raving during the journey. Just forget everything you heard me say.'

Alessandro's driver cleared his throat. 'Actually, it was quite a revelation. Usually His Highness's female friends depart crying. I keep tissues in my glove compartment.'

'Maybe you could add a shotgun.'

'Most women aren't like you, Dr O'Hara.' The man gave a regretful smile. 'Unfortunately. It's been a pleasure driving you these past few weeks.'

'Thanks, Mario. I just hope your bastard boss—sorry, I mean *His Royal Highness*—doesn't fire you for giving me a lift here.'

'No worries, Dr O'Hara. I'll get your cases from the boot.' Mario moved round the car but Tasha was already there.

'I've got it.' She hauled the cases out of the boot so violently that the driver took a step back.

'They're heavy—'

'You'd be amazed how much weight I can lift when I'm steaming mad.'

Alessandro had humiliated her publicly. Again.

She'd trusted him…

Later she knew it was all going to hurt badly, but right now she was running on adrenaline in pure undiluted fury.

She took her surfboard from Mario and tucked it under her arm. 'Thanks.'

'Are you sure you'll be OK?' Concern in his eyes, he watched as she hitched the once-glamorous dress up around her waist. 'I'll just wait while you check your friend is in.'

'No need. I know she's in. I just texted her. Thanks for bringing me here and for being so kind.'

'You're welcome. You have my mobile number. If you need to go anywhere, call and I'll come and pick you up.' With a last concerned look at her face, he drove off and Tasha heard the door of the cottage open.

'Tash?' Megan stood in the doorway and Tasha turned and strode towards her, dragging her cases behind her.

'Thanks so much for letting me come here. I couldn't stay at Sandro's, and if I went to Josh's he just would have said I told you so, and then I would have given him a black eye. And to be honest—' She stopped in mid-rant as she saw the look on Megan's face. 'Oh, my God—what happened to you? You look—you're— *Megan*?'

Megan's eyes were red. 'I don't think you can stay, Tasha,' she said stiffly. 'This is so awkward, but—'

'This is about my brother, isn't it?' Scowling, Tasha yanked her cases through the door, breaking a wheel in the process. She leaned her surfboard against the wall of Megan's hall. 'You can say anything you like and I'm just going to nod and agree with you. He's the one who made me go and look after Alessandro. If it weren't for him, I wouldn't be in this mess.' She kicked the suitcase upright and slammed the door firmly behind them. 'Let's lock it and unplug the phones.'

'I don't need to unplug anything,' Megan said wearily.

'Josh isn't coming back. It's over. He isn't going to come round ever again.'

'No wonder you hate him.'

'I don't, that's the trouble.' Megan's voice cracked and she cleared her throat quickly. 'I love him. I've only ever loved him. All my life. I know you probably can't imagine that, but it's true.'

Stunned by that confession, Tasha slipped her arms around her. 'Don't let him do this to you. No man is worth it. Not even my stupid big brother.'

'I wish I could feel as angry as you.' Megan blew her nose hard. 'I feel as though someone has gouged out my insides with a knife.'

Tasha winced. 'That's not good. I'll try and help you feel angry. It's easier. First you need to stop focusing on the reasons you love him and focus on the bad stuff.'

'I can't bear to think about that.' Megan pulled away. 'And I'm being so selfish. You must be devastated. Do you want to tell me the details?'

'I found out that the Crown Pig Alessandro is virtually engaged to some thin, blonde European princess called Miranda or some other stupid name. He doesn't want to marry her because he doesn't believe in marriage so he used me to send her a clear message that their relationship is over. That's why he invited me to the wedding.' Tasha crashed around Megan's kitchen, helping herself to a bottle of wine from the rack. 'I'm so angry I need to break something, but I can't break anything in your house.'

'Go ahead. It's the least of my worries.'

Tasha glanced at her friend's red eyes. 'How long have you been crying?'

'You don't want to know. It's embarrassing.'

'You'll be dehydrated. You need to drink something.' Tasha popped the cork on the wine and filled two glasses to the brim.

Megan's laugh bordered on the hysterical. 'The usual cure for dehydration is water.'

Tasha gave an airy shrug and handed her a glass. 'This will do fine. It's liquid. Cheers.' She tilted her glass against Megan's, worried by how fragile and broken the other girl looked. 'Drink. To sisterhood. And the therapeutic properties of blazing anger.' *She wasn't going to think about her own pain. She was going to blast her way through it and keep busy.*

'He slept with his wife.' Despite her protests, Megan drank half the wine without pausing. 'She's pregnant. But I expect you already know that.'

Tasha stilled. Guilt shot through her. 'Look—'

'It wasn't your job to tell me. It was his.'

'I know it looks bad, and I'm not trying to defend my brother, but knowing Rebecca as I do I can tell you it was all her doing.'

'It couldn't have been *all* her doing, Tasha.'

'Well, that's true of course. He should have said no. But he's a weak, brainless man.'

'Josh is strong and clever.'

Tasha looked at her with exasperation. 'You're focusing on his qualities again.'

'Sorry. It's just—I really did think he loved me.'

Tasha sighed, wondering whether the truth would make the pain worse or better. 'He does love you. I know he loves you. And if it's any consolation, I'm sure Rebecca was lying in wait on the bed in a skimpy set of underwear or something. Slut.'

'They were married.'

'Their marriage has been over for a long time. She was playing games.' Realising that she was probably making things worse, Tasha picked up the wine and topped up Megan's glass. 'Let's just forget it. Your life is a mess and my life is a mess. You can be sad and I'll be angry. Whatever works. Do you have any chocolate in the house? That's good for either mood.'

'There's a large box of Belgian chocolates given to me by grateful parents.' Her cheeks pale, Megan sipped the wine. 'Do you want them?'

'Urgently. We'll share the box.' Tasha tripped over the hem of her dress and cursed fluently. 'I just need to get a pair of jeans out of my suitcase. I'm going to break my neck if I stay in this.' And break her heart because the dress reminded her of Alessandro. She'd dressed with such hope, never once imagining that this would be the outcome. Because she'd been so careful not to dream, somehow the pain was all the more acute.

Anger, she reminded herself. *Anger was easier.*

Megan looked at the dress. 'We had such fun choosing that. I thought it was perfect.'

Tasha retrieved her suitcase and delved inside for a pair of jeans. 'It was a ridiculous amount of money for something I was only ever going to wear once. And now it's just a reminder of a completely terrible day. I'm going to give it to the charity shop.'

'Do you know the worst thing? When Josh came here today, I thought he was going to tell me he loved me. And he did. Two minutes before he told me his wife was pregnant.'

Still clutching the jeans, Tasha stared at Megan's ashen face and bloodshot eyes and wondered if she could have done something to make it easier. 'I don't know what to say. Right now I want to seriously hurt him.'

'I think he's already hurting.' Megan climbed onto a chair and lifted a box of chocolates from the top shelf of a cupboard. 'If I read this situation in a book, I'd think it was ridiculous. Why does life have to be so hard? Start eating. I'm just going to go and wash my face.'

Tasha stood, staring out across Penhally Bay, feeling numb and exhausted.

When the phone in her bag suddenly rang she scrambled

to answer it, heart racing. When she saw that it was Josh, disappointment thudded through her.

She'd thought—

Her finger hovered over the answer button and then she heard Megan coming back down the stairs and she lifted her chin and switched her phone off.

'Which one of them was it?' Megan's voice was hard and Tasha shrugged and dropped the silent phone back into her pack.

'Doesn't matter.' She helped herself to a chocolate. 'Thanks.' She hesitated. 'What are you going to do, Megan?'

'You mean how am I going to carry on working at St Piran's with Josh there? How am I going to cope with seeing Rebecca pregnant?' Megan dropped onto the edge of the sofa, her fingers plucking at the edge of her cardigan. 'I don't know. I honestly don't know. And how about you? You're living with Alessandro.'

'Not any more. No way am I going back there. I collected my things on the way.' Tasha wriggled out of the dress and winced as the zip tore. 'Oh, dear. Good job I wouldn't have wanted to wear it again.'

'You can stay here as long as you like. It's been years since I had a flatmate.'

'Seriously? I can stay? I was sort of hoping you'd say that. Are you sure it wouldn't be an imposition? Just until I find a job.' She wondered how long it would take for the pain to fade. *Never again*, she vowed as she tugged on her comfortable jeans. She just wasn't going to do this again. She was rubbish at relationships.

'Stay as long as you like, although I suppose that might be awkward for Josh.'

'That's his problem, not mine.'

'But soon you'll be an aunty and…' Megan leaned back against the sofa and closed her eyes. 'God, what a mess. The awful thing is I haven't just lost him, I've lost you. How are we going to stay friends? It's going to be so awkward.'

'I'm used to awkward. You're talking to the girl who told her consultant to get a backbone.'

Megan gave a choked laugh. 'I was forgetting that. You're so gutsy.'

'It's not guts, it's an uncertain temper,' Tasha muttered gloomily. 'And while we're on that subject I probably ought to warn you that I might be arrested for treason. I yelled at Princess Eleanor. And then I punched Alessandro.'

'Oh, Tasha…' Megan started to laugh and Tasha found herself laughing too.

'Will you visit me in prison?'

'You've got to admit it's funny.' Still shaking with laughter, Megan wrapped her arms around her ribs. 'You spent all that time trying to help him heal and then you bruise him again. I'm so glad I met you. Where would we be without girlfriends?'

'We'd be stuck with men and then we'd go slowly mad.'

Megan sprang to her feet and reached for a DVD. 'Let's eat chocolate and watch back-to-back trashy movies.'

'Sounds good to me.'

Megan hugged the DVD to her chest and then turned to look at Tasha. 'I was pregnant once.'

Tasha spilled her wine over her jeans. 'Meg! You can't just make confessions like that without warning.' Without taking her eyes off her friend, she put her wine glass on the carpet. 'Who was—? Oh, God, I'm soaking. Oh, never mind.' Ignoring her wet legs, she bit her lip. 'It was Josh's, wasn't it?'

Megan nodded. 'We had a one-night stand—years ago. He didn't know I was pregnant.'

'But—'

'I lost it. At twenty-three weeks.' Megan drew in a deep breath. 'It was Josh who saved my life. But he couldn't save our son. He was just too little—too sick.'

Tasha felt the tears spill down her cheeks. 'Oh, Meg, I—I'm so sorry. Josh never— I didn't know. I had no idea.'

'Josh only found out recently, although he'd suspected for a while. That morning you banged on the door of the on-call room—'

'You'd spent the night together.'

'I told him then. He overheard something.' Megan shook her head. 'It doesn't matter. It's all in the past now.'

'Is something like that ever in the past?'

'Maybe not. I still ask myself whether the whole thing was my fault.' Megan spoke quietly. 'When I found out I was pregnant I panicked. It wasn't what I wanted. Or at least it wasn't what I wanted right then—and nature took me literally.'

'No! You know that isn't what happened. It wasn't your fault.'

'I developed complications, and...' Megan breathed slowly '...now I can't have children. I'm infertile. I lost our son. So perhaps it's just as well for Josh that he's having this baby with Rebecca.'

'No.' Tasha hugged Megan. 'Josh wants to be with you, I know that.'

'Well, that's never going to happen.' With a sniff, Megan pulled away and fed the DVD into the player. 'You rang me in a state of misery and since you've arrived all I've done is moan. It's the wine. Never give me wine. And stop being so unselfish. Moan to me about Alessandro.'

But Tasha discovered she didn't want to moan, or even talk about what had happened with Alessandro. It was all too raw. And she felt so foolish. Foolish for believing that what they'd shared was real. 'I don't really want to talk. But I do have a question.'

'You want to know why Alessandro behaved like that?'

'No!' Affronted by the suggestion she wanted to talk about Alessandro, Tasha glared. 'I want to ask you if you happen to know who designed this dress I've just ruined. Everyone seems to think I ought to know.'

* * *

Tasha slept badly and awoke early to hear a rhythmic banging sound coming from Megan's kitchen.

With a groan she rolled onto her stomach and stuck her head under the pillow but the banging continued. 'What *is* she doing?' Giving up on sleep, Tasha slid out of the bed and padded barefoot downstairs.

Megan was in the kitchen, attacking a chicken fillet with a rolling pin. 'Good morning.' The rolling pin smashed into the meat again. 'Sleep well?'

'Er—not particularly.' Tasha winced as the sound resonated through her brain. 'Megan—'

'I'm preparing something for our supper.'

Tasha glanced at the clock. 'It's seven in the morning.'

'I'm pretending the chicken is Josh's head.'

'Ah. And is that helping?'

'I think it might be.' Megan gave the chicken an extra-hard thwack and the fillet split in two. 'Oh, dear.'

'It's OK. It will taste the same.' Her head throbbing, Tasha pushed her hair out of her eyes. 'If it's all right with you, I'm going surfing.'

'At this time of the morning? You'll have the beach to yourself.'

'That's the way I like it. Are you working today?'

'Fortunately not. I have two days off.'

Tasha saw that the scrubbed kitchen table was covered in pages from the internet. 'Australia?' She picked one up. 'You're going on holiday to Australia?'

'Not holiday, no.' Megan gave the chicken one more *thwack* for good measure. 'I'm looking at jobs. They need paediatricians, you know. We could both go.'

'To Australia?' Tasha started to laugh. 'I actually think that's a totally genius idea. Let's do it. Are there men in Australia?'

'Apparently, but it's a big country, so if we're really careful we should be able to avoid them.'

'Great. When I get back from surfing, we'll look at it together.'

Tasha thought about it all the way down to the beach and was still thinking about it as she walked onto the damp, cold sand. Just as Megan had predicted, the beach was empty. The wind blew her hair across her face and she heard the plaintive shriek of a seagull.

For a moment she felt a pang at the thought of leaving St Piran, but then she reminded herself that she wouldn't have been working in St Piran anyway. She would have had to go wherever the jobs took her. And that may as well be Australia. Maybe that far away, it wouldn't hurt so much. Presumably the antipodeans weren't remotely interested in a European principality so she was unlikely to be turning on the news and finding herself looking at pictures of Alessandro.

Trying to block it all out, Tasha plunged into the sea, feeling the cold bite through her wetsuit. Australia had some of the best surfing in the world. She could visit the Barrier Reef—maybe learn to dive.

Somehow try and forget about a certain tall, arrogant prince who had played a starring role in her dreams for far too long.

Ignoring the heavy ache in her chest, she paddled out and took up position just outside the breaking waves. Then she sat up, straddling her board as she stared out to sea, waiting for the right moment.

Could she grow to love Australia the way she loved Cornwall?

Her cheeks were wet and she realised that the sea water had mingled with the flow of her tears.

Furious with herself for crying, she turned the nose of the board to catch the oncoming wave, focusing on the sea and not her feelings. The surge of water lifted her and she paddled hard and then hopped up on the board. She dropped down the face of the wave, feeling the speed build, and she rode the water, arms outstretched, knees bent. As she angled along the face of the wave for that single moment there was nothing else in her mind but the rush of speed and the sheer exhilaration of being carried by the erupting swell of water.

She turned and paddled back into the waves, repeating the exercise until she was exhausted.

Wondering whether Megan had finished bashing the chicken, she finally lifted her board under her arm and walked across the cool sand towards the little path that led towards the cottage.

It was the car she noticed first. Long and black, with darkened glass. Bulletproof glass.

Alessandro stood against the car, watching her, four powerfully built bodyguards positioned at strategic positions around him.

They looked so incongruous in this beautiful, wild place that Tasha almost laughed. But she discovered that she couldn't.

As their eyes connected she felt her heart ache as the pain she'd locked away burst free.

Horrified to feel a lump in her throat, she turned her board, deliberately intending to head back out to sea, but his voice travelled across the sand.

'Tasha, wait.'

She closed her eyes, clenched her jaw and kept walking.

Last night she'd held it together and she was proud of the way she'd handled herself. No tears. No begging. Just anger and dignity. She didn't want to sully an otherwise perfect performance.

'Tasha.' He growled her name. 'If you walk away, I'll assume you're a coward.'

She stopped dead and anger shot through her like a live flame. Furious, she turned. 'Coward?' She stalked back to him, eyes blazing. 'You're calling me a coward? Sorry, but were you or were you not the one who invited me to the wedding for the express purpose of sending a message to your fiancée?'

'Miranda isn't, and never was, my fiancée.'

'*Almost* fiancée, then.'

'I would never have married her.'

'But she didn't know that, did she?' Tasha pinned a sweet smile on her face. 'So you thought you'd give her a stronger message. Using me as the messenger.'

'That wasn't what I was doing.'

'Oh, really? Then why did you take me?' She glared at him and he sucked in a breath and glanced over his shoulder towards his bodyguards.

'Walk with me for a few minutes.'

'No way. What the hell are you doing here, Sandro?' The name spilled easily from her tongue and suddenly she was back in his bedroom, in the intimate world they'd created. And she knew from the sudden blaze of awareness in his eyes that his mind was in exactly the same place.

'I'm flying to San Savarre tonight.' Alessandro's expression was grim and serious. 'There's something I want to say to you before I leave.'

'I've said everything I want to say.'

'Fine. I'll do the talking.'

'How did you find me, anyway?'

'I asked my driver where he dropped you. How's Megan?'

'She's doing just fine,' Tasha said coldly, knowing that Alessandro might well speak to Josh. 'Now, just say whatever it is you want to say so that I can get on with my life and you can get back into your bulletproof car.'

'I came to apologise for last night.'

'And you needed bodyguards for that? Now who's the coward?'

Alessandro's mouth flickered at the corners. 'Walk with me.'

She lifted an eyebrow. 'Is that an order?'

'No, it's a request.'

Tasha hesitated and then shrugged. 'All right. If you're

finally going to apologise, this I have to hear.' She put her board down on the path, horribly conscious of his powerful shoulders in the perfectly tailored suit. Dressed formally he looked remote and intimidating, nothing like the man she'd shared midnight picnics with after hot sex. 'Make it quick. Megan is expecting me back.'

'Why didn't you go back to my house?'

Tasha gave an incredulous laugh. 'Er—isn't it obvious? Excuse me, but this is a waste of time.' She turned away but he grabbed her wrist and dragged her close to him.

'I didn't take you to the wedding to make a point.' His voice was lethally soft. 'I took you because I wanted you with me. And because I wanted to see whether you enjoyed yourself at something like that. You're not like most of the women who attend that sort of thing. '

'Thanks for the reminder.' She felt his fingers hard on her wrist and tried to tug herself free. 'I studied for seven years in medical school and I'm still studying—but nowhere in my research have I ever found a benefit for memorising dress designers. I couldn't care less who made my stupid dress. So you were probably right to dump me.'

'I didn't dump you. You dumped me.'

'You made sure I dumped you.'

'No.' He hauled her against him. 'That's my life, Tasha. That's what I do. I go to weddings, I attend fundraising events, I open hospitals, I go on state visits.'

'Why are you telling me this?'

'Because if our relationship is going to work, you need to know what you're getting into.' He drew in a breath. 'I did take you to that wedding to make a point, but it wasn't the point you obviously thought I was making. It was nothing to do with Miranda or anyone else. It was to do with you and me. I wanted to show you my life. This last six weeks—it hasn't been real, Tasha. Yes, we spent time together, and it was special. But we were cocooned in our own little world. I wanted to know if you'd still want to be with me in the other world I inhabit.'

All the air had gone from her lungs. She felt as though she was the one with the broken ribs. 'You—'

'I'm sorry if you felt humiliated.' He took her face in his hands, his eyes holding hers. 'That was never my intention. I know you're not interested in the whole designer-dress thing, that's one of the reasons I love you. But a huge part of my life is attending events. I needed to know that you wouldn't hate the life.'

Tasha felt dizzy. 'Whoa…' Her voice cracked. 'Rewind. Somewhere back there you said something I didn't quite catch.'

A smile touched his mouth. 'I said I love you. I've never said that to a woman before. Ever. Frankly, I never thought I would. But spending that time with you showed me I was wrong. I love you.'

The words had the effect of a drug. Tasha's head spun. She felt decidedly strange. 'If you…love me, why didn't you say something sooner?'

'Because love isn't enough. It isn't that simple. Not for me.' He pushed a strand of hair out of her eyes. 'I'm very aware that when you marry me, you'll have to take on all of it. Not just me, but the whole royal role. It's a lot to ask of anyone.'

'When I…?' Tasha blinked. 'Excuse me, but could you stop saying these completely shocking things with no warning? There's absolutely no way on this planet I'd marry you.'

His eyes held hers. 'Why not?'

'Well, because you're…' Flustered, she waved a hand vaguely. 'And I'm…' She pressed her fingers to her forehead. 'Just—give me a minute here. Yesterday your mother was looking at me as if I were a virus. Now you're suggesting marriage?'

'It may surprise you to learn that my mother is your biggest supporter.'

'You're right. It would surprise me. She turned me to ice with a single glance.'

'Yes, she's good at that. It's her way of keeping people at a distance. But you impressed her, Tash. You were tough. You stood your ground. And she likes the fact that you have your own career.' He gave a short laugh. 'And the fact that you have no idea who designed your dress.'

'Precisely. I have my own career.' Her heart was hammering. She didn't know whether she was feeling terror or excitement. 'I'm not giving that up for anyone.'

'I'm not asking you to. I wouldn't want you to. You're a very talented doctor. I've seen that in the time we've spent at the hospital. I've heard the way people talk about you. But we have hospitals in San Savarre. In the capital we have a brand-new hospital with state-of-the-art equipment. And consultants who are interested in being progressive.' He paused, a wicked gleam in his eye. 'We also have beaches. Incredible surfing. Endless sunshine.'

Seduced by the picture he painted, Tasha glared at him. 'That's not playing fair.'

'I don't want to play fair. I want you.'

Her breath lodged in her throat. 'Well, that's a shame because I hate you.'

'No, you don't. If you hated me you wouldn't have moved in and helped me. You wouldn't have stormed off last night. You stormed off because you love me and I hurt you. I upset you.' He drew breath. 'And I'm sorry. I should have come clean with you.'

'Yes, yes you should.' Tasha faltered. 'So—so you were seeing if I behaved myself at the wedding? You were thinking, Does she use the right knife and fork?'

'No. I was thinking, Could we do this together? Could we have this life?'

'I overheard some girls talking—'

He nodded. 'I thought you might have done. It happens, Tash. When you're a public figure everyone assumes they know everything there is to know about your private life. They think they know you. But they don't. But now I understand why you were so angry.'

'Sometimes I overreact,' Tasha muttered, her face pink. 'Just a little. When it's something I care passionately about.'

'That's all right with me. I'm happy to be someone you care passionately about.' He slipped his hand into his pocket and pulled out a small box. 'I would have followed you yesterday, but I needed to discuss it with my parents.'

'Discuss what?'

'The fact that I was going to ask you to marry me.' Sure and confident, Alessandro flipped open the box and extracted a glittering diamond ring. 'I can't go down on one knee because with this damn ankle I don't think I'd ever be able to get up again.'

Staring at the ring, Tasha lost the ability to breathe. 'Sandro—'

Without pausing, he took her hand and slid the ring onto her finger. 'I want you to marry me. I want you to be my wife and I want to live our lives together.'

'But—'

'For God's sake, Tash, just say yes, will you? For once in your life could you not argue with me?' He took her hands in his and his fingers were cool and strong. 'Princess Tasha. Josh told me you wrote that a few times on your textbooks.'

'That's two reasons I have to kill him when I next see him.'

'Don't do that. He's going to be my brother-in-law.' Alessandro drew her against him. 'I never thought I'd want to get married. I never thought I'd find a woman I wanted to spend the rest of my life with. And then I found you. Being with you feels…right. It always did, even when you were seventeen.'

Melting inside, Tasha lifted her face to his. 'Don't ever mess me around. If you step out of line, I'll hurt you.'

'But at least you'll be able to put me together again after-wards,' Alessandro drawled, smiling as he lowered his mouth to hers. 'I'll take my chances with you. I've always enjoyed dangerous sports.'

'Wait a minute.' She put her fingers against his mouth, delaying the kiss. 'You haven't told me about Miranda. She's the one everyone was talking about. Call me insecure, but I want to know about her.'

He hesitated and then pulled back slightly, his expression serious. 'Miranda was my brother's fiancée, as you know. We were good friends. I hated the way my brother treated her and for a while…' he shrugged '…other people thought it would be neat if we got together. And maybe she thought it, too. But it was never going to happen. She's always been like a sister to me, but I felt as though I owed her something. But I also knew that to go into a marriage without love was the wrong thing to do. You helped me see that.'

'Me?'

'It was the way I feel about you that made up my mind. So the other night I had a long chat with her. It was the most honest talk we've ever had. I told her about you and how I felt.'

'And now she wants to kill me.'

'She wants to meet you.' Smiling, he lowered his forehead to hers. 'You're going to like each other. She didn't really want to marry me any more than I wanted to marry her. We just gave each other support after Antonio died.'

'I yelled at your mother about that.'

'I know.' He gave a low laugh. 'Thanks to you, she and I also had the most honest conversation we've ever had. It cleared the air.'

'So I'm not going to be arrested for treason or whatever and thrown in your dungeons?'

'I might throw you in the dungeons if you don't give me an answer soon.'

Tasha placed her hand against his face and looked at him for a long time. What she saw in his eyes brought tears to her own and happiness burst free inside her. 'Yes,' she muttered. 'I'll marry you. Just don't expect me to call you Your Highness.'

His mouth came down on hers and they kissed until her heart was hammering and her brain was blurred.

Finally Alessandro lifted his head. 'Let's go somewhere more discreet before our most private moment is captured on film by some photographer with a long lens.'

'Wait…' Tasha hesitated, torn between what he was offering and loyalty to her friend. 'I honestly don't think I can leave right now. Megan is in a mess—she's thinking of going to Australia. Making a new life away from Josh and Rebecca.'

'She doesn't have to go that far to make a new life. We need paediatricians in San Savarre. She could rent out the cottage here and make a new life for herself in the Mediterranean.'

Tasha stared at him, touched by his generosity. 'But Josh is your friend. And my brother. Will it be awkward?'

'Josh loves Megan,' Alessandro said quietly. 'He's crushed with guilt. I think right now he'd support any idea that would stand a chance of making her happy. Why don't you invite her? It would be nice for you to have a friend there. She can have an apartment in the palace. I'm not saying it will be easy for her, but at least she won't have to worry about the basics.'

Smiling, Tasha held out her hand. 'I love you, Your Highness, have I told you that?'

'No, but from now on I expect you to do so on an hourly basis.' He lowered his mouth to hers. 'And that's a royal command.'

200 HARLEY STREET: SURGEON IN A TUX

CAROL MARINELLI

PROLOGUE

'ACCOMMODATION PROVIDED' WAS starting to take on a whole new meaning!

Lizzie Birch took the lift to the fifth floor with her heart in her mouth, sure that there must have been some mistake—that this couldn't possibly be her new home.

When she had been given the trendy Marylebone address Lizzie had convinced herself it would be something like the rather drab nursing accommodation she had shared in earlier days—a stunning old building, divided into bedsits perhaps...

This was anything but that.

As she turned the key Lizzie stepped into a tastefully furnished, high-ceilinged flat and caught the scent of flowers. Turning, she swallowed when she saw an elaborate bouquet and a basket of luxurious nibbles and wines there to greet her.

Lizzie walked over and inhaled the gorgeous fragrance of spring, but on a cold January morning. They must have cost a fortune.

The place must be worth a fortune, Lizzie thought, biting into a chocolate champagne truffle and closing her eyes in bliss, but when she opened them she blinked, completely overwhelmed at her new surroundings. Only now was she starting to fully realise the true coup of becoming Head Nurse at the Hunter Clinic at 200 Harley Street.

There was a note to say that the uniforms she had sent her measurements in for were waiting for her at the clinic. It was a far cry from the usual package of white dresses or theatre scrubs that Lizzie was rather more used to. It was all as rich and as expensive as the voice Lizzie had so far only heard on the other end of a telephone.

Leo Hunter.

'You come highly recommended.' There had been an edge to his voice that had made Lizzie frown; after all, the recommendation as to her suitability for the position had come from Leo's own brother, Ethan.

'Thank you.' Lizzie hadn't really known what to say. 'I was very flattered when Ethan suggested that I apply. He said to call and hopefully arrange an interview—'

'The job's yours,' Leo had interrupted. 'There's no need for an interview, unless you want to hop over to Switzerland.' Lizzie hadn't been sure if he'd been joking or had meant it. She'd heard the sound of rich laughter in the background and Leo had apologised for the noise— explaining that, like all good cosmetic surgeons, now that the Christmas rush was over, he was skiing—and then Lizzie had frowned in confusion as he'd told her that he looked forward to seeing her in the New Year.

Was that it?

He hadn't even asked about her employment history! He didn't seem to care that her work with Ethan had simply been agency work and that she was, in fact, a senior nurse in Accident and Emergency.

He'd given the job as easily as that!

'Oh,' Leo added, just before he rang off. 'Did you want accommodation?' As easily as that he tossed it into the conversation—his clipped, well-schooled voice delivering the offer almost as an afterthought. 'As Head Nurse of the Hunter Clinic, we can offer you that.'

'Offer it?' Lizzie checked.

'A furnished flat…'

Lizzie clutched the phone as he thanked someone, presumably for a drink because she could hear the chink of ice cubes as his attention came back to her. 'I'm not sure which one, we've got a few within walking distance of the clinic.' Lizzie was about to decline—anything within walking distance of 200 Harley Street would be way out of her price range—but then Leo continued, 'It's part of the package, though if you already have somewhere to stay, we can come to—'

'That would be great.' It was Lizzie interrupting now. Trying and failing to sound blasé, but a furnished flat within walking distance would save a fortune, not just on rental but on travel. Lizzie had moved from Brighton to London a couple of years ago and had found it fiercely expensive, especially with all her parents' nursing-home bills. She wasn't used to perks and certainly not one of this magnitude. 'The flat would be marvellous.'

'Good,' Leo clipped. 'Gwen, the clinic manager, will be in touch with all the details and I'll see you in the New Year.'

Happy New Year, Lizzie thought as she looked out of the window, marvelling at the glimpse of Regent's Park, unable to believe all this was really happening to her.

Leo's brother, Ethan, had been a patient of Lizzie's. He had returned injured from Afghanistan and Lizzie had been making home visits, treating his badly injured legs. She'd known Ethan was a doctor but had had no idea of his dazzling family history. Ethan had been silent and brooding and, knowing some of what he had been through, Lizzie hadn't taken it remotely personally. Instead she had filled the long silences with chatter about her own life—her aging parents, her mother's Alzheimer's, the on-going concern she had for them despite the fact they were both in a home. How the decision to sell the family home had been a hard one. How expensive it all was. How she tried to get down to Brighton to visit them most of her days off.

How it hurt that her mother rarely recognised her.

Her tongs had paused in mid-dressing, she had been talking more to herself, but it had been Ethan who had, for once, broken the silence.

'They're lucky to have you.'

'No.' Lizzie had smiled, glad to hear him engaging. 'I'm lucky to have them.'

Slowly Ethan had started talking and when he had told her that he was thinking of working in the family business, heading up the charity side of his brother's cosmetic and reconstructive clinic, Lizzie had taken an interest, more because she'd been glad that Ethan was finally communicating.

It had never entered her head that he would put her forward for the position of Head Nurse at the clinic. More than that, she had never thought she would be accepted.

Lizzie was plagued with insecurity about the sudden change in her career, sure that one look at the very fresh-faced Lizzie and Leo Hunter would change his mind.

She wandered through the flat and to the gorgeous

bathroom and stared at her reflection in the large mirror, wondering what head nurse to a renowned cosmetic surgeon ought to look like.

Lizzie looked at her light brown wavy hair and brown eyes and a face that rarely wore make-up and thought of all the celebrities and beauties she would be facing come Monday.

She thought too of facing Leo.

Of course she had looked him up and life hadn't been the same since!

It was rather like the day her blushing mother had told a very naïve Lizzie the facts of life. The autumn crocus in her elderly parents' lives, Lizzie had been cosseted and protected from such things. The day they'd had *the talk*, suddenly it had seemed that periods and sex were everywhere—from adverts on television to full pages in magazines.

It was the same with Leo Hunter—he was everywhere now.

He was the chiselled-jawed, blue-eyed hunk that cavorted on snow-capped mountaintops behind royalty as they were photographed.

Black hair brushed back, he was that beautiful face on the table next to a celebrity, he was that man walking beside a stunning model as she tripped on her way out of a nightclub.

Lizzie had just never paid attention till now.

Leo Hunter was a heartbreaker, surgeon to the stars, irredeemable playboy and, as of Monday, he would also be her boss.

CHAPTER ONE

'I HIRED HER, didn't I?' Leo's response to his brother was terse. 'So why wouldn't I be nice to her?'

'You know what I mean, Leo.'

Rarely was Ethan the one to walk away. He turned on his heel and attempted to stalk out of his brother's plush office but despite the simmering anger, despite ten years, no, a lifetime of rivalry, Leo's jaws clamped together at the painful sight of his brother's attempt to stalk off.

God only knew the mess of Ethan's legs, Leo thought. Ethan certainly never spoke about them and Leo had only read about them. Leo could still remember the pain and humiliation of having to learn from a news article that his brother was recovering in hospital.

So much for being next of kin.

Ethan's time in Afghanistan was something Ethan chose not to discuss but his pain was evident and, yes, Leo wished his brother would share, open up, but why would he? Leo thought.

They'd never been close.

Their father had seen to that long ago.

'You're not proving anything by refusing to use a walking stick.' Leo watched as Ethan's shoulders stiffened but, hell, if his older brother couldn't say it then who could?

'If I want a further opinion I'll go to someone who...' Ethan didn't finish, he didn't have to—that was the dark beauty of being brothers, there was enough history to know exactly what the other meant without having to spell things out. As Ethan's disdain for Leo's work briefly broke through the tense, simmering surface, exposing the rivalry beneath, Leo merely shrugged.

'Mock it all you like,' he said, as Ethan turned to face him. 'But I'll tell you this much—my patients walk out of here feeling one hell of a lot better than they did when they first walked in, and,' he added, 'might I remind you that it's my work and subsequently my patients' word of mouth that have pulled the Hunter name out of the gutter. While you were busy playing soldiers...' Leo broke off, wishing he could retrieve his own words, because Ethan hadn't been playing at anything. Ethan's injuries were a product of war. He was a hero by anyone's standards—especially Leo's. 'That was below the belt,' he admitted.

'Yes, and so is the shrapnel.'

Leo just stood there silent for a moment. His appalling playboy reputation combined with a passion for fast living meant that having a wounded soldier for a younger brother needled on so many levels. 'While you're peering down your nose at your celebrity surgeon brother, just remember that my work allows the charity side of things to happen,' Leo pointed out. 'Without the money coming into the Hunter Clinic those charity beds at the Lighthouse Hospital and Kate's wouldn't be funded and you wouldn't be working here.'

'I get it,' Ethan growled.

'You abhor it, though…' Leo said, as his eyes drifted to the crystal decanter that sat on the walnut table in his office. 'But you don't seem to mind extravagance when you're knocking back the hundred-year-old malt…' He walked over and lifted the decanter. 'I must remember to replace the stopper more carefully in future.' His voice was dripping with sarcasm. 'It seems to be evaporating at a rate of knots.'

Ethan said nothing. It was Leo who chose not to leave it. 'Don't you have a home to go to, Ethan? I'm assuming that you crashed here again last night…'

It was an obvious assumption. Ethan was wearing the same clothes as yesterday and was the antitheses of the impeccably groomed Leo who, despite a late night at an A-list function and an energetic romp with yet another blonde beauty in his bed, had been out for a run at dawn, before showering and heading to work.

Ethan, it would seem, had crashed again on Leo's leather sofa.

'I was working late.' Ethan offered the same excuse as he had on several occasions since coming to work at the Hunter Clinic.

Leo could feel the tension in his jaw, heard his own hiss of breath as he felt the pages of history turning. Yes, Ethan may be a hero but he was very much a wounded one and it wasn't just his legs that were injured, Leo was sure of it. But even if Ethan's mental scars ran deep there was no way that Leo was about to let history repeat itself. He could still remember, as if it had happened yesterday, the time when everything had finally come to a head—their father, James, turning up for work drunk and causing a scene in front of the clients.

Of course he had been sent home, disgraced, but instead of sleeping it off James had carried on with his bender, eventually collapsing and dying. The Hunter reputation had fallen like a house of cards and it had been Leo who had painstakingly rebuilt it brick by brick, client by client, personal recommendation by personal recommendation.

He'd sacrificed way too much to see it fall again.

Leo felt the heavy weight of the stopper in his palm for a moment before he replaced it in the decanter. 'If you ever—' Leo started, but Ethan broke in.

'It's not going to happen.'

'You're quite sure about that?' Leo's eyes were as blue as the ocean and, despite the seemingly decadent lifestyle, just as clear. Unlike Ethan's—his hazel eyes were bloodshot and although Leo appeared unshaven it was designer stubble on his chin, whereas Ethan looked like a man who *had* spent the night on a sofa—albeit an expensive one.

'I shan't be making excuses for you, Ethan.'

'Learned your lesson, have you?' Ethan asked. Yes, there was a dark beauty to being brothers, because in that short question Ethan had demanded answers to the impossible. Why had Leo kept such a lid on things with their father? Why had Leo constantly smoothed over the gaping cracks? Why, when Ethan had wanted to confront their father, had Leo insisted otherwise as their father had spiralled further out of control?

Even as children, Leo had been the same, defusing situations with wit and humour—even pouring his father a drink at times just to knock him out.

Ethan would have preferred different methods to produce the same result.

His fists.

'I don't think now is the time or the place,' Leo said.

'There never has been a right time and place,' Ethan responded, then turned the conversation from the impossible to the practical. 'Just make sure that you're nice to Lizzie.'

'I can't wait to meet her,' Leo clipped. Despite wanting the conversation over, Leo just couldn't help himself, he simply could not resist a dig. Oh, there was history, so much history that threaded every word of his taunt. 'She must be pretty amazing if she's got into that cold black heart of yours.'

'I'm just asking you to go easy on her,' Ethan said. 'Lizzie isn't one of your usual tarts.'

'You really do have a thing for her…' Leo drawled. 'Good in bed, is she?'

Had Ethan thumped Leo it wouldn't have been in defence of Lizzie. Both men's minds had turned now to the woman who had ultimately divided them—so much so that Olivia might just as well be standing in the room watching them, listening to them fight, just as they had ten years ago, almost to the very day.

'How sad that that is your measure of a good woman,' Ethan responded.

'Do I look sad?' Leo's lips sneered into a smile. 'I'm not the one who's turning into a recluse. I'm out every night, I'm living…'

'Really?' Ethan had heard enough. It had been a stupid idea to come back and an even more stupid idea to expose Lizzie to the toxicity. There was a fight waiting to be had, an explosion about to come sometime soon and, were his legs not about to give way, Ethan might have dealt with it then. He looked at Leo—so

arrogant, so assured, so, despite his insistence otherwise, messed up.

What had he been thinking, coming to work here?

'It's not living, Leo, it's existing—I should know!'
Ethan walked out then, calling over his shoulder as he
left, 'Just keep it in your pants for once. Lizzie deserves
better than that.'

Leo stood there as the door slammed.

Their voices hadn't been particularly raised and the
walls were thick but the tension in the clinic was almost
palpable and the staff must surely be noticing it by now.
Had it been a mistake to ask Ethan to come and head
up the charitable side of the business? Leo truly didn't
know. There was no doubt that his brother was a brilliant surgeon and that his skills could be well utilised,
but there was just so much water under the bridge between them.

'Leo...' Gwen, the clinic manager, interrupted his
train of thought as she buzzed through on the intercom. 'I've got—'

'Send her straight in,' Leo broke in, bracing himself
to meet Saint Lizzie—the woman who had got under
his brother's skin.

'Leo.'

Leo's head jerked around at the sound of a low, sensual voice and, no, it wasn't the new head nurse who
stepped into his office, instead it was what he had hoped
was finished business—Flora Franklin, who was as far
removed from a saint as it was possible to be!

Incredibly beautiful, Flora was dressed in a long expensive coat and her heels were so high she was almost as tall as Leo, who stood stock still as she walked

towards him. 'You didn't return my call,' Flora reproached him.

'Because there's nothing more to say. We're finished.' Leo didn't like to have to repeat himself and he already had, once, but twice was one time too many. 'We've been through this…'

'Well, this might change your mind.'

Flora opened her trench coat and let it fall from her shoulders to the floor. Leo looked down at the sight of her spectacular body almost on full display in the sexiest of red underwear, her nipples peeking out between lace, and what man wouldn't be tempted?

Yes, his body might be, there was no denying that fact, but Leo's mind certainly wasn't. Even as she rained kisses on his face and her hands got to work, Leo reminded himself that he was through with Flora. Yes, it had been fun while it had lasted but it was over. He had tried to let her down gently, but it was time to make things very clear.

'Flora…' Leo's voice was as detached as it was firm. 'You really need to…' His voice trailed off to the sound of gentle knocking and as the gap in the partially open door widened and Lizzie stepped in, all Leo could think was that this was *so* not how he had wanted to greet the new head nurse.

'Dr Hunter, I presume?' He saw her tight smile, saw colour flood her rounded cheeks as she took in the situation, and though Lizzie didn't actually say, *your reputation precedes you,* her eyes most certainly did.

'Mister.' Even in the most compromising of situations, Leo corrected mistakes. He'd worked hard for his fellowship after all. 'You must be Lizzie.' Leo returned an equally tight smile as he attempted to peel Flora off, not that Lizzie hung around to watch. With a brief shake of her head she turned and walked out of Leo's office and, unlike Flora, Lizzie did think to close the door properly. There was no door slamming but, just as it had with Ethan, Leo could feel the lingering disapproval.

'Where were we?' Flora purred, not in the least embarrassed by the interruption.

Rarely, Leo was.

'The same place we were a few moments ago,' Leo answered brusquely, getting straight to the brutal point. 'Finished.'

'Leo…' Flora attempted, grabbing the arm that was trying to retract itself, but Leo shook her off—he was in no mood for debate.

'Cover yourself up, make sure that you are out of here by the time I get back. I need to go and sort out this mess.' He marched out of his office and through the plush corridors and because, unlike Lizzie, he knew his way around, Leo had caught up with her before Lizzie made it to the changing rooms.

'Your timing's impeccable,' Leo offered, and gave a wry smile to Lizzie as he tucked in his shirt. 'I'm serious,' he added as she shot him an incredulous look. 'I was actually trying to get rid of her.'

'Really?'

She had a very soft but exceptionally clear voice, though it was, Leo noted, her eyes that did most of the talking and what they had to say was less than flattering—especially as they briefly drifted down and, with a slight purse to her lips, returned to meet his cool gaze. Without needing to check, Leo knew, just *knew* what she had seen—his flies were undone.

Leo could have blushed.

Or cursed.

Perhaps he should have chosen to ignore it.

His response was far less forgivable.

He laughed.

A shameless, deep laugh as he deftly rectified the situation.

Lizzie, he noted, didn't laugh.

He noted a few other things too. She was incredibly... Leo's mind hesitated. As one of Britain's top cosmetic surgeons he was usually able to sum up a woman's looks in an instant. It came as second nature to him to notice any work that might have been done or, perhaps more pointedly, to guess what work a woman might be considering. As a patient walked into his office, Leo's eyes were already assessing their features and had guessed by the end of that first handshake what was on the patient's mind.

He just couldn't work out what might be on Lizzie's.

Rather than noticing very slightly protruding teeth, Leo saw only her full lips. Her creamy complexion didn't come from a bottle—if it did, Leo would have held the patent, and as for that body... With Flora his response had been automatic, clinical, but with Lizzie it was far from that. He'd had no idea what to expect from the new head nurse, but it certainly hasn't been this ball of femininity.

'Flora and I recently broke up,' he explained. 'She just hasn't got used to the idea yet.'

Lizzie really didn't want to hear about his love life. Her cheeks were on fire—a mixture of coming into the warm clinic from a cold January day, nerves at starting her new job, and the sight that had greeted her.

Right now, all she wanted was to get as far away

from Leo Hunter as possible to attempt to get her head together. 'If you will excuse me, I'd like to get changed and then I'll come and introduce myself and we can hopefully start again—more professionally this time.'

'Sure,' Leo responded, realising that in very few words she had stated her case. Lizzie Birch was far from impressed, but right now he had other things to deal with—namely, a near-naked, scorned woman who, Leo thought as he heard the sound of sobbing, was not going to go quietly.

Lizzie was *so* far from impressed.

She stepped into the staff changing room, which looked as if it might belong in some exclusive gymnasium rather than a medical clinic. There were huge mirrors, showers and wall-to-wall fluffy towels. Lizzie half expected an attendant to come out and offer to take her coat.

Thankfully it was empty and Lizzie dragged in a breath. Oh, she was so far from impressed, not just at the scene in his office but at her own response to Leo.

Did he have to be so good-looking? So overpowering, so completely male?

Yes, she'd seen photos but not one of them had adequately captured the beauty or the overwhelming charisma of Leo Hunter close up.

She had expected a slightly older version of Ethan, but instead he seemed younger, lighter and far more reprobate then his serious younger brother. And, unlike Ethan, Leo's eyes were blue but, more than that, they beckoned to bed.

'Oh, no!' Lizzie actually said the words out loud. For all her misgivings about the new position, for all her worry and concern about taking on such a prestigious role, never had it entered her head that on sight her stomach would be doing somersaults and it actually had very little to do with the compromising situation she had found him in.

He'd laughed.

At what should have been the most embarrassing, awkward of moments, when anyone else would have been cringing and red faced, he'd had the audacity to do what, to Lizzie's surprise, she found herself doing now. As a shocked gurgle of laughter filled the room Lizzie's eyes widened in brief surprise at her own reaction to her new boss but then the smile faded.

'He would crush you in the palm of his hand,' Lizzie told her reflection. She was here to work, to make decent money, to finally get ahead.

There was no way she would allow herself to even think of fancying him.

Lizzie was far too sensible for that.

In her new role, Gwen had explained that she would be expected to wear a suit. Lizzie unzipped it from its cover and pulled on the slim charcoal-grey skirt. There was also a cream blouse with a cowl neck and small buttons at the back.

Hardly practical, Lizzie thought, changing from boots to low heels, slipping on the jacket and then stepping back to check her reflection.

Even though she was thirty-two years old, Lizzie felt like a child trying on her mother's clothes. They were tailored, fitted…elegant.

Lizzie didn't normally bother with make-up at work but, having seen Gwen and a couple of the other staff on her entrance, she wished she had thought to bring some.

She walked towards Leo's office, wondering how best to face him.

As it turned out, it wasn't facing Leo that proved to be the problem.

Instead it was Flora!

CHAPTER TWO

'I'VE GOT THIS...' Leo said.

He was attempting to cover Flora with her coat and guide her from the sumptuous reception either out the main door or towards his office. Lizzie wasn't sure which. But, as stubborn as a mule, Flora dug in her stilettoes and stood beneath the chandelier in the reception, telling anyone, who had no choice but to listen, what a bastard Leo was.

'Not here.' Leo was attempting to smooth things and steer her away.

'Yes, here!' Flora insisted.

Leo had been making a coffee, trying to give Flora the chance for a somewhat dignified exit, when the one-woman protest had started.

There was something quite unattractive about a near-naked woman furiously ripping off jewellery and tossing it at a very calm man, Lizzie thought.

'And he was worried about me creating a scene...' Ethan walked out of his own office and made the dry comment as Lizzie joined him. 'Welcome to 200 Harley Street, Lizzie. You've met my brother, I presume?'

'Is it always like this?' Lizzie asked.

'That depends.' Ethan shrugged. 'They've been together for a few weeks, including Christmas, which is a bit of a record for Leo. I hope to God he gets it sorted before patients start to arrive.'

Lizzie was starting to doubt it.

'Flora!' Leo was trying to calm Flora down and failing. 'You're being ridiculous.'

'No.' She hurled a necklace at him and Lizzie realised she was holding her breath as it flew through the air and thankfully missed its target. 'What's ridiculous is you throwing away all we have. Why can't we work on it?'

Leo opened his mouth to say something but then changed his mind and Flora carried on. 'Do you remember what you said when you gave me this?' she demanded, as she wrenched off a ring.

'No,' Leo admitted shamelessly.

'Bastard.' She tossed the ring and this time it did meet its mark. If a diamond could cut glass then it made light work of Leo's cheek—a gash opening as Leo stepped forward to restrain Flora. She was clearly about to hit him but Lizzie got there first. She took the woman's wrist and held it, and for the second time Leo heard the calm ice of Lizzie's voice.

'Now, that really would be stupid,' Lizzie said. 'If this doesn't stop right now I shall have the police called.' Absolutely she meant it. 'I thought I'd left the fights in Accident and Emergency behind when I came to work here.'

'It's not like that,' Flora attempted.

'It's exactly what it's like,' Lizzie said, releasing Flora's hand and watching the woman's anger turn to horror as she realised what she had done. 'Now....' Lizzie quickly put on Flora's coat and did up the buttons, then tied the belt as she spoke. 'I think we've all seen enough drama...' She looked briefly over at Ethan and at Leo, who had blood pouring down his cheek. Seeing Lizzie had control of things, they both gave a brief nod at her dismissal of them but before they disappeared into Ethan's office Leo had a very quiet word with Lizzie.

'See that she gets home okay.'

'Sure.'

All the fight had gone out of Flora and Lizzie couldn't help but feel sorry for her and perhaps embarrassed for her too.

'You need to go home and calm down,' Lizzie said.

'I can't believe it's over.' Flora said. 'He told me—'

'I don't think going over things will be very helpful now,' Lizzie interrupted.

'I thought we were going to get engaged!' Flora sobbed. 'I thought it meant something...'

'This is a medical clinic.' Lizzie kept her voice practical. 'It's not the place to cause a scene. Whatever is going on between you and Leo is to be sorted well away from here.' Lizzie simply refused to prolong the conversation. 'I'll call a taxi for you.'

'I'll take her home.' Gwen walked down the corridor and gave Lizzie a tight smile. 'Come on, Flora.'

'Hold on.' Lizzie picked up the jewellery that was scattered over the floor. 'You don't want to leave these behind.' She was warmed to see a very pale smile on a dazed Flora's lips as Lizzie carefully slipped the jewellery into her coat pocket. 'That really would be a stupid mistake.'

'Thank you.'

Lizzie just nodded.

Before Gwen headed off with Flora she told Lizzie

there was someone watching the front desk as patients would soon be arriving.

Luckily none were here yet.

For a moment Lizzie wondered how to play it when she saw Leo—whether to pretend that it hadn't happened, carry on as if nothing had, or face things.

There really wasn't a choice—yes, she wanted this job but she couldn't work in, let alone be head nurse of, a clinic with this type of thing going on and not state her case.

Lizzie knocked once and opened the door.

'Don't you wait to be called in?' Leo asked, his tone telling Lizzie he was joking. He was leaning back in his leather chair as Ethan opened up a suture pack.

'I don't think there's much point.' Lizzie's response was dry. 'I've seen far more than I wanted to already.'

'Yes, well, sorry about that.'

He gave a slight wince as Ethan probed the wound. 'You need a couple of stitches.'

'I don't.'

'It's deep,' Ethan said. 'If you don't want it opening up…'

'Just do it, then,' Leo snapped, and then his blue eyes opened to Lizzie. 'Things are normally far calmer…'

'He's lying.' Ethan was opening up a vial of local anaesthetic. 'My brother tends to bring out the worst in women.'

'Don't bother with the local.'

'Suit yourself.' Ethan shrugged.

'Why do women always say they want to work on things?' Leo pondered out loud, saying now what he'd been sensible enough not to say to Flora. 'I save work for work.'

'Just what did you say when you gave her the ring?' Ethan asked.

'I said that it *wasn't* an engagement ring. I made it very clear.' Lizzie winced for Leo as Ethan put in a stitch, then she winced for Flora as Leo thought for a moment and then spoke on. 'Actually, I can remember what I said, I said that it was the closest I'd come to one…'

'Leo!' Ethan's exasperation was clear but for the first time since she'd met him, even if Leo couldn't see it, Ethan was actually smiling.

'I didn't mean it like that. What I was trying to say…' Leo jumped to his own defence then gave in. 'Bloody hell, I think I must have had too much *Goldschläger* or something.'

'*What's that*?' Lizzie checked, and Leo actually smiled as the second suture went in and Lizzie picked up some scissors and cut for Ethan.

'Cinnamon schnapps,' Leo said. 'Lethal stuff.'

'How was Switzerland?' Ethan asked, putting in the third.

'Far more romantic than intended, it would seem.' Leo sighed. 'I'll ring her and apologise…'

'Don't,' Lizzie said, and one blue eye peeped open and for the first time she properly met his gaze. 'False hope.'

'Okay.'

'Just leave it,' Lizzie said. 'I think she's got the message.'

'You think?' Leo checked.

'I'm quite sure she's worked out what a top bastard you are.'

She smiled sweetly as she said it.

'Thank you.'

'You're welcome.' Lizzie snipped the stich and then made herself say it. 'Keep arguments away from work.'

'Leo never argues,' Ethan said. 'He ends things long before arguments start.'

'Well, I don't want to walk into that again.' Lizzie knew she had to address it and as she did so he opened the other eye and stared back at Lizzie as she spoke on. 'I'm not just talking about the scene in Reception, I'm talking about what I walked into before—I could have been a patient.'

'But you're not.'

'Even so.' Lizzie put down the scissors as Ethan, tongue in cheek as his brother got a scolding, applied a small dressing. 'It's not very professional.'

'I'm extremely professional,' Leo smarted.

'I can only go by what I've seen.' Lizzie retorted. 'Am I being hired to merely smile or am I to be the head nurse of the clinic?'

'Head nurse,' Leo said through gritted teeth.

'Then let there be no repetitions.' She gave him a smile and then smiled at Ethan. 'I'll go and show myself around.'

She walked out, again closing the door behind her, and let out a long slow breath as, on the other side, Leo did the same.

'You didn't tell me I was hiring an old-school matron,' Leo grumbled, picking up the mirror he usually held up for patients and examining the damage to his cheek as he mimicked Lizzie's voice. '"Let there be no repetitions"—I feel like I'm back at school.'

'God help Lizzie then,' Ethan said, but then the smile faded from his face as he watched Leo's gaze briefly drift to the door Lizzie had just walked out of. Ethan watched as, simply on instinct, Leo dragged in the last dregs of the feminine scent lingering in the air and, not for the first time, Ethan wondered if, by seeing she got this job, he had been doing Lizzie a huge disservice.

Yes, the money might be great but if Leo set his cap on her…

Ethan let out a worried breath. He knew better than most the true cost of a broken heart.

CHAPTER THREE

LIZZIE DID SHOW herself around and chatted to a couple of the staff, who were very friendly.

'Welcome to the Hunter Clinic.' Charlotte, one of the nurses introduced herself. 'I'm just heading over to Kate's or I'd show you around.'

'Kate's?' Lizzie checked—she'd heard that name mentioned a few times in conversation.

'Princess Catherine's Hospital,' Charlotte explained and, as she spoke on, Lizzie was fast finding out how little she knew about her new role. 'Day cases are normally done here but anything other than a twilight sedation is done either at Kate's or the Lighthouse Hospital.'

'Do you do a lot at the Lighthouse?' Lizzie asked, because that was a children's hospital.

'Loads.' Charlotte smiled. 'Rafael De Luca, one of our paediatric surgeons, has a theatre list there this morning and I'm—'

'Charlotte!'

She was interrupted by rather gruff but very good-looking man who popped his head out of a treatment room like a handsome bear peering out of a cave, holding his gloved hands up in front of him and asking in a rich Scottish accent if he might have a hand.

'I'm just on my way out…'

'I can help.' Lizzie smiled, glad of the chance to be useful.

'Lizzie's the new head nurse,' Charlotte explained as she dashed off.

'Hi Lizzie, I'm Iain MacKenzie. I'm removing sutures,' he explained, 'but Jessica, the patient, is very distressed. I need a hand to keep her still. She doesn't want any sedation.'

Jessica was *very* distressed; she was on an examination table and curled up.

'Can we do it tomorrow?' she begged.

'The sooner they come out the less it will scar,' Iain explained. 'It's not going to hurt, there will just be a little bit of tugging. This is Lizzie…'

'Hi, Jessica.' Lizzie smiled. She was about to ask what had happened but Iain shot her a warning look and Lizzie decided otherwise. Instead, she made the woman as comfortable as she could and put a small sterile towel over her face so that she couldn't see the blade Iain was using to remove the numerous tiny sutures from her neck and behind her ear.

'You're doing grand…' Iain said every now and then, but he was a silent type and was concentrating hard so it was Lizzie who did most of the reassuring as the tiny threads were removed.

'How does it look?' Jessica kept asking.

Iain was concentrating and it was Lizzie who spoke for him.

'It's very swollen and tender at the moment,' Lizzie said, 'but the wounds are…' She hesitated. How could she describe them as amazing? Yet she had never seen anything so intricately repaired. 'It's a marvellous job.'

She looked up and Iain gave a grim smile.

He was a man of few words but his work clearly spoke for itself. As he held up the mirror and Jessica carefully examined the wounds, Lizzie was relieved for the patient that she could see an improvement.

'It looks so much better but—'

'Just let it settle and I'll see you in a couple of days and we'll start with ointments and massage, but for now I just want the wound left. How are you?'

'I don't know,' Jessica admitted. 'The thing is…' She glanced over at Lizzie and when it was clear that she'd prefer privacy Lizzie made her excuses and left.

'How is she?' Leo was walking past as Lizzie came out.

'Sorry?'

He nodded in the direction of his office and Lizzie followed. The corridor was perhaps not the best place to speak. 'How is Jessica?' Leo clarified. 'I was going to suture her when she came in but I knew it was going to take hours and I had a function to attend…' He watched as Lizzie's lips tightened a fraction. 'You've been spending far too long listening to my brother about me.' Leo gave a wry smile. 'Anyway, Iain is brilliant for that type of injury. I'm just interested to hear how Jessica is.'

'Her sutures are out,' Lizzie said. 'She's just speaking with Iain. I think she wanted me to leave.'

'You don't recognise her, do you?'

'Should I?' Lizzie said, and then her eyes widened as she recalled the news last week and realised she'd just been looking after the wife of a celebrity who'd been taken in for questioning after a heated argument with his wife.

'From her injuries I thought she must have been in

a car accident.' Lizzie closed her eyes for a moment. 'I thought that working here would be...' She halted, realising Leo might not be the best person to reveal her thoughts to, but he was already one step ahead.

'You thought that it was all fake boobs and anti-aging?' Leo finished for her. 'Domestic violence isn't just for the working classes.'

'I know.' Lizzie's voice was rattled, cross, but more with herself because, yes, Leo was right, people assumed that if you were rich and beautiful of course those sorts of things didn't happen and so, when they did, it was somehow more shocking.

'You'll know it for certain after a couple of months here,' Leo said. 'Right, would you mind stepping outside and then walking in again?' He saw her confusion. 'I'd like to start again.'

'It's really not necessary.'

'It really is,' Leo said. 'Go on, knock and this time wait till I call you in.'

'This is ridiculous,' Lizzie said, walking out and closing the door. She knocked and waited for his summons.

'Come in.'

But kind of fun, Lizzie decided as she opened the door to his smile.

'You must be the new head nurse.' Leo stood from his desk, walked over and shook her hand.

'You must be *Mr* Hunter.' Lizzie smiled. 'It's lovely to meet you... Oh, what on earth happened to your cheek?'

He smiled, and Lizzie's stomach did what it had done at the door to the changing room and simply folded over on itself.

'Oh, that,' Leo said. 'Just a little tumble, skiing.'

'Ouch.' Lizzie winced. 'Poor you!'

Then Leo was serious. He offered her a seat and moved behind his huge walnut table. It really was a lovely office, which looked out onto Harley Street, and Lizzie had to snap her eyes back to Leo when he spoke as she found herself staring out of the window, unable to believe she was actually here.

'I think you'll enjoy working here,' Leo started. 'I have an amazing team —all the staff I have personally chosen for their excellence. From surgeons to receptionists I have hand-picked each one.'

'Except me.'

She didn't mince her words, Leo noted.

'Except you,' Leo admitted. 'But, then, I trust my brother's judgement.' He didn't add it had been a condition of Ethan's that if he was to take the role then Lizzie must be employed. 'So, what made you want to work at the Hunter Clinic?'

Lizzie wondered just how honest she should be— she could hardly admit that it was the dazzling salary that had first attracted her. Neither could she say that the chance for an apartment in such a beautiful part of London had been too good to pass up and that the chance to finally get ahead financially had clinched the deal for her.

'It's a very prestigious clinic,' Lizzie settled for instead.

'It is.' Leo's eyes never left her face. 'You haven't worked in cosmetic or reconstructive surgery, though?' he checked, and watched as her cheeks darkened. 'What attracts you to it?'

'People like Jessica,' Lizzie answered. 'It's wonderful that such an appalling injury—'

'I'm talking about the cosmetic side of things. People who come to the clinic for purely cosmetic reasons. Vanity even…'

'I'm all for it,' Lizzie said.

'Really?' Leo raised an eyebrow. 'You don't sound very sure.'

Lizzie was really struggling. Had she had a formal interview she would have given this question some thought prior to the event, but now it had been thrust upon her. There was no escaping Leo's eyes as her mind raced for a more convincing response.

'Why wouldn't I be all for it?' Lizzie said. 'I've had a little work done myself.'

'Really?' Leo frowned. 'What?'

Lizzie let out a slightly shrill laugh. 'I don't think you'd really expect me to answer that.'

Leo frowned. He could usually spot any work—it was his job after all—and Lizzie had to sit there burning with mortification as his eyes skimmed her face and then dipped briefly before returning to meet her gaze.

'Can I ask who did your work?'

'No,' Lizzie said.

'Well, whatever he did, it was an excellent job.'

'She,' Lizzie said.

'Now you've got me really curious.'

Leo soon got back to being serious as he explained how the clinic ran. 'I take great pride in my work. My patients often live their lives, or have lived their lives in the spotlight,' he explained. 'Like it or not, the world can be a very judgmental place and I do my best for my patients. I respect them immensely for taking care of themselves.' Lizzie looked up at the determination in his voice. 'Though I'm seeing fewer clients now as I focus more on the business side of things.'

'Can I ask why?' Lizzie was curious. 'You're clearly in demand…'

'Two-fold.' He nodded his approval of her question. 'The more elusive I've become the more in demand I am and, on a more serious note, I really do want to build the charitable side of things. That's the reason I've persuaded Ethan to come on board. The Hunter Clinic provides many people with very nice lifestyles but we do give back. It's not just about donating a doctor's time, though, it's the hospital beds, the rehabilitation, the family…'

'I can imagine.'

'Fundraising is a serious part of my role. I'm very good at the social side of things.'

'I had heard.'

'Someone has to be,' Leo said. 'I can hardly send in Edward.'

Lizzie frowned.

'Renowned micro surgeon, absolute genius, lives with his books,' Leo said. 'Then there's Iain.'

'MacKenzie? The Scottish one?'

Leo nodded. 'Another brilliant surgeon but useless at small talk. And can you imagine Ethan drumming up business at an A-list function? He drips disdain.'

Lizzie felt guilty doing so but she did give a small laugh because, yes, Ethan wouldn't be wonderful at schmoozing up to anyone.

'For all he disapproves…' Leo mused out loud, and then halted himself and turned the focus back to

Lizzie. 'Ethan said something about you supporting your parents…'

'He shouldn't have.'

'He wasn't gossiping,' Leo said. 'It must be quite a drain on you.'

'I look out for my parents,' Lizzie said tartly, embarrassed to be discussing this. 'The same way that they have always looked out for me. Like you, there comes a time when it's right to give back.'

'Okay.' He wrote on his pad and Lizzie frowned. 'I was just reminding myself not to go there again.' He turned her visible discomfort into a smile. 'Right, I'd better get on. I do have a patient at two who will expect only the most senior staff.' He opened up a folder and Lizzie saw that despite the effortless small talk this meeting really had been planned because it contained all her paperwork. 'You've signed the confidentiality clause?' Leo checked.

'Yes.'

'You fully understand what you signed?'

'Of course.'

'Good. I'll see you just before two, then. The patient I'm seeing is Marianna Dupont. Have you heard of her?'

Lizzie swallowed. You'd have to be living under a rock not to have heard of Marianna. Since her engagement to Prince Ferdinand of Sirmontane had been announced, their romance had filled the gossip columns. As first in line to the throne, his future wife would one day be queen and from the way Leo was talking, Lizzie was about to meet her.

'I have heard of her,' Lizzie said, attempting nonchalance and failing miserably. The wedding wasn't till next year but it would seem some discreet preparations were being put in place for a woman who would spend the rest of her life living in the eye of the public and on the cover of every magazine.

'Good,' Leo said, and as Lizzie went to go his voice caught up with her at the door.

'The salary.'

'Sorry?' Lizzie turned around.

'You could have just answered that it was the salary that attracted you to the role and I wouldn't have minded. There's nothing wrong with wanting nice things.'

'I know.'

'And a lot of people have no idea what goes on in a clinic like this till they actually work in one.'

'I'm already finding that out.'

'You have to know it to love it,' Leo explained.

She possibly already did.

CHAPTER FOUR

MARIANNA WAS SERIOUSLY beautiful.

Gwen showed her through and Lizzie tried to quieten the flutter of nerves in her stomach, telling herself that all patients wanted, rich or poor, was simply to be well cared for.

It didn't help.

'Leo!' Marianna was charming and greeted him like a friend. 'It's lovely to see you again.' Her voice dropped in concern when she saw the dressing on his cheek. 'What happened there?'

'Just a small tumble, skiing,' Leo said, as he kissed her on both cheeks and gave Lizzie just the tiniest wink. 'How are you?'

'Nervous,' Marianna said in her rich accent.

'This is Lizzie Birch,' Leo introduced them. 'Our new head nurse.'

'It's lovely to meet you, Lizzie.' Marianna smiled but she gave a nervous swallow when she turned back to Leo. 'I am sure that I was photographed coming in.'

'You used the basement?'

'I did, but when I was in the car—'

'You'll leave by the front door,' Leo said. 'Did you wear dark glasses on the way here, like I told you to?'

Marianna nodded. 'If anyone finds out that I'm having work done, it will be awful.'

'No one shall find out from us,' Leo assured her. 'We're very used to dealing with this type of thing, though, as we've discussed, there are always going to be rumours.'

'Of course,' Marianna sighed. 'I have already been pregnant five times.'

'You've kept your figure well,' Lizzie joked, and then blushed, but Marianna just laughed.

'How has it been?' Leo asked, pulling up some images on his computer and then coming over to Marianna to take a closer look.

'Your work is amazing,' Marianna admitted. 'Even I struggle to notice what is different about my nose—I just know that it looks so much better.'

'Marianna had rhinoplasty six weeks ago at Kate's,' Leo explained to Lizzie as he examined the soon-to-be-royal nose. He then took a couple of photos, which he transferred to his computer, and Lizzie marvelled at the change. It was almost imperceptible, yet the difference was very telling.

'I shaved a fraction here...' Leo told Lizzie, using his pen to point to what he had done. 'And then just tweaked the tip and lifted it a millimetre...' He turned to Marianna. 'It's going to just keep getting better,' he said. 'It's still a touch swollen.' He gave his patient a very nice smile. 'You've done the hard part now. The next surgery we can do here. It will just be local anaesthetic and light sedation. We're going to do a blepharoplasty,' Leo said, and then, seeing Lizzie blink, he translated. 'Take away some of the excess on Marianna's eyelids.' He turned back to the images on the screen and addressed Marianna. 'Taking just a sliver will open your eyes up and it will look amazing, especially for profile shots…'

Marianna nodded but she had questions. 'What about the scars?'

'We'll use laser to minimise, but there will be a small scar. It will be easily covered with make-up but if you don't want your staff to know…'

'I do my own make-up,' Marianna said with a nod, 'and I will continue to do so.'

'Well, it won't be a problem, then. The scarring is in the natural crease anyway…' He looked at Lizzie. 'Marianna has to think about constant close-ups.'

'I feel very vain,' Marianna admitted. 'My sister says that I am being ridiculous, but the pressure, honestly…'

'I completely understand.' Leo nodded. 'A little bit of work now will make a huge difference to your confidence.' He looked at Lizzie. 'Can you imagine the whole world watching your every move?'

'No,' Lizzie admitted. 'I'd be terrified.'

'There can be no relaxing when you are out,' Marianna sighed. 'You are always on show.'

'No getting caught with your pants down!' Leo said, and Marianna laughed as Lizzie blushed furiously, wondering if that little reference was in regard to what had taken place earlier. 'When would you like this done?' Leo asked his esteemed patient.

'How soon can you do it?' Marianna asked. 'I am going away at the weekend for a fortnight. I know we were looking at May, but this vacation has just come up and the place is very secluded. Ferdinand says there will be no cameras. I know it is very short notice for you.'

'That's not a problem.' Leo went to his diary and it

was decided the minor surgery would take place at six a.m. the following morning.

'You're to have nothing to eat or drink after midnight,' Leo said. 'That's just as a precaution, though—it will just be very light sedation.'

'So it will be done here?'

'Yes.' Leo nodded. 'Come in at five, while it's still dark. I'll keep you here for the day and then we'll have you back in the hotel by evening. Gwen, our manager, will liaise with the hotel…' He was completely at ease with her, Lizzie noticed—still in charge, despite who he was dealing with. 'Right,' Leo said. 'Before you go I just want to take a closer look at that eye of yours.'

Marinna smiled and leant back in the chair as Leo opened up a small pack. Lizzie was too embarrassed to ask if he needed anything, she didn't have a clue what he was doing! 'Marianna's fiancé bought her a puppy,' Leo said as he opened up a small packet and an eye dressing.

'How lovely,' Lizzie said, frantically trying to work out what was happening. Maybe he had to check her eyes before he operated or something?

'He's a basset hound,' Marianna said. 'He talks to me, I swear.'

'I had a parrot that did that,' Leo said, and it was such a silly joke that Marianna started to laugh and so did Lizzie.

'You didn't have a parrot?' Marianna checked as he put two fluorescein drops into her eyes—it was an indicator and any scratches to her eye would turn green.

'Of course not.'

The laughter mixed with the drops had brought tears to Marianna's eyes and Lizzie watched as the bright orange liquid ran down the side of her face. 'No, there's no scratch,' Leo said. 'Still, keep it covered for a few days, antibiotic drops and mild painkillers if you need them. A scratch to the cornea can be extremely painful. And watch that puppy's claws!'

Lizzie had stopped even trying to hide her frown now—hadn't he just said that she *didn't* have a scratch?

Leo put a large eye patch on and taped it over Marianna's eye. 'Okay, dark glasses back on.'

'Thank you.'

Lizzie saw a little of the stain running down Marianna's cheek and went to wipe it but Leo halted her, his hand lightly dusting hers, and Lizzie pulled her hand back just a little too quickly to even try to pretend his touch hadn't been noted. 'Just leave it…' Leo said.

Only then did Lizzie realise the lengths Marianna had to go to in order to keep this procedure a secret. The puppy, the small smear of fluorescein coming from beneath the eye patch and now the dark glasses. It wasn't her ignorance that had Lizzie's cheeks burning, though, but the brief contact from Leo.

'Thanks, Lizzie.' Marianna smiled as Leo walked her out to the foyer. 'Will I be seeing you in the morning?'

'Of course,' Leo answered for Lizzie.

Well, it looked like she'd better set her alarm early, Lizzie thought as she made her way to her office, but she was excited at the prospect of Marianna arriving under the cover of darkness and just thrilled to be a part of the big charade!

'I assume the future princess was just in?' A terribly handsome man dressed from head to toe in black leathers and carrying a crash helmet under his arm was walking towards her. 'I'm Declan Underwood.' He shook her hand.

'Oh, yes, Leo did tell me about you.' Leo had said that Declan was his second in command. 'I'm Lizzie Birch.'

'I know.' Declan smiled. 'Leo called earlier and told me that you'd started. I hear Flora kicking off was your welcome!'

Lizzie really didn't know what to say but settled for a noncommittal smile as Leo walked over to join them.

'I'm guessing that was Marianna,' Declan said to Leo. 'Lizzie wouldn't tell me.'

'You could be anyone,' Lizzie pointed out.

'Fair enough. But I knew it must be *someone* if Leo was actually rolling up his sleeves to see a patient. He pinches all the good stuff.' Declan smiled. 'Or rather he takes only the good stuff.'

It was good-natured teasing, Lizzie being quite sure that Declan would have more than his fair share of glamorous patients.

Declan headed off to get changed and returned a few moments later looking very suave in a suit. Leo watched as Lizzie, not knowing he was watching, rolled her eyes.

'What?' Leo frowned in fleeting concern. The last thing he needed was his head nurse not getting on with Declan.

'Nothing,' Lizzie said, then, knowing she'd been caught, admitted the truth. 'When you hand-pick your staff...' she shook her head in exasperation '...do they have to be good looking?'

'Do you find me good looking, Lizzie?' Leo teased.

'I think you know that you are.'

Leo just smiled. 'Well, if that is part of my selection criteria then know that you...' He halted. It was her first day and he was determined to heed Ethan's advice and get through it without flirting, but it was starting to prove an impossible ask. 'It's not all about looks, Lizzie,' he scolded.

'That a bit rich, coming from a cosmetic surgeon,' Lizzie retorted lightly.

'Tell me, Lizzie…' He was dying to know. 'What have you had done?'

His finger came and lifted her chin, just slightly, and no there was no teeny scar beneath. She could feel the heat from his fingers and told herself it was second nature for Leo to examine a face.

It just made the air trapped in her lungs burn.

'If I guess correctly, will you—?'

'I still won't tell you.'

Leo dropped the contact and Lizzie was glad that he did but she blushed when she saw the reason he had. A very boot-faced Ethan was walking past.

'Isn't it your home time?' Leo said to Lizzie.

'I was just going to—'

'Go,' he ordered. 'I want you here tomorrow at four. 'I'll have a driver pick you up.'

'A driver?'

'You're not walking alone at that time,' Leo said.

'You don't have to do that.'

'I'm not. It will all go on Prince Ferdinand's account. Oh, and if you come in and someone's crashed on my couch, you have my permission to kick them off.'

'Okay.'

'It's like Piccadilly Circus in here at night,' Leo said, but didn't elaborate. 'Welcome aboard, Lizzie.'

CHAPTER FIVE

WAKING TO HER alarm, Lizzie struggled to remember the last time she had enjoyed waking up way before dawn *and* looking forward to going to work quite as much as she now was.

Yes, it had only been a day, Lizzie thought as she dressed and tied back her hair and, yes, maybe she had got the job by pure default, but it was all so glamorous, and exciting. She was also incredibly impressed with the charitable side of the clinic as well as the care and concern that had been shown to Jessica—the work really was diverse.

As promised, her intercom buzzed at five minutes to four and Lizzie headed down to the car, sinking back into the leather for the impossibly short trip to the clinic.

She felt looked after.

Lizzie blinked at her own admission.

For the first time in an awfully long time she felt as if she was being looked after, rather than the other way round.

It was a guilty admission.

As she'd been growing up, Lizzie's parents had doted on her.

Her mum would even warm her school uniform

every morning in the winter. Lizzie had been wrapped in love by her parents.

Supported.

Stifled.

A bit, Lizzie conceded as she thanked the driver and stepped out of the warm car into the freezing morning. The pavement was icy and the air blew white as she let herself in.

Not stifled in any terrible way, Lizzie guiltily amended as she keyed in the security code to turn off the alarm. Her parents had been wonderful, supporting her in everything, but even her leaving home to do her nursing training had caused such a marked change to their many routines that it had been then, almost at that point, that Lizzie had been more a carer than cared for.

She had worried endlessly about them, telling herself not to as she'd prepared for a trip overseas with her boyfriend.

Her first.

It had never happened.

She had found out at the airport that her mother had had a serious fall and, to Peter's displeasure, she had backed out of their trip and returned to her family, racked with guilt for even thinking of leaving, and had stayed to take care of her mother.

When her mother had gotten to the stage that she'd barely recognised her, and both her parents had gone into a home, Lizzie had realised that it was now or never and had made the move to London, much to her father's distress.

Families, Lizzie thought as she turned on the lights and watched the glittering chandelier sparkle above her, were complicated—even the straightforward ones.

And as for the not so straightforward…

'Ethan!'

He was crashed out on the sofa in Leo's office and she was grateful to Leo for having had the foresight to tell her how to deal with this because otherwise she might have wondered whether it was best to leave Ethan and set up in another office.

'Ethan!' He stirred and, deciding there was only one kind way to wake him, Lizzie went off and made them both a coffee and then woke him as she always had when she had come to do his dressings—by turning on every light.

'Lizzie…'

'Like the old days, isn't it?' Lizzie smiled, handing him the coffee.

'I was working.'

'Hmm…' Lizzie wasn't convinced.

'This time I actually was.' Ethan almost smiled at her doubtful expression. 'I had a conference call at three with a doctor in the Solomon Islands. I thought Leo's office might be a better background than me at home…' He watched as Lizzie turned on Leo's desk lamp and checked all his investigation and prescription pads as Ethan took a grateful drink of his coffee. 'How are you finding it?' Ethan asked.

'Interesting,' Lizzie said. 'I actually really enjoyed yesterday and the flat is amazing.'

'Good.'

'I really am grateful to you for putting me forward for the job.'

'You don't need to be grateful, Lizzie,' Ethan said. 'You deserve a break and after all you did for me I should be the one who's grateful.'

'I did nothing!' Lizzie said. 'Except dress your legs.'

'And talk,' Ethan said, and Lizzie paused, remembering how he had been so shell-shocked, so deep into himself, that she'd just wittered on about her family, her parents, what she was making for dinner. Just every little inane thing as it had come to mind and slowly he had started to converse.

'You helped bring me back from hell.'

'You're still there, though,' Lizzie said, and she turned her back and started pulling back the drapes so that Ethan couldn't see the tears stinging her eyes. Yes, he had come a long way but there was still such a long way to go.

'How come you're in so early?' Ethan asked.

'Leo's got surgery early. Marianna is coming in soon…'

'Ah, the cloak-and-dagger stuff,' Ethan said. 'You might want to leave the curtains closed, then.'

Good point, Lizzie thought, turning around.

'I think he keeps a red carpet in the cupboard in the hall,' Ethan said, and Lizzie heard the slight trace of bitterness.

'She's lovely.'

'I'm sure she is.' Ethan shrugged. 'Lizzie…' Ethan was hesitant, he didn't really know how to play this, but he had seen Leo yesterday, seen his fingers on Lizzie's chin. As much as he had tried to deny it, Ethan had read the instant attraction, not just from Leo but Lizzie too. 'I didn't really tell you much about my brother…'

'He's been great,' Lizzie said, taking a drink of her own coffee. 'Of course, we didn't get off to the best start…'

'You soon get used to that sort of thing with Leo,'

Ethan said, and watched a dull blush spread on her cheeks as she resumed needlessly tidying Leo's desk. 'He's a rake, Lizzie. He goes through women like…' He glanced at the pad she held in her hands. 'That new prescription pad will outlive his next conquest.'

'That's none of my business,' Lizzie pointed out. 'I'm here to run the clinic, not manage his sex life.'

'I'm just letting you know. Leo is what he is…' How did you describe a sun that burnt? 'He's an amazing surgeon, not that he uses it much…'

'He explained all that.'

'Leo likes the fast lane, there's nothing more to him than that.'

Lizzie wasn't so sure. Brilliant surgeon or not, you didn't get to be where Leo was by chance and she was quite sure there was far more to Leo behind that very smooth exterior.

'Lizzie…' Ethan liked Lizzie and decided to get straight to the point. 'He's a bastard. Leo—'

'Ethan,' Lizzie broke in, 'I don't need a big brother looking out for me.'

'Neither do I,' Ethan said, and gave a wry smile. 'I've told him the same thing many times.' Yet she was right. He thought of Lizzie more like a brother would and he didn't want her to get hurt. Ethan knew the damage Leo so easily wreaked and he could not stand that for Lizzie so he pressed on when, with anyone else, he wouldn't have. 'I've never known Leo serious about anyone…' Ethan hesitated and then corrected his lie by omission. 'Actually, there was one…' Lizzie glanced up at the tentative note to his voice '…but they were never serious.' God, Ethan hated talking about personal things and he certainly wasn't going to tell Lizzie about Olivia. 'All you need to know is that Leo—'

'I get the message.'

'Good,' Ethan said. 'So long as you do.'

They both fell silent as they heard a car pull up and a few moments later Leo stepped in.

His hair was damp and he smelt as fresh as if he'd just that second stepped from the shower and sprayed cologne on himself.

'Bitching about me?' he said, for his entrance.

'It's so very easy to do,' Ethan responded.

'Don't believe a word,' Leo quipped to Lizzie, but he was unusually rattled, a smidge jealous at the sight of Ethan and Lizzie gossiping over coffee, and not for the first time he wondered about the nature of their relationship.

'I'll get you a coffee.' Lizzie headed off and Leo took off his heavy coat and hung it up.

'Here again?' he said to Ethan.

'I had a conference call,' Ethan said. 'So you've got Marianna coming in for *major* surgery this morning?'

'I do.' Leo refused to be drawn; he knew how little Ethan thought of his work and that his skills could be far better utilised. Leo certainly wasn't about to justify himself, especially not at this hour!

'Have a look at this,' Leo said, as Lizzie returned with coffee. 'Hot off the press.'

'Oh, my goodness!' Lizzie smiled. There was a picture of Marianna wearing her eye patch and a white arrow pointing to the streak of fluorescein running down her cheek. There was an extraordinarily long piece about corneal scratches and how she would have to keep her eye covered and wear dark glasses. The Sirmontane royal spokesperson neither confirmed nor denied the reports that Marianna had been scratched by the puppy Prince Ferdinand had bought her.

'There's even a photo of her puppy!'

She couldn't help but laugh but a less than impressed Ethan limped off. He could hear them laughing and chatting through the empty clinic, hear their easy conversation as Lizzie set up for the surgery, and he wondered if he'd been clear enough in his warning.

No, he wasn't overreacting and it wasn't far too soon, he'd seen the way Leo had first responded to her.

They'd known each other close to twenty-four hours now.

For Leo, that could be considered contained!

Gwen arrived early too and then, a short while later, Marianna arrived via the basement, with her security, and very soon the procedure would be under way.

Marianna really was delightful.

'Well done!' she said to Leo as he marked her eyes with his purple pen for the procedure. 'I read the article on the way here.'

'Good, isn't it?' Leo smiled. 'By the time most people are waking up to read it, you'll already be done. I'll let you know how many journalists we have calling to make an appointment with the ophthalmologist.'

'Do you have one here?' Lizzie asked, and Leo nodded.

'He comes in twice a week. It works out great for this type of thing. They'll all be ringing to make appointments, just trying to catch us out. They won't, though.'

Leo really did have everything worked out, Lizzie was fast realising.

He was very good with Marianna. She lay down and he chatted with her easily as he put in an IV. Incredibly stoic, she asked for only minimum sedation.

'You're sure?' Leo checked. 'You can sleep through it.'

'I'd really rather not.'

'That's fine,' Leo said. 'I'll give you lots of local and just enough sedation to make sure you're relaxed. You can always change your mind.'

'Thank you,' Marianna said, but Lizzie guessed she wouldn't be changing her mind. Marianna was a woman who clearly liked to be in control at all times.

Leo and Lizzie set up for the procedure, chatting to Marianna as they did so.

'How are you enjoying your work?' Marianna asked.

'Very much,' Lizzie said, keeping a careful eye on their patient as Leo administered the sedation.

'How are you feeling?' Leo checked.

'Good.'

'Okay. I'm just going to put in the local anaesthetic around your eyes.'

'The things we have to go through…' Marianna said, as Lizzie wiped a few tears away and they waited for the anaesthetic to take effect. 'I am hoping once the wedding is over the press will get tired of me.'

Leo's eyebrows rose above his mask and Marianna smiled. 'Yes, I know they will go crazy again when we have children but, like you, I have my secret weapons.'

'Do tell.' Leo grinned.

'Marco.'

Leo laughed and glanced over at Lizzie. 'That's Prince Ferdinand's younger brother. He's a bit of a wild card—I can see he could help take the spotlight off the two of you.'

'Ferdinand is much quieter.' Marianna yawned, the sedation making her feel a little drowsy. 'Marco is the one who makes the headlines.'

'I haven't heard much about him lately,' Leo mused, checking around Marianna's eyes to be sure they were numb before starting. 'What's he up to these days?'

Marianna didn't answer. Lizzie wondered if she'd dozed off but, no, she was still awake, telling Leo that she couldn't feel anything as he dabbed at the area with a needle.

'We'll start then,' Leo said. He had worked with celebrities and royalty long enough to know when a question was deliberately ignored—whatever Prince Marco was up to, Marianna did not want it discussed.

'Okay, keep your eyes closed, Marianna, unless I tell you otherwise.'

Lizzie had never seen such steady hands as Leo's. He was incredibly precise.

Leo too was enjoying working with Lizzie. The mood in the room was relaxed and he knew Marianna was being well taken care of as he focused on her eyes, removing the smallest sliver of her upper lids. Even as he tied off one long suture, Lizzie could see the difference.

'Less is more,' Leo explained to Lizzie as he worked. 'In this case we're not trying to change anything, just enhance.'

'Will there be any more procedures?' Lizzie asked now that Marianna was dozing quietly as Leo worked.

Leo shook his head. 'I've already zapped a few capillaries and I'm sure Marianna won't mind me telling you she had some work done with the most impressive ceramist. I might have to pay him a visit.'

Lizzie smiled behind her mask, Leo needed no work done on his teeth, which were white and very even, but not so falsely perfect that she really couldn't be sure if he'd had work done.

'Have you ever thought of having anything done, Lizzie?' Marianna asked groggily.

'I have.' Lizzie refused to look at Leo.

'Have you had anything done yourself?'

It was Lizzie who chose not to answer this time.

'That's what I'm trying to work out,' Leo answered for her.

It was all good-natured teasing, just the sort of idle chatter that took place during a straightforward procedure, and in less than an hour Marianna was sitting up, a little woozy but looking into the mirror as Leo outlined what he had done.

'You will get a little bruising and swelling but not too much, I think.'

'Will I be able to cover it with make-up?'

'No make-up yet,' Leo warned. 'It's going to look worse before it looks better. We'll keep you here for today…' He wrote his operation notes and gave Lizzie his instructions. 'Lots of iced eye masks and if Marianna can rest in a recliner, that would be great. I'd like her head up.'

'Sure.'

Lizzie watched as he wrote on a small card. She assumed it was the instructions but he clipped it to the operation notes.

'Okay, call someone to help you take Marianna to the recovery area.'

It was nothing like anywhere Lizzie had worked.

She didn't even have to push the wheelchair.

Charlotte was waiting in the sumptuous recovery room, which was more like a day spa than anything Lizzie was used to. She welcomed Marianna and they helped her into a chair and checked her obs and then, as Marianna slept, Charlotte showed Lizzie a few things—such as letting the chef know that they had a patient back from Theatre after twilight sedation.

'Iced water.' Charlotte read Marianna's choices to the chef and Lizzie hid her amazement—you even ordered water here! 'Could you send some chamomile tea in half an hour and I'll let you know when she's ready for breakfast. Poached eggs and salmon and brown bread, no crusts, no butter.'

'I want to get my eyes done just so I can lie in that chair and have poached eggs and salmon brought up to me.' Lizzie smiled. 'But I'll have butter, please.'

'You can,' Charlotte answered. 'Leo lets us have one procedure a year on the house…it doesn't have to be you, you can use it for a family member.'

Lizzie wondered if she should get a T-shirt with *I LOVE MY JOB!'* printed on the front.

'Usually a patient who has had a blepharoplasty would just stay till around lunchtime but Leo wants Marianna here all day and you'll take her back to the hotel this evening.'

'Okay.'

There was a knock at the door and Gwen came in, smiling. 'Have you got something for me?'

'I do.'

Charlotte removed the little card from the patient notes and handed it to Gwen, who headed off. 'It's just a note to attach to flowers,' Charlotte explained. 'Gwen will have them sent to the hotel.'

'Do all patients come home to flowers and handwritten notes from the surgeon?'

'Leo's Ladies do,' Charlotte said with a smile. 'I'll leave you, then.'

Lizzie was completely unused to doing nothing at work but, for this esteemed patient, the head nurse was with her at all times and Lizzie found herself checking cupboards for something to do.

'You *can* sit and read,' Leo said, when he came in later in the afternoon to check in on Marianna. 'You don't have to pretend to be busy. You may as well enjoy the quiet times, it's not always like this.'

'Thanks.'

He went over and checked on Marianna.

'I think I can go back to the hotel now,' Marianna said, and Leo agreed. Really, she could have gone home a while ago but naturally Leo had wanted to make sure everything was fine.

'Lizzie will see you back to your hotel. If you have any concerns at all, don't hesitate to call me. Otherwise I'll see you tomorrow.'

He gave his instructions to Lizzie before they headed off.

'Don't worry about coming back,' Leo said. 'Thank you for coming in so early. It all went very well. I'll give you a call a bit later.'

'A call?'

'To make sure the transfer to the hotel went okay.'

Why else would he be calling her? Lizzie thought, trying to tame a sudden blush.

The hotel ensured everything went seamlessly too

and, completely unseen by any prying eyes, Lizzie transferred her patient from Harley Street to a gorgeous suite at the hotel, where flowers were waiting from Ferdinand and, of course, from Leo too.

'How sweet!' Marianna said as she read the card and whatever Leo had written made her laugh. 'He says my puppy *really* needs his nails trimmed. Leo is gorgeous, isn't he?'

Lizzie didn't really know how to answer. 'He's a great boss,' she said. 'Well, so far...' And then her voice trailed off. Really, their start had been terrible, she'd been thinking of walking out on the job there and then, but in less than two days somehow all had been forgiven.

Not forgotten, though.

As she slipped eye masks into the fridge for Marianna to use overnight Lizzie recalled Ethan's words this morning—he'd been warning her, Lizzie knew.

He didn't have to.

Of course Leo was gorgeous and of course she fancied him, but there was no way Lizzie was going to add herself to the list of *Leo's Ladies*. And anyway, she told herself, as if someone as stunning and delicious and as in demand as Leo Hunter might be remotely interested in her.

He was, though.

Lizzie swallowed and then corrected herself.

Leo Hunter would have been flirting from the cradle—those blue eyes, that slow smile certainly weren't exclusive to her.

Two days in and Lizzie was in love...

With her job!

And she had every intention of keeping it.

She applied some ointment to Marianna's eyes and made sure she was settled before saying goodbye then heading out to the street and into a taxi and home.

Lizzie was just sinking into the bath with the last of the champagne chocolate truffles and wondering if it was true that she could have a procedure done, and what she might choose if it was, when her phone rang.

Of course she had to race through to the lounge and stood naked and dripping wet as the very unruffled voice of Leo came on the line.

'Did I disturb you?'

'Of course not,' Lizzie lied.

'How was Marianna?'

'Fine. Everything went well,' Lizzie said, trying to tell herself she was freezing, that it wasn't his voice that had her shivering and made her toes curl.

'Good.'

There wasn't much to say really. It had been a very simple procedure and just as she thought she was done thinking about Leo Hunter for the day, he made sure that he would spend the rest of the night and days to come perpetually lodged in her thoughts.

'Did Gwen discuss the ball with you?'

'The ball?'

'There's a charity ball for Princess Catherine's next weekend. You'll be attending as my guest.'

'Me?'

'Yes.'

Lizzie just stood there as Leo calmly explained that as head nurse it was right that she accompany him.

It was pretty ironic that she was naked and soaked as he invited her to such a prestigious event—a fish out of water was exactly how she'd be, and she knew it.

'I don't think you…' How could she explain that she'd never been to a ball in her life, let alone on the arm of someone as glamorous as he? How could she properly explain to someone as sophisticated and worldly as Leo that she would stand out like a sore thumb? 'I think I'm away that weekend…' Lizzie frantically attempted.

'I'm not asking you if you'd like to go, Lizzie,' Leo said, and she realised that she might have witnessed his might but only now was she glimpsing his power. No one said no to Leo, unless they had an exceptionally good reason. 'There's an important work function coming up—I'm hoping you'll be able to attend.'

'Of course,' Lizzie responded.

'Good.'

He rang off then and instead of running back to her bath Lizzie headed to her wardrobe and then the computer and logged into her bank account.

She might be working in the most luxurious surroundings but her pay didn't go in till next Thursday and… Lizzie winced as she saw the damage Christmas had wreaked on her credit card, and her mother's hairdresser was booked for this weekend and she charged like a wounded bull.

Leo might call it a mere work function but it was the renowned Princess Catherine's Charity Ball he was referring to. It wasn't just that she had no idea what to wear that had her head spinning, it was also that she would be attending *with* Leo.

No, Lizzie didn't sleep well.

CHAPTER SIX

'I THINK THAT Lizzie seems an excellent choice.' Declan didn't hold back on his praise. They were having a medical staff meeting and Leo was trying to wrap it up, yet the conversation kept turning to the new head nurse.

'I agree.' Rafael nodded. 'I had a few problems with my schedule on Monday and it was all swiftly dealt with without anyone being upset.'

'Okay, can we move things along? We're not just here for the Lizzie Birch Admiration Society,' Leo said, irritated and not sure why.

They discussed a few internal matters. With so many eminent surgeons working there, often they would talk about a particularly difficult case but this morning they were discussing the charity side of things. 'How are things going?' he asked Ethan.

'Slowly,' Ethan admitted. He loathed meetings and sat turning his pen over and over. 'But then again, most people I need to speak to are still away for the Christmas break. Things should start to kick into gear next week but I'm having trouble deciding the next patient. I've narrowed it down to two possibilities and I'm waiting for some test results to come back for the insurance companies.' They spoke for a little while longer but as the meeting wound up, despite Leo's best efforts Ethan got back to the one topic Leo would rather not discuss. He looked at Leo, his eyes black with anger, and Leo guessed what was coming before Ethan even said it. 'I hear that you're taking Lizzie to the ball.'

'Of course.' Leo didn't bat an eyelid. 'It's an important function, and I think that she should be there to represent the clinic.' Rather abruptly Leo stood. 'I've got a patient to see.'

He did have a patient to see but he was also questioning his decision last night. It had seemed an obvious choice at the time but as he saw Lizzie chatting to Charlotte in a treatment room as he walked past, saw her throw her head back and laugh at something that was being said, Leo knew the decision hadn't just been about representing the Hunter Clinic well. But did he really need the complication of an aggrieved head nurse?

Yes, Leo had enough insight to know that she'd soon be aggrieved. The only thing he took seriously was work, not that Ethan could get that. Ethan seemed to think it all just magically happened, no one really understood the effort that he put in.

'Darling Leo!'

His favourite patient stood when she saw him. Tiny, petite, she was trailing scarves and expensive scent as they walked to his office and past Lizzie, who, with a brief nod at them, was heading into hers.

'Francesca…' Leo helped her off with her luxurious coat. She had once been his father's patient and more recently Leo had done a lot of work on her. Last year Francesca had had a full facelift and they both were thrilled with the result. She often popped in for a smudge of cosmetic filler or to have her lips plumped up a fraction. Francesca only ever saw Leo, even for the tiniest procedures. 'It's lovely to see you,' Leo said.

'And you, darling. It's terribly cold.' She shivered without her coat and Leo suppressed a smile. The routine never changed.

'I can have the heating turned up.'

'No, no…' Francesca waved her hands. 'I don't want to cause trouble. I am always cold, you know that.'

'Perhaps a small brandy might warm you?' Leo suggested.

'Just a small one maybe,' Francesca said, and Leo duly headed to the decanter.

'It really is freezing out there,' he added, as he handed Francesca a drink.

'How are you, Leo?' Francesca asked once she'd taken a sip. 'How's the love life?'

'You know I don't have a love life, Francesca.' Leo grinned. 'The social life's amazing, though.'

Francesca laughed and then got to the real reason she was there. 'I have a wedding to go to in the summer,' Francesca started, and Leo sighed inwardly as he realised that she wasn't just there for a little top-up. Francesca knew enough about procedures to know she would need a few months for the swelling and bruising to go down fully and the effect to show properly, except Leo didn't want to do any more surgery on her. Francesca looked amazing as she was.

'Just here…' Francesca ran her fingers along non-existent jowls. 'And I think if I had more volume in my cheeks—'

'Francesca,' Leo interrupted, 'you never had much volume in your cheeks even when you were younger.' Leo came over and examined Francesca's face carefully.

Objectively.

He tried to ignore the fact that he had done her previous surgery and to look at Francesca as if she were a new patient who was coming to see him for the first time. He asked himself what he would advise if that were the case.

Nothing.

Leo had taken care of everything in last year's surgery. He was incredibly proud of his work. Francesca, from a distance, could pass as a woman in her late forties or early fifties, thanks to the amazing care she took of herself. Even examining Francesca close up, even scrutinising her features carefully, the work she'd had done, combined with her already breath-taking features, meant that she looked two decades younger then she was.

'Francesca.' Leo went and sat back behind his desk—he knew this was going to be difficult, knew just how volatile Francesca could be. 'You don't need any work.'

'I want it, though.'

'You don't need surgery.' Leo would not budge. Ethan might consider most of Leo's work unnecessary but what his brother did not understand was that Leo would never put a patient through an unnecessary procedure. Yes, he catered for vanity but not insanity and in this case absolutely nothing needed to be done. 'We can maybe do a small touch-up with fillers before the wedding and naturally I will see you a month before so that your cosmetic filler is at its optimum, but—'

'Leo!' Francesca interrupted impatiently. 'I want this surgery. This wedding is very important to me. Tony is going to be there. I haven't seen him in years. I want to take his breath away.'

'You'll more than take his breath away if you look like Cat Woman.' Leo could be very direct when needed, though he did try to soften it with a touch of humour. 'He'll choke on his hors d'oeuvre.'

'Leo, you are not listening to me.'

'You are the one who is not listening to me, Francesca. Do you remember when I took over your care from my father? You made me promise that no one would ever be able to guess that you'd had some work done. I've kept that promise. You look stunning. Even knowing the work you have had done, I still can't really see it and I'm the surgeon. What you're asking me to do will have everybody knowing that you've been under the knife and that you've got a face pumped up with fillers, and I'm just not prepared to put my name to it.'

'Leo, please!'

'Francesca, we can arrange for some skin treatments in the lead-up to the wedding and as I said I will make sure that your—'

'I want to have the surgery.'

'And I'm not prepared to operate,' Leo said. 'There are risks with any surgery, Francesca, and at seventy-two years of age...' Don't mention the war, Leo thought as he watched her furious eyes widen, but Leo simply would not be swayed and he continued on with the truth. 'It would be foolish at best to operate for absolutely no reason.'

'So you are saying that I'm too old for surgery?'

'For completely unnecessary surgery, yes,' Leo said. 'Francesca, why don't we—?'

But Francesca wasn't listening. First making sure to drain the last of her brandy, angrily she stood. 'You can't say no to me.'

'I can,' Leo answered. 'I just have. But I will—' He didn't get to finish. Francesca didn't want to hear about fillers or skin treatments, she wanted surgery and she wanted it booked now! She stormed out in rage, hurling out her anger as she left.

'I have been good to you, Leo! This is how you repay my loyalty, this is how you treat me...'

Lizzie heard the fracas and chose not to ignore it. 'Is everything okay?' Lizzie checked, popping her head in.

Leo rolled his eyes.

'No jewellery to pick up?' Lizzie checked.

'Not this time.' Leo gave a tight smile.

'Not another lovers' tiff, I hope!'

'God, no.' Leo actually laughed. 'I do have some morals. Not many...' Then his face went serious. 'I refused to do the surgery she wanted.'

'Oh.'

'I did a full facelift on her last year. Francesca is seventy-two!'

'Oh, my...' Lizzie blinked. She could not believe that the woman she had seen was in her seventies. 'I knew you were a good surgeon but...' She shook her head. 'She looks amazing.'

'I'd love to take all the credit but, the fact is Francesca has the most amazing bone structure I've ever seen and still exercises daily and keeps herself in shape. She was a prima ballerina,' Leo explained. 'When I took over her care we both agreed to keep it minimal. Part of the reason she looks so good is that she *doesn't* look as if she has had surgery—her face moves, she's got lines...' He let out a sigh. 'Not for long, though.'

'Meaning.'

'The trouble with saying no to someone like Francesca is that she'll find someone who is only too happy to say yes. The double trouble is…' he shrugged '…she's my favourite patient and I can't stand to think of anyone else treating her. I know I'm the best and I want the best for her. I really do think a lot of her.'

'Really?' Lizzie smiled.

'She's so eccentric.' He rolled his eyes. 'She tells me all about Tony, the love of her life. How he wanted her to give up dancing yet she refused to. He wanted lots of bambinos and she wanted the stage so she ended it. There have been numerous young lovers and husbands since then but Tony is the love of her life. It turns out Tony is going to be at a wedding and she wants to look like she did the day she left him.'

He headed over to a huge bookshelf and pulled down a ballet programme. 'Signed.' Leo smiled. 'I asked her to bring in old photos to work from…' He laughed at the memory. 'I'd still be looking through them now if I hadn't narrowed it down to this. She's as neurotic and vain as most dancers are, and twice as temperamental. God, I hope she doesn't go anywhere else.'

He really did care about her, Lizzie thought, looking through the programme. Francesca was seriously beautiful now and in her day had been breath-taking. 'A major part of her appeal is her gamine features,' Leo explained, still flicking through the photos. 'Look at that symmetry.'

'Look at those eyes…' Lizzie said.

'They weren't looking so doleful a few moments ago,' Leo said. 'She's furious with me.'

'But surely Francesca knows that you've got her best interests covered?' Lizzie said, but Leo shook his head.

'She determined that this is what she needs and,

believe me, when Francesca sets her mind on something...' He replaced the programme then chewed around the base of his thumbnail, pondering what to do.

'Will you give Francesca a follow-up call?' Leo asked. 'See if she will come in and speak with me again—she'll just hang up on me if I try to call.'

'Sure.'

'Women,' Leo said.

'Men,' Lizzie sighed.

'We're not all bad.'

'*You* are!'

'I'm afraid so.'

It was a warning and Lizzie heeded it but they stared at each other for a very long moment, a moment when Lizzie felt he might just lower that head and kiss her.

She was imagining things surely.

Except she was having to hold onto her tongue just to stop herself licking her lips in delicious anticipation.

How did he do it? How, with just a look, could she almost taste his mouth?

The door knocked and Ethan came in. Lizzie could feel the crackling tension between the brothers and she didn't really understand Ethan's slightly disapproving look that he shot in her direction.

'I wanted to talk to you, Leo, about the patients I've got in mind. We can only take one and it's proving impossible to choose...' He had two files with him and on the front were images of two terribly disfigured children. 'Burns,' Ethan explained to Lizzie. 'There aren't any too many fireguards where they come from. Both need surgery, it's just hell trying to decide...'

'That one.' Lizzie blinked as Leo's finger jabbed at an image.

'Why that one?' Ethan asked.

'Why not?' Leo shrugged.

'You're an arrogant jerk…'

There had always been tension between them, Lizzie was in no doubt as to that, but it was the first time she'd actually witnessed such a terse exchange. Maybe it was because Leo assumed Ethan and she had actually spoken about him, but in truth, till the morning of Marianna's surgery, Ethan never really had.

'No,' Leo said evenly. 'I'm practical. You can't save the world, Ethan.' He glanced at Lizzie. 'Go and get your coat.'

'My coat?'

'I've got a couple of house calls to make.'

As Lizzie went to get her coat, Leo pulled his on as Ethan stood there.

'Since when have you taken the head nurse on house calls?'

'I'm seeing Marianna,' Leo hissed. 'Continuity of care.'

'And you're taking Lizzie to the ball.'

'I'm trying to be more serious about our charity work,' Leo said. 'I thought it might be more professional to take staff…' He turned. 'Does it bother you?'

'You know it does. I warned you to leave well alone.'

Leo needed to know more. There was a part of their past they both avoided discussing, but if Ethan had dated Lizzie, well, she was off limits.

'Are you worried history might repeat itself?' Leo said carefully, loathed, even now, to mention Olivia's name.

Leo had fallen hard for the paediatric plastics nurse but she'd only ever seen him as a friend.

It had been Ethan that Olivia had fallen for.

Leo closed his eyes for a brief moment, recalling the terrible row that had erupted and Olivia's horror when she had walked in on it in time to hear Ethan telling Leo that he was only using her anyway.

Leo and Ethan's already fractured relationship had from that point seemed broken beyond repair.

Maybe it was, Leo thought as he opened his eyes to his brother.

'There's nothing between Lizzie and I,' Ethan said. 'But she's probably the best thing that could happen to this place and I don't want my elder brother screwing it up.'

'I don't screw,' Leo said. 'I make love…'

'It's all a joke to you,' Ethan said. 'I'm warning you, Leo.'

'I don't take warnings from my little brother.'

'Take this one!'

'We really are very protective of Lizzie,' Leo sneered.

'Of course I am—she was the one who got me talking, she was the one—'

'Ethan.' Leo was serious now. 'What the hell happened to you out there?' But Ethan didn't answer. 'You've changed…'

'War tends to do that to you.'

It was all Leo was going to get because Ethan moved back to the original conversation. 'Why *are* you taking Lizzie to the ball? Why can't you just leave her alone?'

This time it was Leo who was evasive.

Without answering, he walked out into the foyer where Lizzie was waiting and they stepped out into the grey wintery morning. Lizzie shivered and stamped her feet as they waited for a taxi. Leo knew full well the answer and it was a very inconvenient one.

He wanted Lizzie in bed.

CHAPTER SEVEN

THEY TOOK A taxi and he felt her eyes on him and Leo knew she thought he had been unkind to Ethan about choosing the charity patient. 'If you thought about it you'd never be able to choose and my brother proves my point.' He looked at her tight lips. 'I don't have to beat myself up to do charity work.'

'Okay.' Lizzie turned and gazed out of the window but Leo prolonged the conversation. 'Was he as cheerful when you were looking after him?' he asked, and sighed when Lizzie didn't answer. 'I'm not asking you to break confidence, I'm just making idle conversation…'

'Terrible weather,' Lizzie said. '*That's* idle conversation.'

Leo was wise enough to know that Lizzie wasn't going to reveal anything and so they drove in silence to the hotel. Leo spoke to a receptionist and Lizzie noticed he didn't use his title and neither did he give the patient's name.

It was just all very smooth and discreet.

They walked to the lift and Leo explained that it wasn't just Marianna they would be visiting but Jessica too.

'Hello.' Leo smiled at Jessica as she let them in. 'As

Gwen explained, Iain's in Theatre all day but I wanted to see for myself how you are doing.'

'I'm feeling much better.' Jessica smiled and she really did seem a whole lot better than she had on Monday. 'And thank you, Lizzie, for the other day, I'm sorry—I was in a right state.'

'You did really well,' Lizzie said, because Jessica had—it had taken ages to remove the tiny sutures and even though Iain had soaked them, it had still been uncomfortable and unpleasant, on top of everything else Jessica was already going through.

Leo washed his hands and Jessica lifted her hair as Leo examined the wound carefully.

'Iain has done an amazing job,' Leo said. 'How are you?'

This time she didn't look at Lizzie to leave, and it was good to see Jessica looking far more relaxed.

'Better. My mum's staying with me and I've spoken to a lawyer…' Then she did glance at Lizzie.

'Lizzie's fine,' Leo said.

'It wasn't the first time,' Jessica admitted.

'It rarely is,' Leo said.

'That time I said that I fell down the stairs…' Jessica said, and Leo nodded. 'Did you know?'

'I asked you outright.'

'I know.' Jessica screwed up her face. 'I just wasn't ready to tell anyone. I am now, though.'

'Good for you. You know that if there's anything we can do…'

'Thank you.'

'I mean it,' Leo said. 'And not just with paperwork for lawyers—we've got a marvellous psychologist at the clinic, Tanya is…'

'I spoke to her.'

'Good,' Leo said. 'Keep speaking to her.'

He was extremely nice to Jessica and they chatted some more but Leo declined when she offered to ring down for coffee.

'I'm afraid we have to go.' He glanced at his watch but still didn't dash off.

'Of course you do.' Jessica smiled. 'It's just so nice to have company. I'm getting cabin fever.'

'Have you been out?'

Jessica shook her head.

'You should go for a little walk.'

'I'm worried I'll be seen or photographed. It's all over the papers, it's just all so embarrassing…'

'Not for you it isn't.' Leo stood. 'You have absolutely nothing to be embarrassed about.' He did stand then. 'Put a big scarf on and go for a walk with your head held high.'

He wasn't smiling when they took the lift.

'Bastard,' Leo grumbled. 'I re-set his nose once. I'd love to break it again.' Instead of going down, they were going up.

'Are we going to see Marianna?'

'Why else would we be going up to the top floor?' Leo winked. 'Unless…' He didn't finish. He saw her blush and, unbelievably, Leo almost did the same.

Though, of course, it must be the heating!

'Come on, now for the nicer part of the job,' Leo said.

He really loved his work, and there was so much more to it than Lizzie had realised.

'I can't believe how good it already looks!' Marianna exclaimed. 'I thought I would have two black eyes…'

'I'm just brilliant.' Leo smiled and carefully checked them. 'I'm really pleased.' Marianna was flying out to join Ferdinand the next day and they chatted for a little while longer before Lizzie and Leo headed back to the clinic, but as they walked through the hotel foyer and reached the doors, Leo suddenly changed his mind.

'How about afternoon tea?'

'We'll never get a table,' Lizzie said, because she'd rung up at the weekend and found out that if you weren't a guest you had to book weeks in advance.

Not if your name was Leo Hunter, apparently.

'They should pay me commission.' Leo grinned as they took a seat. 'I've sent more clients their way than I can count.'

Lizzie wasn't used to being spoiled.

Afternoon tea was sumptuous and Leo was very good company. 'Do you do this a lot?' Lizzie asked.

'Not too often,' Leo said. 'It's nice to pause sometimes.'

She felt dreadfully gauche. It was a pause in Leo's day and yet Lizzie felt tempted to whip out her phone and take a photo as afternoon tea was delivered to their table and the china cups filled. 'My mum would have loved this.' She glanced up. 'Sorry, that sounds really maudlin. My mum loved anything to do with food—she was a wonderful cook.'

'Was?'

'She has Alzheimer's.'

'How bad is she?'

'She had good days and bad,' Lizzie said. 'Mainly she has no idea who I am but every now and then her face lights up and we talk, though it's mainly a teenage Lizzie she's talking about. It's good to know that she does recognise me sometimes.'

'What about your father?'

He's in the same home as Mum. He's relatively well, though...' She didn't really want to discuss it. Yes, she'd chatted away to Ethan about how her father, despite her best efforts, refused to even come out for a coffee with her. How he didn't even want to go out to the shops. But she just didn't want to bore Leo. 'This is lovely.' She looked at the gorgeous surroundings. 'It's a big change from my old job.'

'You're from Brighton?' Leo checked, recalling her résumé.

'I came to London a couple of years ago, once my...' She stopped. All her conversations seemed to lead back to her parents. 'Mind you, I'm seeing a different side to things since I started the job. I've never been to a formal ball.'

'It will be fun,' Leo said, taking out a sweetener and flicking it into his tea.

Lizzie let out her breath and asked the question that had been plaguing her, though of course she knew the answer. She was just fishing for a hint about what Leo would expect her to wear. 'What's the dress code for the ball?'

'Evening wear, formal.' Leo was spreading jam on a scone when he glanced up. 'You'll be fine.'

It was all so easy for him.

'I'm just a bit worried—'

'You'll look stunning,' Leo interrupted, doing his best to put her at ease and failing miserably.

For Lizzie things came to a head just before home time when she heard Kara, one of the plastic surgeons, talking about the ball. She kindly tried to bring Lizzie into the conversation. 'Do you know what you're wearing yet, Lizzie? I hear Leo's taking you.'

'That's right.' Lizzie nodded. 'I haven't decided yet.'

God, she had to say something to him. She wouldn't just be letting herself down. Leo expected glamour on his arm and later in that afternoon Lizzie finally caved, knocking on his door.

'Who is it?'

'Lizzie.'

'Come in.' He turned briefly from the basin as she entered. 'I'm surprised you bothered knocking.'

'What are you doing?' Lizzie asked, and if she sounded brusque it was to cover up her embarrassment at the sight of Leo. He was naked from the hips up, his suit pants sat low on his hips and there was a fresh shirt over the chair. He had, she presumed, just finished shaving and was now trying to take out his own stitches. 'You can't take your own stitches out.'

'It's harder than I thought,' Leo admitted.

They were tiny sutures, and Leo was having more trouble than he'd expected, getting the tiny blade to snip the thread, but, given where he was going, it was essential he looked his best.

'I'll do it.' Lizzie sighed.

'Sorry to trouble you!' Leo quipped, and well he might. After all, he was paying her extremely well, but only as he sat down and put his head back did he realise her discomfort, only then was he suddenly aware of his own naked skin, because Lizzie was leaning over him, and trying not to touch him as she soaked the wound to soften it so that the stitches wouldn't stick or catch on their way out.

Breast implants? Leo wondered as one hovered above his view, and he desperately tried to quash that thought, not just because it was inappropriate but rather more the effect it was starting to have on him. 'Just take them out.'

'I'm going to.'

No, there were no implants, Leo knew his silicone from his saline and these were just soft and ripe, and his jaw clamped down as he focused on the blade in an effort to keep things down!

Lizzie's hands were shaking slightly. She could smell his cologne and his bare arm seemed to burn her skirted thigh as she leant over and tried to slip the blade beneath the suture.

'Stay still,' she warned.

'I am staying still,' Leo snapped, because ninety nine per cent of him was, it was just the flood to his groin that was the problem. He lay there refuting the body surface area charts he'd studied in his medical training, because that part of his anatomy certainly accounted for more than one per cent right now.

He did his twelve-times table backwards and breathed in the scent of antiseptic rather than focusing on the fresh smell of her, and when that didn't work he reminded himself that Lizzie could be sleeping with Ethan.

Olivia.

With just one word he averted disaster.

'Done.'

'Thank you.'

'You need a little adhesive strip here,' Lizzie said. 'It's a teeny bit open in the middle.'

'It's fine.'

'Whatever.' Lizzie shrugged.

No!

Both said it in their heads as their eyes met.

This is so not going to happen.

'You should keep it dry...'

'I know the drill.'

'Of course.'

'Lizzie?'

'What?'

He didn't know how to ask her, yet he had to know if there was more between her and Ethan, but the time wasn't right now—there was somewhere else he needed to be. 'I'd better get on.' He stood and pulled on his shirt as she cleared the dressing pack away and put the blade in the sharps box.

'Are you going somewhere nice?' Lizzie asked, as he opened a bag and pulled out three new ties, with the extortionate price tags still on.

'Somewhere *very* nice,' Leo said. 'And I'm actually nervous.'

'Oh?'

'Which tie? I asked them to send a selection.'

'Grey...' Lizzie said, then changed her mind. 'I like the silver one.'

'Nope.' Leo shook his head. 'Too much.'

'You really are nervous!' She grinned. 'So where are you going?'

'I actually can't tell you,' he admitted. 'I've another house call to make.'

'You're going to see a patient?' Lizzie frowned because he truly did seem tense.

'Yep.'

He was knotting his tie and kept having to redo it.

'So why can't you tell me?'

'Completely confidential,' Leo said.

'Isn't everyone?'

'Of course.'

He wasn't saying any more and Lizzie loathed herself for being so curious, but who on earth could it be? After all they'd had Marianna, you didn't get any more prestigious than a soon-to-be European princess…maybe another royal?

'What time do you have to be there?'

'Six,' Leo said. 'On the dot. How's that?' He stood there, looking absolutely stunning, his hair brushed back, his suit to die for and, yes, his tie was perfect.

'Can't beat a good old Windsor knot,' she said, and gave him an almost imperceptible wink. 'Though maybe you should have gone for royal blue.'

Still he refused to be drawn but she did see his tongue roll in his cheek as he suppressed a smile. 'See you, Lizzie.'

'Good luck,' she called out to him as he headed off, and, rather than nervous now, Leo was actually smiling.

Lizzie was far too perceptive!

CHAPTER EIGHT

INSTEAD OF WORKING out what she would be wearing for the ball or getting a pedicure and her nails done, Lizzie's weekend was spent in Brighton.

'I'm going to a ball next weekend,' Lizzie told her mum, chatting away as she sorted out her mother's clothes for the week.

'Do you hear that, Faye?' her father, Thomas, asked. 'Lizzie's going to a ball in London.'

But Faye wasn't interested in anything other than the thought that someone had taken her watch.

'It's being fixed, Mum,' Lizzie attempted *again,* but Faye wouldn't accept that. Today everyone was a thief, including Lizzie—who she thought was a stranger rifling through her wardrobe in broad daylight.

'It's Lizzie,' Thomas said when Faye angrily confronted her.

'Mum, I'm just trying to sort out your clothes,' Lizzie explained patiently.

'I'm not your mother,' Faye shouted, and then walked off and Thomas followed her. It was normal that she didn't recognise her, Lizzie more than knew that, and the anger and aggression was part of her illness too, but it *hurt* to see her mother so angry and fearful, and to not even be recognised was an agony that couldn't always be rationalised away.

'She's having a cup of tea with the nurses.' Thomas came back and gave Lizzie a smile. 'So, you're going out next week to a ball?'

'It's a work function,' Lizzie said, 'but it sounds very glamorous.'

'Are you going with anyone?'

'My boss.'

'And does your boss have a name?'

'Leo,' Lizzie said. 'Leo Hunter.' She saw her dad's eyebrow rise and Lizzie frowned but then realised that, of course, her dad would have heard of Leo. Even before Faye had taken ill they had lived their lives through magazines and newspapers.

'Watch yourself, Lizzie.'

'Leo's lovely.'

'Hmmph,' her dad said. 'He comes from bad stock. I remember reading about his mother. Above all the rules everyone else lived by, out partying…'

'It's a work do.'

'Even so,' her dad huffed. 'I don't want you getting hurt again. I remember Peter…'

Lizzie bit her tongue. Peter had been her boyfriend nearly ten years ago and, yes, the break-up had hurt but life hurt sometimes whether or not you lived it.

Her father just chose to live his life reading about everyone else.

'Why don't you come over to see the Hewitts when Mum's resting this afternoon?' Lizzie asked. 'Just for a coffee.' The Hewitts were old family friends who ran the bed and breakfast Lizzie stayed at when visiting, but her dad shook his head. 'What about a walk on the beach, then?' Lizzie attempted. 'It would be nice to get some fresh air.'

'I like to stay close to your mum.'

'I know but…'

Lizzie gave in. Even a small walk was a major event for her father. It was a long weekend and a depressing one. She loved her parents dearly and the Hewitts were lovely people too, but they were almost as locked in the past as her parents and Lizzie was guilty with relief at how nice it felt to be back in London. As she headed to 200 Harley Street on Monday morning she was certainly looking forward to work, and, even though she was trying hard to deny it, she was also looking forward to seeing Leo.

'How was your weekend?' Leo asked her as she took off her scarf and coat.

'It was fine,' she answered. 'How was yours?'

'I need another one to recover from it.' He yawned.

'Any house calls today?' Lizzie asked.

'Nope.'

'You never did tell me how things went the other evening on your *house* call,' she fished.

'I deliberately didn't.'

'Please…' Lizzie whimpered. 'I have to know where you went.'

'I'll tell you if you tell me who did your surgery.'

She poked out her tongue and then stopped because banter was just too easy with Leo and it was starting to look a lot like flirting.

Leo had actually had an unusually quiet weekend. Yes, there had been drinks after work on Friday and he'd been out to a very glamorous dinner on Saturday but, unusually for Leo, he'd returned to his apartment alone and on Sunday he'd found himself racking his brains for a reason, or rather an excuse, to ring Lizzie.

It would be a terrible idea, Leo knew that. Especially as he didn't yet know the full extent of her friendship with Ethan. Yes, his brother had said it had all been professional but Ethan seemed terribly keen to look out for her.

All morning the question built for Leo. He simply could not get Lizzie out of his mind and, as lunchtime approached, Leo came up with a very simple solution.

He'd just ask her, Leo decided.

But not here.

'Do you want to go out for lunch?' Leo didn't mince his words, he was very used to asking women to join him, it was Lizzie's response that he wasn't used to.

'Er, no,' Lizzie said. 'I've got plans…' She frantically searched for an excuse because she was already struggling to keep things professional. 'I'm going to the zoo.'

'The zoo?'

'I've been meaning to since I got here. It's so close…'

'It's freezing,' Leo said, 'you won't see anything.'

'How do you know?' Lizzie asked. 'Have you ever been to the zoo in January?'

'No.'

'Then don't comment on what you don't know.' Lizzie said. 'It will be nice without the crowds. Anyway, I'm not going to look at the animals today, I'm taking out a membership.'

She turned to go and Leo watched her, saw the curve of her bottom and with two words he confirmed the mood in the room.

'Buttock implants?'

It was a little game they'd invented—Leo was still

trying to guess what work Lizzie had done, but even he inwardly cringed as he said it. He was either outright flirting with Lizzie or being completely inappropriate with a colleague, and he held his breath as he leapt over the line, wondering what her reaction would be.

It surprised him.

More pointedly, it surprised Lizzie.

'Maybe!' She didn't turn around, just paused momentarily and gave a little wiggle that sent all his blood rushing south..

What on earth was that?

Lizzie almost ran to her office and retrieved her coat, astounded at her own brazenness, asking herself how, with one smouldering look, he so easily tripped the switch.

No! she told herself as she took a taxi to the zoo.

No, no, no, she thought as she filled in the forms and paid for her membership, which would give her unlimited visits for the year.

The zoo actually served as a very pertinent reminder.

Do not feed the lions.

Especially one called Leo.

'How was the zoo?' Leo asked when she returned an hour later.

'I'll tell you when I've been properly.'

'Leo…' Gwen knocked on the open door. 'I've got Francesca on the telephone—she's terribly upset. I can't make sense…'

'Put her through,' Leo said, dismissing them both, but a few minutes later he found Lizzie and brought her up to speed.

'Francesca had surgery on Friday and she thinks it's

infected. She's completely hysterical and she won't go back to the surgeon who did the operation and she's refusing to go to Kate's. I've told her to get into a taxi and come here. I'll see her in one of the treatment rooms. She won't be long.'

Francesca wasn't.

Gwen went out to help her in and Leo gave a small eye roll to Lizzie. 'Hold onto that while I examine her, please.'

'Hold onto what?'

'My ego,' Leo said. 'And you have my permission to kick me if I look like I'm about to say, "I told you so".'

In fact, he was nothing but kind to her.

Francesca was absolutely distraught and sat huddled behind dark glasses and with a scarf around her face.

'Please don't be cross with me, Leo.'

'Why would I be cross?'

'Disappointed, then.'

'I'm not a parent for a reason, Francesca. I don't do guilt trips.'

'No, you don't,' Francesca conceded.

'Tell me what happened.'

'I had surgery on Friday; he was able to fit me in the next day as he had a cancellation. I didn't go to just anyone. He comes highly recommended...' She gave the surgeon's name.

'Geoff's a fantastic surgeon,' Leo said. 'Right, I need to take a look at it.'

Lizzie helped Francesca with her glasses and scarf as she told them the work she'd had done. 'He said it was just a small lift and some fillers but now the wound is oozing.'

Leo washed his hands as Lizzie checked Francesca's

temperature and pulse—both were high—then Leo sat on a stool opposite Francesca and examined her face very carefully.

'I agree it looks terrible at the moment but...' As Francesca started sobbing Leo overrode her. 'From what I can see, Geoff has done a good job.'

Francesca's eyes snapped open.

'I wouldn't have done it, but, then, I possibly go overboard on subtle and natural, but he hasn't gone over the top. There's a lot of swelling and a lot of bruising but when that all settles, I think it will be far better than you're now expecting.'

Not for the first time, Leo surprised her—he didn't criticise the other surgeon. If anything, he spoke well of his work and, as promised, he didn't take Francesca on a guilt trip, he just slowly calmed the terrified woman down.

'What about the infection?' Francesca asked.

'Unfortunate,' Leo said, 'but it happens sometimes...' He took a swab. 'I want to have a listen to your chest...' He took her pulse for quite a long time and then looked at Lizzie. 'Actually, could you help Francesca into a gown? I'd like to examine her properly.'

'Leo...' Francesca shook her head to decline but Leo was adamant.

'I'm not arguing with you again, Francesca. I want to examine you and I'll be honest—I think you need a couple of days in hospital.' When Francesca started to argue Leo pushed on. 'My only criticism, and this isn't just Geoff, but people seem to think surgery like this is a day procedure.'

'Leo, I don't want to go to hospital. I don't want anyone seeing me like this.'

He would not be swayed. Buzzing through to Gwen, he asked her to order a private ambulance for the short trip to Kate's as, behind a curtain, Lizzie helped Francesca into a gown and onto the examination table.

'I'm a stupid old fool,' Francesca said, as Lizzie pulled off her boots, but a very agile Francesca needed no help swinging her legs up.

'I think you're amazing,' Lizzie admitted.

'You just say that to be kind.'

'No.' Lizzie shook her head, forgetting that Leo was listening as she did her best to put Francesca at ease. 'Even before my mum got ill, my parents were always acting older than they were—always set in their ways. My father won't even go for a walk. At least you do things,' Lizzie said. 'You live your life and make mistakes...' She said it so nicely and gently that even Francesca smiled. 'I think you're glamorous and wonderful and everything I'd like to be when I'm—'

'Careful!' came Francesca's friendly warning.

'Fifty-two,' Lizzie said, and both women laughed.

'What's wrong with your mum?' Francesca asked, but just as Lizzie went to answer, the other woman started to cough. 'Here,' Lizzie said, 'let me help you sit up.'

'I can't...' Francesca was struggling to get in air.

And just at the moment Lizzie thought that she had a handle on her job and knew more or less what to expect, she was in the middle of an emergency. 'Leo...'

He must have heard the concern in Lizzie's voice because he was behind the curtain in an instant.

'It's okay, Francesca,' he said immediately, and he sounded so calm that for a second Lizzie wondered if he'd actually noticed that Francesca's lips were blue and her skin a deathly grey.

'I can't breathe…' Francesca gasped.

'I know,' Leo said, his fingers taking the pulse on her neck as his other hand reached for his stethoscope. 'Don't try and speak. Just nod or shake your head. Do you have pain?' Leo asked.

She shook her head. 'Leo…'

'Press the intercom,' Leo said once Lizzie had put on a probe to read Francesca's oxygen levels—and they were dire. 'Gwen!' His voice was calm and clipped. 'Call 999 and see who else is around.'

Lizzie slipped an oxygen mask on Francesca as Leo inserted an IV. Despite his calm demeanour, Lizzie could see the flare of worry in his eyes as more and more it looked as if Francesca was suffering from a potentially fatal pulmonary embolism—a complication that sometimes happened after surgery when a clot deep in the veins of the leg flicked off and travelled to the lung.

'What have we got?' Mitchell Cooper, an American surgeon who Lizzie had had few dealings with, came in with the crash trolley and set to work pulling up emergency drugs.

'Query PE in a seventy-two-year-old, three days post facelift and fillers. The wound looks infected…'

'When was she last seen?' Mitchell glanced up from the syringe he was filling.

'I'm not sure.' Lizzie saw Mitchell frown at Leo's irregular response because post-operative care was taken very seriously at the Hunter Clinic.

'What do you mean, you're not sure when she was last seen?' Mitchell demanded—he clearly had no qualms questioning Leo about something as serious as this.

'I didn't do the surgery,' Leo said.

But he was dealing with the consequences of it.

Still, they didn't think of that now, they just concentrated on keeping Francesca as comfortable as possible until the ambulance arrived. Francesca was gripping tightly onto Leo's hand as she struggled to get air in. 'It's okay, Francesca.' He just kept saying it over and over and from the way she was holding onto him, it was clearly helping. 'The ambulance is here.'

The paramedics were skilled and calm and soon had her on the stretcher.

'Who do you want me to contact?' Leo asked Francesca. 'Your niece?'

'No.' An exhausted Francesca shook her head, still determined that no one must ever find out.

'Francesca, your family need to know what's happening. This could be serious. Amelia would want to know that you were ill. It would be awful not to know...' Lizzie looked up as Leo fell silent, surprised because he seemed to be struggling, but he soon regained his composure. 'You must let me tell her.'

Clearly Francesca trusted Leo because she gave a weary nod.

'Can you text Amelia's details to me?' Leo looked over at Lizzie. 'I'll call her when we get to the hospital.'

'You're going with Francesca?' Mitchell checked.

'Of course,' Leo said. 'She's my patient.'

Lizzie was shaken and terribly worried for Francesca. She turned to see Ethan and Rafael, who had just come back from the Lighthouse Hospital to the sight of a blue light ambulance leaving the clinic, and Mitchell quickly brought them up to speed.

'Didn't Leo do a full facelift on her just last year?' Rafael asked, and Mitchell nodded.

'Leo didn't do the surgery this time.'

'He refused to,' Lizzie said.

'Well, we all know what that means at times...' Mitchell's face was grim, in fact, all three surgeons seemed very concerned. 'I'd better go and speak with Lexi.'

'Why Lexi?' Lizzie asked, as Mitchell headed off to speak to the head of PR for the Hunter Clinic.

'The proverbial is about to hit the fan,' Ethan said darkly. 'Mark my words.'

CHAPTER NINE

LIZZIE DID HER best to get on with her day, but she was very worried. Not about the publicity, given Leo hadn't been the surgeon who'd operated, but about Francesca. Late in the evening, long after the patients had gone, she was still reluctant to go home till she knew what was happing.

'Why don't you call Leo?' Gwen suggested, as she headed out the door.

'I might,' Lizzie said, but when she tried she just got his voicemail.

It felt strange to be alone in the clinic. Lizzie tried to find something to do but there wasn't much. She took the files of the patients Leo would be seeing tomorrow into his office and placed them on the table. She couldn't help but walk over to the shelf and take down the ballet programme. She started to flick through it then became so engrossed she hardly heard Leo coming through the door.

'She's stable.'

Lizzie turned around at the sound of Leo's voice.

'Several clots, but small ones, thank God.' He closed his eyes briefly. Both had worked in medicine long enough to know that had it been a large clot, nothing anyone could have done would have changed the out-come. 'I'm just so glad she came to the clinic. Had that happened at home…' He walked over and looked at the programme Lizzie was holding. 'It's not often that I question my work but on days like today…'

'Leo, you didn't even do the surgery.'

'I know that, but I could easily have. There is a risk. I say it every day but on days like today you just ques-tion things.'

'Lexi seems to think it might look bad for the clinic if it gets out.'

'It's already out,' Leo said. 'Lexi just rang and told me. She's had two journalists call in the last hour.'

'She's telling them that Francesca didn't have the surgery here?'

'No,' Leo said. 'I never comment on any patients.'

'But—'

'No buts,' Leo said. 'You can't play that card only when it suits and I'm certainly not going to put the blame on Geoff. It's a post-operative complication—it could be any one of us.'

'Even so,' Lizzie said. 'It's your reputation…'

'My reputation can take it,' Leo said. 'It's par for the course, Lizzie. If I couldn't handle this sort of thing I'd have given up on surgery ages ago.' He sounded so as-sured and confident but she could tell he was deeply concerned.

It was all just so unfair.

'Do you want a drink?' Lizzie offered.

'I'd kill for a coffee.' Leo yawned. 'I'll give Franc-esca's niece another call and see how she is and then I'm going to ring Geoff and speak with him.'

'I meant…' She looked at the decanter.

'That's for the patients, oh, and Ethan,' Leo said, then nodded. 'Go on, then, if you'll join me.'

She shouldn't be joining him, both knew that. They were heading into dangerous territory and it had been a long and emotional day, but she wanted to talk to him more than she wanted to go home.

Lizzie poured them both a drink while Leo scrolled through his tablet.

'Have you seen this?'

As she walked over Lizzie wondered which of their famous clients she was about to see, or whether it was something about Francesca, but instead it was an article she had read several months ago.

'That's how I found out about Ethan,' Leo said. 'From a news article. That's why I was so insistent that Francesca ring Amelia—I know how it feels not to be told. How could the hospital not tell me?'

Lizzie said nothing, though she knew much more. Not that Ethan had ever been particularly effusive, but he had opened up a little to her and of course she'd read his notes.

What had happened to Ethan was so much worse than the little Leo knew.

'I don't know how we grew so far apart,' Leo mused. 'Actually, I do. I never wanted him to go into the military,' he admitted. 'I wanted him here, working in the family business...'

'It means a lot to you, doesn't it?' Lizzie offered. 'The family name.'

'Didn't you look me up before you came to work here?' He loved it that she blushed as she admitted that she had. 'You should have read back further. The Hunter name was mud for years. I wanted Ethan to help rebuild it.'

'Mud?' Lizzie frowned. 'Your father was an esteemed surgeon and your mother...' She blushed again, remembering her own father's less than complimentary description of Leo's mother, though she could hardly say that now, but Leo got in first.

'My parents' marriage was a disaster. Not to the outside world at first, but they soon got to see it, warts and all. You really don't know about them?' Leo asked, and Lizzie admitted to having done a little research before plucking up the courage to ring him. 'I read his obituary.'

'Obituaries tend to gloss over certain things. Yes, the Hunter name was prestigious, yes, we catered to the rich and wealthy and had a stunning reputation, till my father forgot to leave the less pleasant side of his personality at home.'

He didn't mean to elaborate further, he had already said far more than he usually did, but, yes, Leo told himself, it had been a long day and so he continued.

'You know how people say they build a place from nothing?' He looked directly at her and normally she averted her eyes but tonight she felt as if she was looking at the real Leo Hunter and instead of looking away she nodded.

'I built this from less than nothing. Not that your lover seems very impressed...'

Had she agreed to lunch he'd have asked the question far more nicely. Instead, his eyes were just a touch accusing as he awaited her response.

'He's not my lover.'

'Has he ever been?'

'No! Anyway, what is it to you?' Her voice trailed off because it was a stupid question, a very stupid question given the attraction crackling between herself and Leo, and this time Lizzie did pull her eyes away. 'What is it with you and Ethan?' In a desperate attempt to distract Leo from her previous question, she asked what few would dare. Something needed to be said—even Ethan had joked that he had thought his days of unexploded land mines were over. 'Why don't the two of you get on?'

'Is that the head nurse asking?'

'No,' Lizzie said. 'It's me.'

He wanted to tell her, or maybe he just needed to speak with someone, Leo rationalised, because having Ethan working here was proving way harder than he had thought it would. He felt as if someone had taken a rake through the clinic and turfed every inch of it. The only thing that had made coming to work bearable lately was sitting in front of him now.

'All the time we were growing up—' Leo was clearly uncomfortable discussing it '—I did everything I could to appease my father. I guess that's the best way to describe it. He was a mean drunk and for all our mother's dazzling ways she wasn't exactly a stable parent—there were endless parties, affairs, all glossed over, of course. After our mother died there could be no glossing over. It just got worse.'

'His drinking?'

'That and the moods and the anger. Ethan loves confrontation, I rely on smooth talk…'

'I had noticed.'

He gave a thin smile. 'I spent my life trying to keep

him calm, trying to smooth things over, stop the whole thing from exploding, and Ethan loathes me for it.'

'Why were you the peacekeeper?'

'Honestly?' Leo asked, and Lizzie nodded. 'If confronted, I thought my father might kill him.'

Lizzie swallowed. It was just so far from the love she had known growing up.

'I remember one time when I was thirteen and we were home for the school holidays.' Leo shook his head, not wanting to go there ever again. 'Ethan was ten years old!' He offered little by way of explanation but the agony was clear. 'That was no match for my father in a rage.'

'Ethan needs to get over himself,' Lizzie said. 'He's lucky to have had an older brother looking out for him— who would light the tail of a lion and send someone they love in to deal with it.'

'I guess.' Leo pondered on that for a moment then pulled his phone from his pocket. 'I'd better ring Francesca's niece and then Geoff.'

'I'll go when you've rung Amelia.'

She waited while he made the call and it was clear even from the one-sided conversation that Francesca was doing well, though she was being carefully monitored in ICU and given medication to disperse the clots.

'I'm so pleased to hear she's improving,' Leo said to Francesca's niece. 'Let her know that I'll come in and visit…' He chatted a moment longer and then ended the call.

'She's stable.'

'I heard,' Lizzie said. 'That's great news.'

'Tony's on his way!' Leo grinned. 'Things looked pretty grim for a while when we first got to Kate's and

Amelia ended up calling him and he wants to see her. I doubt Francesca will be too pleased! She's certainly looking nothing like she'd hoped to for the wedding.'

'You really do have a soft spot for her.'

'I do.' Leo nodded. 'She's got the same name as my mother—who I'm turning into, apparently…' He gave a black smile. 'She was a bit of a party girl and, as I said, there were a lot of affairs.'

'That sounds like one of Ethan's comparisons,' Lizzie said, and Leo's eyes jerked up.

'Actually, it was.'

'You're not married, Leo. You're not being unfaithful to anyone.'

'Just a top bastard.'

'I was wrong about that,' Lizzie admitted. 'It was Flora who got the wrong idea about things. From what I've heard since then, you don't make any promises that you don't keep.'

'Never,' Leo said, and he watched the swallow in her throat as he spelt things out, as he always had and always would. 'I'll never have an affair because I'll never be with one person long enough. I've seen first hand what a bad relationship can do.'

'There are good ones too.'

'I have no intention of finding out,' Leo dismissed. 'I like the nice things in life,' he continued. 'I don't wait for things to turn sour.'

Her eyes never left his face as she stood up.

'I'm going to go,' Lizzie said.

'Sure—I need to ring Geoff.'

He didn't blame her in the least for going—he had pretty much told her how they would be and he didn't blame Lizzie in the least for wanting no part of it.

He just didn't want her to go.

'Night, Leo…'

'I'll walk you out,' Leo offered, standing up to do just that.

'There's no need.'

She should go, simply walk, yet instead she stood there. Lizzie didn't do mixed messages but Leo was certainly mixing her up.

'Night, Lizzie.'

When still she didn't move his hand lifted to her cheek and Lizzie had plenty of time to turn but instead her cheek met his skin and moved into it like a cat nudging his palm.

'You should go,' Leo warned, but his hand remained.

'I am going,' Lizzie said. 'But first…'

Lizzie had never made first moves, always she held back, but tonight she did not. Slowly, softly she touched her lips to his.

His hand slid to her waist and her mouth opened, and the first taste of his tongue was more potent than brandy. It warmed but it did not comfort; instead, it made her crave. It was a kiss that lingered and with reason—for Leo, never had the darkness been lit by a kiss.

She wanted the bag that was on her shoulder to slip to the floor and for the hand that was on her waist to pull her further into him, she wanted him to press her with his mouth and lead her to his sofa.

In a kiss that remained a kiss there were so many thoughts to be had.

He smelt of that expensive cologne, yet there was a base note that was exclusive to Leo and was driving her wild, along with the knowledge that right now he could easily have her on the floor.

She pulled back, knew she had to play it casual if they were going to continue as normal at work.

'What was that?' Leo smiled, running the tip of his tongue over his lips and tasting her over again.

'A kiss,' Lizzie said. 'Just a kiss,' she said, trying to pretend a kiss was all their bodies required. 'You looked like you could do with one.'

He was about to make one of his usual quips, how he'd do better with two, or that it would be very thoughtless to leave him like this, to drag her hand to feel the strain of his erection, to push her head back to his mouth and let his tongue in detail tell her what he wanted to do, except he wanted more than that from Lizzie. He actually wanted the conversations, the meals and the moments, getting to know each other.

Yet he did not.

And certainly he didn't want the fall-out afterwards.

''Night, Lizzie.'

It was why he let her go.

CHAPTER TEN

WHAT HAD SEEMED not just appropriate at the time but natural was worrying her by the time Lizzie had got home.

She loved her job.

More than that, for the first time in a long time she was panicking about what to wear to a ball, rather than panicking about the bills from the nursing home and making the month's rent.

More than that, though, she liked Leo and had no idea how things would be at work if they—

Stop.

Over and over she told herself not to go there, but working alongside him the next week and pretending their kiss hadn't happened, or that it had meant very little, would be hard enough. Imagine what it would be like if they—

Stop.

By Thursday Lizzie wondered if she should just walk around with a stop sign to hold up at five-minute intervals throughout the day. She was finishing up some notes on a patient when Leo walked past and paused to give her an update on Francesca. 'She's been moved to a ward and is improving.'

'And Tony?'

'I didn't actually see Francesca, I just called.'

Lizzie noted his tense features and didn't blame him in the least for not adding fuel to the fire by visiting Francesca. The press were all over it and the interest wasn't abating—the Hunter name was, yet again, being held to question. Only, as it turned out, that wasn't the reason he hadn't visited his favourite patient.

'She's really upset,' Leo explained. 'Francesca's no fool and she's really upset by all the drama and, on top of everything, now the whole world knows she's been under the knife. Amelia said she'd just burst into tears and get all upset if she saw me.'

'I could go in and visit.'

'Would you?' Leo seemed to like that idea. 'That would be great and, please, tell her she's not to worry about me.' He looked at Lizzie. He wanted to speak with her, he wanted to take up where they had left off, but in a rare occurrence his conscience was pricking.

Ethan was right.

Lizzie wasn't his usual type—far from it. He was now more than questioning his decision to ask her to the ball. It was hard enough just stopping by and chatting to her.

'I meant to ask you something,' Lizzie said, before he walked away. 'I've had a couple of patients asking when Abbie would be back. I assume she's a doctor here?'

Leo nodded. 'She's a paediatric surgeon. Abbie de Luca…'

'Oh!' Lizzie's eyes widened in question because de Luca was Rafael's surname.

'They've got a very sick baby.'

'Oh, no…' Lizzie really hadn't had too many dealings with Rafael. His theatre list was spilling over and he was constantly at the hospital or closed in behind his office door. 'Is there anything we can do...?' She didn't really know how to broach it—but shouldn't he be home more with his family than working around the clock? 'He seems to have a terribly heavy workload.'

'Yes, well, he's taken on a lot of Abbie's patients.' Leo felt uncomfortable discussing something so private but as head nurse Lizzie perhaps ought to be told. 'We're not keeping him from his family. Abbie is in America, there's a new treatment but it's...' Leo gave an uncomfortable shrug, it was a very sensitive topic. 'It's probably better that you don't ask Rafael how things are going. If he chooses to talk...'

'Sure.'

'And as for the patients, just say if they ask that she's taking care of their daughter,' Leo said, 'which she is.'

'Fine.'

'Lizzie, about the ball...' Leo hesitated, He really couldn't retract his offer and anyway, apart from good manners, he assumed she'd already bought her dress and booked the million appointments women did before a ball such as this one. 'I'll pick you up at six.'

'We could meet there.'

'I'll pick you up at six,' he repeated.

Even though her pay had gone in, instead of venturing to the shops after work Lizzie headed over to the private wing at Kate's and braced herself for tears and drama, but instead it was a beaming Francesca who greeted her!

'Lizzie!' She held out her arms. 'Thank you so much for all you did for me.'

'It's just lovely to see you looking so well.' It was—

Francesca was sitting up in bed with her eyeliner and red lipstick on and even with an IV pump attached to her she still looked rather stunning. 'Do you ever *not* wear make-up?' Lizzie asked.

'Never.' Francesca laughed. 'How is Leo?'

'He's just concerned about you,' Lizzie said. 'And he's told me to let you know that you're not to worry. It will all sort itself out. Leo wanted to come in and see you himself but thought it might cause you more upset…'

'You haven't heard, have you?'

'Heard what?' Lizzie frowned.

'I just did a radio interview.' Francesca beamed. 'I said that Leo didn't do the surgery. I said that he had operated on me in the past and I was thrilled with his work but why would I be faithful to my surgeon when I couldn't even manage to be faithful to my husbands and lovers…' She gave a wicked laugh. 'I said that I was not ashamed to admit that I accept a little help for my appearance. I also told them that when I felt unwell last Monday, I went to the man I trust most with my health. I said that darling Leo took wonderful care of me and that it tears at my heart that he is being blamed for something that had nothing to do with him. Leo saved my life.'

'Oh, Francesca!' Lizzie's eyes filled with tears. 'You didn't have to speak to the media.'

'Of course I did.' Francesca shrugged. 'And it wasn't so bad…' Her face brightened into a beaming smile as she looked over her shoulder. 'Lizzie, this is Tony. The cause of all this.'

A very dashing, very elegant man came into the

room. 'It's all my fault, of course,' Tony said, smiling as he shook Lizzie's hand.

'Of course it is,' Francesca happily agreed. 'I had to nearly die to get him to come and see me.'

Lizzie could just imagine the tempestuous rows—Francesca and a fiery Italian was a passionate combination.

'You could have just picked up the telephone,' Tony said, then turned back to Lizzie. 'Thank you so much for saving her. Thank you to all at the Hunter Clinic.'

'We really did very little.'

'Nonsense,' Francesca scolded. 'Tony, can you give us a minute?' The moment Tony had left, Francesca asked for Lizzie to fetch her bag. 'Can I ask you to do a couple of little jobs for me?' She was a star, a diva, and she made Lizzie smile. 'Amelia has to go and look after her children but I have run out of my body lotion and naturally I don't want to ask Tony.'

'Of course.'

'And I need my favourite hair conditioner.' She wrote quite a list as she spoke on. 'I hope it's no trouble.'

'It's not,' Lizzie answered truthfully. 'I have to get a few things anyway. I'm going to a ball...'

'The Princess Catherine's ball?' Francesca beamed. 'What are you wearing?'

'I'm not sure,' Lizzie admitted. 'I've got my black dress...' Francesca's rather shocked features weren't helping matters.

'You're not getting something new to wear?'

'I'm going to look for something tonight,' Lizzie admitted. 'I'll make up my mind then. I might find something I like...'

'Who's doing your hair and make-up?'

'Me.'

'No, no,' Francesca, rather frantically, shook her head. 'You *have* to plan this. It's not just a dress, think of it as a costume, think of who you are going to be that night… If I wasn't so drained I could help you with your make-up.'

Lizzie smothered a smile as she imagined Leo's expression if he picked her up in full prima ballerina make-up mode. 'I'll manage,' Lizzie said, but she had lost her audience. Francesca was looking over her shoulder and beaming again and Lizzie assumed that Tony was back but jumped slightly when she heard Leo's voice.

'You didn't have to do that.'

'Leo!' Francesca dismissed his concerns with a flick of the wrist. 'As I said to Lizzie, it wasn't so bad. I nearly died on Monday and I am vain enough that, dying or not, the last thing I wanted was Tony to see me looking as I did. It was embarrassing, it was awful, but I survived it. I don't think anything could embarrass me after that.' She gave a cheeky smile. 'According to the lady who interviewed me, I am the new face of ageing apparently—seventy is the new fifty!'

'You're scandalous!' Leo said.

'I intend to be to the day I die.'

'I'm going to go.' Lizzie gave Francesca a kiss as she took the list and an awful lot of cash. 'I'll pop in later with your things.'

'Thank you, darling.'

When Lizzie had gone, Leo came and took a seat. 'Thank you,' he said. Despite insisting to everyone he was fine and that his reputation could handle it, the week had been hell. An *unnamed source* had gone to great lengths to tell the press that he'd long thought the surgeons at the Hunter Clinic were a touch over-zealous and Leo's gut had churned at the thought of the ball and facing so many peers with his integrity up to such public scrutiny. Still, now that Francesca had spoken to the press, it would be all false smiles and hand-pumping.

'You're sure you're okay with people knowing?' Leo checked.

'I like attention.' Francesca smiled then turned serious. 'Thank you, Leo—you saved my life but, even so, I am cross with you.'

'Why?'

'Sending that beautiful woman into that snake pit when she hasn't a clue. Lizzie is talking about doing her own make-up and hair and she still hasn't worked out what she will be wearing.'

'Lizzie's not some hick.' Leo was surprised by the defensiveness in his voice. 'Stop trying to control the world from your hospital bed.'

'You have no idea about women.'

'Hey,' Leo snapped. 'I work with women, I know exactly—'

'I'll tell you exactly,' Francesca interrupted. 'Sort this, Leo.'

'How?' Leo asked, just a little bit worried now and not for himself, more for the stress he would have caused Lizzie. 'I can't tell her I'm worried that she's not going to look the part…' He rolled his eyes. 'I can't do this without offending her.'

'Of course you can,' Francesca said. 'And you will do it now.'

Lizzie answered her phone just as she was buying body lotion for Francesca—the price of which would feed a family of four for a week and it certainly wasn't available at the chemist!

'Where are you?' Leo asked, and Lizzie frowned at his response when she told him the name of the iconic store. 'That's convenient.'

'Why?' Lizzie asked. 'Do you need something?'

'You've got an appointment on the fourth floor.'

'With who?'

'Her name's Melinda, she'll help you pick a dress and make appointments for make-up and things.'

'Excuse me?'

He tried a fib. 'Francesca said that you are worried about going to the ball.'

'I never said that I was worried,' Lizzie said tartly. 'I think it's Francesca who's worried about me.' Her face was on fire in embarrassment. 'Don't worry, Leo, I shan't let the side down.'

'So you don't want a new dress and shoes and your hair and make-up done on the day, all paid for by the boss?' Leo said. 'What woman wouldn't want that?'

'Well, if you put it like that…' Her angry blush was fading, a smile stretching her lips at the deep purr of his voice.

'Goldilocks, you shall go to the ball.'

'It's Cinderella.' Lizzie laughed.

'Yes, well, I don't think reading fairy-tales was my mother's forte. Enjoy yourself, Cinderella,' Leo said. 'That's an order!'

CHAPTER ELEVEN

To the letter!

Lizzie stood back from the mirror. She had followed Leo's order to the letter to enjoy herself and had taken Melinda's advice, because never in month of Sundays would she have even tried on this dress and coat, and that was aside from the price tag!

It was either beige or pink, Lizzie couldn't decide which. The fabric was the softest velvet and it clung everywhere and was so low at the back she had been worried it bordered on indecent.

'It's stunning,' Melinda had assured her.

It was. And seeing it with her new hair and make-up, Lizzie couldn't believe that the woman in the mirror was really her.

Her body had been waxed and massaged and that had been just the start. Her brown hair had been curled and pinned up and her make-up was amazing—Lizzie's eyes had been dressed in smoky grey eye shadow and her lips...well, she couldn't decide if they were beige or pink either.

She was shaking, she was nervous and excited too, but that had more to do with the fact that in ten minutes she'd be facing Leo. And then there was the question of dancing with him…

Stop.

She didn't need an evening bag, she needed a table-tennis bat to flick away the thoughts about dancing with him. Even spraying on her perfume, she imagined his face in her neck, inhaling it…

No.

Again she said it to herself.

This week had been awkward enough and it had just been a kiss. Imagine if they…

The buzz of her intercom had her heart beating faster and Lizzie didn't know whether she should say she was on her way down or invite him up.

'I hope I'm getting asked in?' Leo said, making the decision for her.

'Of course,' Lizzie said. 'After all, you're my land-lord.'

She opened the door and Leo rather wished she'd settled for her usual black dress—it would have cer-tainly been safer.

'Oh, my!' he said, and Lizzie squirmed at the ap-proval in his eyes.

'Oh, my, to you too!' He was wearing a tux and he was so clean-shaven she wanted to put her hand to his jaw, or run her fingers through his silken black hair, or just smother his collar in her lipstick.

'Come through…' Lizzie settled for that instead.

He passed the coat and boots that she wore for walk-ing to work and followed her, getting the sight of her bare back, and she could feel the tingle the length of her spine as it blistered under his gaze.

'Do you want a drink?' Lizzie had splurged and

bought some decent whisky, just in case he wanted one, but Leo declined.

'Not for me.' He stood by the fireplace and saw the pictures of her family and friends, and small talk was supremely difficult when all he wanted was to pull her into his arms.

'I'm ready whenever…'

'No rush,' Leo said. 'We'll be in plenty of time.' He tried again. 'Your dress is lovely.'

'Thank you,' Lizzie said. 'And thank you for…' She stopped when Leo gave a brief shake of his head. 'I'm not sure if it's beige or pink.'

He didn't answer.

'Look at my shoes.' She lifted her dress a fraction and Leo looked at her ankles and the smooth skin of her calves rather than the shoes, and he couldn't manage small talk. If he did it would be something like, 'Fancy a quickie before we go?' She was wiggling her feet and he wanted the shoes off, he wanted that foot in his mouth and, before he put his own in his, he glanced at his watch. 'Actually, I think we should get going.'

He helped Lizzie on with her coat as much as he could without touching her, smelling her, turning her round or just taking her against the wall, and then there was the agony of the lift and he couldn't not touch her.

'Rapunzel,' Leo said, gently lifting a curl.

'She had long blonde hair,' Lizzie corrected him. His fingers weren't even touching her skin but she could feel their energy and warmth and she tried to joke her way out of it. 'You need to go on a fairy-tale workshop.'

She did feel like something out of a fairy-tale, though, as the driver came round and she climbed into the back and then sat with Leo as the car swished through the London streets. Never had she looked more beautiful and neither had Lizzie.

'The Christmas lights are gone,' Lizzie said. 'If I'm still living here next year, I'll be able to—'

'Why wouldn't you still be living here?' Leo asked, and she just kept on looking out of the window because the answer was an impossible one to give.

'Lizzie?'

She was aware of the glitter of tears in her eyes, a combination of tension and passion and the absolute unfairness of it all. God, she wished she'd met him in a bar or something—why did he have to be her boss? But, then, she didn't frequent the type of bars that Leo Hunter did, and if she had, Lizzie frantically thought, she'd still have run a mile if someone as drop-dead gorgeous as Leo had approached her.

'Are you okay?'

'A bit nervous,' Lizzie said, which was a lie. His presence meant she'd forgotten her nerves about the ball.

'You'll be fine.'

She was more than fine, Leo soon realised. Heads turned for all the right reasons. Lizzie was as in demand as he was because, as soon as he introduced her as a work colleague, you could see male smiles widen.

'Bit of a scare for you this week.' A woman who'd introduced herself as Matilda batted her eyelashes at Leo.

'A scare?' Leo frowned, pretending he had no idea what Matilda was referring to.

'Of course it all turned out well.'

But Leo remained noncommittal and, as the conversation progressed, Lizzie realised Matilda was, in fact, a journalist and of course Leo would never talk about his patients. He did, though, Lizzie noticed, give a subtle nod for Lexi to come over. She saw too his tight smile as a *friend* patted him on the back and said he'd never doubted him for a moment.

'His name should be Janus,' Leo said when they were briefly alone. 'He was one of the *experts* that *chose not to be named* but were only too happy to talk to the press.' Though he did smile a little while later when Janus asked Lizzie to dance and she politely but rather publicly declined him.

She didn't decline everyone, though.

'So you're not...?' one particular rake checked with Leo, before taking Lizzie off to dance.

Unfortunately not, Leo thought as he did duty dances with the women he must.

Lizzie danced and danced, just not with the man she wanted to be with.

It was work, Lizzie reminded herself, making her way over to the bar, where she sat on a stool and watched the room, though her eyes were drawn all too often to Leo.

He worked the room so well and, Lizzie realised, apart from a very occasional sip, more often than not he replaced his full glass and got a fresh one. Lizzie glanced over and saw Kara and Declan. Kara looked amazing in a long gold dress, her blonde hair in curls and worn loose. Declan was stunning in the requisite tuxedo. They were doing tequila shots at the bar and Lizzie was about to go over and say hi but, almost as soon as she thought it, Lizzie realised that they didn't look as if they'd appreciate being disturbed!

She had never noticed anything between Kara and Declan till now.

She watched as they headed to the dance floor and

just as she was starting to feel like a wallflower an astonishingly good-looking man asked her to dance.

It was just the wrong good-looking man, though, Lizzie thought. Her eyes drifted around the room, seeking Leo, but instead they landed on Declan and Kara, locked in a searing kiss, and Lizzie wanted to be as bold as them, to not care what tomorrow might bring.

Or maybe they did care because suddenly Kara left, leaving Declan standing on the dance floor, a *what the hell was that* look on his face.

Lizzie couldn't dwell on others, though, all she could think about was Leo and, no, she didn't want a second dance with this good-looking stranger. Politely she declined and as she did so Lizzie turned, and it was to Leo. Finally she got to dance with the one she wanted.

'You look as if you're enjoying yourself,' Leo said to her hair.

'I am.'

'Not so scary after all.'

It wasn't, Lizzie thought. She liked being back in his arms.

All the self-enforced warnings were diminishing— for both of them.

Leo could feel her spine beneath his hand and he resisted the urge to run the pad of his fingers along it.

Then he stopped resisting.

She felt her stomach curl over as his fingers lightly dusted her back and then hesitate, and she breathed deeply and sank further into him which was permission for Leo to gently resume his exploration.

'I've wanted you all night,' Leo said.

'I'm here now.' She could feel her heart pounding

in her chest, feel the wobble in her voice as she tried to keep it light.

'I wasn't just talking about dancing.'

Leo didn't need to look down to know that Lizzie was blushing—he felt the heat race up her exposed back and he stroked the blushing skin with the pads of his fingers, his touch subtle yet almost indecent.

'What's stopping us, Lizzie?'

'Your track record,' she admitted. 'My job.'

'It would never jeopardise your job,' Leo said. 'But I can't do a thing about my track record. It's there for a reason—I don't do for ever.' He thought how best to proceed. 'Lizzie…' He had to make things clear. He *had* to do the 'I'm a bastard nothing will ever come of it' talk, right here right now, but she halted him.

'Leo, I'm thirty-two, I don't need to hear the warnings.'

'They're not warnings, Lizzie. They're certainties.'

'Heeded. This,' she said, 'is going nowhere except bed.'

'You're sure?'

Till now, sex had been pleasant at times, at others a chore.

With Leo she knew she was heading towards bliss.

She felt bold, she felt wanton, she felt sexy. Francesca was right—it wasn't just a dress and make-up, tonight she was in costume. Tonight, Lizzie realised, she could be anyone she wanted to be. And she wanted to be a woman who could do the no-strings thing, who could give in to want because…she could.

And so she answered him.

'There's nothing stopping us.'

She felt the warmth of his body as he pulled her in

closer and closed her eyes in decadent bliss as they both stopped fighting their attraction.

'I know what colour your dress is.' His mouth was close to her ear and she wanted his tongue, her eyes closing as Leo stopped holding back and it was sublime. 'It's the colour of your skin when you get out of the bath.' His fingers were still working her back. 'Were you in the bath that night I called?'

'You know that I was.'

'I did know and I *was* right about Rapunzel,' Leo said, 'because all I want to do is let down your hair.'

She felt almost dizzy, her body a hand grenade, and as his hand moved to her hair, if he pulled even one pin Lizzie thought she might just explode.

As might Leo.

'We've got to go.'

'It's too soon,' Lizzie said.

'I don't care.'

For the first time in forever his focus wasn't on the Hunter Clinic; for the first time in forever there was a woman who came before it.

Even if just for tonight.

They didn't care about the driver and they were too far gone for seat belts. They were a tangle of arms and tongues, both *desperate* to get to Leo's home. And to tomorrow's shame for Lizzie, she had no idea if there was anyone in the lift when they entered because, quite simply, their lips could not be parted.

Keys were very inconvenient things.

Condoms too.

They were at his door, Lizzie patting him down as if she was about to arrest him, Leo honestly wondering if they were going to make it inside and would it matter if they didn't, and then sense drifted in and he pulled out the key.

'Here…' He put the key in upside down, for his next attempt he used the Harley Street one, until finally he located the correct key and they were in.

Then a triumphant Lizzie located the second essential item, if Leo wanted in!

Still they kissed. She held his face in her hands and for a moment she moved him back just a fraction from her and met his eyes.

Leo thought she was about to halt things, to say too fast, too soon, but he smiled at her stern warning.

'If you tear my dress…'

It was her favourite thing in the world, apart from this. She shrugged off her coat and then as his hands roamed her body Lizzie's were equally as direct. Unzipping him, freeing him, she held him in her hands for a brief slice of time, and as she slid the condom down his delicious length it was as if the word shy had never been invented. Lizzie actually felt as if she knew who she was as he lifted her dress and hauled down her panties.

'I'll fall…' Lizzie said, not exactly used to being taken up against a wall.

'I won't let you.'

He lifted her onto him and she wrapped her legs around him. It had to be fast, they were both on the edge of orgasm and there could be no other way, but as he filled her, as she wrapped her legs tightly around him and he pressed her down, Lizzie knew it had had to be this way for another reason—there was no changing their minds now, whatever the future, they had a past. There was no turning back.

'Lizzie.' His teeth were gritted in an effort to hold on

but holding her buttocks in his hands, hearing the squeal escape her throat as she started to come, Leo gave in. She felt him swell further inside and Leo heard the tiny scream that had his seed race to fill her.

Lizzie had never felt anything like it—had never been taken with such force and passion. As she came she was less than a lady and when he lowered one of her legs, as her lovely shoe hit the floor, he was able to thrust more deeply. So deeply he demanded an encore, her orgasm dashing back from the wings to take centre stage. So deep and long was the second time Leo was able to open his eyes to watch, before kissing her back to the world.

By the time she walked, on shaky legs, into his lounge, they were already lovers.

CHAPTER TWELVE

Leo had been right—it *was* Goldilocks.

After a blissful night of lovemaking Lizzie woke to a silver-grey morning and lay warmed by Leo's body spooned into hers. As she felt him stir and wake up she then felt him become still as he perhaps realised just who was sleeping in his bed.

And was still there.

Lizzie stared at her dress. Her beautiful dress, which lay like a puddle on the floor, and she remembered him taking it off. She thought of her coat still on the floor in his hallway and she hoped its magic would last, that the costume she had worn last night, where she had been so bold and brave, could see her through this morning.

They had to face each other at work on Monday, which meant things had to play out well today—it was that or run screaming into the woods, never to be seen again.

She could do this, Lizzie decided. In the painful times when her mum had first been diagnosed Lizzie had learnt how to act. How to not notice her mum's errors in conversations, how to say nothing except thank you when her third birthday card appeared in the post, because her mother had forgotten that she'd already sent one.

Yes, Lizzie could act.

'Morning.' She didn't turn, just stared out of the floor-to-ceiling windows. 'I won't ask how you slept, given you've had as little as me.'

'Coffee?' Leo asked, and Lizzie nodded.

'Two sugars, please.'

It was an unusual request from a bedfellow! Normally, Leo thought, yawning as he spooned sugar into her cup, it was black coffee and a sweetener, or green tea. He thought of Lizzie's curves and last night and, really, there was no regret.

Now came the awkward part.

He walked into his bedroom and she was still gazing out of the window and the view from behind was stunning. Her hair fell in thick, still-lacquered curls and as he put her coffee down he was treated to the sight of Lizzie with panda eyes and a mark low on her neck and a slow smile on a mouth that now knew him intimately. Recalling last night's surprising lack of inhibition, the furthest thing from Leo's mind now was feeling awkward.

'Your view is so amazing,' Lizzie said. 'I feel like I'm on the London Eye.'

'If at any time you require assistance...' Leo made her laugh as he put on an automated woman's voice '...press the button at either end of the capsule...'

'What happens then?'

'I'm not sure.' Leo climbed back into bed and took a very welcome drink of coffee. 'How much champagne did we have?'

'Well, I had three glasses so there goes my excuse...'

She rolled over and he watched as the sheet slipped and one breast beckoned him but he took another sip of his drink instead. 'And you had about two sips…' His cup hesitated as he realised she'd rumbled his game. 'You just keep taking a fresh glass…'

'I like to stay sharp.'

'So I noticed.'

A smile spread his lips and Lizzie found she was biting down on hers. God, he looked sexy in the morning, unshaven, rumpled and, despite his attempts to halt it, one hand was playing with her breast, which had slipped out from under the sheet.

'Do you want to go out for breakfast?' Leo asked, because maybe it would be easier to clear the air for Monday somewhere public. He wasn't concentrating very well in bed. 'We could go to Drakes,' he suggested, then gave a brief shake of his head. 'Actually, that's not such a good idea. Half of the Hunter Clinic will be there, nursing their hangovers and trying to work out who got off with who last night.'

'And we don't want to fan the flames…' Lizzie said.

'No,' Leo agreed.

'Where shall we go, then?' Lizzie asked.

'How about here?' He put down his coffee and suggested that she do the same. 'Beside mine,' Leo said, and he slid down on the bed as she leant over him, caught the breast with his mouth and Lizzie, one hand beside his head the other on the bedside, knelt and revelled in the sensation, tried to remember to breathe as he pulled her hips so she was over him.

She wanted him to pull her down, she loathed how he had to stop a second to put on another condom, she almost told him not to bother, that she was on the Pill, she just wanted him inside her now.

'Where were we?' Leo said, and pulled her down onto him, his hands working her breasts and then down to her hips and then back to her breasts because she rode him so perfectly he could just enjoy and watch her enjoyment too.

'So much for feeling awkward...' Leo said, loving her breathless laugh, loving looking down and watching, then cursing as he saw the condom wrapped low around his thick base. 'Lizzie...' She was coming as he grabbed her hips and lifted her off him; she didn't want to get off, didn't really understand what was happening till she looked down to the gorgeous sight of Leo pulsing over her.

'More...' She just said the first thing on her mind.

'Here.' He stroked *more* out onto her and then rubbed it in with his fingers and for Lizzie it was shockingly intimate and it was the same for Leo too.

He rubbed in silver, he looked up to eyes that looked golden, and for the first time Leo wanted more too.

More of the same.

Over and over.

He drove them to Lizzie's apartment but this was no awkward car ride home, they were just going so that she could change into jeans and boots, and brunch had been well earned, it was no wonder they were starving.

This should be ending about now, both knew it, but walking along the Thames a little while later Leo wanted to keep pulling the scarf she had over her face down just so he could see her mouth.

So he did.

And warmed it with his.

'Shouldn't we be regretting this about now?' Leo checked as they walked alongside the river.

'Probably,' Lizzie said. 'How on earth am I going to face you at work tomorrow?'

'You won't have to,' Leo said. 'I'll just turn you over your desk…'

She hit him with her hand; he made her laugh, and she hadn't laughed like this in a very long time.

Ever.

'Do you want to go to the zoo?' Leo asked.

'The zoo?'

'You're a cheap date,' Leo said, 'given you've got a life membership.'

They had lunch there and just walked and talked and she gave a wry smile at the do-not-feed-the-lion sign.

'Too late for that,' Leo said.

'Where to now?' Lizzie asked.

'The reptile house?' Leo suggested.

'I don't like snakes.'

'What are you doing here, then?' It was the closest they'd come today since broaching the subject.

'You're not a snake,' Lizzie said. 'You won't hurt me, Leo. We can just enjoy it while it lasts.'

Enjoy it they did.

They watched as three female gorillas attempted to gain attention from one very impressive silverback male and the irony was lost on neither of them.

'I'd make a terrible gorilla,' Lizzie said, and she gave her one warning. 'I don't like to share.'

'You'll never have to,' Leo assured her, and he looked at her profile—saw that she was tense for the first time today and he told her how it would be. 'I've told you I don't stay around for the rows to start, and it's served me well—it's the reason I can still be friendly with my exes.'

'Apart from Flora.'

'Yes, apart from Flora.'

Who had been foolish enough to read more into them. This was Leo, like it or leave it, take it or not, he made no excuses and Lizzie was grateful for that, she truly didn't want them. She would far prefer the painful truth than cruel lies.

She watched the huge silverback gorilla assert himself. 'He's so arrogant.'

'I think he's rather magnificent,' Leo said.

So too did Lizzie.

It was evening, their magical wonderful night, extended by a day, except they were heading to his apartment and, yes, a drink would be nice.

'I could call ahead,' Leo said. 'Have some dinner delivered.'

'Sounds great.'

'Do you want to stop by your place?' Leo suggested. 'Let the fish out?'

A small joke and Lizzie laughed but they both knew what they were there for.

Lizzie collected her uniform, her toothbrush and hairbrush...

'Is that it?' Leo was incredibly impressed by the paltry size of her overnight bag.

'I'm hardly moving in.'

Yes, the view from his apartment was like being on the London Eye as later that night, lying on his couch, she watched the moon drift across London as he stroked her hair with one hand and slid down the zipper of her jeans with the other.

Yes, he had been right, it was Goldilocks.

Too soft the beats of pressure on her clitoris, and he loved it that she was open enough in the bed to tell him that.

Too hard the erection at her entrance to even think of getting off the sofa and finding condoms—after all, he used them all the time and Lizzie was on the Pill.

And as he slipped inside her, she didn't care about tomorrow and how difficult things might be at some future time.

For now, right now as Leo spilled inside her, it was just right.

CHAPTER THIRTEEN

'YOU'RE LOOKING VERY pleased with yourself,' Ethan commented as Leo arrived at the Hunter Clinic.

'Have you seen some of the donations raised?' Leo said, and gave a brief nod to Lizzie, who was trying to remember how she usually acted when Leo was around.

Oh, yes—blushing and on edge! Strangest of all, now that she'd slept with him she was neither of those things.

'How did you enjoy the ball?' Ethan asked, as Leo headed for his office.

'It was great,' Lizzie answered, then excused herself, but she felt a little like she had when her father had asked questions when she'd first gone out with Peter.

'I'm allowed to be concerned, Lizzie,' Thomas had said. 'I know his type and I just don't see any good coming from it.'

Ethan didn't need to be concerned, Lizzie told herself.

She knew what she was getting into. If anything, there was less tension between Lizzie and Leo, there was no flirting, it was all very business-like now.

Until home time.

Lizzie was wrapping her scarf around her neck and chatting with Rafael about her parents as Leo walked past.

'I'll go and see them at the weekend.'

'You go each weekend?' Rafael asked.

'Not every weekend,' Lizzie said, but there was guilt, because the build-up to Christmas had been crazy and then between moving and starting her new job, she hadn't been going so much lately.

Leo headed for his office and tried to ignore what he was thinking because he had been hoping to see her again at the weekend. While, of course, Lizzie had to do what was right for her, it just left no time for them, unless…

'Night, Leo.' Lizzie smiled and walked past his office.

'Night, Lizzie.'

She wanted him to call her back.

He didn't.

She got home and peeled off her coat and then ran a bath and ate a bowl of cereal for dinner. Exhausted, and seriously so, after the most incredible weekend of her life, it was blissful to slip into bed and finally catch up with her thoughts.

Leo.

She waited for guilt, for self-recrimination, for common sense to make her bolt upright with an anxiety attack. Instead she lay in bed actually smiling, laughing, just on the crest of a wave and riding it, wherever it might take her. Such was her sudden longing for him it came as no surprise when her phone rang and it was Leo.

His apartment was lit by the moon. On coming home

Leo had scanned the apartment for a piece of Lizzie, but the cleaners were thorough and very used to tidying up after one of Leo's weekends.

'Loser,' Leo muttered to himself as he found himself picking up her deodorant can and spraying it.

What was the problem again? Leo checked.

That's right, her weekend was taken.

'Hi, there…' He was almost brusque when he called her.

'Hi, Leo.'

"What are you doing?'

'I'm in bed.'

'It's eight.'

'I'm tired.'

'About the weekend…'

'I've got plans.'

'I know that,' Leo said. 'What about Thursday?'

'I've got drinks with friends,' Lizzie said, which was true—it was her friend Brenda's birthday. They'd shared a flat when Lizzie had first arrived in London and they got together now and then. Though not one of her friends would mind in the least if she stood them up for such a glorious cause.

'What are you wearing?' Leo asked. 'And if it's one of those awful all-in-one things you have my permission to lie.'

'I'm not,' Lizzie said.

'Good.'

'I'm not wearing anything.' She waited, closed her eyes and almost willed his reply.

'Well, I'd suggest you amend that,' Leo said. 'I don't want you scaring my driver.'

It was the serious bonking time of a new romance,

Lizzie told herself. That time when you just can't bear to be apart.

And they used every minute.

It was dizzying, enlightening, freeing, and between steamy encounters as they waited for rancour to hit and for both of them to admit to it all being a terrible mistake, sometimes they actually managed to talk.

'You were at the airport?'

Leo was watching her get ready for birthday drinks with Brenda. It had meant another trip to her flat to get more of her things and very soon she would have spent more nights at Leo's than her own home. He had suggested they go to Paris for Valentine's Day, which was looming, and Lizzie was explaining why she didn't like to be too far away.

'Yes,' Lizzie said, pulling down her lower eyelid and applying black kohl on the inner rim. 'We were going to travel for a year—see the world.' They had spoken about exes and, as innocent as Lizzie was compared to Leo, it had come as a surprise to both that neither had lived with another person. Not that they were living together, both had hastily agreed, it had been just little while after all.

But it was heading into record time for Leo.

The lack of condoms was already a new record.

So too making plans that fell into next month.

He lay on the bed, half listening, half thinking, as Lizzie spoke on.

'My neighbour called and said that Mum had fallen,'

'What did Peter say?'

'Not much,' Lizzie admitted, putting down her eyeliner, remembering that awful time. She had been so excited about her trip but also so nervous to leave her parents—sure that something would go wrong. And it had. She hadn't even made it onto the plane. 'Mum had fractured her hip and was going to Theatre. Peter seemed to think I should ring and see how she was doing when we landed…'

'Clearly, Peter didn't know you very well.' She turned and gave a pale smile at his comment because in the short time they had been seeing each other Leo seemed to understand her more than anyone else ever had.

'He said that it was him or them. That if I didn't get on the plane…'

'Hadn't he heard of rescheduling?' Leo drawled. 'Didn't you have flight insurance?'

'It was a bit more complicated than that,' Lizzie said, but he did make her giggle about even the most serious thing.

'So you chose your parents?'

'Of course,' Lizzie said. 'I could never have gone away knowing my mum was about to have surgery. Now do you see why I don't want to go to Paris?'

'No.' He came over and looked at her. She was all dressed up and ready to go out and her freshly painted lips really begged to be made naked by his mouth. 'If anyone should have a hang-up about going to Paris then I win—my mother died in a helicopter crash, coming back from a party there.' He took her cheeks in his hands as she gave a shocked gasp. 'Does that mean I'm supposed to boycott France?' Despite the dark subject matter, he still made her smile. 'Only take the Euro Tunnel just so that history never repeats itself?'

'I don't know,' Lizzie admitted. 'I just remember the guilt, how awful I felt. I don't expect anyone to understand but I'm all they've got. Even my moving to London was so massive to them...' She was truly shocked at what he had just told her. 'Do you miss them?'

'I've never really had the time to miss them,' Leo said. 'I've been too busy cleaning up after their mistakes.'

Lizzie looked at him for a long moment. No wonder he dreaded the thought of commitment—he was still bearing the cost of his parents' lack of commitment to anything other than themselves.

'Not all relationships are like your parents', Leo.'

'Of course not,' Leo quipped. 'Take...' He pretended to think for a moment then gave a very wry smile. 'I can't think of too many shining examples. Think about Paris...'

'I already have.' It was getting late, she had to go. 'The answer's no.'

It wasn't a row, it wasn't even close to one, but as Lizzie sat in the taxi on her way to visit her friends she felt as if the clock was ticking towards the end of them. They were both so completely different. Leo often said his only responsibility was to his patients and he intended to keep it that way. She had been born responsible.

'Where have you been?' Brenda scooped her into a hug. 'Have you dropped off the planet or something?'

'I'm here now.' Lizzie grinned, handing over her present and ordering a drink.

'You're seeing someone.' Haley was straight onto it. 'Come on, Lizzie, who?'

And she almost told them but changed her mind, because that would make what she and Leo had more real—maybe in a few weeks she could tell them about her crazy time with Leo Hunter, maybe she could sob into her margarita with friends, but for now all Lizzie wanted to do was protect whatever she had with Leo, instead of handing it over to others for discussion.

It was the same with her parents.

Lizzie walked along Brighton beach at the weekend, trying to come up for breath after a dizzying time with Leo.

It was so cold that her teeth were chattering as she looked out to the grey churn of the sea. Lizzie had always loved this time of year in her home town—the summer tourists were long gone, the Christmas shoppers had left and it was just bare and beautiful and recovering, getting ready to start all over again.

She wanted to share it with Leo, she wanted to walk along the pier and go on rides that would be almost empty now. She wanted to take him to her favourite coffee shop and share this part of herself with him.

She missed him and it was just a weekend, Lizzie thought. Soon she'd have to miss him for the rest of her life.

How are they?

A text from Leo maybe meant he was missing her at this moment too but as she answered Lizzie kept the details sparse. Leo was out with some prominent people tonight and he was being interviewed on television tomorrow about the hazards of cosmetic surgery and people who went overseas for cheap procedures. She didn't share that her mum had broken her watch again and kept forgetting it was being repaired and so was frantically searching for it, or that her father kept asking questions about the ball and Leo. Lizzie knew as she fired back a suitably upbeat reply that Leo didn't need to hear it and she also knew something else—he'd been right about Paris.

Her world really was too small.

CHAPTER FOURTEEN

'WE COULD JUST keep it simple—red roses and choc-olates.' Leo only briefly looked up as Lizzie walked in. It had been a couple of weeks since she'd visited her parents and she was going again this weekend for her mother's birthday. 'Shan't be a moment,' he said to Lizzie, then resumed his conversation with Lexi.

'Won't it be an issue if their partners don't know that they're coming to the clinic?' Lexi said.

'They can always say no,' Leo commented. 'I'm not having gifts sent to their house or anything.' He looked at Lizzie. 'We're discussing Valentine's Day,' he ex-plained, and Lizzie gave a wry smile, because Leo had no problem giving his heart to his patients. 'Lexi's wor-ried that I'm going to upset a few husbands.'

'Well, it wouldn't be the first time.' Lexi smiled and stood. 'I'll have a think and get back to you.'

'Would you have liked flowers and chocolates on Valentine's Day if you'd had your surgery scheduled then?' Leo asked when Lexi had closed the door.

'Keep trying, Leo,' Lizzie teased as he resumed their game. 'I'm never going to tell you.'

'Tonight.' Leo's blue eyes turned black as he looked at her, lust turned on like a laser that in an instant made her burn. His voice was very matter-of-fact as he told her exactly what he was going to do. 'All lights on, I'm going to strip you naked and I'm going to explore every inch of you, and this time,' unlike the countless other times, 'I won't get distracted. I *am* going to find out.' He opened a desk and pulled out his ophthalmoscope. 'I haven't used this in a while.' He pressed the intercom on his desk. 'Gwen, could you bring me some batteries for my ophthalmoscope, please?' He gave her a wicked smile. 'Every inch,' he said, and Lizzie stood there, heat washing through her at the thought of Leo exploring every inch of her skin. 'So, what *do* you want to do for Valentine's Day—or do I have to surprise you?' Leo asked.

'Actually…'

'I assume Paris is still out of bounds?'

'Leo…' She tried to get back to the reason she had come into see him in the first place. 'I actually came into say that I needed that afternoon off. My mum's having a small procedure and it's scheduled for four p.m. on that day…'

Leo just looked. He wanted to say 'It's Valentine's Day' but he knew it wasn't his place, that would sound like a ten-year-old whining. It was her mother, for God's sake, but he certainly wasn't used to spending Valentine's Day alone.

'I can pick you up from Brighton.'

'Leo, she'll be confused. I'll probably spend the night there…' It was actually a tiny procedure her mother was having—the removal of a tiny basal cell carcinoma on her forehead—and in truth Lizzie probably didn't even need to be here. Yes, she was hiding because she didn't want the hearts and roses and to be made love to, didn't want the perfect Valentine's Day to happen because every one after that would be a pale comparison.

With each passing day and certainly with each passing night, Lizzie was becoming more aware that every single Valentine's Day, no matter her future, would not compare to *one* spent with Leo.

'Lizzie.' Leo was struggling, he wanted her in a way he never had another woman, and that unnerved him too. An ever-efficient Gwen came in with the batteries for his ophthalmoscope and a message for Lizzie, and he registered Lizzie's rapid blink as she read it.

'Is everything okay?'

'I'm not sure,' Lizzie said, as she read the brief message. 'I'd better get on.' She saw his concern and moved to reassure him. 'It's nothing to with the clinic.'

Which should reassure him, but this time it didn't.

He shouldn't be getting so involved, Leo told himself, but he sought her out a little while later and found her hiding in her office, trying to pretend everything was okay, though it was clear to Leo she was close to crying.

'It's nothing too major,' Lizzie said when pressed. 'They think Mum's got a UTI.'

'A urinary tract infection can be serious in the elderly,' Leo said. 'How bad is she?'

'More confused than ever,' Lizzie said. 'They've got a nurse specialling her and they've started antibiotics, but if she gets worse they're going to have to transfer her to hospital.'

'Are you going to go and see her?' He didn't understand the shrill laugh that came out of her mouth. 'Lizzie, if your mother's not well…'

'She's never well,' Lizzie said. 'Yes, maybe I should

go and see her now or do I wait till she's worse and see
her in the hospital or do I...?' Her shoulders were shaking as he took them in his hands, glimpsing the never-
ending quandary she was in. 'I can't drop everything
all the time but the one time I don't dash to see her I
know it will be the time...'

'Get your coat,' Leo said.

She gave a weary nod. It was almost four. If she left
now she might miss the worst of the traffic and if she
left really early tomorrow she could be back in time
for work...

'What are you doing?' Lizzie asked, as Leo came
back, his jacket on, telling Gwen he was going on a
house call and wouldn't be back, and then he led her to
his car. 'I live two minutes away.'

'I'm taking you to see your mother,' Leo said. 'You're
upset, I don't want you driving.'

'No.' Lizzie shook her head. 'I was going to stay
the night and drive back in the morning. You wouldn't
want...' She couldn't imagine him at the Hewitts and
she couldn't imagine the Hewitts if she and Leo shared
a bed! 'I stay at a bed and breakfast, they're old family friends.'

'Why don't we just see how she is first?' Leo was
practical. 'If you need to stay you can make a booking;
if not, we'll come back. We can stop at home and get
our things just in case...' He pulled out into the heavy
London traffic and, realising what he had just said, corrected himself. 'Do you want to go to your place first?'

'No.'

There wasn't any point—everything she needed for
an overnight stay was already at Leo's.

It was a long, slow drive but they were chatting so

much that a traffic jam didn't really matter. She showed him the bed and breakfast they might be staying in that night and forewarned him about the nylon sheets and the rules of the kitchen.

'Last booking is at seven-thirty,' Lizzie said. 'I always want to tell them that I'll eat out but they take it so personally.'

'So you eat there to please them?' Leo grinned.

'No,' Lizzie corrected. 'I eat there so as not to offend them.'

They pulled up at the nursing home and Lizzie hesitated as Leo turned off the engine and went to get out.

'You don't have to visit.'

'I know.'

'It might just…' She didn't know how to put it delicately. 'Dad might have some questions.'

'I'm a friend,' Leo said. 'I'm also your boss. Won't your father be pleased to know that you didn't have to drive yourself? Won't it help him to know that you've got people who care about you?'

He did care, that much he was more than willing to admit.

'Of course,' Lizzie lied.

Leo simply didn't get it. The only person he answered to was himself and his mere presence would set off a whole load of questions—not tonight but in the future.

'Lizzie!' Shelby, the nurse, gave her a beaming smile as Lizzie and Leo walked in, and went a little bit pink when she saw Leo. 'Your mum's actually picking up a bit. The antibiotics seem to be kicking in and we've been giving her lots to drink. I'm so sorry for scaring you…'

'Don't be,' Lizzie said. 'I'd far rather you rang and let me know what's happening than not. Is the nurse still specialling her?'

'No. Your dad's in there with her. She's a lot more settled and her temperature has started to come down.'

A little bit more gingerly than usual, Lizzie went in.

'Lizzie!' Her dad stood, clearly shocked at the sight of a man with his daughter, but, then, Lizzie reasoned as she made the introductions, her dad would be shocked if she'd had her hair cut—he simply loathed any change in routine.

He always had, Lizzie thought as she approached Faye.

'Hi, Mum.'

'Have you got my watch?'

'I'm trying to find it,' Lizzie answered patiently. 'I hear you haven't been feeling well.'

'Who are you?'

Even the ten thousandth time hurt and Leo saw the brief flicker of pain in her eyes.

'It's me, Lizzie.'

'And who are you?' She looked at Leo. 'Have you got my watch?'

'I haven't got your watch, Mrs Birch,' Leo said. 'I'm Leo, a friend of Lizzie's.' He could see the tension in her father's face. 'She was upset so I offered to drive her.'

'Are you staying at the Hewitts'?' her father snapped to Lizzie, but it was Leo who answered.

'Lizzie was going to stay if her mother wasn't well but I have to get back tonight.'

'Oh,' Thomas huffed, only slightly appeased, but then he turned to his wife when she surprised everyone.

'Lizzie!' Faye's smile was wide.

'Hi, Mum.' Lizzie went over and kissed her again as if she'd just walked in. 'How are you feeling?'

'Not so bad...' She looked at Leo. 'Who's this?'

'I'm Leo,' Leo answered again. 'I'm a friend of Lizzie's.'

'It's lovely to see you with someone...' Faye said to her daughter, and Lizzie cringed. She usually craved her mother's rare moments of near-lucidity—the times when Faye actually recognised her daughter, and they could have an almost normal conversation, but did she have to do her reminiscing in front of Leo? 'Better looking than that Peter,' Faye said. 'He was no good for Lizzie,' she told Leo. 'Lizzie has wanted a husband and children since the day she was born and all Peter wanted....' Her voice trailed off as she lost her train of thought. 'Have you seen my watch, Lizzie?'

Leo was actually fantastic with them but, then, naturally he would be, Lizzie reminded herself. He had a fantastic bedside manner. He chatted with her father about the traffic and it was a relief for Lizzie not to have to go over and over every detail of the journey down to Brighton for once. She left it to Leo and sorted her mum's hair and encouraged a couple of drinks of lemonade into her.

'Has she got any cranberry juice?' Lizzie asked, because she always brought some with her but yet again it had gone missing.

'I'll go and get some,' Leo offered.

'The shop will be closed.'

'I'll find somewhere.'

He did. Leo was back ten minutes later.

'The garage had some.'

Lizzie could only smile. Leo would have no idea

how much cranberry juice cost, let alone care that it was double the price at the garage.

It was all these tiny things that constantly rammed home to Lizzie that their worlds were completely different.

The drive home was a slightly strained one. Leo might not know much about the cost of cranberry juice but he did know the cost of other things. The home her parents were in would cost a small fortune and, as they chatted, he soon worked out that, no, it hadn't all been covered by the sale of their house and Lizzie was paying for a lot of things.

'It must be a strain.'

'It is.' Lizzie could now admit it. 'But growing up they gave me everything—it's the least I can do.'

Her selflessness unnerved him. That she would give everything she had to ensure her parents' comfort, that she would drop everything for what had turned out to be a simple UTI.

'Well, at least you won't have to go this weekend.' He turned and briefly looked at her. 'Given that you've already been. Which is good because I've got a dinner to go to on Saturday and—'

'Today was a bonus visit,' Lizzie interrupted, with an edge to her voice. 'Of course I'm still going this weekend, it's Mum's birthday.'

'You are allowed to have a life, Lizzie.'

'I do have a life,' Lizzie snapped back. 'And this is it.'

It wasn't a row, it was an almost row.

Both confirmed it when, for the first time, that night they didn't make love.

Or have sex.

Or whatever Leo told himself it was.

He lay on his back as she slept beside him, going over all that her mother had said about Lizzie wanting a husband and babies.

Lizzie, Leo decided as he finally drifted off to sleep, really had terrible taste in men, because if it was a husband and babies she wanted, what on earth was she doing here with him?

Lizzie woke to the sound of Leo's phone buzzing and listened as he took a call from Ethan.

'I can see them when I get into work…' Leo yawned, his hand moving to Lizzie and stroking her bottom, their almost row forgotten, his mouth working the back of her shoulder as Ethan spoke on. 'I don't care if it's the end of the working day in the Solomon Islands…' He put his hand over her mouth to stifle Lizzie's giggle. 'Okay,' Leo snapped. 'I'll take a look now.' He let out a long sigh as he ended the call. 'Ethan wants me to go over some details on a patient he thinks the clinic might be able to help.'

'Is he coming over?'

'I'm afraid so. My brother with a cause is like a…'

'A what?'

'I don't know.' Leo yawned. 'I haven't had a coffee yet.'

'I'll get us one.' Lizzie would far prefer he got back to kissing her, but she could use a coffee too.

'Actually…' Leo's voice was rarely tentative. 'He'll be here soon.'

'Getting kicked out without so much as a coffee!' Lizzie kept her voice light but there was an edge to it she couldn't hide as she climbed out of bed.

'You've said many times that you don't want anyone at work knowing.'

'I know.'

She *didn't* want anyone at working knowing.

What was the point?

It would be over soon. It was bad enough trying to get over a guy like Leo, without the world watching, guessing your reaction, asking how you felt.

They were in this strange arena.

Caught somewhere between a fling and a relationship.

Only relationships Leo didn't really do, except it was starting to feel a lot like one. Lizzie was staying at his place most nights and when they decided otherwise, when Lizzie had gone out with friends and come home to her apartment, Leo had caved at one a.m. and called her and ended up coming over to hers.

And as for a fling, yes, it might feel like that way to Leo, but her heart was saying otherwise.

Stupidly Lizzie was close to tears as she took *her* toothbrush from his cupboard and *her* deodorant and, after the quickest wash, pulled her dress on.

'Lizzie…'

He was at the bathroom door, two coffees in hand as she pulled her hair back into a ponytail and fiddled with it for something to do. She was wearing a tight black dress with a high neck. Last night she'd had a smoky grey top over it, but now he could see her bare arms and the slight shake of her hand as she pulled a couple of strands of hair out and tried to make herself look, to commuters' eyes, as if she was going to work, rather than going home after a night not spent in her own bed.

'I found this.' He handed her a missing earring.

Yes, they were at the precipice and it had come far more rapidly than either had thought it might.

All or nothing and neither wanted to make that choice.

She put in her earring and then fiddled with her hair as he stood behind her in the mirror, his trousers on, his chest bare, though she did everything she could not to look. She would give anything rather than have him see her with tears in her eyes over them.

'Have your coffee.' He put a mug down beside the sink.

'It's fine,' Lizzie said. 'I'll grab one on the way.'

'Lizzie.'

Her teeth gritted but to prove she wasn't upset she took a drink.

'Would it be so terrible if Ethan found out?' Leo asked.

'I don't think terrible is the word,' Lizzie said. 'More...' she thought for a moment, '...awkward.'

'I'm sure he's not going to go shouting it to all the staff...'

Which was the whole damn point, Lizzie thought, and she turned to him. 'Would it be so terrible if he did?'

'No,' Leo said carefully. 'As you said, it might just make things a bit awkward.'

'Why?' Lizzie frowned. 'Is it awkward when Abbie and Rafael are there?'

'Of course not,' Leo said. 'They're a team, they're married...' He closed his eyes, not sure where this row had come from, not sure he deserved the label of bad guy here. 'I'm just thinking of you,' Leo said. 'You're the head nurse and—'

'It might not look so good that I'm shagging the boss?'

'Lizzie.'

'You're right.' Lizzie turned around. 'It is better that I go before Ethan gets here—it would make things terribly awkward if he found out, so thanks for the coffee but, no, thanks.' She brushed past him and sat on the sofa and pulled on her boots and then added the grey top and coat and scarf. 'We should have done this in summer.'

'Sorry?'

'It's not very easy to make a rapid exit in the middle of winter. I'll be climbing down the fire escape at this rate,' she said, picking up her bag.

'I don't know what's going on here, Lizzie.' As always, he got to the point. 'I've said stay, I've said let Ethan know…'

'I know.' She breathed out loudly. This anger in her stomach just had to be released, she just wanted to get away from him.

'Come over tonight,' Leo said, and he did something he never had before. 'I'm operating this afternoon.' He took a key from the dresser in the hall. 'Just…' Those stupid tears were back as she watched him close her fingers around the metal. 'Let yourself in.'

She wanted to argue, wanted to tell him she didn't want his key, that it was killing her to get closer, that there was more and more she'd have to give back—the key, the suit he'd left at her flat, the cufflinks, the tie, and there were her favourite shoes under his bed. She couldn't end it and leave them here. And there were a couple of movies she'd brought over…

'See you.' She almost turned her head as he went to give her a kiss but he captured her cheeks and kissed her properly, nicely, deeply, and then, before he asked her a question, he wisely held her wrists.

'Are you getting your period?'

She almost went to lift her hand but his grip tightened and she gave a wry smile at his foresight. She was in a dangerous mood, an unpredictable mood.

'Are you worried that I might be pregnant?'

'No,' Leo said. 'I'm just trying to account for your mood.'

'It's not very twenty-first century to ask a woman—'

'I don't care.'

'Yes, Leo,' Lizzie duly said. 'I have raging PMS, of course that's what's wrong.' She pulled her hands away and opened the door. 'I'll see you at work.' She heard the lift and guessing it could well be Ethan she headed for the stairs, but Leo halted her.

'You're not, are you?'

And she looked at him, a man who, no doubt, could not think of anything worse.

'No, Leo. I'm not pregnant. Your carefree days aren't over.'

She loathed the breath he let out and the relief in his eyes at her answer and ran down the stairs as if someone was chasing her.

Something was.

Lizzie stepped onto the street and the tears she'd been holding back tumbled out there and then. So much for dressing for the commuters. There was a mad woman sobbing as she walked, because, of all the stupid things to go and do, she was head over heels in love with him.

Real love.

A few weeks in and despite her best efforts not to she was thinking stupid things—like a life with Leo, and babies and having that heart to herself. And it was stupid, it was mad, and she'd waited this long because she wanted Mr Right.

She'd just never known Mr Right would also be Mr Completely Wrong and Never Want to be Tied Down.

It wasn't his fault.

Leo was who he was.

She just happened to love him.

CHAPTER FIFTEEN

IT WAS A bad day at the office.

Leo and Ethan were bunkered down in Leo's office for most of the day but the tension from behind the door seemed to seep out and attach itself to everyone.

Rafael looked almost grey as he dashed back between theatre cases to check on a child who had a post-operative fever. Lizzie was trying to calm the mother down more than the baby when a grim-faced Rafael pulled her aside.

'I asked you to tell her to take the baby over to the Lighthouse for me to examine him.'

'I know that,' Lizzie said, 'but she thought I said we would see him here and then, if needed, transfer him to hospital. It was a simple miscommunication.'

Lizzie could see he was holding onto his temper—a simple miscommunication, with Rafael's heavy operating list, was something he simply did not need. On top of that he had a wife in America and a very sick baby of his own to worry about.

'Will you give him his first dose of antibiotic and arrange for him to be admitted?' Rafael asked.

'Of course,' Lizzie said. 'Rafael…' She wanted to ask how things were but Leo had said not to and she saw too the warning in Rafael's eyes for Lizzie not to go there so she changed what she was about to say. 'I am sorry for the mix-up.'

His anger dimmed then and he gave a small nod of thanks for her about turn and gave a wry smile and Lizzie saw a glimpse of the real Rafael—gorgeous, passionate, and terribly Italian. He apologised for his non-outburst with his smile and his eyes. 'That's not a problem—it *was* a simple miscommunication.'

It was more of the same all day. Ethan left looking boot-faced and then Leo headed over to Kate's, where he had surgery scheduled into the evening, but he did stop by her office to say goodbye.

'I don't know what happened this morning.'

Lizzie looked up at him.

'I think…' He just looked at her and she looked back at him—a man who didn't hang around waiting for the rows to start, a man who saved work for work, not relationships.

'Maybe it's better not to think sometimes,' Lizzie said.

Leo nodded.

He didn't want to think about that morning's row, he didn't want to acknowledge they'd lain in his bed together but apart last night, bristling with rancour—like some miserable married couple who saved sex for birthdays and anniversaries.

It was just one night, he reasoned.

Couples rowed sometimes.

He just didn't want to be half of that couple that rowed sometimes.

'That function I have to attend on Saturday,' Leo said. 'Lexi's pushing for a response…'

'I told you.' Lizzie looked up at him. 'I'm seeing my parents this weekend.'

Leo just looked at her. 'These things are bad enough at the best of times,' he attempted, 'without having to go alone.' He was trying to keep his voice even, what the hell was the point of having a plus one if she couldn't even attend? What the hell was the point in committing to a relationship if she was never around?

And Lizzie looked at him. Why should she drop her visit to her parents for a man who was going to drop her any time soon?

It was unsustainable.

The both knew it.

'Come over tonight,' Leo said, but she shook her head. 'Come over,' Leo repeated. 'You know that we need to talk.'

'Talk, then.'

'We can't here.'

She blew out a breath and nodded. They had to work together after all so they had to end it, and neatly.

Nicely.

Lizzie did consider just heading home, maybe they should write today off as a bad one, yet she knew it was more than that.

Cracks were appearing and Leo wasn't one for papering over them, whereas she had the sudden image of her rushing around with a trowel in a frantic attempt to repair them before everything was broken.

It had to be over, Lizzie knew that.

How, though?

How did you end something so wonderful just because you knew it couldn't last?

Wait till it's horrible, wait till the rows start?

They were almost there.

Lizzie took the lift up to his flat and as she stepped out she blinked as she saw a huge bunch of roses and chocolates there and was reminded just how very nice Leo could be—that in the middle of a very long day he had taken the time to think of her.

Of them.

Lizzie wasn't really one for red roses but she read the card.

'Seeing as you can't make it for Valentine's I thought we could have our own tonight. Lx'

They couldn't make it.

Both of them knew.

Oh, God.

They were over, and both knew it.

Tonight was their goodbye, their Valentine's. Before they took to fighting, before things turned bitter, they would end it nicely.

She wasn't overthinking things—in the little time they'd been together they had come to know each other well.

Too well perhaps, Leo thought as he finished operating and headed to the changing rooms.

Rafael was there, getting changed to head over to the Lighthouse, he told Leo.

'How are Abbie and Ella?' Leo asked, but Rafael was in no mood to talk. He just gave some vague answer and then said he was in a rush.

Leo wished Rafael would speak with him but really he couldn't blame him for not doing so. After all, the last thing Leo wanted to do was discuss his feelings for Lizzie with anyone.

Maybe Ethan?

Yeah, that would go down well.

He and Lizzie were too close for comfort, Leo thought as he drove home.

The traffic was bad, he'd have been quicker walking or at least taking the Tube, but he was actually glad of the pause before he got home to Lizzie.

Home to Lizzie.

He was growing far too used to that and Leo wasn't used to relying on anyone.

How, in just a few weeks, had she come to be such a part of his life? Leo didn't like it, loathed the thought that he might ever need another person.

As he pulled up his phone rang and, seeing it was Lexi, Leo took the call.

'I need a response for Saturday,' Lexi said. 'I've been putting it off.'

So had Leo.

'Yes, I'll be attending.'

'Who's your guest?' Lexi asked. 'They need it for the table plan.'

He sat and stared out of the window. The wipers were still going and he watched the light bouncing off the black roads and he paused for a long moment before answering.

'I'm not sure yet. I'll let you know in the morning.'

Lexi didn't turn a hair. It was a regular response from Leo. He always left things like this till the last minute—his low attention span with women ensured that names could not be given weeks in advance.

He'd asked Lizzie, but she'd said no.

You could always go alone, a voice that sounded like his own told him.

'Why?' Leo said to the silence. 'Why should I?'

Because that's what relationships are about, that small voice told him.

Compromise.

It wasn't something he did well.

As the door opened Lizzie's back was towards him. He saw her putting roses in the vase, he could see her slender arms and the curve of her bottom in the fitted skirt, and he just wanted to go over, turn her around and just bury himself in her, yet he held back.

'They're for you.'

'I know,' Lizzie said, 'but for all the time I'm at home…' She halted, saw the brief look in his eyes and simply didn't want go there just yet. Neither did Leo. 'Let's just enjoy them tonight.'

She walked towards him, smiling, and he pulled her into his arms, inhaled the fragrance of her hair, held the woman he had come home to and hated it that he wasn't capable of making their relationship last but he just did not believe in forever.

He was hurting her. Every day that they were together would simply make the parting harder, and so instead of diving into a kiss he headed over to the dresser and, rarely for Leo, poured a drink. 'Do you want one?' he offered.

'Not if I'm driving.'

He hesitated but poured two.

'It's not working, is it?' Lizzie was the one who broached the subject. 'It hasn't been since you visited the nursing home.'

'It's not that.'

Lizzie didn't believe him. 'Leo, what my mum said about a husband and babies was a ten-year-old Lizzie she was remembering.'

'So you don't want that?' Leo glanced over.

'I do.' Lizzie was honest enough to admit it. 'But I know that's not for you—I know what she said freaked you out.'

He held his breath. It had freaked him out but not in the way Lizzie was thinking—it was more that she deserved someone who could give her all that she wanted when he honestly didn't think he could. 'Why would it freak me out?' he asked. 'I already told you it's not for me.'

They stood there and the usual response would have been, *So where are we going, then*? Except Lizzie had always known the answer.

Nowhere.

'I don't want to fight,' Leo said. He loathed arguments more than anything, loathed the sound of raised voices as people hurtled out of control.

Leo was always in control—always a step ahead, always making sure that it never came to that.

It had possibly saved Ethan's life.

It had certainly messed up his own.

He looked at Lizzie, so loving and warm, so where he wanted to be, yet the gap between them was a chasm he could not breach.

'We're not fighting, Leo, we're talking.'

Ah, but about their relationship, he thought.

'Can you come on Saturday?' he asked. 'I have to give Lexi the name of the person accompanying me by the morning.'

She could do it, Lizzie knew that. She could head down to Brighton on Friday instead of Saturday, hit the worst of the traffic, and then race back Saturday afternoon, but they had birthday cake after dinner at the nursing home. Her father would be devastated if she wasn't there—and for what?

Another night in Leo's bed, then perhaps another.

For a glimpse of a future, she'd do it, but he denied them both that.

'Leo…'

As she went to answer he walked over to her. He didn't want to hear that, no, she couldn't come, neither did he want the question about where they were heading, because it was a path he'd always refused to take.

So he kissed her.

A kiss that offered more escape than the brandy he'd barely touched.

'Leo…' She pulled back a bit and then gave in, because she wanted him so much, wanted that mouth that was on hers, that was kissing her top lip, over and over. Lizzie wanted him every bit as much as he wanted her.

They were frenzied as they set themselves free from an impossible conversation. He pushed her down so they were half leaning on the sofa, half kneeling on the floor, so their mouths barely need to part to undress each other. Frantic, deep kisses, till Lizzie was down to her bra and shoes and Leo was kissing her chest and up to her neck. He should rise, should get out of his trousers, but the taste of her skin and her hands pressing into his back were the only things Leo could think of.

His lips trailed a path from her neck to a mouth that was waiting and then he moved back down, over and over, tasting her skin till her neck was arching. Just inhaling her and crushing her as she pulled at his zipper and freed him, and continuing to kiss her. Concentrating on the same areas over and over—the neck he would never again kiss, the breasts that would tease and the mouth that would, from tomorrow, forever taunt him.

He didn't do for ever, Leo reminded himself, except he wasn't listening to himself now.

Lizzie wrapped a leg around him and sobbed as Leo stabbed into her. She rose to him, tightened her leg around him, and she almost just wanted this done, because his mouth was driving her crazy. Dizzy and crazy, because how could he kiss her with such passion when soon he would want her gone?

Lizzie curved into him, pressed herself to him, but then he slowed things down, thrusting slowly and deeply inside her, his mouth to her ear as her body urged him on.

'Please…' Lizzie said.

She wanted this done.

She lied.

'Please…' she begged to a groin that thrust slowly, to a mouth that was roaming her ear. She was coming and Leo refused to and she *hated* his control. *Hated it* that he could now look down and watch her come as he still moved deep inside her. Hated how his blue eyes could reproach her as they made love, as if it was she who was messing with his head, rather than the other way around.

Then she saw him, felt him briefly still, and watched the moment when Leo gave in—the grimace and the pleasure and the bliss of escape as he moved now and filled her with the most intimate part of him.

She didn't want it to end.

It just had.

'Lizzie…' He looked down at her. He didn't even know what it was he was going to say, he had never wanted to hurt her and whatever way it went now, surely he would.

He kissed her eyes and her cheeks and then met her gaze, and he could see the tears in her eyes that he'd put there.

She wriggled from under him, but he didn't let her go.

The trowel had been passed to him now—it was Leo frantically plastering over the cracks. 'I was thinking, if you went and saw your parents early and then came back…'

'Leo, it's Mum's birthday on Saturday.'

Leo's jaw gritted.

'They do a cake at dinnertime,' Lizzie explained.

'Can't they do it at lunch?'

He let her go then, sat on the sofa as she moved for her clothes, it was all so easy for him.

He tried, though. 'I'm not saying don't go, just that you were there yesterday, you could be there for her birthday—you don't have to drop everything…'

'But I do,' Lizzie said, and stood to pull on her skirt. 'And I will continue to do so. Leo, you seem to think yesterday was an anomaly, a brief inconvenience, but the last few weeks have actually been very quiet for me. Often I'm there every weekend with one drama or another…'

'You make it harder on yourself.'

'I never said it was hard.'

'Actually, you did.' Leo could be a bastard sometimes. 'Several times.'

'Oh, I'm to drop everything because you've got a dinner on Saturday with the directors of Kate's?'

'You drop everything for them.'

'And I will continue to do so.' Lizzie was dressed now. 'For as long as they're alive I will drop everything if they need me.'

'That's your choice.'

'Yes, it is.'

'If you ask me—'

'I'm not.' Lizzie just stood there. 'I'm not asking your opinion on family. I'm not asking someone who's so royally screwed up every relationship he's ever had to tell me how I should handle mine. Yes, my parents are a huge part of my life, yes, I might have not much to show for it, but I'm content with my choices.'

'Content.'

'Too boring for you, Leo?' Lizzie challenged. 'I happen to like content, I happen to like sleeping and waking and living guilt-free. I've always known what I wanted—whether I'll get it might be another thing, but I wanted to be a nurse and I wanted a family of my own, and a career, not screwing and partying and trying to outrun hell. It catches up, Leo…'

'Not if you don't let it.' Leo shrugged. 'I was right the first time.'

'What?' Lizzie's head snapped round as she picked up her bag to go, to walk out. 'Yes, I'm running into the woods, never to be seen again,' she snarled. 'Don't worry, I'll be fine at work.'

Only Leo wasn't referring to a fairy-tale, he was referring to a conversation that had taken place even before he'd met her.

'Saint Lizzie…' Leo drawled, his scalpel sharpened, ready to lance this once and for all. 'You're a martyr, Lizzie…' He could be very scathing at times. 'You really do need to get out more…'

'Oh, I'm getting out, Leo,' Lizzie said. 'Just a little too late.'

She walked away and he wanted to call her back, to catch her and turn her around, but he just stood there.

He heard the door slam.

The lift bell pinged and he should run and stop her, tell her they could sort something out.

But what?

He looked at the roses, taunting him because romance was the only part he could do. The compromise, the rows, he did not.

Ah, but the making up afterwards?

It had never dawned on him that you could.

Leo wrenched open the door, went to run down the stairs, but for what?

Lizzie knew what she wanted from life.

He walked back into the apartment to the scent of her mingled with roses and he unleashed his anger at himself, slamming the vase from the table with his hand. The crash and splinter of the glass barely registered, such was the noise in his head.

Back to being single.

Again.

CHAPTER SIXTEEN

STEPPING INTO 200 Harley Street the next morning was amongst the hardest things Lizzie had ever done.

Thankfully the door to Leo's office was closed and remained so.

She got through the morning as best she could but, of course, Ethan noticed.

'Are you okay?' Ethan checked, and Lizzie forced a smile.

'Of course I am,' Lizzie said. 'Mum's been a bit unwell,' she offered, and then halted, very aware she was using her parents as an excuse.

When Ethan had gone she sat at the desk in her office and the tears came, not about the row the previous night but because, damn him, Leo was right. Oh, he'd put it terribly, but she was hiding behind her parents. Of course they could have had cake at lunchtime and, yes, she could have had her mother's surgery rescheduled, of course she didn't have to stay overnight. It had been the excuse she'd needed to shield her from the full blaze of Leo, the distance between them necessary if she was somehow to protect her heart.

It hadn't worked, though.

Her heart, for the first time ever, was truly broken.

Ethan heard her tears from behind her closed door and, incensed, marched into Leo's office.

'What's going on with Lizzie?' Ethan demanded.

'Nothing, as far as I know.'

'Come off it, Leo. I know you two are on together—everyone knows.'

'Were on,' Leo corrected him. 'We just finished.'

'I told you to back off.'

'And I chose not to listen.' Leo shrugged, guilt at his handling of things making him more cutting than usual. 'Anyway, what does it have to do with you?' Leo frowned. 'Is there something I'm missing here? Because you seem terribly attached to your little nurse. Did a bit more than dressings go on during the home visits?'

'You know they didn't.'

'Was she taking care of more than your legs?' Leo jeered, and, war hero or not, injured or not, Leo had his brother against the wall.

'What does it matter to you?' Ethan taunted. 'You just said you two were finished.' They were stepping into very dangerous territory, the same anger and jealousy that had ripped through Leo when he'd found out that the woman he had fallen hard for had been on with Ethan was coming between them again. 'Go on,' Ethan goaded, 'hit me.' Leo raised his fist. 'We both know you won't.'

'You're not worth it,' Leo snarled, dropping his fist.

'Backing off, are you, Leo?' Ethan's lip curled. 'Let's see how you smooth this over. Let's see you charm your way out of it, or,' he said, talking now about Leo's handling of their father, 'why don't you pour me a drink?'

Leo nearly did hit him then, but instead he fought with his mouth.

Ethan would have far preferred his fist.

'You know what, Ethan, for all that you loathe me, your anger's misdirected. I stopped him—I wasn't enabling him, I preferred him unconscious at times. Do you really think I wanted that drunk bastard's temper unleashed on you?' Leo had him back up against the wall again but this time with words. 'You're my brother—my younger brother. Do you really think I'd just step back and let you at him?'

Ethan's face screwed up in fury but Leo didn't relent. 'Hate me all you like, Ethan.' He thought of Lizzie, there wasn't a moment that he wasn't thinking of her but right now it was as if she was in the room, her words replaying, Leo's truth coming out now. 'At least you're alive. You blame me for talking him down or knocking him out with his beverage of choice, instead of letting the whole mess blow up. Would you light the tail of a lion and send someone you love in to deal with it?'

Ethan stood there as Leo said, in the most backward of ways, that he loved him. 'Would you?'

Still Ethan said nothing, so Leo answered for him.

'No, you'd do everything in your power to keep someone you love safe. Hate me if you must, get your kicks that way if it suits you. Just know I stopped that drunk from exploding, not because I'm ignorant or a fool. Instead, I played him, I smooth-talked him round, not because I wanted to appease the drunk but because I was trying to protect you.'

'Okay, I get it...'

'Sure about that?' Leo stepped back. He was breathless. He felt as if his head was exploding, not just from all he had revealed but at the taunt from Ethan about Lizzie.

Ethan was a bit stunned himself to find out that be-hind Leo's mask there were feelings, and perhaps not just for him. He'd never seen Leo explode like that. Oh, he'd come close, but beneath the vitriol there had been real anguish in Leo's voice. At least there he could put him out of his misery.

'Nothing has ever happened between Lizzie and I,' Ethan said.

'It doesn't matter anyway. We're finished.'

'Because?'

'Lizzie's a bit busy with her parents for the next de-cade.'

'She's not going to change things for someone who's not going to change.'

Leo gave a bitter laugh. 'Since when did you get so wise?'

Ethan wasn't going to answer that question. Instead, he answered the other one. 'I promise you there has never been anything at all between Lizzie and I. I think of her more like a sister—I care about her because she was there when I was in a dark place.'

'It's looking pretty black now,' Leo said, looking at his brother who worried him so.

'Yeah, it's black now but I was in hell then, Leo, maybe I still am. Lizzie used to come over to do my dressings and she'd talk and I wouldn't answer, but I did listen. She'd tell me about her parents, little things, nor-mal things, real things. She brought me back to a world that I'd forgotten existed.' Leo wanted to know more but knew better than to push for now—it was the most Ethan had ever spoken about the effects of Afghanistan. 'You know what? You can't keep going like this, Leo.'

'Like what?' Leo said. 'You're the messed up one,

remember?' And then let out a mirthless laugh. He was through talking his way out of it, through fighting it, through pretending that everything was okay. 'I think it's far safer for Lizzie that I carry on as I have been, rather than testing my heart out on her. I should have listened,' he conceded. 'I should have stayed well away.'

CHAPTER SEVENTEEN

TOO LATE, LEO stayed well away.

A pale-faced, red-eyed Lizzie did her best to avoid him as he threw himself back into work and his social life, got straight back on the horse and asked a favourite blonde who knew the rules to join him on Saturday.

And Lizzie did the same.

Or rather she checked herself into the bed and breakfast and spent a weekend trying to assuage the guilt that she'd rather be with Leo than with her parents.

She walked on the beach and remembered getting a text from him, recalling all the thrill and excitement that had been there then, and, instead of crying, she lugged her broken heart into a wheelbarrow and left it sitting there for a little while as she thought about Leo without pain in the mix. She walked and thought of dancing and dressing up and the bliss of that night and every night she had spent with Leo.

With her heart on hold she could examine it without pain. Their time together had been amazing, for the first time she'd had a glimpse of freedom, had tasted exhilaration—how could she possibly regret that?

So she fetched the wheelbarrow and replaced her heart and, yes, she was still better for her time with him.

One big cry, Lizzie decided.

Tonight, after she'd had birthday cake with her parents, she'd head to the shops and get supplies. With chocolate and wine and her favourite movie, she'd lie on nylon sheets and howl, but on Monday, if she valued her job, she'd better work out rather quickly how to face him better.

'I'll be up on Friday.' Lizzie kissed her father goodbye.

'We'll look forward to it, won't we, Faye?' Thomas said to his wife. 'Lizzie's coming up early next weekend. We'll have three days of her.'

'No.' Lizzie's face was on fire. 'I'll be going home on Saturday morning. I'm just coming up for the procedure.'

'I just thought…' Thomas huffed. 'We haven't been seeing so much of you lately.'

'I've got a new job, Dad,' Lizzie said. 'Sometimes I have to go to work functions…' And she just stopped making excuses to her father for actually having a life. 'I need to catch up with some of my friends too.' She gave him a kiss. 'I'll see you on Friday.'

No, she would not be a martyr, Lizzie told herself on Monday as she walked past Leo's office. The door was open and there he was, looking a little seedy.

'Busy weekend?' Lizzie smiled.

'Er, a bit.' He was caught unawares. She'd been busily avoiding him late last week and Leo had been only too happy with that, but it was a very together Lizzie who greeted him now.

She saw his slightly guarded expression as she unbuttoned her coat. 'It's okay, Leo, I'm not going to do a Flora.'

He was surprised at how easily she still made him smile and he bit back his response because he'd been about to say, 'Pity.'

'You're okay?' Leo settled for instead.

'I'm fine.'

'I mean…' Leo wasn't brilliant at apologies. 'I was a bit harsh,' he admitted. 'The things I said about your parents…'

'Were spot on.' Lizzie rolled her eyes. 'I just want to be clear about one thing—you won't get a better head nurse than me.'

'I know that,' Leo said. 'Ethan's worried I've upset you.'

'You can tell Ethan to call off the firing squad. I just needed a few days to lick my wounds.'

'And you're really okay?' Leo checked, not sure if he was actually pleased that she seemed to be.

'Of course,' Lizzie said. 'I know it sounds like a line, but it really was good while it lasted.'

'I hate it that it ended in a row,' Leo admitted.

'It didn't.' Lizzie did the hardest, bravest thing she had ever done. She went over to Leo and with a smile she bent over and gave him a very brief kiss.

'That's how it ended,' Lizzie said.

'How?' Leo frowned. 'Show me again.'

'Nope.' Lizzie stood straight and then headed to her office and breathed out loudly. Yes, it had been amongst the hardest things she had ever done but it had been necessary.

Very necessary to appear completely fine, but it was terribly hard at times.

The chocolates for the patients were delivered on Wednesday, the scent of them driving her crazy, and, of course, Leo had to catch her when she caved in.

'What's behind your hand?' Leo asked as he knocked and without waiting walked into her office.

'Nothing!' But it didn't come out very well with a mouth that was full.

Leo actually had to stop himself from going over and having a little wrestle to get to the chocolates or prising her mouth open with his tongue to get a taste.

Instead, he remembered what he had come in for. 'I need a new prescription pad.'

Not even chocolate on her tongue could disguise the bitter taste as she went and replaced the pad she'd out-lived only marginally.

Ethan had almost been right.

Valentine's Day dawned and Lizzie had to get there early and watch as the florist and her assistant carried bucket after bucket of red roses through the clinic.

It hurt.

She just couldn't let it show.

Though Leo made her laugh when he saw all the roses. 'God, I hope no one's got hay fever.'

'You'd better check the expiry date on the adrenaline shots,' Declan said, and then asked Lizzie what she was up to for Valentine's Day.

'I'm visiting my mum,' Lizzie said. 'So it's not ex-actly a romantic one for me.'

'Oh, well, you can always do Valentine's tomorrow,' Declan said. 'Free and single in London is a very nice place to be.'

'It is.' Lizzie smiled and Leo felt his back straighten a touch. She was trying to make him jealous was his first thought, but, then, Lizzie didn't have to try, he already was.

'You're staying the weekend in Brighton?' Leo asked.

'Nope.' Lizzie kept that smile on. 'Just tonight. I've been a bit absent of late with my friends...'

Leo loathed the thought of Lizzie let loose in London and paced his office floor, stopping as she popped her head in to say goodbye before leaving early for the weekend.

'You've got Francesca at two,' Lizzie reminded him. 'Have a great weekend.'

'Don't forget your flowers,' Leo said, because he'd made sure there was a bouquet for each of the women who worked at the clinic, but, realising it might be a bit insensitive, he added, 'You could take them for your mum.'

He stood there, rigid, as Lizzie just laughed and because it was Friday she let rip just a little some of the hurt she was holding onto, just enough to confuse him.

'If you weren't such a good boss, Leo, I'd tell you where you could shove your flowers. Happy Valentine's Day!'

Wry was the smile on his face when he watched from the window as Lizzie walked down the steps and into the street.

No, she hadn't taken her flowers but, of course, she'd taken the chocolate! He was so busy watching her that he didn't even notice, till he heard a voice, that Ethan had come in and was standing behind him.

'Lizzie,' Ethan said, 'would be the best thing that ever happened to you.'

'I thought you wanted me away from her.'

'It's way too late for that, but if you do love her...'

'What do you know about love?' Leo quipped. Ethan had so easily admitted to Leo that time that he'd only been using Olivia. Ethan's heart was pretty much closed.

'Oh, I know…'

Something in Ethan's voice was enough to tear Leo's gaze from the spectacular sight of Lizzie's rear end and turn round. 'Ethan?'

'Leave it,' Ethan said.

Which meant leave it.

It really did.

Francesca had all her sparkle back.

'Leo!' she greeted him warmly. 'Where's Lizzie?'

'Lizzie's got the afternoon off.' Leo had to stop himself from snapping out his reply.

'Getting herself ready for Valentine's night?' Francesca asked. 'I hope you are taking her somewhere nice.'

'Francesca, the ball we attended together was a work function.'

'Please!' Francesca rolled her eyes but he moved the conversation on. 'What can I do for you, Francesca? And please tell me it doesn't involve surgery.'

Francesca gave a little shiver. 'It's cold.'

'It's a beautiful day,' Leo corrected her, but headed over to the brandy and poured her one.

'Of course I don't want surgery,' Francesca said, 'but I was reading in my magazine abut cosmetic tattooing. My hands are a little shaky these days…'

'You could just have one of these before you put your make-up on,' Leo teased, handing her the brandy.

'It has nothing to do with brandy.' Francesca laughed. 'It is age.'

When it suited her, Leo thought dryly. 'I don't do tattooing.'

'I thought not—it's hardly a tattoo parlour. I just hate Tony seeing me without my eyeliner on,' she said.

'I can give you a name,' Leo said. 'How are you two doing?'

'That's the real reason I'm here.' Francesca smiled. 'We're getting married, Leo!'

He was over in an instant. His favourite patient was getting married, *this time* to a man she loved, and he couldn't be happier for her.

'I'm thrilled for you.' He gave her a hug. 'Hell, you didn't need to make an appointment to come in and tell me that!'

'I know. It's just a small wedding,' Francesca said, and she took out an invitation. 'I put Leo and Lizzie…'

'Just change it and put Leo plus one.'

'I want Lizzie to come.'

'Well, invite Lizzie, then,' Leo said, but his collar suddenly felt tight at the thought of Lizzie's plus one.

'Leo, please listen.'

'Francesca, you are one of my most valued clients but that doesn't mean—'

'I remember your father, Leo. I remember waiting for the first of many facelifts and him falling down drunk. He was a fool.'

'You're not telling me anything I don't know.'

'And I remember your mother.' Francesca would not stop. 'Her affairs and her social life and all the things she put before your brother and you.'

'Just leave it.'

'Is that how you want to be?'

'I don't have affairs.'

'I'm not talking about cheating, I'm talking about family. How old are you, Leo?'

'A lady never asks a gentleman his age...' Leo smiled but he was smarting a little inside. Thirty-eight and a brilliant career to show for it, but a reputation with women that had had Lizzie running off into the woods, or rather choosing a weekend in a nursing home than being in Paris with him.

'I regret and I regret and I regret,' Francesca said, 'because I was too stupidly proud to admit what a fool I'd been and too vain and too young...'

Leo stood to halt her, to let her know his valuable time was up, but Francesca stood too.

'I *am* your friend, Leo,' Francesca said, 'which is why I'm going to tell you this. Do you know one of the reasons I'm so scared of getting old?'

Leo didn't answer.

'There is no more a selfish profession than that of a ballerina...although a surgeon might come a close second.' Leo swallowed as Francesca spoke on. 'I'm not talking about the back end of a chorus line, Leo. I'm talking about being centre stage. These hands...' she held hers up to him '...this face, this body, this neck... do you know how many people were counting on me to be on form?'

'I get it.'

'No, you don't,' Francesca said. 'Because I didn't and now that I am old I realise all the love I let slip through my hands.'

'So, what?' Leo wasn't going to be swayed by Francesca's dramatic musings. 'I'm supposed to marry Lizzie and have lots of children so when I'm old and mad I'm not alone?'

'No,' Francesca said. 'So when you're old and sane you don't spend every day regretting the choices you made.'

'Thanks for the lecture, Francesca.' He was not about to be dictated to by some eccentric patient, but he softened his abruptness with a smile and it was back to doctor mode. Carefully he examined her face. 'Geoff has done a good job,' Leo admitted, but still held his own. 'I wouldn't have put in as much filler, though.'

'I like it,' Francesca said, 'but I think the glow isn't from Geoff's filler, more Tony and I making—'

'I get the picture,' Leo interrupted. That image he really didn't need! 'Right, I'll give you that name of the tattooist and if you decide you *need* something done for your wedding, I hope, this time, you'll listen to me.'

'I will come in and see you.'

'And if I say no, will you listen?'

'Yes, Leo.'

'Because there's no point otherwise,' Leo scolded. 'If I know you're just going to take yourself off to someone else every time you don't get your own way...'

'I will listen to you, Leo.'

'Good.' He went to walk her out then realised he'd almost forgotten. 'Happy Valentine's Day, Francesca...' He kissed his favourite patient on the cheek as he handed her her flowers and chocolates. 'Of course I shan't be offended if you don't take them—I don't want to cause any friction between you and Tony.'

'Ah, a little mystery is a good thing in a relationship.' She held the bouquet and inhaled the scent, just as if she were accepting the accolade on stage. 'But isn't there someone else who you should be giving these to?'

Leo didn't have the heart to tell Francesca the staff-room was filled with the blooms. 'As I said…' Leo gave a tight smile. 'I don't need you to sort out my love life.'

'Love life?' Francesca checked. 'I thought Leo Hunter only had a social life.' She shook her head before walking off. 'You'd be mad to let her go.'

CHAPTER EIGHTEEN

LIZZIE DROPPED OFF her things at the bed and breakfast and told Mrs Hewitt that, no, she didn't want dinner tonight, before heading off to visit her parents.

It was the tiniest procedure.

A visiting surgeon was there for lumps-and-bumps day and Lizzie held her mother's hand as the small lesion was removed.

You missed Valentine's Night in Paris with Leo Hunter for this.

She watched as a small sticking plaster was applied, and stupid tears filled Lizzie's eyes.

'It's not hurting her,' Shelby, the nurse, said. 'He put in lots of anaesthetic.'

'I know,' Lizzie answered. What was hurting was the full realisation that she *had* been hiding, had been trying to stop the hurt—and causing it in the end.

Lizzie took her mum back to her room, helped her into bed and then brought her in some biscuits and tea.

'So you're off in the morning?' Thomas asked.

'Yes, but I'll come and see you before I go,' Lizzie said, dunking the biscuit and feeding it to her mum and seeing her smile from the simple pleasure of a tea-soaked biscuit.

'Nice?' Lizzie asked her mum.

'Lovely,' Faye said. 'Thank you for being here today, Lizzie.'

As clear as a bell Faye said it and Lizzie started to cry because, yes, she'd missed Valentine's night in Paris with Leo but it was now actually worth it for this.

Worth it to see her mum to take out a tissue and wipe her daughter's tears—worth it for a brief moment with her mum that was how it should be.

Not how it was.

'Have you got my watch?'

'Actually, I do.' Lizzie could only laugh. 'I picked it up this afternoon.' She put the watch on her mother's wrist and wished that she could superglue it there. 'I love you, Mum,' Lizzie said, but Faye was back to wherever it was she went.

When the residents had all had dinner and her mum was settled, Lizzie said goodnight.

Lizzie waved to a couple of the other residents as she left and then headed back to the Hewitts', drained and exhausted from a week of pretending to be fine with Leo, and then the sound of her mother's clear voice.

One more big cry, Lizzie decided, and stopped for supplies—she already had chocolate but she bought some more and a nice bottle of wine too.

Oh, and a DVD.

Oh, and a big box of tissues with aloe vera in them so her nose wouldn't be all cracked on Monday.

'Evening, Lizzie.' Mrs Hewitt's eyes lingered on the bag as if she was smuggling in contraband. 'You just made it. Howard was about to close the kitchen.'

'I didn't want dinner,' Lizzie said, even though she was starving, but sitting alone on Valentines night really was about the limit. She could hear the sound of laughter and the chink of glasses coming from the dining room.

'Howard waited for you,' Mrs Hewitt said. Which meant, in her oh-so-passive-aggressive way, "get through there now and eat your dinner!"

'Okay, thanks…' Lizzie said. 'I'll just go and put my coat away.' And sign up for a course on self-assertion, Lizzie thought darkly as she climbed the stairs. She just wanted to be alone and to think about Leo.

Oh, Leo.

She missed him.

Missed his snobbish sense of humour and missed being the other person in his life.

She understood Flora totally now because it would be terribly easy to make a fool of herself, Lizzie thought as she took her phone out of her bag.

Terribly easy to text him and plead for that helicopter to come and whizz her away and to promise she could handle it for a little while longer, even though it could never last.

Put down the phone, Lizzie!

She did as pride told her and put some lip-gloss on instead then chewed it off as she made her way down to the dining room, bracing herself to enter couple's world alone on Valentine's night.

She was sure she was seeing things.

There, rising to stand as she walked in, was Leo.

'He told me to say nothing,' Mrs Hewitt said.

'What are you doing here?' Lizzie asked, trying to tame her heart, trying not to rush over and burst into tears and read far more into this than there was.

'I felt like splurging,' Leo said. 'I ordered three courses and we get a free bread roll and coffee.'

'Stop it.' Lizzie laughed.

'I haven't told you the best bit.' His face was completely deadpan. 'Howard made rum balls with our coffee, given it's Valentine's Day.'

'What *are* you doing here?' Lizzie asked, after Howard had served them their tomato soup, with a very wobbly cream heart drizzled on top.

'I miss you,' Leo answered simply.

'You saw me this morning.'

'You know what I mean.'

She did.

'Mrs Hewitt wouldn't let me into your room…' He always had and always would make her smile. 'I'm across the hall. Can I sneak over?'

'I can't have sex here, Leo. It would be like doing it at home.'

'We'll be very quiet,' Leo said, pressing his knee into hers, 'but we'll have to do it on the floor or we'll self-combust with those nylon sheets.' He saw the glitter of tears in her eyes even as she laughed. 'How was your mum?' he asked, as the second course was served.

'I was just sitting there feeling sorry for myself that I'd missed Paris with you, but then she smiled and thanked me for being there. She really did recognise me.'

'Worth it, then,' Leo said, and it was without even a trace of sarcasm.

'Yes.'

'But it doesn't make it easier.' His insight shocked Lizzie. 'That she does know that you're there sometimes must make you wonder if she misses you when you're not.'

Lizzie nodded and she felt his hand on her cheek but she moved her face, she just couldn't pretend it wasn't agonising. 'The thing is…' Soup was a terribly hard ask and she shredded her roll instead and wondered how best to tell someone you desperately wanted to be with that it hurt too much to pretend. How to tell him that she loved him, which meant she couldn't have sex with him because it came with her heart attached and it was soul-destroying, trying to guard it. 'The thing is,' Lizzie started again. 'You remember when we said it might be awkward, us working together—I think, if we prolong things, we could get to that stage and I still want to work at the clinic so I think we need to—'

'It isn't awkward for Rafael and Abbie.'

'No,' Lizzie said, 'but they're a real couple. Leo…'

'If we were married, would it be less awkward?'

Lizzie's eyes jerked up, sure he was teasing, that she was supposed to give some witty reply—but she was all out of them.

'Please, don't joke.'

'If you knew how nervous I was, you'd know I wasn't joking. Look.' He showed her a small mark on his chin. 'I cut myself shaving.'

'Wow!'

'I mean it,' Leo said. 'I want you to marry me.'

'Leo?' She didn't understand. 'You don't want to get married. You don't want be tied down…' She giggled at his expression. 'You know what I mean, Leo. I have commitments.'

'I know,' Leo said, and Lizzie blinked because he didn't seem fazed.

'Of course, I have to get the mix better, I realise that, but when my parents need me...'

'You'll be here when they do,' Leo said. 'Lizzie, I'm never going to ask you to choose me over them.' He saw the doubt in her eyes and decided to smooth-talk his way around it. 'Lizzie, look at the positives—I have no parents, yours are in a home, we're never going to have to do that awful juggle-the-parents on Christmas Day that other couples have to. I am selfish, but I'm not that selfish that I would keep you from them. We can do it,' he said. 'I'm here, aren't I? On Valentine's Day.'

He was.

'I want to be with you,' Leo said. 'That's all I know. I've never come close to feeling the way I do and I never thought I would. It's true, what you said. I've messed up every relationship I've ever been in—I just know that I'm not going to mess things up with you.

'I love you,' he confessed. 'I don't know what you do to me, Lizzie—I practically told Ethan I loved him last week...'

'You should tell him properly.'

'Yeah, one day.' He looked at her. 'You know there can be no secrets between a husband and wife...'

'Oh, Leo, you shan't get me that way, I've been nursing long enough to know there are plenty of secrets between most husbands and wives.' Then she was serious. 'Please don't ask me about Ethan.'

She watched his jaw tighten, wondered if he'd falter at their first hurdle.

'I won't.' He gave her his word and looked up as Howard came over with their desserts.

'Not for us, thanks,' Leo said.

'But you ordered three courses.'

'We're full.'

Leo took her by the hand and led her up the stairs. 'You can't do that,' Lizzie hissed.

'Well, if I'm going to be staying here at times, they'd better get used to me—I *can* do that!' Leo said, and Lizzie glowed inside as she realised he'd meant every word he'd said back there. The thought of him staying here with her, through all the difficult times to come, made the world suddenly so much easier.

'Let's melt those sheets,' Leo said, as she let him into her room. 'Oh, Lizzie.' He tutted as he went through her bag of contraband and found her wine and chocolate and tragic movie, and she winced when he pulled out the tissues. 'You did miss me.'

He kissed her to the bed, and she wasn't sure if it was the nylon sheets or just the Leo effect but every hair on her skin stood up as he undressed her as they slid into bed.

'Like an old married couple,' Leo said, only he wasn't leaning over to turn off the lamp; instead, he was picking it up.

'What are you doing?' Lizzie asked.

'I forgot my ophthalmoscope. I'm going to find out what you've had done and then you're going to tell me who did it.'

He parted her legs and the Hewitts would have had a fit if they'd known where he shone that lamp. 'Labiaplasty?' Leo said. 'If it was, she did a *fantastic* job.' Lizzie was laughing so hard, turned on so much and so just happy that she nearly forget to tell him the truth.

'No,' Lizzie said, as his fingers admired the handiwork. 'I mean, no, I haven't had any surgery.'

'You lied?' Leo was a touch incredulous. Of all the

things he'd wondered, Lizzie lying to him hadn't entered his head, and to Leo's surprise he found himself smiling. 'You looked me in the eye and you lied.'

'I did!' Lizzie smiled back.

'Why?'

'I wanted the job, I thought you might think I would be a bit more empathetic to the patients.'

He laughed and then he was serious because a more empathetic person you could not meet.

Only Lizzie could have saved his heart.

Yes, the bed creaked terribly and Lizzie didn't come quietly. She wanted to wear dark glasses as they sat the next morning eating breakfast.

'What time are you checking out?' Mrs Hewitt asked, as Lizzie blushed into her scrambled eggs.

'Actually, if there's availability,' Leo said, 'we'd like to stay tonight. Just the one room, though.'

'Tonight?' Lizzie glanced up at him. She'd been sure they'd be leaving tyre marks in his haste to get away. Instead, he wasn't rushing her.

Leo took himself off after breakfast and, just a little back to front, did the right thing, asking Thomas for Lizzie's hand in marriage.

He couldn't blame Thomas for his caution.

Leo knew his own reputation.

'I understand your reservations,' Leo said, 'but I love your daughter and I want you to know I would never hurt her.'

'See you don't, then.'

It was her perfect day—they walked along the beach and went on all the rides on the pier and then she took Leo for coffee at her favourite place. They walked past the house where she had grown up and, after a suitable pause, returned to the nursing home, where Lizzie shared the lovely news with her parents. Then it was back to the Hewitts' B&B for an afternoon in bed and to the future that was waiting for them.

'I miss our game,' Leo said.

'What game?' Lizzie asked, as he started to undress her, those beautiful blue eyes examining her.

'Our game.'

'Oh, that one.' She smiled. 'There's nothing to miss, Leo. We've only just started.'

EPILOGUE

'NERVOUS?' ETHAN ASKED as Leo pulled on his jacket, and Leo paused.

'Not in the least.'

For the first time that black churning in his gut was gone. A rapid wedding should be stressful to arrange, yet it had been seamless. When Lizzie had realised that a wedding in her home town and her father giving her away was causing Thomas so much stress, Leo had suggested they marry at Claridge's and that they could go and visit her family before their honeymoon.

'I never thought I'd see the day,' Ethan said as he checked that he had the rings.

'Neither did I,' Leo admitted.

'I'm pleased for you,' Ethan said. 'I always felt bad about—'

'Not today,' Leo interrupted. He didn't want to think about Olivia on his wedding day and he didn't need Ethan's apology. All Leo wanted was for his brother to know the peace and happiness that he himself had found, but happiness, for Ethan, still seemed a very long way off.

'Can I ask one thing?' Leo watched as Ethan's face

shuttered as he braced himself to answer one of Leo's many questions on this his wedding day.

'You can try.'

'It's been bugging me.' Leo looked at the tension in his brother's face. There was so much he wanted to know, just not today. 'Why does everyone always end up crashing on my sofa?'

He watched as Ethan's face broke into its first genuine smile of the day.

'I mean,' Leo continued, 'everyone's got a sofa in their office, the place is littered with them, yet you all end up on mine.'

'It's longer,' Ethan said. 'And wider. When you're over six foot there aren't many sofas where you can actually stretch out.'

'Oh.'

'And you keep your drinks topped up.'

'Okay,' Leo said. 'Good to know.'

'Come on, then,' Ethan said. 'You don't want to keep Lizzie waiting.'

It was Leo who was kept waiting.

Lizzie actually felt sick at the thought of all eyes being on her, and even though she was relieved that her father didn't have the stress of her wedding to deal with, today, especially, she missed them.

'Have a brandy,' Brenda, who was her bridesmaid, suggested. Lizzie was booked into a hotel suite, where *nothing* was too much trouble and a brandy was soon poured.

She took a sip and felt the burn but it did nothing to calm her and she took another. 'I'm scared I'll be sick or faint,' Lizzie admitted. She knew all brides were nervous on their wedding day but this was ridiculous.

She stood and looked in the mirror, worried she wasn't a suitable society bride.

'You look beautiful,' Brenda said. 'I'm so jealous *I* could be sick.'

Lizzie smiled—she loved her friends so much.

'Your dress is perfect,' Brenda said.

It had been the first one Lizzie had tried on—instantly she had known it was the right one. Very simple, it had delicately capped sleeves and was tied with a very thin silver belt. It was stunning in its simplicity. She carried white roses and her hair had been coiled and everything was perfect, except... Lizzie closed her eyes and took another sip of her brandy. She didn't want to dwell on the sad parts today.

'Come on,' Lizzie said, or she'd start panicking again.

She made her way down the steps and as the huge doors were opened she was briefly aware of all the people—nothing in Leo's world was small. There were people from the clinic and some terribly impressive people and there, smiling widely, was Francesca. Just one look at her and Lizzie straightened her back and walked forward.

Then she saw Leo standing beside Ethan—two brothers for today united. They both looked beautiful, but she only had eyes for Leo—a man who, even when she was completely and utterly petrified, could still make her smile. 'Been drinking, darling?' he said, as he caught a waft of brandy when she finally stood beside him. Then he took her hand and squeezed it. 'You look beautiful.'

When Leo was beside her, she knew that she was.

'About time,' he muttered when he was told he could kiss the bride, and then, very nicely, he kissed her.

There were photos and congratulations and as they stepped outside, Lizzie assumed it was for more photos, except she was being ushered into a car.

'Where are we going?'

'More photos.'

'Won't the guests mind us disappearing?' Lizzie asked. She knew he was up to something.

'It's our wedding, we can do what we want to.'

'Are we going to have photos at the zoo?'

'Nope,' Leo said, watching her face as she realised they were about to get into a helicopter. 'We're going to where you want to be.'

Lizzie had never been in a helicopter before and had never thought her first ride in one might be in her wedding dress.

In less than half an hour they were there, walking into the nursing home. All the guests and even the staff were dressed up for a wedding. There was sparkling apple juice and sandwiches and a stunning wedding cake.

'Catering by the Hewitts,' Leo said, out of the side of his mouth.

It could not have been more wonderful, especially when her mother took her hand and looked at the ring and then admired her dress.

'You look beautiful,' Faye said.

'So do you,' Lizzie said, because the staff had been busy, making sure Faye was a very beautiful mother of the bride, even if Lizzie couldn't be sure her mother knew that she was one.

A photographer had also been arranged and the photos he took of Lizzie and Leo with her family on their actual wedding day were ones that would be treasured for ever.

'Where are you going for your honeymoon?' Thomas checked a little while later, as they got ready to leave.

'Not far,' Lizzie said.

Finally she would see Paris.

'Take care of her,' Thomas warned Leo as they said their goodbyes.

'I will,' Leo said.

He meant it.

From the helicopter Lizzie looked down as London came into view and she thought of the dancing and the fun night ahead, while Leo looked at his bride and thought of the hours after the dancing and that part of the fun night ahead.

'Happy?' Leo asked, as they drove back to the hotel.

'Very,' Lizzie said. 'You?'

'Very,' Leo said. 'It's nice to already know who I'm going to be getting off with tonight.' He nodded to the door, where their reception was waiting. 'Unlike most of that lot.'

Oh, and there would be scandal, of course there would be scandal tonight—there were too many guests from 200 Harley Street for there not to be.

'I was right,' Leo said, giving her a kiss before they walked in.

Lizzie looked up at him.

'It is like Goldilocks.'

'No.' Lizzie shook her head. 'She ran off at the end.'

'What happened to Cinderella?'

'She married her prince.'

'Rapunzel?'

'She lived happily ever after…' Lizzie said. 'I'm not Goldilocks.'

'You are,' Leo said, taking her hand. 'When you ran into the woods a big lion chased you and caught you for life…'

He wasn't joking, though he sort of was, but Lizzie knew he had never been more serious in his life.

'I'm rewriting the ending,' Leo said. 'If Goldilocks agrees?'

She most certainly did.

* * * * *

200 HARLEY STREET: GIRL FROM THE RED CARPET

SCARLET WILSON

This book is dedicated to the newest addition of our family Lleyton John Hyndman, a beautiful boy who I'm wishing a long, healthy and happy life. Welcome to the family!

CHAPTER ONE

LEXI TAPPED HER pink fingernails on the desk with impatience. The clinic was in complete darkness. All caused by a little '*phoof*' when she'd tried to switch on the lights in one of the consulting rooms. If only she knew where the main trip switch was.

She squinted at her watch, using the light from her phone. Just after eleven o'clock at night. Where was he? He had to be here somewhere—his car was parked just down the road. She'd already phoned the few members of staff that were currently in Drake's wine bar and he wasn't with them.

She spun on her heel, a new determination causing her stomach to clench.

'Iain McKenzie, you can run but you can't hide.'

He'd been avoiding her all day.

She knew that.

And he knew that.

But two could play at that game. No one escaped Lexi Robbins, Head of PR at the Hunter Clinic. She'd got tired of dodging his lame excuses via his devoted and sergeant-majorish secretary. She'd looked at his theatre lists today and knew exactly when he'd be available.

Except he'd been in a meeting, then taking a conference call, then out buying a sandwich. The final straw had been when his secretary had said he'd left to pick up his dry-cleaning!

So she'd waited. Lexi Robbins could be very patient. She was also very persistent. So far she'd been through the three operating theatres, the recovery room and the anaesthetic room—even though there were no patients in the building—all in her search for Iain.

She'd checked his room four times today. She'd checked the waiting room, the kitchen, the changing rooms and the treatment rooms. She'd been down to the gym and private swimming pool too—the thought of catching Iain McKenzie in a state of undress wasn't exactly unappealing. Now she'd started checking the *other* consultants' rooms in the hope she'd catch him hiding somewhere.

As a kid she'd been the best at hide and seek and she'd no intention of being beaten now.

Iain McKenzie had met his match.

It was infuriating. *He* was infuriating. She was only trying to do her job and help raise the profile of the clinic to try and attract some more overseas clients. So far, she'd managed to persuade several celebrity friends, a few TV film stars, an international politician and the sheikh of Amal to use the services of the Hunter Clinic. Interviewing and filming some of the staff members would help her publicity drive to even bigger audiences.

And with his shaggy hair, muscular build and Scottish accent Iain McKenzie was to die for. Women would love him and flock to this clinic from miles around if only she could get him on screen and online.

She'd worked hard for this job and had no intention of failing. Leo Hunter had just let her know that they were linking with a charity, so raising the profile and income of the Hunter Clinic would be even more crucial than before. She was determined not to let him down, not when he'd given her an opportunity that others hadn't.

Being the daughter of a family constantly in the media meant she had her own cross to bear. If she had a pound for every time someone had said the words 'You're Penelope Crosby's daughter?', usually with an expression of disbelief in their eyes, she would never need to work again. Being the daughter of a former famous model with one of the world's top-selling range of beauty products was tough—having a father who interviewed all the top celebrities in the world, along with his billionaire status, was even tougher.

No one in her family had respected her decision to go to university and get her degree. No one in the family respected the work she did at the Hunter Clinic. The only time her parents had ever been happy with her choices was when she'd spent a few summers doing charity work because it had given them more good publicity than they would ever need.

That's why she was so determined not to let Leo down.

No matter how hard Iain McKenzie tried to hide from her.

She could see it in her head right now. The publicity shot she wanted to use—Iain McKenzie in that dark grey suit he wore, with a white shirt and red tie, arms folded across his chest in front of the Hunter Clinic sign. He would look fabulous.

Or maybe she should put him in a set of navy scrubs—all his athletic muscles would be clearly on show. Or maybe she could persuade him to wear a kilt.

No. Scratch that. Old prickly guts would never agree to wear a kilt for her.

She pushed open the door to Mitchell Cooper's room. Even though the lights were out there was plenty of light from the outside streetlights in Harley Street. She could see around the room easily. Empty. Just like all the others.

There was only one place left. Leo Hunter's office. The boss.

She felt a flutter of excitement. Leo's office was the most gorgeous in the building. Spectacular views over Harley Street, hand-picked opulent furniture and gorgeous soft furnishings.

She turned the handle carefully. It almost felt wrong, creeping into the boss's office while he wasn't around. But she was determined to check every inch of this clinic.

But something was wrong. There were no gentle lights from the street bathing the office in a partly orange glow.

The curtains were pulled tightly, leaving the office in complete darkness. She fumbled with her phone, trying to pull it from her pocket and use the torch to see her way around.

A flicker of nerves danced across her skin. What was that faint noise? She held her breath, leaning forward a little and straining to hear. But after more than sixteen hours in stiletto heels her balance had deserted her. She tripped on the large Turkish rug Leo kept in the middle of his floor. She fell forward and let out a gasp, reaching out towards the blackness in front of her and hitting the edge of the chesterfield lounge—and a whole lot more.

There was movement. Sudden, powerful movement and none of it was hers. Lexi felt the breath leave her body as she found herself spun around and pushed flat on her back onto the chesterfield lounge.

Her heart pounded in her chest, the thudding reverberating in her ears. She tried to reach out and fight her attacker as an adrenaline surge hit her body. Fight or flight had never seemed more apt. But the arms holding her down were fierce. Fierce and strong, very strong.

Her breath seemed caught in her throat, her tongue stuck to the roof of her mouth. Her attacker's weight was pressing down on her chest, affecting her ability to take a deep breath.

She still couldn't see. It was just darkness, pure and utter darkness. Like your worst nightmare and most hated horror movie all rolled into one.

She heard a grunt. And it gave her the faintest glimmer of hope.

It was a grunt she thought she recognised. Usually when she was trying to persuade him to acknowledge her existence.

She fought to push the word from her throat. 'Iain?' she croaked.

Iain had finally managed to grab a few minutes' precious sleep. There was no point in going home. No matter how exhausted he was—or how many hours he'd spent in theatre, making the world look 'more beautiful'—sleep evaded him the second he stepped through his doorway.

Too much quiet. Too much time to let his brain spin around and around, going over all aspects of his past. Every decision made, every conversation, every cross word, every pleaded case. If only he'd taken the road less travelled.

It didn't matter that he'd moved from Edinburgh to London. His house had too many memories and too many familiar knick-knacks that he couldn't face putting away. That would be like a betrayal.

So he'd spent half the day playing cat and mouse with Lexi Robbins. The woman wouldn't give him a moment's peace. Boy, was she tenacious—his gran would have loved her. All over an interview that he'd cancelled at the last minute and publicity that he couldn't really care less about.

And just when the muscles in his body had finally started to relax—just when the last remnants of tension had finally managed to exit his body—this.

Noise. In the Hunter Clinic in the middle of the night.

Noise. In a place where he was supposed to be alone.

The assailant was smaller than he expected. Lighter than he expected too. Probably in search of drugs or the elusive cosmetic fillers that Harley Street was so famous for.

Then it hit him. That smell.

The smell that had been haunting him around the clinic for the last few days.

Strike that. Actually, for the last few months. Ever since Lexi Robbins had started working there.

Sensual woody amber distinctive notes with gentle floral notes of jasmine. Along with the feel of some very distinctive soft curves that only a plastic surgeon could recognise merely by touch.

He could feel the assailant's soft breath beneath him, along with the strangled voice. 'Iain?'

'Lexi?' He sprang backwards, moving swiftly to

the door and trying to flick on the light. Nothing. Still darkness.

'I think I blew the lights,' came the whisper from the couch. She was still breathless. He'd obviously winded her.

After a few seconds she fumbled for her phone and pressed the button to light up the room. She held it towards him. 'Do you know where the master switch is?'

Rage was circulating in his belly. What on earth was she doing? He snatched the phone from her hand and strode down the corridor towards the electricity box, opening it quickly and flicking the master switch, allowing instant illumination in parts of the clinic.

Bright. White. Everywhere.

Sometimes he could groan out loud about the décor in the clinic. Leo Hunter had wanted brilliant white and clean lines everywhere—thank goodness he'd been allowed to decorate his office to his own taste.

But now that he could actually see what he was doing he was furious.

'What were you thinking of, Lexi?' He stormed back into the room.

But Lexi hadn't moved. Even though the room was now flooded with light she was still lying on the couch, her hands pressed to her chest, her face as white as a sheet. One shoe was twisted on the floor , the other dangling from the end of her foot. Her usually pristine suit was a little askew and it looked as if the top button had popped from her shirt.

Yikes! He'd thought he was tackling a burglar. Maybe he'd been a little more forceful than he thought.

'Lexi? Are you okay?' He stood over her, giving her a few seconds to collect herself.

After what seemed like an age she finally blinked. Colour flooded into her face and she pushed herself up. 'Wow. Talk about sweeping the legs from under a girl.'

Iain felt colour come to his own cheeks. He was trying hard not to stare at Lexi's cleavage. He was a plastic surgeon. He spent his days with his hands on women's breasts. But he'd never clocked Lexi Robbins as a boob job kind of girl. She'd surprised him.

In all the time she'd been around him in the last few months, wearing her designer suits, he'd never noticed her additions. But then again, he'd never seen her undressed.

He pushed the thoughts that sprang to mind aside instantly. He sat down on one of the leather armchairs and put his head in his hands. 'What on earth are you doing here at this time of night, Lexi?' He was tired. And he was definitely feeling crabbit.

She straightened on the couch, looking down at her shirt and frowning at the missing button. 'I could ask you the same thing.'

She was obviously feeling a bit better. Lexi Robbins could give as good as she got. He raised his eyebrows at her and gave her a cheeky smile. 'Avoiding you?'

She shot him a glare.

He held up his hands. 'Seriously, Lexi. I thought you were a burglar. You're lucky I didn't do you some permanent damage.'

'Who says you didn't?'

She was adjusting herself on the couch and he felt instantly uncomfortable. What did she mean? He hadn't done anything more than push her onto the couch and hold her down. There was no way he could have damaged her implants.

Her blonde tousled hair fell over her face as she shuffled on the edge of the couch. Iain was torn between panic and embarrassment. It didn't help that his curiosity was naturally piqued.

He'd heard of Lexi before she'd started work here. Even for a man who had as little interest in celebrities as humanly possible—other than to contemplate what procedures they'd had done—it was impossible to miss Lexi Robbins.

If there was an event she was at it. Albeit usually trying to fade into the background behind her mother and father, but dazzling all the same. He'd instantly dismissed her as a wannabe and had been more than a little surprised when Leo had hired her as their head of PR.

But Leo Hunter only hired the best. And Iain could vouch for that as Leo had pursued him relentlessly to get him here.

She lifted her head and gave her hair a shake, catching him with her blue eyes and winking. 'Gotcha!'

He couldn't stop the instant smile that appeared on his lips. Even this late at night, after pursuing him all day, she could still joke with him.

She slid off the chesterfield and moved over towards him, folding her arms across her depleted shirt. 'So, Iain McKenzie, your mission to avoid me has failed. Resistance is futile.'

He raised his eyebrows. Surprised by her knowledge of his favourite TV show. Lexi Robbins did her homework.

'You're going to have to agree to the interview *and* to me shadowing you for a few days. I mean, after all, some people could be very upset about being mishandled.'

He sighed. 'Ms Robbins, are you trying to black-mail me?'

She gave a perfunctory nod. 'You bet I am.'

He shook his head. 'Lexi, find someone else. Some happy, shiny person who likes doing this kind of thing. I just want to do my job.'

'And so do I. Believe it or not, Ethan Hunter is even more difficult than you. Would you call him happy and shiny? Because he's my other potential interviewee.' She raised her eyebrows at him.

His head was spinning. She'd moved closer and he was getting a waft of that perfume again. Predator perfume. At least that was what his brain was telling him.

It was making him uneasy, on edge. Or maybe it was just reminding him of how up close and personal they'd just been.

When was the last time he'd been up close and personal with a woman?

He didn't even want to think about that. He'd known from the second he'd laid eyes on her that Lexi Robbins meant trouble for him. His body reacted in ways it shouldn't when she was around. The sound of her voice, the smell of her distinctive perfume, even the sound of her stiletto heels clicking along the corridor were enough to send his imagination into overdrive and remind him of why he'd been avoiding her at all costs.

He rubbed his sleep-heavy eyes. Maybe his night-mares had taken a new turn and an alien was about to burst from her stomach and eat him alive. Nope. She was still there. Still staring at him with her big blue eyes and pink lips.

She held out her hand towards him.

'What?'

'Let's go, Iain.'

For a second he was confused. 'Go where?'

She shot him a dazzling smile. 'Home. I'm going to take you home.'

CHAPTER TWO

SHE WAS TRYING not to show her nerves. Trying to pretend that this was an everyday occurrence.

But Iain McKenzie wasn't helping. His brow was wrinkled, deep furrowed wrinkles that marred his handsome complexion.

She leaned forward and grabbed hold of one his hands, bending down in front of him. 'Iain, I'm worried about you. You spent hours in surgery today, then you spent another few hours avoiding me, and now I catch you here...' she held up her other hand '...fast asleep in another office.' She looked up into his face, seeing tiny lines of exhaustion around his eyes that instantly tugged at her heart. 'It's not good, Iain. You are one of our greatest assets. I wouldn't be doing my job if I didn't take you home.'

The confused and uptight expression on his face relaxed a little. Oh, no. What had he thought she'd meant?

She patted his hand. It was meant to be reassuring, motherly. But it wasn't working for her, and she doubted it was working for him. It was only making her sluggish veins pick up tempo and send the blood flowing more quickly back to her heart.

The long day had obviously caused her brain to become fuddled. The sooner she got Iain McKenzie home safely the better.

He stood up next to her and she was instantly swamped by his large athletic frame. 'Don't be silly, Lexi. You're not going to drive me home. My car is down the street. I'll go and get it.'

That accent. That Scottish burr sent shivers down her spine. She could happily listen to it all day. And she could bet that potential clients could too. She had to persuade him to take part in the publicity campaign. Iain was pure gold.

It was time for a firm approach. 'Iain, I meant what I said. From what I can gather, you've put in a sixteen-hour day so far. You were sleeping soundly before I disturbed you.' Then she wrinkled her nose. 'And, truth be told, I'd already staked out your car. It looks as if it's got a flat. There's no way you're changing that at this time of night.' She gave a little laugh. 'Not in the dark anyway, with those surgeon's hands. How much are they worth?'

She saw his shoulders sag a little and it gave her a spurt of hope. Maybe tomorrow he could forgive her little white lie? In the meantime, she had to use her best tactics to persuade him to take part in the publicity.

He gave his forehead another rub and arched his back. 'Okay, Lexi. Thanks for the offer. I guess spending the night in the clinic isn't ideal.' He bent over and picked up his jacket, which was lying across a chair, then held the door open for her.

She gave a little nod, straightened her blouse and jacket and slipped her feet back into her shoes. It only took a few minutes to reach her car, which she'd moved near the clinic entrance.

He nodded in approval. 'Sports car? Nice, Lexi. Did you pick this yourself?'

She gave an embarrassed shake of her head as she pressed the button to open the doors. 'Not exactly. It was a birthday present.'

He let out a sigh as he sat down in the passenger seat, folding his long legs into the small footwell. 'That's some birthday present. From a man?'

The question hung in the air between them. Was he curious about her love life, or was he just making small talk? The air in the car seemed to instantly close around them as she slammed her door. Iain McKenzie was a big man in the small space. The sleeve of his jacket was brushing against hers.

Her brain was ready to drift back to the office. To the feel of the hard planes of his chest against her firm breasts.

She pushed the gearstick into reverse and looked at him sideways. 'The car was from my father. I'd like to think he spent hours thinking about it, but the reality is his PA probably picked the make, model and colour and all he had to do was sign the cheque.'

She pulled out into the street. It was practically empty at this time in the morning and her natural instinct was to floor it. Talking about her parents brought out the worst in her.

Iain surprised her. He let out a deep, hearty laugh. She glanced over, raising her eyebrows in surprise.

'So you're a cynic, then, Lexi Robbins. I never had you down for that. I thought you lived a remarkably charmed life.'

Her instant reaction was to bristle and put him promptly in his place. But this was her chance to work on him—not alienate him. Plus with that face she was still curious as to why a man as hard working and good looking as Iain didn't have someone to rush home to. Why on earth would anyone like him want to sleep at the clinic? It just didn't make sense.

'I know you've been avoiding me. I'm not an idiot, you know.'

'I'm sorry. I just don't have the time. And to be honest, I can't really see the point. Get someone else to do it. Someone who likes a bit of the limelight on them.'

'Like who, Ethan?'

She let the question hang in the air. If Iain was prickly then Ethan Hunter was a floating underwater mine.

A former soldier, who was still recuperating from an injury he really refused to acknowledge. His heart was in the right place and he was committed to all the charity work the clinic was involved in—most of it he'd referred himself. But putting Ethan on screen for the clinic's publicity would be a complete no-no. She'd already tried to interview him twice with no success. Ethan just wasn't a people person.

Whatever had happened in his past meant he just wasn't ready for this kind of thing, and Lexi knew enough about people to know when to leave it alone. Hence her relentless pursuit of Iain. He was her current golden goose—whether he liked it or not.

Iain eventually let out a long sigh. 'Okay. Agreed, Ethan probably isn't the best person right now. He asked me to be involved in his charity work and obviously I agreed—who wouldn't? I can make a real difference to some of those patients' lives. I'm happy to help. I'm happy to give up my time and do the surgery free. It's just the rest of the stuff I don't like so much.'

Lexi lifted her hands off the steering-wheel of the car and made quote marks with her fingers in the air. 'You mean the "rest of the stuff" like me?'

Iain ran his fingers through his dark hair. It was obvious he was tired and she was putting him on the spot. But maybe, just maybe, in a moment of weakness he would relent and agree to what she wanted.

She indicated and turned the car into the nearest street. It would only be a few more minutes before they reached Iain's townhouse. It was time to turn the screw. 'I don't think you understand how hard I'm working at all this, Iain. You might do the surgery for free, but what about everything else? We need to pay for theatre time, equipment use, other staff salaries and all the aftercare. We need the publicity to raise funds for all other aspects of the charity work. These interviews are really important.

'Leo has just agreed to take on another charity for one of his friends. Did he talk to you about Fair Go— Olivia Fairchild's charity? She's doing some stellar work in Africa. There are children out there who really need our help. Kids who've been victims of the violence— victims of war. The kind of kids who fall through the cracks. Their conditions aren't life-threatening or emergencies—but think of the difference we could make to their lives by doing what in this country would be seen as basic surgery. If we can do some interviews with staff members, focus on their special skills and surgeries, get the information out there for the world and media to see, it could really raise the profile of the Hunter Clinic. The more international customers we have, the more disposable income the clinic can use to help aid these charities.

'The Hunter Clinic has finally managed to regain its reputation and polish. Things are looking even better now people know that Leo and Ethan are working together. It does wonders for the whole ethos of the place. Just think, Iain, if a clinic that's known as the best of the best is going all out for some of these charities, don't you think that will make people stop and think? It'll make people look more closely at these charities and wonder what they could do to help too. That's exactly the kind of publicity that they need, Iain. This isn't just about your surgical skills and time, it's about the bigger picture. It's about what everyone else can do to help.'

She couldn't stop the enthusiasm and passion that was coming through in her voice. She was excited just thinking about this and the huge realm of possibilities. She could tell she was getting to him. He wasn't so quick to answer back, as if he were mulling over what she'd just said. Exactly the way she'd hoped he would.

Her brain was whirring again and her tongue itching to fill the silence in the car. But this was exactly the time to be quiet. To leave him with no excuse but to mull it over.

She changed gear and her hand brushed against his thigh. Wow. Now there were a hundred reasons for a girl not to concentrate on the road.

For a second she felt a little panicked. She could smell him. His scent was invading her senses and she was starting to feel swamped by his presence in her car. She could remember his firm hands on her shoulders, holding her down on the couch. It had been terrifying. All rational thought had flown out of the window.

Of course it had to have been Iain. He was the person she'd been hunting for in the clinic—who else could it possibly have been?

And once the terror had left her, all she'd been left with had been the whoosh.

That feeling of being close to a man again. How long had it been since she'd let a man touch her? And how much had her senses fired in Iain's powerful arms?

She tried to shake the intimate thoughts from her head. She was a professional. She had a job to do. And Iain McKenzie was part of that job.

Her PR head started to buzz. Should she have concerns about Iain McKenzie? Why on earth was one of their top surgeons sleeping at the clinic? She'd read the information in his personnel file. She knew he was originally from Edinburgh and had a broad general experience before specialising in plastics. He'd printed several professional papers, spoke at conferences and conducted scientific clinical studies into different techniques for various types of plastic surgery. Technically, he was brilliant.

So why did she feel as if something was wrong? More importantly, why did it make her stomach twist?

That was the thing about Iain's personnel file. There was hardly a 'personal' thing in it. All professional. It just didn't sit right with her.

She pulled up outside his townhouse.

'How did you know where I stay, Lexi? I never told you.'

The frown was etched on his brow again. If he wasn't careful it would become a permanent fixture.

She smiled. 'I'm the Head of PR, Iain. I know everything about everybody.' She looked up at the dark townhouse. It wasn't exactly welcoming.

Bleak and sombre. A bit like Iain.

She'd expected him to more or less jump from the car the second they arrived but he didn't. He sat for a few moments then turned to face her. With so little space between them in the car she was almost afraid to turn round.

'I appreciate what you're trying to do for the charities. Really, I do, Lexi. And if Leo hired you then he must think you're good at your job.'

'And you don't?' Was that the implication? Because that train of thought alarmed her.

He shook his head and lifted his hand. 'Don't be so defensive. What exactly is it you want from me?'

She took a deep breath. Finally. She was going to get somewhere with him.

'I want to shadow you for a few days. See your consultations with patients. Watch you perform surgery. Once I've had a chance to get to see the real you, I'll interview you on camera. It will work better that way, I'll know you—you'll know me. The interview will go more smoothly.'

He frowned. 'That's a bit more in-depth than I expected. I can't have you disturbing things with my patients. If they don't want you around you have to leave.' His words were absolutely definite.

She nodded quickly. 'Agreed.'

'And I'll need my patients' consent for you to watch any surgeries.'

'Will that be difficult?'

He let out a slow stream of air through his lips. 'Not tomorrow it won't. I'm performing surgery on Aida Atkins. You know how fame-hungry she is. She'll be falling all over herself at the mere thought of some publicity for herself.' He paused. 'You signed a confidentiality agreement when you started at the clinic?'

She nodded.

'I think you'll find with Aida Atkins you may as well throw it out the window.'

Aida Atkins. The latest model-cum-actress-cum-trophy wife. Lexi had seen more of them than she'd eaten home-cooked meals. Hardly difficult.

'This publicity is really about the clinic, the work you do and the associated charities.'

'Aida won't care. If she gets her five minutes of fame she'll be happy. Her type are all the same.'

'What does that mean?' There was a horrible little gnawing feeling at the pit of her stomach. She could almost predict what he was about to say.

'Vain. Pretentious. Fixed ideas about what a perfect body should look like.'

'If you feel like that, why are you operating on her?'

'Because it's what she wants. Because she's medically and psychologically competent to make a decision about surgery and she's not an anaesthetic risk. As simple as that.'

Lexi could feel a wave of disappointment sweep over her body. Was that what he thought about all his plastic-surgery clients? That they were all superficial and vain? Was that what he thought about her because she'd had a boob job?

He shook his head as if he realised his words sounded unnecessarily harsh. 'Wait until tomorrow. You'll understand then. There's a reason I'm doing Aida's surgery instead of a general plastic surgeon.'

Iain put his hand on the door handle. 'Princess Catherine's. Seven a.m. tomorrow. And bring something to eat. It will be a long day.' It took him a few seconds to release his long legs from the foot well. He straightened up and pulled some house keys from his pocket.

She watched as he looked over at the house. There was no look of relief to finally be home. More a look of resignation. He bent back down. 'Thanks for the lift, Lexi. See you tomorrow.' Then he slammed the door and trudged up his steps.

Lexi took a deep breath. There was so much more hidden behind the handsome façade of Iain McKenzie. The question was, how much did she want to find out?

CHAPTER THREE

THE DARKNESS PERVADED him as soon as he set foot in his house. It was such a shame as it was a beautiful home and, in theory, all his dark memories should have been left behind in Edinburgh.

Coming to London was supposed to be the start of something new for him. He just couldn't seem to shake off the big black thundercloud of guilt that hung permanently above his head.

He flicked on a light and looked out at the road. Lexi hadn't pulled away yet. Should he have invited her in? Had he been impolite? It had been so long since he'd done any of the social niceties with women that he'd probably forgotten what most of them were.

He watched as she indicated and pulled out onto the quiet street. It was after midnight. If he'd invited her in it might have been misconstrued as something else entirely. And whether he admitted it or not, he was trying to avoid the woman who was causing uncomfortable flarings in his libido, not invite her into his home.

He paused at the dark polished sideboard, which held a photograph of himself and his wife, Bonnie. They were sitting on the grass in their garden in Edinburgh, her back leaning against him and his arms wrapped around her enlarged abdomen. Bonnie had the most contented look on her face. The look of a woman who had finally got the thing she'd always dreamed of. They *both* looked like that, but Iain knew the truth behind that photo.

One of his friends had suggested he put that picture away. A friend who'd been close enough to both of them to know what had actually happened.

But Iain couldn't do that. His guilt didn't matter. This was still his favourite picture of them both. They looked so relaxed. They looked so happy. As if they had their whole lives ahead of them.

If only he'd known…

His fingers touched the glass in front of the photograph. 'Three years, Bonnie,' he whispered. And not a single day had gone by that he hadn't thought of her.

They'd been childhood sweethearts. Destined to be together for ever. Or so they had thought.

When Leo Hunter had pursued him to work at the Hunter Clinic he'd thought the guy was crazy. His world had just collapsed around him and Leo had wanted him to up sticks and move to another part of the country?

But Leo had understood him better than he'd understood himself. He'd known he would never be able to pull himself up if he stayed in the family home, with the same work colleagues with their averted eyes and sad expressions. The move to London had been exactly what he'd needed at the time. Apart from Leo, no one knew about his wife. He'd skirted around the edges of any potentially difficult conversations, avoiding any personal details.

London was easy to lose yourself in. And the clientele coming to and from the Hunter Clinic had more to worry about than the personal background of their surgeon. And it was better that way. It really was.

Iain walked into his vast kitchen and pulled a glass from the cupboard, pressing it against the dispenser on his stainless-steel fridge. A beautiful kitchen that he hardly used. Just like the rest of this house.

He climbed the staircase to his bedroom, peeled off his jacket, trousers, shirt and tie, not bothering to hang them up. He'd have to be up in a few hours to get to Princess Catherine's for surgery and he had a whole rail of identical business suits in the cupboard.

He sank into the bed with white Egyptian cotton sheets. Praying that tonight—even for a few hours— he might get a few hours' precious sleep.

But it wasn't to be.

It seemed that it wasn't only the scent of Lexi Robbins that had pervaded his memory. He sat bolt upright in bed, sweat pouring from his body.

This was why he'd purposefully been avoiding Lexi Robbins.

He'd known it. Right from the first time he'd seen her and he'd felt a skitter of impulses across his shoulders that he couldn't be around her. He couldn't be near her.

He leant forward and wiped the sweat from his brow. Erotic dreams weren't the norm for Iain. But when Lexi's firm breasts had pressed against the planes of his chest it had left an indelible imprint. Not just on his skin.

Those tiny, fleeting thoughts that hadn't even taken up a second in his brain when he'd had her pressed down on the examination couch had just taken front and centre stage in his mind in all their erotic beauty. Dreams like that had more than one obvious effect on the body.

He'd never be able to look Lexi Robbins in the eye today. It was almost as if he could smell her here, now.

He jumped from the bed and walked through to the en suite, flicking the switch on the shower then coming back and gulping the glass of water at the side of his bed. Was he going crazy? He *could* smell Lexi Robbins.

Then he remembered how close they'd been. He snatched his crumpled shirt from the floor and pressed it to his nose. There. Not the smell of his own after-shave. The smell of her.

That heady, exotic smell that left an invisible pied-piper trail wherever she went. That was what had caused the dream. Nothing else.

The shirt had been lying at his bedside and her scent had obviously drifted up and around him while he'd slept. How could this woman find a way into his dreams?

Guilt flooded through him, seeping in through every pore on his body. The hot sweat instantly turned cold, chilling his skin. Bonnie. That's who he should have been dreaming about. No one else.

Steam was starting to billow from the shower. He stalked back through and instantly turned the switch to cold. That was what he needed. Icy, cold, blasting water to wash away any unwanted thoughts or feelings.

He stepped into the freezing water, shuddering as it came into contact with his skin. There was no point going back to sleep now.

Not if Lexi Robbins was going to feature in his dreams again.

CHAPTER FOUR

'MORNING, MORNING.' LEXI nodded at the sea of faces in and around the theatres at Princess Catherine's, or Kate's, where the Hunter Clinic had an arrangement to perform adult surgery. Children's surgery was carried out at the Lighthouse Children's Hospital.

Lexi had thought she'd be in good stead, turning up early. But early seemed to be normal in the theatres here.

She'd followed all the instructions carefully. Even though she wouldn't be near any patients, she'd removed the nail varnish from her fingernails, ensured her face was scrubbed clean of any make-up and left her perfume and jewellery at home. She didn't want to give Iain McKenzie any reason not to let her shadow him today.

And her stomach was churning a little. Nerves. Lots of them. Most of the world saw Lexi Robbins as a together, sorted woman. She didn't reveal the insecure woman that hid away underneath. The person who was horrified to be here with a bare face and pulled-back hair.

It was odd, but she felt strangely safe here. No paparazzi were going to jump out from a corner and snap her, showing the world she wasn't as beautiful as her mother. No one here cared. Everyone here had one purpose in mind—excellent patient care. It was almost a relief to know she could fade into the background.

Kate's was buzzing. There was a rainbow of coloured scrubs around her. She'd been under the illusion that everyone wore the same-coloured scrubs, but Kate's had scrubs in every colour, shape and size. One of the theatre nurses had pointed her to a laundry cupboard and told her to help herself. So she had, and she was currently sporting pale pink scrubs and white clogs.

'Ready?'

The deep voice behind her made her jump. 'Oh, Iain. Great. I was waiting for you.'

The words seemed to come out all wrong and she could feel the colour rushing into her face. She might have guessed it. Even dressed in navy scrubs there was no disguising his broad frame and muscles. If she was going to have to watch that muscled back all day she might as well just go and lie down in a corner now.

'I've already spoken to Aida. She signed a disclaimer. She's more than happy for you to watch her surgery—you can even film it if you like.'

Lexi cleared her throat. 'Actually, it's you we would be filming, Iain. We don't intend to focus on the patient. Just let people see your expertise at work.'

'Whatever.' He gave a shrug and pushed open the door to the theatre. 'After you...'

She nodded and brushed past his arm as he held the door open for her. *No contact.* That's what she'd been telling herself all night. Seems like she'd broken her first rule already.

She tried to back herself into a corner as the rest of the staff moved in perfect unison around the theatre.

Iain and one of his colleagues scrubbing meticulously at the sinks. The nurses opening up theatre packs, the anaesthetist and his assistant bringing Aida into Theatre and talking to her quietly and calmly as they put her under.

Lexi could feel herself holding her breath as the drapes were placed around Aida and her skin cleaned with betadine. Wow. Scars like she'd never seen before.

Iain's brown eyes connected with hers above his mask. He nodded towards her. 'Step a little closer, Lexi.'

Her feet moved forward, even though her body wanted to remain pinned against the wall.

'This is the reason that Aida isn't being operated on by a general plastic surgeon.' His gloved hand pointed at her scarring. 'She has significant scarring caused by her previous surgery. This operation isn't just about replacing her implants, it's about reducing the scarring and trying to give her the best possible outcome.'

Lexi nodded behind her mask. 'Why does she have scars like that?'

Iain spoke slowly. 'All patients react differently to surgery. Some form thick, keloid scars, others hypertrophic scars like these. It's to do with collagen in the skin. The most important aspect for Aida isn't what I do today—although that's obviously important—it's more about her aftercare to minimise scarring.'

'But if she's prone to scarring, is there anything you can do to avoid it?'

'We'll monitor Aida very closely. We can use various things after surgery to reduce inflammation and scarring. A series of steroid injections might be appropriate or silicone gel sheeting used to flatten the scar. Aida knows that she has to follow my instructions to the letter for her aftercare. It was the only reason I agreed to do her surgery in the first place.'

Lexi could feel the hairs rise at the back of her neck. Iain wasn't joking. She could just imagine how stern he'd been with Aida before agreeing to her surgery. The scarring was a complete surprise to her. She was sure she'd seen semi-naked pictures of Aida before, and nothing had been noticeable. How had she managed that?

Of course. The beauty of photographic touch-ups. She knew better than anyone how fickle the beauty industry was. As long as they got the picture they wanted it didn't matter how they got it—or whether it was an accurate portrayal of the person or not.

Her feet moved slowly backwards, edging towards the wall again. She wished she'd known about the surgery beforehand and had given herself a little time to prepare. Watching breast surgery and having breast surgery were two entirely different things. In a way she was glad she'd slept through her own surgery and had never had to think too much about it all. She had to press her hands against the cool wall to stop herself automatically lifting them and holding them against her breasts.

She glanced downwards. There they were. Perfect, in every way.

If only she'd got them because *she*'d wanted them and not because someone else had criticised her. It almost made her feel like a fool.

But she was stronger now. More resilient.

She was happy with her shape and regardless of anyone else's opinion she had more confidence like this.

Iain's concentration was intense in Theatre. Woe betide anyone who interrupted the master at work. But the theatre staff were comfortable with him, obviously used to his techniques and procedures. He hardly needed to utter an instruction.

The surgery flew past. Quickly followed by another, more standard breast enlargement. He turned to face her as he scrubbed for yet another surgery.

'Now would be a good time to grab a quick bite,' he said to Lexi.

As if on cue, her stomach gave a low rumble. 'Haven't you finished yet?'

He shook his head. 'Not by a long shot. I've got some reconstructive surgery to do on a professional football player's knee and then some facial surgery on a lady with head and neck cancer. That one will last around four hours.'

Lexi tried to stop her jaw from hitting the floor when she realised exactly how long Iain would be in Theatre. 'I didn't know you did things like that. If that surgery will take so long, shouldn't it have been done first?'

He gave a little nod of acknowledgement. 'You're right. We normally do the most complicated surgery first but Carol Kennedy has enough on her plate. She wanted to keep things as normal as possible. She wanted to drop her kids at school today and has told them that she's got business in the city for a few days.'

Lexi felt a little tug at her heart as she recognised the name of the well-known TV presenter. 'She has head and neck cancer?' Her voice came out as a squeak, even though she was trying to be as professional as possible. News like that usually spread like wildfire and she was surprised she hadn't heard a thing.

Iain gave a curt nod. 'I'll talk you through it later. Now, go and eat.'

One of the theatre nurses gestured towards the door and held it open for her as she walked towards it. 'Come with me. I'll show you where you can grab a coffee. We'll have to be quick, mind. Iain will be starting again within ten minutes.'

Lexi followed her quickly to the nearby kitchen. This would be an ideal time to see how much she could find out about Iain from his colleagues. She hadn't really met many of the staff from Kate's before.

She gave a grateful smile as the nurse poured out some coffee and handed her a cup. 'Take some biscuits. They're on the table. It's a free for all in here.'

Lexi smiled. 'Thanks for that. Have you worked with Iain long?'

The nurse lifted her eyebrows. 'Happy Harry?'

Lexi nearly choked. 'Is that what you call him?'

The nurse laughed. 'Actually, he's not the worst. Leo Hunter used to be much more grumpy but since he's met Lizzie he's all smiles. His brother Ethan seems to have taken on the mantle of biggest bear.' She walked over to the table and sat down next to Lexi. 'But to be fair to him he's still not recovered and he works far too long hours—they all do—but Ethan's trouble is he's far too stubborn to use his stick.'

Lexi frowned. 'I've never seen Ethan walking with a stick.'

'Exactly. I've worked in orthopaedic theatres for too many years not to know when someone should be using a stick.'

Lexi pressed her lips together. It was time for a subject change, but the nurse was already back on her feet and washing her cup. No one got to hang around for long here. 'Let's go, Lexi.' She gave her a quick wink. 'Let's not keep our Scots laird waiting.'

Lexi followed her pale green scrubs out the door. Iain was near the end of scrubbing and his premiership footballer was being wheeled in the door. She almost couldn't believe the range of operations that Iain was involved in.

The surgery on the footballer player took several hours and her legs were already beginning to ache by the time a very nervous-looking Carol Kennedy was wheeled in. It was obvious she recognised Lexi immediately, and if she was surprised to see her she didn't show it. Instead, she gestured to her to come over.

Lexi's stomach was churning. She'd met Carol at numerous charity events over the years and had always found her to be as charming in person as she was on television. She reached over and gave Carol's hand a little squeeze. 'I'm so sorry to see you here, Carol.'

Carol nodded nervously, tears pooling in her eyes. 'Iain spoke to me beforehand about the filming. It's fine with me. I'll have some time to explain to the children when I go home.'

'Are you sure, Carol? The last thing I want to do is invade your privacy. If this is something you want kept out of the media, I completely understand. You know that my lips are sealed and I'll never breathe a word.'

Carol nodded gratefully. 'I appreciate that, Lexi. I've been fighting this cancer in private for quite some time. But after the surgery today I'll have some scars. Iain will do whatever he can, but I will have some scars around my neck that I don't want to have to spend my life telling lies about.' She shook her head. 'In a few days' time I'll be home and will have told my children. If filming the surgery helps other people and helps raise the profile of the clinic for the charities, it's fine with me.'

Carol gave a little nod as the anaesthetist signalled to her to lie back against the pillow. Lexi gave a final squeeze of her hand as the anaesthetist started slowing injecting the milky substance into her vein. A few seconds later Carol's body relaxed and her breathing was assisted. Lexi watched as Carol's head was tilted backwards but instead of sliding a tube down Carol's throat, as she'd expected, the anaesthetist slid a tube down her nose.

Iain saw the expression on her face. 'When we're doing surgery on the head and neck we often use nasotracheal intubation. It means we can maintain the patient's airway but still have access to do surgery in and around the face, mouth and neck.'

Lexi nodded. It made sense. If Iain needed access to the inside of Carol's mouth, it would be virtually impossible if a tube was down her throat.

'So what are you going to do for Carol?'

There was something so strange about seeing someone she knew lying on the operating table. Even though she'd recognised the footballer from earlier, she'd never met him before in person.

Iain and his team were positioning themselves around the table, a wide variety of surgical instruments around them. Even though Iain's mask was in place and all she could see were his brown eyes, his thick Scottish accent carried clearly across the theatre. 'All head and neck cancers are different. The extent of the surgery depends on the size of the cancer and where it is. If it's a small cancer of the mouth, there is often no scarring. But if the cancer has spread from the head or neck, the most likely place for it to go to is the lymph nodes in the neck—that's what has happened in Carol's case.'

It sounded so ominous when he said it like that. She couldn't bring herself to ask the obvious question. If this cancer was curable.

Iain was pointing inside Carol's mouth. 'I'm going to do to two types of surgery on Carol today. Transoral laser surgery is used to treat smaller cancers on the lip, mouth or throat. The laser removes the tumour using a high-power beam of light. The light is attached to a microscope so that I can see the tissue in detail when I'm operating. Carol's tumour is near the back of her throat near her larynx. We need to be very careful and precise. Anything we do could affect her speech. Once we've dealt with that tumour we need to deal with the spread.

'Neck dissection is necessary to remove all the affected lymph nodes in both sides of the neck. Tests have shown the cancer has spread to both sides. The nerve that helps move the lower lip can sometimes be affected. This can cause weakness on one side of the mouth and could potentially make her smile crooked. It would usually return to normal after a few months but I want to avoid that for Carol if I can.'

Lexi nodded. He was thinking about his patient and the impact this surgery could have on her livelihood. If Carol had problems with her speech, it would affect her ability to do her job. Things would be hard enough with her scarring. She didn't need any further complications.

She watched as the team draped Carol's skin and cleaned it prior to any incision. Iain attached the light and microscope to his visor and positioned himself at the entrance to her mouth. He gave his registrar, who was assisting, a nod and then looked around the theatre. 'People, I don't need to tell you how important my concentration is right now. No noise. No interruptions.'

For the next twenty minutes Lexi was scared to breathe. The theatre was eerily quiet. Occasionally Iain spoke quietly to his registrar and they adjusted their positions. She could see the intense focus of the laser. It was almost unthinkable that the slightest movement could mean the laser hitting healthy tissue instead of the tumour.

How could the theatre staff remain so calm? How could Iain keep his nerves in check? She felt sick just thinking about it, and from the look of her cameraman, he felt exactly the same.

Eventually Iain lifted his head, gave a nod and removed his head and eye set. He leaned back as far as he could, his back giving a painful crick.

Even beneath his mask she could see the corners of his eyes lift as he smiled. 'That's it, folks. You can talk again. We'll move on to the next part of the surgery.' The sigh of relief around the room was audible. Tense shoulders sagged and bad jokes started to circulate around the room again.

But Iain was in no way finished. He was joined at one point by Carol's cancer specialist and the two of them reviewed the earlier CT scan to ensure Iain would capture all the lymph nodes affected. The surgery was painstaking. Iain was more exacting, more precise than she could have ever have imagined. The surgery that had been expected to take four hours actually took six, all because Iain was determined not only to remove every possible trace of cancer but also to give Carol the best cosmetic outcome possible.

When he finally finished he inserted a small plastic drain on either side of her neck. After the care and attention to detail Lexi was surprised. It seemed almost unsightly. Iain caught her expression and gave a little shake of his head. 'We'll need to keep these in place for the next twenty-four hours to help drain any excess fluid. It will give Carol a better result overall, even though it doesn't look too pretty right now.'

He gave a final nod at the anaesthetist. 'All yours, Tony. Let's get some analgesia in and bring Carol round. I'll be around for the next two hours if you have any concerns.' He peeled off his gloves and mask. 'Thank you, everyone, for your hard work and attention to detail today. Let's do it all again on Thursday.'

It was almost as if his words gave her permission to sag against the wall. She'd found the day long, tiring, even though she'd been standing virtually in one spot. And this was just one day out of her life. Iain did this most days—sometimes every day—as well as seeing patients at the Hunter Clinic. No wonder he fell asleep in the office.

She watched as Iain moved back over to the theatre sinks to wash up. She could see the way the thin navy scrubs clung to every muscle, every sinew of his lithe body. He was chatting away to one of the scrub nurses as she cleaned the theatre around him. Not flirting. Just easy banter, the way they must act every day.

He was more relaxed in here than he was at the Hunter Clinic. And it didn't take her long to realise why. This was home for Iain. This was his comfort zone.

Iain wasn't renowned for his charm or easygoing

manner. Quite the opposite, in fact. He was known for being gruff, sometimes downright blunt with colleagues and occasionally with patients. But his surgery spoke for itself. As did his patient recovery stories. No one could argue with those.

But if she wanted to increase publicity for the Hunter Clinic she was going to have to dig beneath the surface a little. Reveal a little of what she'd seen in Theatre today. The question was—how to do that? Iain was fiercely private and she was going to have to persuade him to lower his barriers just a touch to let their patients see the human side of the brilliant surgeon.

With the filming today she'd had a clear demonstration of his surgical skills and his commitment to the task. They'd even managed to capture some of his lighter moments with the theatre staff. All of this would be pure television gold, if only she could capture a little of the man as well.

She arched her back, just as he had done earlier. It didn't make the same alarming cricking noise but it certainly stretched her aching muscles. She dragged her eyes away from Iain. From the shaggy hair that had been released from the theatre cap. The hair that she was imagining running her fingers through.

This would never do. She was a professional.

She was always a professional. She'd met numerous celebrities throughout her life and very few of them had impressed her. Very few of them had made her imagination run wild. Not like the way it was at the moment. It must just be fatigue. She was tired—that was all. She'd had a late night last night, after dropping Iain home, and then an early start again this morning. It couldn't be anything else, could it?

She pushed open the door to the changing room and stripped off her pink scrubs and jumped into the shower. It only took a few minutes for the cool water to wake her up a little and she pulled on her red business suit and untied her hair, turning her head upside and down and giving it a good shake. After being confined up all day in a theatre cap, it felt good to finally have it loose again. Last she took her perfume from her bag and squirted liberally, finishing with her red lipstick.

There. Barely human again after how long? She checked her watch. Nearly twelve hours. Her stomach gave a loud rumble.

She was starving. And getting food—preferably of the unhealthy kind—was first on her list.

Iain was waiting at the changing-room doors, hoping he hadn't missed her. Lexi Robbins had been on his radar all day. It was the first time anyone had been in his operating theatre who had actually threatened his focus.

Iain McKenzie was a surgeon who slid into 'the zone' whenever he operated. The patient was his absolute focus—and nothing else penetrated.

But today had been a little different. Even though his focus had still been on his patients, for the first time he'd been conscious of his peripheral vision. The set of pale pink scrubs and wide blue eyes that had occasionally caught his attention.

It had been like a constant, persistent itch. And in Iain's mind the only way to deal with an itch was to scratch it. Maybe if he bent just a little and gave Lexi the interview she wanted she would move on to the next person on her hit list and he could return to a little sanity.

He smelt her first. Her scent permeating through the female changing-room doors. Seconds later the door opened and Lexi, a vision in red with her blonde hair tumbling around her shoulders, appeared.

He hesitated for a second. Lexi Robbins might have spent the day hidden in shapeless scrubs with her hair tucked away and no make-up on, but half an hour later the transformation into gorgeous sex princess was complete.

'Oh, Iain. I wasn't expecting to see you again. Is something wrong? Is Carol okay?'

He smiled. It was nice that her first thought was for the patient that she knew. He nodded his head. 'Carol is doing fine. I'm happy to leave her for the evening and check on her again in the morning. I think she'll have a comfortable night. Tomorrow we'll get her drains out and her husband will bring her kids in for a visit. A few days' rest with staff who will take good care of her will do her the world of good.'

Lexi's face brightened, the smile reaching from ear to ear. It was obvious her concern was genuine and he liked that about her.

'So what can I do for you, Iain? I thought you would be exhausted and want to get home.'

'I do. I mean, I would. But I'd like to get our interview over with first.'

'Really? After the day you've had?' She seemed genuinely surprised.

He nodded. 'Is that OK? Can we do it now?'

She seemed momentarily stunned then she reached into her bag to fumble with her phone. She pulled it out and stared at it for a second.

'Something wrong?'

She shrugged. 'Just the usual. Seventeen messages, I'll get to them later.' She looked around. 'John, the cameraman, will still be about. I'll send him a quick text. Is there somewhere around here we can set up?'

He pointed down the corridor. 'I've already sorted it. The staff at the Hunter Clinic have the use of some office space here. We can use a room just down the corridor.'

'Perfect.' She pressed the details into her phone, sent the message to John and followed him down the corridor.

The office space was standard for any hospital. Not particularly big, with a desk, a phone and a chair. But the pièce de résistance was a picture window with a stunning backdrop of the Thames. Iain watched the expression on her face as she knew instantly it was the ideal setting for the interview. Not only did it give a really traditional view of London, it let patients know the setting for their potential hospital stay if they used the Hunter Clinic. What better selling point could there be?

He should have mentioned it to her earlier, but it hadn't even crossed his mind until his registrar had realised he was going to be interviewed and mentioned the spectacular view.

Lexi started pulling a chair over to the window, nodding at John as he appeared with his camera and instantly began setting up. 'The light will fade soon. We'd better be quick.'

Lexi, ever the professional, nodded and pulled out her notebook. She gave Iain a cheeky wink. 'Want me to sort out some make-up for you before your big screen debut?'

He laughed. 'I think I'll stick with the natural look.'

'And the scrubs?' She pointed to his navy scrubs. He hadn't even given them a second thought. For the sake of the clinic Lexi would probably have preferred him polished and scrubbed in his business suit. More associated with a Harley Street clinic. But that wasn't for Iain.

He lifted his hands. 'I'd prefer it if patients see me the way that I spend most of my day. They don't expect me to operate with the business suit on.'

She nodded. 'True. But I might need you to put on a business suit for some publicity shots later. Deal?' She lifted her eyebrows as her cheeky smile got even wider. 'Or how about a kilt, Iain? Because once the ladies have heard that Scottish accent…'

He lifted his hand. 'Enough. I might agree to the suit, but that's it.'

She sat down and waited for the signal from John to say that he was ready. 'How about we negotiate on the kilt?'

He tried not to laugh. Did she have any idea how appealing she looked right now? With her designer red suit, black stilettos and red lipstick? Lexi Robbins didn't look like a girl who'd just spent the last twelve hours on her feet. Especially with those loose waves of blonde hair and sultry perfume floating in the air.

'I've negotiated on the interview. That's enough for now.'

John gave Lexi the nod and the light came on at the top of the camera. Iain adjusted his position under its glare.

'Let's start simply,' Lexi said. 'Start by telling us your name, what you do at Hunter Clinic and how long you've worked there.'

Iain nodded and took a deep breath. If he could get

this over and done with tonight then this could be the end of his contact with Lexi Robbins.

This itch just didn't need scratched. It was like a chicken pox. It needed the head knocked clean off it.

He looked towards the camera. Smiling just wasn't his natural instinct. 'I'm Iain McKenzie and you might guess by the accent that I'm from Edinburgh. I've worked at the Hunter Clinic for the last two years, specialising in reconstructive surgery.'

Lexi nodded. 'Iain, can you tell us the difference between general plastic surgery and reconstructive surgery?'

He nodded curtly, trying to choose his words carefully. Trying to use terms that people would be familiar with instead of medical jargon. 'I can do all the things that a general plastic surgeon can do—face lifts, tummy tucks, breast enhancements—but I specialise in surgery that's a bit more complicated. For example, lots of my patients have had surgery in other places—other countries—that might not have given them the outcome they wanted or expected. Some of the surgery I do would be termed corrective surgery.'

Lexi made some circling motions with her hand, urging him to continue.

He took a deep breath. 'I also deal with a number of patients who've had cancer that's affected various parts of their bodies. That can be anywhere, their breasts, their faces, head and neck. All areas that might require reconstruction after the cancer has been removed and treatment has been completed. Often these surgeries require rebuilding, reshaping or prosthetic implants to give the patient back the body that they want.'

'Is it purely cosmetic reconstructive surgery that you do at the Hunter Clinic, Iain?'

He shook his head. 'I also specialise in functional surgery. I've treated a number of patients with oral and cleft-palate defects. In this country, most children would have surgery done at a young age. The same facilities aren't available in all countries and I've dealt with a number of adult patients who've come to the Hunter Clinic to have these corrected later in life. It can make a huge difference to their ability to eat and to their speech to have these corrected later in life.

'Of course, we also have a number of rehabilitation services, such as speech therapists and dieticians, available to support the care of these patients. All our services are about giving people the best possible outcome from their surgeries.' He shook his head firmly. 'I wouldn't perform any surgery that I didn't believe would have a positive impact on the patient.'

He was trying his absolute best not to say anything that would make Lexi throw her hands up in horror. He didn't want to have to repeat this interview over and over again because he'd been way too blunt about some of the vanity-driven requests of clients.

Lexi shifted in her chair, crossing her legs and giving him an unexpectedly good view of her shapely calves and thighs.

'That's great, Iain, thanks. Now, can you tell us a little more about yourself?'

She was staring at him with those big blue eyes. Smiling, with her open face and manner. He could almost forget that the camera was in the room with them.

'Well, there's not much to tell. I grew up in Edinburgh, Scotland. I did my university and medical training at hospitals in Edinburgh. I was a Scout—though not a very good one. I could never master the art of lighting a fire.' He raised his eyebrows at Lexi, who let out a little laugh.

'Our patients would like to know a little more about the man behind the surgeon's mask. How about I ask you some questions?'

He shifted in his chair a little uncomfortably. From this position it was still too easy to keep his eyes on Lexi's legs.

She leaned forward a little, as if she was trying to encourage him. It also gave him the slightest hint of her cleavage down her firmly fastened white blouse. Cleavage that he would love to get his hands on—to see who had done her surgery and whether it met with his approval. To see whether it was right for Lexi.

Those legs again and the thoughts of having his hands on her breasts was causing a familiar sensation. One that a camera certainly shouldn't see. He shifted his position.

'Let's try some quick-fire questions.'

'Yes, let's.' The words came out almost unconsciously. It must be fatigue. That must be why he was being so pliable. That, or the fact he needed to try some distraction techniques right now. Normally, by this point he would have got up and walked away. Personal questions really went against all his principles.

'Movies—action or drama?'

He shook his head. 'Neither. Sci-fi. Every single time.' These kinds of question were fine. They were harmless. Inane.

'Italian, Chinese or Indian food?'

'Depends entirely what day of the week it is—and,

what I'm doing the next day. Italian, with no garlic, if I'm operating the next day. Chinese if it's heading towards a weekend. And Indian food on a Saturday night, preferably with a pint.'

'A pint?'

'You know.' He lifted and gestured with his wrist. 'Like all good Scotsmen. A pint of beer.'

She smiled again. 'Just the one?'

He shrugged. 'Normally, depends on the company.'

She paused, as if taking in those words, then glanced back down at her notes. 'Best job—apart from the Hunter Clinic, of course.'

He frowned, racking his brain. 'There are two—completely different from each other. One, as a trainee I spent two months with the mountain rescue team in the Swiss Alps. Learnt more in those two months than I did at any other point in my training. It was fabulous.'

Lexi nodded. 'And the second?'

'Voluntary work. I visited one of the Romanian orphanages a number of years ago and did some of the specialist cleft-lip and palate surgeries that I described earlier.' His voice lowered. 'It was a real eye-opener. And a really rewarding time. I'm planning on going back next summer.'

Lexi was looking excited. 'The Hunter Clinic will be supporting some charity work and has just joined up with Olivia Fairchild's charity Fair Go. Will you be available to do some work for that charity, Iain?'

The way she said the words was so innocent. So off the cuff. But he knew fine well she was capturing him on tape. Just as well he'd already had this conversation with Leo Hunter and had agreed to help in any way he could. 'I'm happy to help the Hunter Clinic in any charity that they choose to support—just as they are happy to help me, in any charity I choose to support.' Touché. These things worked both ways.

Lexi was still leaning forward. Still making him feel as if it were only the two of them in the room. It was starting to fire his imagination again. Make him remember the things that had kept him from sleeping last night.

She gave him her dazzling smile. 'What about your favourite holiday?'

It was an innocent question. A completely innocuous question. But for Iain it hit a nerve he was unprepared for. Pictures were instantly conjured up in his mind. Pictures of a perfect honeymoon in Venice, with thousands of images of the multicoloured houses, the islands, the canals, the gondolas and the wonders of St Mark's Square. If he breathed in deeply enough he could practically smell the place. The words formed on his lips without him even thinking. 'Venice, for my honeymoon. It was beautiful. The most perfect city in the world.'

'You were married?'

The surprised tone in Lexi's voice brought him to his senses. He knew he should answer this casually. It had been a slip. His fault, something he didn't normally reveal, and he could have kicked himself for saying the words out loud.

But there was something else. Something hanging in the air between them. Something that he hadn't quite yet managed to fathom.

And as Lexi sat there in the dimming light, with her wide blue eyes, designer red suit and long, lithe limbs, all he could remember was the Lexi from his dream last night. The one who had been straddling him with those long legs. The one who had danced those red lips across his forehead and chest. Taking him to a whole place he hadn't visited in a long time.

His reaction was automatic. He stood up, causing both Lexi and John to start in their positions. Trying to erase all those thoughts from his head and trying to push the aroma of her perfume from his senses.

He needed to get out of there. He needed space. More importantly, he needed to get away from *her*. As far away as possible.

'Iain? Iain, what's wrong?' She stood up, straightening her skirt and taking a step towards him.

He couldn't let her touch him. He couldn't let her be near him at all right now.

'Interview over,' he growled as he strode to the door and flung it open, letting it slam off the wall as his steps ate up the corridor outside.

CHAPTER FIVE

'As if this day could get any worse.' Lexi let out a sigh as the buzzer sounded loudly again. It was almost as if someone upstairs was laughing at her, waiting until her toe was perfectly poised above the millions of lavender-scented bubbles and her satin dressing gown had just hit the floor.

The buzzing was becoming more incessant, more desperate. So she picked the dressing-gown back off the floor and knotted it tightly around her waist. 'This had better be good,' she muttered as she made her way to the door.

She swung the door open, fatigue stopping her from putting her sensible head in place. The one that would make her put all her locks in place and check through the peephole before opening the door, half-dressed.

'Iain!'

The very last person she had expected to see tonight.

The cool night air swept around her thin dressing-gown, making it billow against her legs. She tried to grab it, tried to hide the swathes of skin it was threatening to expose.

Iain was leaning against her doorjamb, his shaggy

hair looking as if he'd spent the last two hours running his fingers through it.

Twenty minutes. That was how long the interview had lasted. And while what she'd captured initially was just what she'd hoped for and would be perfect for the publicity campaign, the ending had been more than a little abrupt.

She'd been left standing with her jaw bouncing off the floor as John had shrugged, packed up his camera and left for the night. Iain had vanished. No one in the hospital had known where he was and Lexi had been left to make her way home wondering what on earth she'd done wrong.

A long hot bubble bath, a glass of wine and a mountain of pizza had been on the cards.

'Can I come in?' His manner was still abrupt but he was looking at her with those big brown eyes that sucked you in and made you forget how to give appropriate answers. It didn't help that every hair on her skin was standing on end and she couldn't bear to look down and see the effects on her nipples.

She stood aside. 'If you want,' she muttered, unsure whether this was a good idea or not.

Iain walked into her flat, instantly filling it with his large frame. It wasn't as if she lived somewhere small. By most people's proportions Lexi's London flat was positively comfortable. But just having Iain in it seemed to make the air close in around her. She was feeling completely and utterly underdressed.

He was pacing. Pacing around her flat. He had the obligatory grey suit on, with a dark blue shirt, his top button open and tie askew. 'Look, Lexi, about earlier—'

'What about earlier?' she interrupted, folding her

arms across her chest as it seemed the safest position for them.

He stopped pacing and took a step towards her, closing the space between them in an instant. His voice was low. 'I'm not very good at this.'

'Not very good at what?' Was that her voice that sounded all squeaky? How embarrassing. He was too close. She could reach right out and put her hand on the plane of his chest. *So not a good idea.* It was better to keep her eyes fixed on her dark wooden floor and bare feet with their painted toenails.

She heard him sigh. 'Saying sorry.'

Her head snapped back up in time to see him run his fingers through his hair and fix his brown eyes on hers. So not what she was expecting.

Being this close to Iain McKenzie was more than a little disconcerting. Particularly when she was partially dressed.

'Lexi?' he said softly.

'What?'

'Would you mind putting some clothes on? It's kind of distracting, seeing you like this.'

She felt the colour rush into her cheeks. On one hand she should be glad that he found her distracting—on the other? She wasn't entirely sure if that was a good or a bad thing.

'I was just about to step into the bath,' she said by way of explanation.

'Have you eaten?' He glanced at the clock.

She shook her head. 'Ordering pizza was next on my list.'

He reached over and touched her arm, his warm hand

circling her cold wrist. 'Then let me take you out to dinner.'

She pulled back a little, trying not to focus on the electricity shooting up her arm. 'It's nearly nine o'clock. Where are you going to find somewhere that still has a table?'

He gave her a knowing smile and tapped the edge of his nose. 'Leave that to me. Will you come, Lexi? We need to talk.'

For a second she hesitated. Was this a good idea? Maybe she could persuade Iain McKenzie that the job she was doing was actually a worthwhile one. Maybe she could persuade him to be a little more involved. Anything that would help the charity work of the clinic would surely be worth a dinner. No matter how blunt her dinner partner was.

She looked down at her pink toes. 'What do I need to wear?'

'You could wear a plastic bin bag, Lexi, you'd still look good.' The words tripped off his tongue as easily as could be. He didn't even seem embarrassed by them.

She walked off towards the bedroom. 'That didn't help!' she shouted over her shoulder.

Fifteen minutes later he walked her down a street in London she'd never visited before. A warm and enveloping smell started to surround them as Iain walked towards a red-painted door and pushed it open. There was no traditional restaurant window looking out onto the street and advertising its presence. Instead there was a winding staircase up to what felt like the top of a private townhouse.

The smell was intriguing her. 'What is this place?'

She looked around for a restaurant name or menu but there was nothing obvious.

A man appeared at Iain's side and pulled a curtain aside for them, revealing a small intimate restaurant. 'Nice to see you again, mate. Find yourself a table.'

She smiled at the rich Australian accent and informality of it all. The restaurant was busy, with only a few free tables.

Then reality started to hit and she took a little step backwards. 'Isn't that Georgie Perkins, the Oscar-winning actress?' The woman was dressed in a green suit and drinking wine with her husband and another couple.

Iain gave a nod and pulled out a chair for her. Lexi smoothed the front of her red jersey dress as she sat down, yet again feeling instantly underdressed.

'Hey, Iain.'

'Hey, Kevin, nice to see you.' He gave the man on their right a curt nod.

Lexi leaned forward and gritted her teeth. 'Sir Kevin Bain? Chairman of the richest football club in the country?'

Iain reached over and grabbed some bread out of the basket sitting on the table. 'Yup, him and wife number three.' He leaned forward and winked. 'She's one of ours, you know.'

'What is this place?' Lexi asked, looking around and realising she still hadn't seen a name anywhere.

'It's Frank's,' he said simply.

'And who is Frank?' she asked. 'And how come I've never heard of this place?' She pointed over at the other diners. 'Other people obviously have.'

'Take it from me, this place is for good eating and

good wine. You won't find any paparazzi hanging around outside the door, and it never needs to advertise.'

Lexi settled back into her chair. He was right. The place had a certain ambience about it, as if the celebrities who were there knew their privacy would be guarded. She had dined around lots of people like this, but she'd never seen them quite so relaxed—quite so unguarded. Would the same rules apply to Iain? Was this why he'd brought her here?

The guy from the door appeared and handed them menus. He looked at Lexi and held out his hand. 'I haven't met you before, have I?'

She shook her head and met his firm handshake. 'Lexi Robbins. I work with Iain.'

'Lucky man. I'm Frank. If it's not on the menu—just ask and I'll make it for you. I can handle all the allergy quirks, all the special diets, but if you're a crazy who just doesn't want any calories then I'll pour you a glass of water and charge you a hundred bucks.'

She laughed, instantly liking the big Australian, then grabbed her stomach as it let out a little grumble.

He looked skyward. 'My favourite noise in the world. What will it be, lady?'

Lexi handed him back the menu. She'd barely even glanced at it but felt as if she could trust his judgement. 'I'm a chicken girl. Do anything you like with it—except give me bones.'

Frank blew some of his hair off his forehead. 'Amateur!' He turned to Iain, 'Go on, master of the universe. Surprise me.'

Iain rolled his eyes. 'If you keep talking to me like that, I won't come back.'

'Fat chance.'

He nodded and handed over his menu. 'You're right. I'll have the usual.'

Frank disappeared muttering, only to reappear and plonk a bottle of red wine on the table along with a couple of glasses.

Iain lifted the bottle and gave a smile. 'Are you okay with red, or would you prefer something else?'

She lifted her glass towards him. 'Red's fine. Just not too much.'

Iain filled her glass part way then did the same with his own.

'To Frank's?'

She smiled and clinked glasses with him. 'To Frank's. Here's hoping the food is as good as you promised.'

Iain nodded with confidence. 'You've nothing to worry about here.' He looked around at their surroundings. 'This place is all about chilling and relaxing. That's why I brought you here. We could have gone to Drake's but the food, and the company, are infinitely better here.'

She smiled. Drake's would be packed to the rafters right now—probably with most of the staff from the Hunter Clinic and St Catherine's. It was unlikely they would have managed to have any kind of conversation in there.

'Who is Frank?'

'Just a sad Australian who needed an op one day. He told me he owned a restaurant and invited me for dinner after that.'

'You're not going to reveal?'

He shook his head. 'Only if you get me drunk.'

There it was. That little hint of humour that appeared on the rarest of occasions. She liked it. It proved that the gruff exterior of Iain McKenzie wasn't as rock solid as it first seemed and the man could actually laugh at himself.

He set his glass on the table. 'So, Lexi Robbins. I'm curious about you.'

'Why?'

'Because I don't know much about you.'

She sighed. 'Haven't you ever read a newspaper or a gossip magazine? My life's been pretty much an open book since the second I was born.'

'Yeah, but that's not the kind of thing I want to know.'

She leaned forward a little. 'So what do you want to know, Iain McKenzie?'

She hadn't meant it to come out that way. Slightly flirtatious. Slightly coy. But they were sitting in a darkened candlelit restaurant in the middle of London after a stressful day. She really didn't want to have to think too hard. She was only doing what came naturally.

His eyes skimmed over her. She could feel them. Taking in her loose curls and comfortably fitted dress. She hadn't bothered with much make-up, only reapplying her lipstick and adding some mascara.

His finger ran round the rim of his glass. 'I'm curious why Leo Hunter hired you to be the head of PR. You must be good—you must be very good, because everyone working at the clinic was handpicked by Leo.'

'And the implication is that I don't seem that good?' Her reaction was instant. She could get angry. She could get upset and tearful. But to be frank she'd heard it all before and was far too tired to fight. She leaned back in her seat and took a sip of her wine.

'I didn't say that.' His voice was quiet. Controlled. As if he was trying to get the measure of her.

She let out a sigh. 'You didn't have to, Iain. A million others have implied it before you.'

His eyebrow rose ever so slightly. 'Why would they do that?'

She took another sip of wine. It was official. A few sips were definitely hitting the right spot and relaxing her. That's what happened when you hardly managed to eat all day.

'Let's start at the very beginning. You might have guessed I was a bit of an accessory to my parents.'

'That seems a bit harsh.'

She let out a snort. 'Try living it. It gets a bit much when they constantly tell you you're not pretty enough or good enough.'

Iain leaned forward, his eyes practically smoking. 'Your parents did that?'

She shook her head a little. 'Not in so many words. It was implied—in a lot of ways. I was constantly in the press, being compared to my mother, the supermodel. What girl really wants to spend her life being told she's not as pretty as her mother?' Lexi lowered her eyes. 'I focused on other things. I was academic. I liked school, I guess in that respect I took after my father. Then I had a bit of an accident and I was out of school for a while.'

'What happened?' She could see the concern on his face and felt a lump forming in her throat. So much time had passed. It had been so long ago. She'd got over this and put it behind her, she didn't feel the need to go into details.

'I had a horse-riding accident and needed some major surgery.' It was best to leave the specifics out. 'My mum and dad were there for a few days, but they were busy. They both had contractual obligations. So once they knew I would live but need some serious recuperation, they handed me over to my Aunt Jo.'

Iain wrinkled his nose. 'I thought you said your family was permanently in the papers. I've not heard of your Aunt Jo.'

Lexi smiled. 'I bet you have. Josephine Kirk. She's my father's sister.'

His eyes widened. 'Wasn't she an ambassador for children for the UN?'

Lexi nodded. 'After I recovered from surgery I still wasn't really fit for school. I spent the summer with Aunt Jo—and almost every summer after that. We're close.'

'Closer than you are to your mum and dad?'

'Absolutely.' There was no hesitation in the word.

Iain sucked in his breath. He had a great relationship with his mum and dad. They'd been his absolute backbone when he'd lost his wife. He couldn't imagine not knowing that they would always be there for him. Lexi had described herself as an 'accessory'—what kind of parents did she have?

He watched her in the flickering candlelight. She seemed totally at ease, totally oblivious to the casual, admiring glances she was receiving. He'd never given Lexi much thought. Even when she'd started working at the clinic he hadn't really taken much notice of her credentials or her work ethic. But she was rapidly turning into the most interesting woman he'd met in a long time.

Lexi was tempted to fill the silence. Should she tell Iain more?

He was a doctor. He would understand.

But she wasn't really ready to share any personal details. Her aunt was the wisest woman she'd known.

Lexi's surgery had been extensive—a horseshoe in her lower abdomen had caused tremendous damage to her young body, meaning that she would never be able to have children of her own. But her aunt had taken her to a place to show her the little children in this world who would need someone like her—someone to love and care for them in future years.

And it had helped Lexi move on. To stop thinking about the fact she'd never be pregnant and give birth, but to realise that not everyone became a mother in the same way. To realise that if her dream was to have a family then the possibility was there.

Very few people knew that detail about her. And even though Iain was watching her with those big chocolate-brown eyes, lulling her into a false sense of security that might make her reveal her innermost secrets, she just couldn't say anything else.

This was about protecting herself and protecting the decisions that she made. She'd learned from her mistakes. So no matter what spark she currently felt towards the sexy Scot, it wouldn't make her reveal her most intimate secrets.

'Here we go, folks. Chicken with no bones, and my own special concoction, and the usual for you.' Frank placed the plates down on the table with a flourish and then melted into the back ground once again.

Lexi leaned forward and breathed deeply. 'Oh, this smells great. I'm starved. What have you got?'

Iain smiled. 'Pulled pork with spicy sauce and hand-cut chips. Can't beat it. It's perfect every time I come here.' He picked up his knife and fork. 'What did Frank make for you?'

Lexi smiled. 'I think he secretly switched on his

telepathic powers and invaded my brain. He's given me something that I'll love, chicken with mushrooms and some spicy potato bravas. I can't wait.'

Iain nodded. 'Frank always seems to get it just right.' He waved his fork at her. 'Dig in.'

She did. And Iain watched with enjoyment as she cleared her plate and then sat back and gave a sigh. 'That was much better than pizza.'

A woman who wasn't scared to eat. What a relief. At least fifty per cent of the women he saw at the Hunter Clinic had some weird ideas about diets and eating. Some of them were even refused surgery because their BMIs were so low it made them anaesthetic risks. It was nice to be in the company of a woman who seemed comfortable in her own skin.

The strange thing was, it obviously hadn't always been the case. She'd already told him about her experiences of being compared to her mother, and there was the fact she'd obviously had implants. Why would someone like Lexi think she needed to have surgery?

But the more time he spent in her company the more he was drawn to her. She was warm and charming with a good sense of humour. And even though she'd spent part of her life in the spotlight she certainly wasn't the vacant blonde she was sometimes portrayed as in the press.

Lexi was highly intelligent, well read with an opinion on everything. And pushing aside the breasts and fabulous legs, there was just more and more to like about her.

'What did your parents think about you doing your degree?'

She stared at him and the edges of her lips curled

upwards. 'Why do I get the impression that you already know?'

'I'm just guessing your mother might have had other plans for you.'

'Oh, she did. And they all involved being her personal assistant and PR girl. She was most annoyed when I passed my exams with flying colours and got a place to study international business.'

Iain nodded slowly. 'Interesting choice.'

'It was fabulous. And in the final year you had a placement in a real business for six months. I loved it. They offered me a job straight after uni.'

'And did you take it?'

'I did for a few years.' She took another sip of her wine. 'Funny thing was, I actually found myself drawn towards PR work. Maybe my mother knew me better than I knew myself all along.'

'So did you work for her?'

Lexi smiled. And it was the best smile of the evening, reaching all the way into her eyes and giving her a cheeky sparkle. 'Not a chance.'

He laughed. There were so many qualities here that he hadn't seen before. Hadn't taken the chance to see. All because from the second he'd set eyes on Lexi she'd woken up his libido like a shrieking alarm clock. Something he definitely hadn't been prepared for. And something he definitely hadn't been ready to acknowledge.

'So how did you end up being head-hunted by Leo Hunter at the clinic?'

She nodded. 'Leo is very persuasive. I was working for a variety of charities when he approached me. At first I wasn't interested in trying to raise the profile of a private clinic. It seemed almost the exact opposite of what I was currently doing. But Leo told me about the work they wanted to fund and the people he wanted to help by increasing the client base of the clinic...' Her voice tailed off and Iain smiled.

'I get it. Leo is very persuasive.'

She smiled again, her blue eyes fixed on his face. He pushed his wine glass aside. Lexi Robbins was beginning to wreak havoc on his senses.

'I like the clinic. I'm proud of the job I do. I want to be known for me, Lexi Robbins. I hate it when a newspaper article starts, "Lexi Robbins, daughter of..."' She shook her head. 'I'm my own person. But I'm also wise enough to know that some of the clients I've brought to the clinic saw me in the first instance because I'm my father's—or my mother's—daughter.'

Iain lifted his glass and held it up to her. 'Well, in that case I want to make a toast. To Lexi Robbins, PR genius of Hunter Clinic, who will bring in thousands of pounds to help fund the charity projects.'

She lifted her glass and gave him a wink. '*Tens* of thousands of pounds.'

They clinked glasses.

'Dessert?' Frank appeared at their side again, clearing their dinner plates. 'Could I tempt you with a beautiful pear tart with chocolate sauce?'

Lexi shook her head. 'It sounds heavenly, Frank, but I'm all chickened out.'

'Too much?' he asked.

'No, just perfect. But I honestly couldn't eat another bite.' She glanced at her watch. 'It's been a long day and I'm feeling kind of tired.' She looked apologetically at Iain and he stood immediately to come to her side and pull her chair out.

'No problem at all.' He pulled some money from his wallet to pay Frank and gave him a wave as he helped Lexi on with her coat. It was late. He should have paid more attention to the time. Not everyone was an insomniac like him. Not everyone did anything possible rather than go to bed and stare at the ceiling, hoping to have a dreamless night.

'I hope you don't mind, Iain.' She spun round to face him and her big blue eyes and blonde curls were directly under his nose. Just inches away from him.

'Of course not, Lexi. I'll walk you home. I should have kept my eye on the time.' He held out his arm as they walked down the stairs and out onto the street and was secretly glad when she slid her arm through his.

He was telling himself he was only being polite. It didn't mean anything else. It didn't mean anything at all.

But walking through the darkened London streets with a beautiful woman on his arm gave him a little buzz. And not in the traditional sense. As a surgeon Iain knew better than most that true beauty came from the inside. And tonight he'd been well and truly exposed to the true beauty of Lexi Robbins.

He'd watched a programme once where people sat behind a screen and described how they looked to an artist who drew a picture of them from their description. Then one of their friends described them to the same artist. The programme ended with the pictures hanging side by side. It truly reflected that people often didn't see themselves the way others saw them. The pictures where the people had described themselves were nowhere near as beautiful as the ones where their friends had described them. And the friends' pictures were a much more accurate reflection of the individual.

Why had this sprung to mind? Because he could tell—just from tonight and their conversation—that Lexi couldn't see the beauty he could, both inside and out.

It still intrigued him why she'd felt the need to get implants. But it seemed too personal a question to ask. It could be that Lexi had had other reasons for surgery and the implants were a consequence of that.

They rounded the corner into her street.

'You're awfully quiet, Iain. Something wrong?' Even her voice sounded merry. Lexi was a pleasure to be around.

'Not at all. I'm just enjoying the company.'

'That'll be a first. You're usually playing hide and seek with me.'

Yes. She was nobody's fool, even if she was usually too polite to say so. It seemed the wine had loosened her tongue.

He stopped and spun her round, catching her around the waist. 'Lexi Robbins, I have no idea what you mean,' he said in mock horror.

She pointed her finger at his wide chest. 'I'll have you know, Iain McKenzie, that I was the champion hide-and-seeker as a kid.' She lifted her hands in the air. 'You can run but you can't hide.'

'Who says I want to hide?' he said, closing the space between them in an instant and pulling her hard against his chest.

This time the sensation of her firm breasts wasn't a surprise. But the way her body melded into his was. It was almost as if she…fitted.

This time her hands rested on his shoulders. The initial flash of surprise disappeared from her eyes and her gaze remained steady on his.

Her voice was a little breathless. 'Admit it, Iain, you have been hiding from me.' There wasn't another person on the street. It was just the two of them. Nothing and no one to interrupt them.

'And all of a sudden I can't imagine why,' he said quietly.

Silence. The tension between them was almost palpable. The air was practically crackling.

Then she almost tipped him over the edge. Her tongue ran along her red lips, moistening them and making them glisten in the dim light. Her voice was hoarse. 'Neither can I,' she whispered, as her fingers pressed into his shoulder bones.

He didn't think. He didn't stop to think for a second.

This was all about instinct. And his instinct was to make her his.

He bent his head, taking her lips as his own. Claiming them in every way possible. His hands pulled her hips close against his then he lifted them and wound them through her blonde hair. So soft, so silky between his fingers.

She let out a little gasp and raised herself up on tiptoe, trying to get herself even closer to him. Her hands left his shoulders and slid around to the back of his neck, curving themselves across the expanse of his back.

There was nothing tender and gentle about this kiss. This was pure and utter unbridled lust. That scent was under his nose again, drifting through his senses. It had followed him for days, driving him slowly and utterly crazy with the thoughts it evoked in his brain.

Lexi was matching him every step of the way. He

pushed her back from the pavement towards the entrance of her flat. His hands were drifting under her coat, up the sensual curves of her waist and hips, relishing the feel of the clingy jersey dress beneath his fingertips. Then his hands met her breasts, the rational part of his brain wondering if she would react to his touch but the sensual part of his brain already on a mission he had to complete. Beneath the thin material her nipples reacted in his palms, making him stifle a groan in the back of his throat.

He pressed her further against the wall, one of her legs rising up and hitching on his hip, his hardness pushing against her core. His head had fallen to her neck now, to the source of that delicious sensual scent. He could taste it under his lips as his tongue moved around the soft skin at the bottom of her neck and along her fine clavicle. Her hands were moving in one direction—with a distinct purpose—and his back arched towards her.

His fingers were following suit, pushing up her dress and edging along the inside of her thigh.

'Iain,' she panted.

'What?' He didn't even look up, didn't want to stop what was happening.

Her body was reacting to his every touch, completely and utterly responding to every single move he made.

A cool breeze danced across his skin where she'd opened a few buttons on his shirt and the sweep of air caused him to stiffen.

He looked up. Lexi's gaze was fixed on his. Part of it passion, part of it confusion. He could see the wealth of emotions behind her blue eyes and it brought him crashing to earth with an almighty thump.

Lexi. It was Lexi Robbins standing in front of him now.

It was Lexi Robbins who had stoked his emotions so high he'd almost choked on them.

Blonde hair, blue eyes. Staring at him with a look of expectation, a look of reciprocation of the feelings that were bubbling inside him.

It was like a bucketful of ice chips tumbling over his body. The horrible, stomach-churning realisation that not once this evening—not once—had he given Bonnie a second thought.

He stepped backwards, trying to put some distance between him and Lexi. Distance that had already formed in his mind a mile wide.

For the last few years he'd thought about Bonnie every single day. *Every single day.*

Whether it was first thing in the morning when he woke up, at some quiet time snatched in the middle of the day, or late at night when he was home alone, Bonnie had appeared in his thoughts every day. Sometimes the memories were good ones, happy thoughts of places they'd been, things they'd experienced together.

Other times he was in Theatre when he relived those horrendous moments. Losing his precious wife and losing his twins in one fell swoop.

Other times he was racked with guilt, replaying conversations when he'd persuaded her to give IVF one last go. To give that particular chance of having a family that way one last try.

So many steps in his life that he wanted to rewind. Wanted to turn back the clock and do differently.

But no matter what the thoughts, no matter whether

the memories were good or bad, they had been there. Every single day. Until now.

The guilt was horrendous. From the second he'd got up that morning he'd thought about Lexi, knowing that she was meeting him at Kate's.

He'd even thought about her at some points today during surgery. Unthinkable.

The only time today he'd given Bonnie any thought had been the tiniest fleeting moment at the end of the interview when he'd walked out.

But it had vanished in a flash when he'd realised his reaction had been over the top and his priority had been to apologise to Lexi. Not to sit down for a few seconds and wonder why he was so mixed up. Wonder why he was reacting in such an irrational way.

Somewhere along the way an invisible line had been crossed without him even realising it. A line that he'd drawn in the sand years ago to protect himself from taking actions that could affect the life of another. The consequences were too big a cross to bear.

Casual relationships were fine. But Lexi was no one's casual relationship. And he'd known that from the second he'd seen her and realised the affect she had on him.

Avoiding her had been a self-preservation technique—one he should have stuck to.

'Iain? Iain, what's wrong?' Her voice was still breathy, panting, as if she was full of pent-up frustration. The last thing he needed right now. What he needed right now was space. Distance. As much as possible.

'This was a mistake. A big mistake.' With every word he stepped back a little further, as if it helped him say the words.

A splash of rain landed on his nose and he looked upwards at the dark sky above him. Clouds were circling above his head in more ways than one.

'I have to go. I'm sorry, Lexi. Let's just leave it. Just leave it alone.'

She started to shake her head. Utter confusion was painted across her face and his gut clenched at the fact he'd hurt her. It had never been his intention. Things had just got out of control.

'But, Iain—'

He whipped away as the rain started to deluge the pavement around him, his stride lengthening with every step.

He didn't care about the weather, he didn't care about the rain.

He just needed to get away from her. Get away from her intoxicating scent. Even as he walked down the street he could still smell her—smell her perfume on his clothes.

He lifted his hand and something reflected under the orange streetlight. A strand of shiny blonde hair, glittering like a moonlit stream. She was everywhere.

Not just in his head.

Guilt ground away at him. He should be thinking of Bonnie and his lost children. He should be remembering the terrible impact he'd had on three lives, all because he'd persuaded his beautiful wife to give IVF one last try. She hadn't been sure. The previous two attempts had been tougher than either of them had anticipated, and they'd almost resigned themselves to the fact that they wouldn't have a family by a natural means.

And he'd felt fine about that.

So, why, why had he pushed for one last try? Even

he couldn't fathom out the details now. The decision seemed so ridiculous, so misguided. And that had been before the eventual outcome.

Carrying two tiny white coffins next to his wife's had been the end of Iain McKenzie.

It had been the end of the light-hearted, laughter-filled man that he'd become thanks to Bonnie. She had always been the person to lift his sometimes dark moods. She'd always been the glass-half-full kind of girl.

She'd been his shining light. And look what he'd done to her.

'Beloved Wife. Beloved Son. Beloved Daughter.'

The words etched in gold on the black granite, along with the three red poppies, were forever in the back of his mind.

Maybe he'd been wrong to come to London. Maybe he should have stayed in Edinburgh, where he could have visited the grave every day?

But the smoky strands of depression had been circling around his brain. Creeping up on him with their strangulating hands. His parents, his friends and his family had all urged him to go with Leo. They had told him it was for the best. They had told him he needed a fresh start.

They hadn't counted on Lexi Robbins.

And, three years later, neither had he.

CHAPTER SIX

THE DEMONS WERE whispering in Lexi's ear again. Those horrible little voices of self-doubt and self-deprecation.

She'd fought hard to keep them at bay as it seemed as if there had been constant reinforcement of them in her life.

First from her parents. Then from her boyfriend. The one who'd liked her name and standing instead of Lexi Robbins the person, Lexi Robbins, the human being.

Jack Parker had spent most of his time mocking her bedroom performance and mocking her flat chest. It had taken her a long time to get the measure of him. And it had been at his insistence that she'd gone for the boob job.

Her hands went automatically to her breasts. Automatically to the over-sensitised skin that Iain McKenzie had just been touching.

The rain was pelting down, soaking straight through her thin raincoat and even thinner jersey dress. But Lexi didn't care about the rain.

She was feeling a surge of anger in her belly.

It had taken too long, too many years for her to come to terms with who she really was and not who people thought she should be. The gentle, steady support from her aunt had been invaluable. She wasn't about to stand back and let those old feelings invade her life again.

She was strong now. She was determined.

She leaned back against the wall as her legs gave way a little under the maelstrom of emotions that were threatening to overwhelm her.

She could see her ex's face in her mind. The super-confident Jack Parker squeezing her small breasts contemptuously and comparing them to the latest model in the newspaper. Telling her that she'd never look good in their holiday shots in the Bahamas. The ones that he'd tipped the newspapers off about.

And his caustic, consistent putdowns had chipped away at her already low self-esteem.

She had already worn two sets of chicken fillets in her bra. She hadn't particularly liked her body shape herself. Dresses that had fitted her around the hips and thighs had sagged over her chest—unless she'd worn her chicken fillets. But she could have lived with that because the rest of the world hadn't seen her naked.

Only Jack had. But he hadn't liked what he'd seen.

It had taken all her strength and resilience to get rid of him. Once she'd had the breast implants he'd started suggesting other improvements. So she'd made the ultimate improvement and got rid of him—tossing his clothes out onto the street—before he'd dragged her down any further.

She would never, ever let another man do that to her.

Let another man make her feel that way.

Not even Iain McKenzie.

It had taken her time to accept the changes to her body. To finally realise that she did actually like the shape she had now. She only wished she'd made the decision for herself. She wouldn't let anyone chip away at her self-esteem again.

She started to walk in the rain. Striding down the same street that he'd taken, following the road to his townhouse. She didn't care that it was late at night. She didn't care that she was the only person crazy enough to be out in weather like this—right now it matched her mood.

And as if to magnify her building temper, there was a flash of lightning above her, closely followed by a rumble of thunder.

Her anger built with every step she took.

She knew there was something between them. Any fool could see that.

How dared he call what had just happened a mistake?

He'd felt every single thing that she'd felt. He'd felt every tiny little spark and electric current that she had.

He'd been every bit as turned on as she'd been.

Did he think this was something she did every day—in the middle of the street?

No. She wouldn't let him treat her like that. Not for a second. Not in this lifetime.

Her footsteps quickened. Her normally bouncy curled hair was drenched, hanging in bedraggled rope-like swaths around her head. She reached up and rubbed her eye, coming away with a dark-washed smudge. What little mascara had been there was now obviously streaked down her face. But she didn't care.

She had no desire to go home and get changed. To strip off her wet clothes and climb under a warm duvet. The lightning flashed again. It was spurring her on, guiding her path straight to his door.

She climbed up his steps and put one finger on his

doorbell, pressing hard and leaving it there. The other hand she clenched into a fist and banged on the door. She wouldn't be ignored. She wouldn't let Iain ignore whatever this was between them.

The door creaked open just as a rumble of thunder sounded overhead again and the dark clouds pitched above her.

Iain was bare-chested, obviously in the middle of stripping off his clothes. The dark circles under his eyes and shadow along his jaw only fed her fury even more.

'Lexi! What are you doing here?'

She pushed past him—not waiting to be asked to come in, and stood in the middle of his wide hallway, letting a huge puddle of rainwater form at her feet.

She clenched her jaw. 'You. Won't. Treat. Me. Like. That.' Every word was forced. Every word angrily controlled.

His hands were trembling as he closed the door behind her, shutting out the storm outside but not the one inside.

She said nothing. Stared him down. Watched the changing emotions on his face. She was strong enough for this. Whatever it might be.

She could see the pulse throbbing at the base of his neck, see every dark, curly chest hair standing on end.

But he didn't say a word. Not a single thing.

He just moved. And started kissing her like she'd never been kissed before.

CHAPTER SEVEN

IT WAS FIVE O'CLOCK in the morning and the first early streams of light were edging their way through the gap in the curtains. Lexi turned over in bed, her hand coming up automatically and touching her still-damp hair. It seemed impossible to believe that shaggy-haired Iain didn't possess a hairdryer, and her thick, long hair held the dampness, causing her to spend most of the night turning her pillow over.

'Wanna swap?' Iain was watching her with his dark brown eyes.

'Absolutely.' She smiled. 'I'm ruthless when it comes to bedding.' She grabbed the pillow he offered and sank down into the soft dryness, pushing the still-damp one in his direction.

He picked up a lock of her blonde hair. 'Doesn't matter if your hair is damp, Lexi. You still look beautiful.'

She shifted in the bed, instantly uncomfortable. 'You don't need to talk me into bed, Iain, I'm already here.'

His eyes widened. 'Why on earth would you think that?'

She pulled the light sheet a little closer to her body and sighed. 'I know I'm not beautiful, Iain. I've spent my life living in the shadow of the "world's most beautiful woman"',' She lifted her fingers in the air to make imaginary quote marks. 'You just learn to accept that will never be you.'

Ian lifted his head and propped it up on his hand. 'What do you see when you look in the mirror, Lexi?'

She frowned. 'What do you mean?'

He shook his head. 'I'm betting you don't see what I do. Not even close.'

She pulled the sheet up above her breasts, as if shielding herself from him. She was almost too scared to ask the next question. 'What do you see?' she whispered.

He lifted a finger and traced it lightly down the side of her cheek. 'I see a gorgeous young woman, with beautiful skin, perfectly intact—not damaged by the sun in any way.' He ran his finger over her eyelids. 'I see the most beautiful blue eyes. There's a little hint of turquoise and they remind me of the sea next to a Caribbean island.' His finger dusted her eyelids. 'I see thick, dark lashes that most women would give their eye teeth for and a pair of lips that were exclusively designed for kissing me.'

She smiled and he leaned over and kissed her gently on the lips. She closed her eyes a little. 'Okay, so I'm starting to like that.'

His hand drifted under the sheet and she felt herself tense a little. He hadn't mentioned her surgery. Hadn't mentioned it at all. And it struck her as strange. He was a surgeon. He'd known from the very first time their bodies had made contact that she'd had surgery. And he had certainly appreciated her breasts last night.

The pads of his fingers caressed her shoulders then followed the curves of her body. He pulled the sheet back a little. 'I'd ask you who did them, but I might get a little jealous. Because they're perfect.' His finger danced along the almost invisible scar under one of her breasts.

'You really think so?' Her voice was hesitant. She'd expected him to criticise. For all he was a surgeon himself, he didn't seem to rate cosmetic surgery very highly.

He nodded slowly, his eyelids still heavy with fatigue. 'I just wonder why you felt as if you needed them.'

It was a natural question, particularly for a surgeon, but it instantly caused her to bristle.

For a second it crossed her mind to lie. To act with a whole lot of bravado. But she was done with pretending to be something she was not. She was Lexi Robbins and she was proud of who she was.

'I didn't want them. Not to begin with. My ex—Jack told me to get them. He wore me down, kept telling me my flat chest did nothing for him and it made me feel as if I wasn't worthy of our relationship.'

Anger flared instantly in Iain's eyes. 'What?' He sat up, his voice incredulous. 'Why on earth would he do that? You're gorgeous, Lexi—and I'm sure you were absolutely perfect. What a complete—'

Her hand reached up and cut him off. 'Iain. Don't. I've spent a long time coming to terms with this. Jack never really loved me and it took a long time for me to understand that. Jack loved the *idea* of me. Who my parents were. The fact my name attracted attention. The fact my name meant we got invited to every fancy party in town.'

Iain's expletives filled the room. 'Of all the low-down, monkey-brained—'

'Stop that. Don't insult monkeys. They're highly intelligent creatures.'

But she could see the fire was still burning in his belly. 'I don't get it, Lexi. Why would you let anyone persuade you to have surgery? Didn't your surgeon ask you questions about why you were there? I thought he'd done a good job but now I'm not so sure.'

She shook her head. 'I gave him all the right answers, Iain. He didn't do anything wrong.' She sighed and lay back against the pillow again, her hands coming up and resting on her breasts. 'I've come to like my boobs. They've given me more confidence. They've made me feel better about myself. Deep down, I was never really happy with my shape—Jack just amplified my own feelings in a cruel way.'

There must have been something on her face, something about the way she said the words.

Iain's face darkened even further. 'Was that all he did?'

She hesitated as she felt a little flush of colour come to her cheeks. It seemed ridiculous. She'd just spent the night with Iain, was lying naked in bed with him, and she was embarrassed to say the words.

'What is it?' he coaxed, intertwining his fingers with hers.

'He said other things too. He didn't just comment on my breasts—or lack of them. He told me I should be taking lessons…for other things.'

It took a few seconds for the penny to drop and Lexi was cringing. It was bad enough that Jack had said those things in the first place. She'd never told another living soul about them.

Iain looked incredulous. 'He said what? How dared he?'

She looked down and shrugged her shoulders. 'I'm

not the most experienced. I've only ever had a few long-term relationships.'

'And he thought he would criticise you?' Iain's voice was aghast. 'Lexi, he should have been grateful, honoured even that you let him get that close to you. That you trusted him enough to share yourself with him. He shouldn't have been criticising your technique!'

The fury of his words made her want to bury her head under the pillow. She kept her eyes averted. 'This isn't normal for me, Iain. This isn't what I do. I don't do—*this*.'

He put his finger under her chin and tilted her face up to look at his. 'I get that. And I didn't get that because I thought you were inexperienced.' He gave her little smile. 'I have no complaints at all—quite the contrary, in fact. I enjoyed every second. You were perfect.'

Was it wrong that those words gave her a little buzz all the way down to her toes? Was it wrong that she couldn't help but smile? Smile at the gorgeous, handsome, strapping man who was lying next to her in bed, telling her that he thought she was perfect?

Even though she hadn't realised she'd been holding it, her breath came out in a long, steady stream.

She looked back into his eyes. 'Everything has changed. I'm a different person than I used to be—and not just physically. I like how I look now. I'm comfortable in my own skin. I love the fact that I'm doing a job that makes me happy. I don't care that my parents don't appreciate it. I know the value of the job I do. I've raised more money in the last few weeks than even I thought possible. I've got another few trips overseas to speak to some more potential clients.' She ran her fingers along the stubble on his jaw. 'And I've got a whole host of plans for raising the profile of the Harley Street clinic, some of which include a hunky Scotsman…' she gave him a wink '…who might even wear a kilt for me.'

He rolled his eyes and she laughed, before rolling back onto her back and putting her hands on her breasts again. 'This is me, Lexi Robbins. Take me or leave me.'

Iain's hand came over and rested over one of hers. 'So you're happy?'

She nodded. 'Yes, Iain, I'm happy.'

His hand ran down the outside of the sheet, resting on her hip. She wondered if he was about to ask other questions about her abdominal scar. Would she answer truthfully? Did she feel as if she could?

He wrinkled his nose at her. 'Well, I'm not.'

Her stomach gave a little clench. What did he mean?

'I want to find Jack Parker and wring his neck with my bare hands until I squeeze every last breath out of him. I want to bang his head off a wall to try and knock some sense into him. I want to take a walk down a dark alley late at night and show him what I think about how he treated you.'

She was struck by the intensity of his words. Maybe it was the aftermath of their lovemaking that had provoked such deep emotions in him but she could tell from the sincerity in his brown eyes that he'd meant every word.

'Thank you,' she whispered. 'But this was about me dealing with things. I had to learn for myself that he wasn't what I thought. I had to value myself enough to not allow him to treat me that way. He was never physical, he never laid a hand on me. But his constant comments on my face and figure wore me down. I've never felt so free than when I flung him out of our flat and dumped his designer wardrobe out of the window. At that point, it was probably the best moment of my life.'

Iain lifted his hand and rested it between her breasts. 'But we both know that all beauty is superficial. I can make the most hideous person in the world look stunning on the outside. But it doesn't change what's in here. Who that person really is. There have never been truer words than "Beauty is only skin deep".'

There was genuine warmth in his words, a warmth that swept around her like a comfortable blanket, shielding her from everything else. She could get used to this. She could get used to being shielded by Iain McKenzie.

'I want you to know, Lexi Robbins, that you are one of the most beautiful people I've ever met. Both inside and out. And no matter what happens in the future, where we both end up, I want you to keep that with you. And if any time you're feeling down, if you've had a bad day and can't face things, I want you to come back and remember *this* moment, here and now.'

In one way the words were a comfort, and in another they made her stomach clench again. She'd no idea what she expected from Iain—none of this had been planned. But there seemed to be a little edge to those words. As if he knew there would never be a future for them so he was just giving her this moment instead.

And the fact was she'd never felt so perfect as she did at this moment. She'd never felt so valued.

He stroked his fingers down her face again. 'We need to talk. There are some other things I need to tell you. But first I want to show you just how special you are.'

And for the next few hours he did.

* * *

By the time Iain woke up the sun was streaming through the windows. He turned to face Lexi. She was smiling. A real, genuine smile of contentment.

'How long have you been awake?'

She looked over at the clock. 'About ten minutes.' She lay back and stretched her arms above her head. 'I was waiting for you to make me breakfast,' she said with a glint in her eye.

'Do you have any preferences?'

'Do you have any food?'

He cringed. 'Have you already been up and looked through my cupboards?'

She touched his chin. 'You just strike me as a guy who doesn't do a weekly shop.'

He laughed. 'You're right. If you wanted dinner right now we'd be in trouble. But breakfast I can do. How does poached egg, toast and bacon sound?'

'Heavenly.' She glanced towards his en suite. 'Can I use your shower while you make breakfast?'

'Of course.' Iain pulled on his dressing-gown and headed to the kitchen. His stomach was churning. He'd never brought a woman back to his London house before, let alone back to his bedroom. He'd spent so long partitioning these parts of his life and keeping himself away from people.

Of course he socialised when he had to. He kept in contact with some of his old friends in Edinburgh—but those were fleeting hello-goodbye moments. But since moving down to London he hadn't really been seeking the company of friends. He wasn't really looking for friends. He was only looking for partial distractions.

And his gut told him Lexi Robbins could never fit into that category.

He started boiling water in one pan, put the bacon under the grill and the bread in the toaster. The coffee was easy, he had a bright and shiny machine he hardly used. All he had to do was flick a switch.

He turned, his eyes catching on a photo on the window ledge. A photo of Bonnie, sitting on top of a hill in Edinburgh on a sunny day. She had wrapped her long pink flowered dress around her legs to stop it flapping in the wind and her hair was completely windswept.

Something curled inside him. It was going to be the three of them sitting in this kitchen, having breakfast. He wasn't sure how he felt about that. He wasn't sure if he was ready for that.

Everything with Lexi was so new. Attraction aside, he didn't even know how he felt about her yet. Sure, she was beautiful. Sure, she was intelligent. But did that add up to anything else?

For a split second he considered putting the photo in a drawer. But as quickly as the thought flew into his head he pushed it aside. He could never treat Bonnie as if she hadn't existed. He owed her so much more than that.

And Lexi was no fool. She knew nothing about his past. She would ask about the photo on the window ledge. It was if a dozen little pinpricks started on his shoulders at once. He would tell her. He would tell her about Bonnie. She'd been a big part of his life and she deserved her place there.

The bacon sizzled just as the coffee machine started to splutter and the water in the pot boiled. He dropped in the eggs and pulled out some plates and cutlery.

Lexi appeared a few minutes later, looking like the kind of pin-up poster a teenage boy would have on his bedroom wall.

She'd clipped her hair haphazardly on top of her head and pulled one of his long-sleeved blue shirts from his cupboard. The bottom buttons were fastened and the top two left tantalisingly open. Along with her long legs and pink toenails, the effect was stunning.

She shrugged. 'I don't think my dress will ever recover. It's spent the night on the floor in a sodden mess. Hope you don't mind.'

'Of course I don't.' He set the coffee on the table. 'Cappuccino okay for you?'

'Of course.' She lifted the coffee cup to her lips and smiled. 'Don't be too good at this. I might get comfortable.'

There was that little tumble in his stomach again. He didn't know how to react to that. The toast popped and he buttered it and placed it on the table, alongside the bacon and the newly poached eggs.

Lexi started piling food on her plate and Iain watched with pleasure. It was the second time he'd eaten with Lexi, and for all her slim frame she wasn't afraid to eat. Thank goodness. He couldn't stand being around a picky eater.

Iain took a few mouthfuls then set his fork down. He didn't even get a chance to say a word.

'You said you wanted to talk, Iain. What is it? Is this where you tell me this is a wham-bam, thank you, ma'am?'

Boy, she was direct. Another thing he liked about her. This was getting harder all the time.

He shook his head and took a quick drink of his

thick, strong coffee. He took a deep breath, but when he exhaled it came out more like a sigh.

'Spit it out, Scots boy.'

He nodded and pointed to the window ledge before he changed his mind. 'I wanted to introduce you to someone.'

Lexi looked up at the photo of the pretty dark-haired woman. 'She's lovely. Who is she? Your sister?'

'My wife.'

Lexi set her cup on the table, her face frozen. 'Please tell me you're not still married. I don't sleep with married men.' She was deadly serious and her face was deathly pale.

'I'm widowed,' he said quickly.

There was a visible sigh of relief from across the table. She took a deep breath, her eyes full of sympathy for him. He wasn't sure that was what he wanted. He'd had enough darned sympathy to last a lifetime. He just wanted her to understand.

'I'm really sorry about your loss, Iain. I can't imagine what that feels like.'

There was a tight feeling in his chest. A kettlebell from the gym had just positioned itself on his chest, pushing the air out of his lungs and making him struggle for breath. He was going to see this through. He was. Once he'd told her, that was it—it was out there.

'It won't surprise you to know I don't talk about my personal life much. That's why I came down to London. To get away from things. The only person who knows what happened is Leo.'

'Don't worry. I won't breathe a word.'

He tried to find the words in his head. He wasn't just doing this for himself, he was doing it for her too. 'Bonnie—my wife—died giving birth to our twins. There were complications. My son and daughter died too.'

Her hand had gone automatically to her mouth and her eyes had widened in shock. This wasn't your everyday conversation.

He put his elbows on the table for a second and put his head in his hands. He was trying not to let the familiar wave of emotions wash over him. He needed to keep himself together.

He ran his tongue along his dry lips. 'I wanted you to know that when I walked away last night—I wasn't walking away from you. It wasn't about you.' He pressed his hand to his chest. 'It was about me feeling guilty. I haven't been with anyone since my wife died.'

'Oh, Iain...' There were tears glistening in her eyes and in a second she was up on her bare feet, walking round the kitchen table and standing behind him, linking her hands around his neck and resting her head on his shoulder.

They stayed like that for a few minutes. He could feel the rise and fall of her chest behind him, feel her warm breath on his cheek. He lifted up his hand and linked it with hers.

'Lexi, I just want you to know—'

'Don't say it.'

He pulled her hand, adjusting his position in the chair until he was sitting sideways and could pull her onto his lap.

'I don't know about anything. I can't promise you anything. Because I don't know if I'm ready. I don't know if I'm there yet.' She looked so young, so vulnerable. The very last thing he wanted to do was hurt her.

He put his finger under her chin and pulled her head

up to meet his eyes. They were almost nose to nose and he had the clearest view he'd ever had of her beautiful blue eyes. 'I want you to know that I think you're gorgeous. I think you're very desirable. And if I make a mess of things here, it's because there's something wrong with *me*, not you. You're every man's dream come true.' He lowered his voice. 'But not every man deserves you, Lexi. And not every man is ready for you.'

There was a waver in her eyes, a sign of hesitation. Then she took a deep breath, her chest rose and her shoulders straightened. Her fingers wound their way through his shaggy brown hair. 'Thank you for telling me about your wife, Iain. I appreciate this is hard. And it's new. I won't tell anyone about your wife. And I guess we can just wait to see how things go.'

She smiled at him, and it was an older, more resigned smile. 'I'm not looking for you to save me. After my last experience I'm just looking for someone to treat me with respect and value my opinions. How about we go from there?'

He could see she was holding back. He could see there was something in her eyes that she was keeping from him. Guarding herself and guarding her heart. The sensible option. And he respected that. He could live with that, because he hadn't told her everything yet. That might come later.

She stood up. 'You're still going to be grumpy at the clinic, though, aren't you?'

He took a bite of his toast. 'Obviously. Why change the habit of a lifetime?' He looked at the clock. 'Are you due there today?'

She nodded and looked down at the pale blue shirt.

'I don't have any appointments until later today—and then some into the evening. I have a few interviews lined up with some national papers and I still need to edit your interview. Oh, and get you to pose for some publicity shots.'

'I am *not* wearing a kilt.'

She tilted her head to the side and folded her arms. 'I might be able to think of a way to persuade you. How much time have you got?'

'A few hours. I need to go to the Lighthouse to check on one of my patients. But they aren't expecting me until around eleven.' He abandoned the toast. He much preferred the other offer. 'How do you think you can persuade me?'

'Have you got a bath? A big bath?' She had that gleam in her eye as she took his hand and led him towards the stairs.

Her voice drifted along the corridor. 'And what I'd really like is some bubbles…'

CHAPTER EIGHT

IAIN GLANCED AT the clock on the wall. 'Lexi, are you ready?' He didn't want to be late.

She appeared instantly at his side. He tried not to let his eyes automatically run up and down the length of her body—but, boy, was it hard. Her perfume was already assaulting his senses and rejigging his memory from the night before.

It was making his skin prickle and resurrecting a whole host of feelings of guilt. He tried to push them away. She was dressed conservatively. A plain cream blouse, knee-length navy skirt and flats. But she still managed to carry it off with panache. The sooner he finished with this the better. He hated the fact he didn't think he could control his body's responses around her. The last thing he needed was other people suspecting something was going on.

This was the last part of the filming—a review of a little Chinese boy he'd performed surgery on a few days ago. He stopped just outside the door and nodded to the cameraman, who started filming.

'Okay, today we're going to look in on An. He's a six-year-old Chinese boy with a facial deformity—hemifacial microsomia. It's a condition that affects the bone, muscle, fat and nerves of the lower part of the face. The deformities are on a spectrum. They can range from a mild presentation with slight asymmetry to severe absence of facial structures. It's a progressive disorder and becomes more apparent as the child grows.'

'How common is it?' asked Lexi.

'It's the second most common facial deformity and affects around one in five thousand six hundred births. It's equally common in males and females.'

Lexi halted at the door and he wondered about her reaction. Please don't let her grimace when she sees the child. An's asymmetrical features were apparent, even at a young age. He had many more years of surgery ahead of him.

He tapped her shoulder as they walked in and kept talking to the camera. 'One side of An's face is growing normally. The other isn't. The surgery I did a few days ago was a mandibular correction to allow for normal maxillary growth. It means An's dental structures and jaw will be in better alignment.'

He was still watching Lexi from the corner of his eye. She had her head tilted to one side and looked as if she was concentrating fiercely. She was watching An and his mother talk in hushed voices. He glanced towards the doorway again, waiting for the translator. Speaking Chinese was not in his repertoire.

But it appeared to be in Lexi's.

She walked over and knelt next to the little boy and his mother, trying a few hesitant words. The woman's eyebrows shot skywards and after a few seconds she replied haltingly.

Lexi smiled and tried again. This time she was a little more relaxed and the words flowed more freely. The exchange lasted a few minutes. Iain couldn't believe his eyes. How did she know Chinese?

He took a few steps closer. 'Lexi?'

She looked up. 'I thought I recognised the language. It's Gan with a Nanchang dialect.'

'How on earth do you know that?'

A wrinkle appeared across her brow. It was obvious she was choosing her words carefully. 'Do you remember I told you I spent the summer with my aunt?'

He nodded.

'My aunt did lots of charity work. At that time most of her work was in some of the Chinese orphanages. She took me over there for a whole summer. It was the best summer of my life.'

'You learned a Chinese dialect in one summer?'

'I still go back,' she said quietly. 'Away from the spotlight. Every few years Jo and I go back to that same orphanage. I feel a real connection with it. I've spent a long time learning the language, the particular dialect. It makes the work so much more rewarding when I can converse with the children.

'Some of those children were taken away from their parents against their will. The parents couldn't afford to pay the fine for having more than one child. It's awful. But we've tried to make things better. We have links with social services around the world and some of the children get adopted internationally.'

'So, An is from the same area?'

She nodded. 'Yes. I'm not completely fluent, but I can easily make myself understood. You don't need to wait for an interpreter.'

Iain hesitated for a second. He was trying not to let

his mouth hang open. But Lexi had just rendered him speechless.

This was not what he had expected. And he was almost ashamed to think that.

He'd been up close and personal with her. He knew she was much deeper than people assumed. But it was obvious he'd only scratched the surface—only got to know a little about the woman underneath the pretty façade.

From her teenage years Lexi had spent summer after summer helping out at a Chinese orphanage. This was more than charity work for her. She was committed to this. Committed enough to learn the language.

He'd spent a summer at a Romanian orphanage himself, operating on children with cleft lips and palates. He knew how much it sucked you in. How you would do anything to help. How you could think about nothing else.

This was a whole new part of Lexi Robbins he hadn't counted on.

'Iain? Are we doing this?'

He nodded, embarrassed by his long silence. 'Of course...thank you.'

He knelt down next to An, who was perched on his mother's knee. The stitches on the skin along the little boy's jaw had healed well. 'Ask him how he's managing to eat.'

Lexi nodded and spoke quietly to his mother, listening to her reply and letting An answer too. She turned to Iain. 'He's fed up with soft foods.' She gave him a smile. 'He wants some chips.'

Iain smiled. 'Can you ask him to open his mouth so I

can have a look at his dentition? Some of his teeth have been affected by the repositioning of his jaw.'

Lexi only took a second to ask the question and An opened his mouth a little hesitantly. Iain bent down and looked inside, using a small torch, 'Everything looks as though it's healing well. I see no reason he can't have a more substantial diet.'

Lexi translated quickly. An's face was still bruised and slightly swollen and his attempt at a smile lopsided. But it was the most satisfying thing that Iain could see.

'Can you ask him about pain relief? If he's going to eat a bit more he might need his analgesics adjusted for the next few days.'

Lexi took a few minutes, taking her time while she spoke to An and his mother. She made it seem like the most natural thing in the world. It was obvious she wasn't completely fluent, but she had more than a grasp of the language, and An and his mother seemed to appreciate being able to communicate with a member of staff.

Lexi turned around from where she was kneeling on the floor and touched Iain's leg. The warmth of her hand startled him, as did her position. He moved quickly out of her reach, before her touch could have any affect. 'An hasn't been talking too much as he finds the jaw movements painful. He probably does need his analgesics adjusted.'

Iain nodded. 'Let them know I'll take care of that now.' He lifted the chart and walked over the nurses' station to talk to the nurse allocated to An. Lexi stayed where she was, continuing to talk to An and his mother.

They loved her already. It was obvious. She was writing a few things on a piece of paper along with a little picture and telling them what they meant. It was obvious there had been a few key things they had wanted to communicate to the staff and hadn't been able to. Lexi was doing her best to facilitate that. She was doing her very best for an unknown mother and child she'd just met.

It made his stomach twist. Lexi's nature was sweet and kind. This shouldn't be unexpected for him. But seeing it, right before his eyes, was just a little different.

He was used to Lexi Robbins, Head of PR. He'd also experienced Lexi Robbins, sultry, sexy woman.

But Lexi Robbins, humanitarian, was a whole different ball game. Now he understood where the passion in her eyes came from when she spoke about the charity work. It wasn't just all part of her PR game. It was how she really *felt*.

And that made him uncomfortable.

It made him feel too close.

She was unsettling him, in more ways than one. She was much more than a pretty face.

But the thing that worried him most was just how much more he wanted to know.

The knock on the door work her up. Eek! She'd overslept.

She dashed to the door, trying to shove her arms into her dressing-gown. She pulled the door open. 'Iain. I'm sorry. Give me five minutes and I promise you I'll be ready.' She didn't wait for an answer, just dashed to the bedroom to throw on some jeans and a jumper.

A few minutes later she found him in her kitchen, stirring a cup of black of coffee. 'Inside or out?'

'What?' He looked confused.

'You haven't told me where we're going. What kind of jacket do I need?'

He smiled. 'Dress up warm.'

She raised her eyebrows and ducked back into her bedroom, pulling out a pair of red leather gloves and a red woolly hat with a huge pom-pom on top and big flaps to cover her ears. She stuffed it on top of her blonde hair and pulled on a thick black jacket and fleecy black boots.

It was freezing in London. Not wet or drizzly. It was completely dry, just very, very cold.

'I'm ready.' She marched into the kitchen and took a quick drink of the coffee Iain had made for her. It wasn't a skinny caramel latte, but he'd made it perfectly. Maybe this was all just a little too good to be true.

Iain held the door open for her. 'Then let's go. Time to have some fun.'

They rode on the Tube and got off at Tower Hill. They walked out of the Tube station and round the corner to face the impressive façade of the Tower of London.

'We're going sightseeing?'

He nodded. 'I haven't been yet. I've been in London two years and I've hardly seen a thing.' He walked up to the ticket booth. 'Do we want to see the Crown Jewels too?'

She didn't hesitate for a second. 'Absolutely. It's my favourite part.'

He took their tickets and reached out to take her hand as they walked towards the main entrance, where impressive Beefeaters in their black and red outfits stood.

Iain stopped for a few seconds. 'Wow. It's some place. Have you been here much?'

She nodded. 'Not as much as you think. Last time was around eight years ago.' She stopped and looked back at the impressive White Tower. 'Why did you pick here?'

He looked a little sheepish. 'I actually wanted to go to Buckingham Palace but I didn't realise it's only open in the summer for tours.'

'It's fabulous.' Something tickled in her stomach. July would be the time for the tours to start at Buckingham Palace. That was five months away. 'Maybe we can go some other time.'

'Maybe.' It sounded so noncommittal and she tried not to feel disappointed. Iain had already told her he didn't know where this would go.

She pulled him further along where she could see a small crowd gathering. 'Let's listen to one of the Yeoman tours. They know everything about the Tower's history, it's great fun.'

They joined the crowd and waited for a few minutes for the tour to start. Lexi was right. It was fascinating. He'd never realised just how treacherous a place the Tower of London had been. He watched as the Yeoman showed them where the boats used to moor with their prisoners and royal victims at Traitor's Gate. He showed them the place where the two young princes were supposedly imprisoned and perhaps killed.

Lexi leaned her head against his shoulder as they listened to the tour. There was a young woman next to her, trying to juggle three kids—a baby in a pouch next to her breasts, a toddler strapped into a buggy and a four-year-old who was looking distinctly bored and kept wandering off. The woman looked tired and was struggling to hear what the Yeoman was saying. Lexi touched her arm and gave her a smile. 'If it's okay with you, how about I entertain your oldest for a little while?'

The woman nodded and gave her a grateful smile. They were standing on Tower Green. Lexi could walk about freely and still be safely in the mother's sight.

She walked over and bent down next to the dark-headed little girl. Her heart gave a squeeze. The little girl was gorgeous. Her hair was in bunches and wearing a purple coat. 'Hi, there. I'm Lexi. How about I tell you some stories about this place?'

The little girl scowled at her. Lexi pointed over at her mother. 'Your mum says it's okay.' She gave her mother a wave. 'What's your name.'

'Lucy.'

Lexi held out her hand. 'Good. I'm Lexi. Pleased to meet you.'

Lucy gave a sigh. 'My feet are sore and Damian is in the buggy.' She rolled her eyes.

Lexi held out her hands. 'Fancy a carry?'

Lucy's eyes brightened and she let her herself be lifted into Lexi's arms. As the tour moved along little by little, Lexi stayed only a few feet away from the mother, whispering in Lucy's ear and pointing out various things along the way.

Iain watched carefully. Lexi seemed so at ease. She was obviously used to children. She'd already told Iain about her work at the Chinese orphanage and everything she did showed him her natural affinity for children.

A heavy feeling started to descend over him. Lexi was his first step back to a normal life. He'd promised her nothing.

She spun Lucy backwards in her arms, letting her

lean back and throw her arms out, imitating the ravens around about them. Their hair flew outwards as they spun, the smiles on their faces completely and utterly spontaneous. Lexi was a natural.

And he didn't like it.

It was a horrible admission. But Iain hadn't planned on thinking such thoughts on what he'd wanted to be a nice day out.

But watching Lexi was making him ache. He was wasting his time with her. Here was a woman who had the word 'mother' stamped all over her. What would she think when she found out what he'd done? If she'd any sense at all she would run in the other direction.

What woman would want to be with a man who'd persuaded his wife to take the final chance of IVF that had led to her death?

He looked around Tower Green. Families everywhere. Families happy and smiling. And he knew. He knew he could never set foot in a delivery room again. Not after his last experience.

And Lexi would want a family of her own. How could he explain? She was kneeling on the ground with Lucy right now, telling her some long and obviously gory tale by the actions she was doing. Right on cue, Lucy's mouth formed a wide O. She slapped her hand across her mouth as Lexi let out a peal of laughter.

Right before his eyes was the reason he should stop all this. He could never be the man that she needed.

But Lexi turned and pushed her hat further back on her head. Her blonde hair was sticking out all round and she shot him the most dazzling smile. The Yeoman was reaching the end of the walking tour at the Medieval Tower.

She mouthed over to him, 'Crown jewels?'

He nodded. She'd already told him it was her favourite part. They joined the queue with Lucy's mother behind them. She was looking calmer, more relaxed. She leaned over and whispered to the two of them, 'It's dark in here, isn't it? The two little ones will fall asleep as soon as we get inside.'

They queued quietly as Lexi started to whisper stories of secret princesses to Lucy. The inside of the display was dark, surrounded by armed guards, who were happy to talk to the visitors about some of the jewels on display.

Lucy's little face gaped at the huge glittering Cullianan diamond in the sovereign's sceptre.

'I don't think there is a magical fairy kingdom inside the stone,' Iain whispered.

'Shh!' Lexi put her finger to her lips, 'Spoilsport,' she whispered.

They oohed over the Imperial state crown and Lucy was highly disappointed she couldn't try it on. 'But I'm a princess too,' she said huffily.

'I know you are,' said Lexi, 'and I'm sure when we get to the gift shop I'll be able to buy you a crown of your own.'

And sure enough she did. It was early afternoon by the time they'd finished at the Tower. 'I'm sorry our afternoon got hijacked,' she said to Iain as they made their way to the exit.

'No, you're not,' he said, shaking his head. 'You looked like you were having the time of your life. What stories were you telling her?'

Lexi smiled. 'Stories about the evil ravens stealing

fairies and the fairies fighting back by hiding in the crown jewels.'

'All totally based on reality, then?'

She nodded solemnly. 'Based on a four-year-old girl's reality.' She tapped the side of her nose. 'That's the trick to keeping them quiet.'

'Well, you certainly managed to master that.'

She smiled up at him as he reached for her hand and gave it a little squeeze. 'Let's go for a walk down to Tower Bridge,' she said.

Even though it was still cold, the day was bright and sunny. The path down next to the bridge was busy, filled with street acts and various parties on tours. They bought coffee from a street vendor and sat on a bench, people-watching.

Lexi seemed relaxed and happy next to him. If they looked along the river a little they could see Kate's. 'Are you going there today?'

Iain nodded. 'I'll go in later. I have a few patients to check over. It won't take long.'

She ran her tongue along her lips. Her hat was sitting in her lap now and her blonde hair was blowing in the breeze. She didn't seem to mind at all that it was all over the place. In fact, for the daughter of a supermodel, Lexi didn't seem to care at all about her appearance. She hadn't looked in a mirror once since they'd met today.

She was gorgeous, of course. But it helped him realise how far down the list she put superficial things. Another plus point for Lexi.

If only that didn't make him squirm. Because every good point about Lexi made him realise how they couldn't really be a match. There must be a whole host of guys out there who would want to snatch her up. To admire her beauty, good spirit and work ethic. A hundred guys out there who want to settle down with her and have a family.

She leaned over and gave him a gentle kiss on the lips. There was a kind of glazed look behind her smile. She was squinting at him in the sunshine as she reached up and ran her fingers through his hair.

'It's not exactly the usual look, is it?' she said, tugging at his shaggy hair.

'What do you mean?' He was distracted by her lips and blue eyes and only looked up when she gave his hair an extra tug.

'Most surgeons go for the ultra-short look.'

'I'm not most surgeons,' he growled.

'I get that.'

'Just imagine me shipwrecked on a mysterious island. This is the natural look for me.'

'Good, because I like it. It suits you.' She gave him a cheeky wink. 'Now, don't ever cut it. I might go off you.' She stood up. 'So, fancy a late dinner at mine?'

She said the words so easily. Probably never expecting him to hesitate. But he did. This was his chance. This was his opportunity to let her spread her wings and fly. To stop any chance of him hurting her. But there was still a little something in her eyes. Still a little lack of confidence.

So he smiled, standing up and taking her hand. 'I think I can manage that.' He changed his mind, dropping her hand and wrapping his arm around her shoulder. She was closer this way.

Eventually he would have to let her go.

Eventually he would have to tell her the truth.

Just not right now.

CHAPTER NINE

'LEXI, CAN I speak to you a minute, please?'

Ethan Hunter was leaning on her doorframe. *He's still not using his stick.* It was her first thought and she quickly pushed it out of her head. It was none of her business.

She pushed her chair back and stood up, walking over towards the door. 'No problem, Ethan. What can I do for you?'

She was very busy, and between an influx of high-profile clients, thanks to her PR campaign, her nights with Iain and her charity work, she hardly had a moment to think. But Ethan very rarely bothered her and she wanted to give him the attention he deserved.

Ethan looked a little uncomfortable. Was that his leg again, or was he just choosing his words carefully?

'Lexi, I wanted to ask you about something. I've seen some paperwork lying about and heard some of the other surgeons talking about Fair Go. Can you tell me what it is?'

Lexi straightened her shoulders and put on her brightest smile. 'Why don't you come and sit down, Ethan? I'm happy to fill you in on all the details of Fair Go. Can I get you some tea or coffee?'

Ethan shook his head and sat down in the leather high-backed armchair opposite her desk. He probably didn't even realise the visible sweep of relief that came across his face as he took the weight off his leg.

Lexi shuffled some papers on her desk until she found what she was looking for. 'Here it is. Fair Go— it's a great name, isn't it? Named after Olivia Fairchild, the nurse who started it.'

She looked up in time to see Ethan visibly pale. Maybe his leg gave him more pain than he let on?

She moved on. 'It's an African-based charity focusing on helping adults and children affected by war. It's a small charity right now, but with our backing Olivia is hoping she will be able to assist more victims. She has several cases already that could do with transport to the UK for specialist surgery.' She smiled over at Ethan. 'I take it you'll be keen to take part?'

It seemed an obvious question. She knew that Ethan had been a victim of war himself so it seemed only natural he would want to help others. It just seemed odd his brother hadn't mentioned it—but, then again, she couldn't really fathom the relationship between the brothers. And she knew better than to interfere in other families' problems.

Ethan's voice was strained. 'Of course I'll take part. I knew another charity was being proposed for the clinic—I just hadn't heard the details yet. That's why I asked Iain if he'd be willing to participate too. I take it he was happy to help?'

Lexi felt an odd rush of colour to her cheeks. Oh, no. Just the mention of Iain's name was causing her to blush. Talk about giving herself away.

'Yes, yes. Well, you know Iain. I had to persuade

him a little.' Had she really managed to say that without turning beetroot red?

'I'm sorry I haven't done your interview yet, Lexi.' Ethan had the good grace to look a little shame-faced. 'It's just not really my thing. I prefer to stay out of the spotlight. I am happy to support the charity work, though.'

He was staring at the paper on her desk—the one with the details of Olivia Fairchild's charity. And he was looking at it with such ferocity that she knew something else was going on entirely. She wouldn't like to be in Leo Hunter's shoes right now.

She decided to give him an out. 'I spent three weeks chasing you for an interview, Ethan—I can take a hint. Iain gave in after two. I think we'll be able to use his interview for some very effective publicity. I finished the edits on it last night and we're ready to release it online in a few days. So I think I can release you from your obligation.'

She saw a little tension sag out of his shoulders and he stood up from the chair. 'Lexi, just to let you know. We had news yesterday of some other big-name clients. Sheikh Abdullah's wife, Lydia Jones the newscaster and Violet Ingram the equestrian who fell in the recent Games, to name a few. They're all coming here for surgery. I don't know what you've been doing out there—but it's obviously working.'

His dark hazel eyes were full of sincerity. 'Thanks, Lexi. This will make a world of difference for us, particularly around our charity work.'

'That's why you pay me, Ethan. I'm just happy you think I'm doing a good job.' She watched as he walked to the door, his limp still visible.

This was the longest conversation she'd ever had with Ethan Hunter. She didn't know if he'd always been this quiet or if it was since his return from his tour of duty in Afghanistan. It was obvious he'd been injured in the field. But she wasn't entirely sure what those injuries were. Just that while it was obvious he wasn't back to full fitness yet, it was equally obvious that he wasn't really ready to accept that.

She just hoped she hadn't stoked some still-smouldering fire between the brothers by telling Ethan about the Fair Go charity.

It seemed ridiculous. A number of other members of the clinic knew about Fair Go. Any one of them could have told Ethan about it.

So why was she hoping against hope that he wouldn't tell Leo it had been her?

'Time for coffee?'

The voice at the door startled her and she smiled as Carrie, one of the receptionists, appeared. Truth was, she didn't really have time to breathe let alone have coffee but she needed a break. And she needed some fresh air. She nodded. 'How about the coffee house at the end of the street? I could do with a walk.'

Carrie nodded and waved the purse she was holding in her hand. 'I was hoping you might say that. Let's go.'

They walked down the street swiftly. Lexi never did anything slowly and she was trying her best not to glance at her watch.

'So where have you been? I've hardly seen you these last few weeks.'

'I know. I've been rushed off my feet with the publicity campaign for the clinic and the charities.' She counted off on her fingers. 'In the last fourteen days I've been to Spain, Switzerland, Dubai and Belgium. I'm frazzled. And I'm due to launch the video interview of Iain in the next few days.'

Carrie nodded. She was smiling but Lexi could tell she wasn't really taking in everything she said.

She pushed open the door to the coffee house at the end of the street and grabbed the only free table. Neither of them needed to look at the menu. Lexi smiled at the waitress. 'Usual coffee—skinny latte with sugar-free caramel and…' she smiled over at the cake counter '…I'll have the raspberry and cream sponge, please.'

'And I'll have a cappuccino and a piece of the carrot cake, please.'

Lexi smiled as Carrie adjusted herself in the chair. 'Ooh, you're eating today. You never normally eat mid-morning.'

Carrie fumbled in her bag and pulled a white envelope out and pushed it across the table with a nervous smile.

Lexi felt her stomach flip over. *Keep smiling*, she told herself. She already knew what would be in the envelope. This had happened to her too many times already.

She went onto automatic pilot. She pulled the scan image from the envelope and let out a little gasp of surprise, trying the whole time not to think about how this moment would never be hers. She placed the black and white print out down, easily seeing the shape of the little baby with its curved spine, larger than average head and little limbs pointing upwards. She leaned over the table. 'Congratulations, Carrie, I'm delighted for you. When is your due date?'

Carrie's face flushed with pleasure. 'Tenth of September. I had my scan last week when I was twelve weeks.'

'And are you keeping okay?'

Carrie shrugged. 'I can't eat first thing in the morning because I feel really lousy. But by now—mid-morning—I'm ravenous.'

'So that's why the change in eating habits.'

The waitress appeared and put the coffees and cakes on the table, and Carrie didn't waste any time in digging in.

Lexi pressed her lips together. She was happy for her friend. She really was. And she'd been through this a dozen times before. She'd resigned herself years before to the fact she wouldn't have kids naturally. She kept close ties with the orphanages—adoption would be her way to a future family. And she was looking forward to it—when the time was right.

But something had happened in the last two weeks, since she'd sat in that kitchen with Iain and looked into his eyes as he'd told her about losing his wife and twins. Her heart had broken for him. It truly had.

But something else had happened.

Her confidence and inner strength now had a tiny chip in the armour.

Iain and his wife had obviously wanted to have a family. Which meant that Iain had wanted a family of his own. Logic told her that even though his wife was gone, eventually his brain would go down that path again. That path of wanting to share his life with a woman who could have his children.

A path it wasn't possible for her to go down.

Carrie was guzzling her cake and coffee. And she did look different. Lexi wondered why she hadn't noticed.

Carrie had a little glow about her, her hair was thick and glossy and there was added sparkle in her eyes.

Carrie looked up. 'I wanted to tell you first before I tell anyone else. I know they will be fine about maternity leave and everything, but I just wanted to talk to you first.'

Lexi reached across the table and squeezed her hand. 'Thank you. I'm delighted for you—really I am.' Even though there were a million tiny butterflies taking flight in her stomach. The raspberry and cream sponge was beautiful but she could barely touch it.

She hated herself right now. She'd never felt more than a fleeting pang before when a friend had told her they were pregnant.

But what she hated more than anything right now was the remote possibility that because of her budding relationship with Iain, she might be feeling a tiny bit jealous.

Jealous. What a horrible word.

'What's going on with Iain McKenzie?'

'What?' She dropped the fork she'd been holding for the last few minutes.

Carrie was smiling. 'Our grumpy Scotsman isn't quite so grumpy. We're all wondering what's happened. Do you know anything?'

'Me? No.' The words came out too quickly, falling over themselves in their haste.

Carrie put her fork down. 'Lexi?' Her eyebrows were raised.

Oh, no. Carrie had that look on her face. That you'd-better-tell-me-everything-right-now look.

Lexi started shaking her head and focusing intently on the raspberry sponge, which all of a sudden she could eat easily. 'I've no idea what's going on with Iain. I've just told you I've not been around. I've been flying everywhere and barely had a minute to myself.' She popped a big piece of sponge into her mouth to stop herself saying anything else.

'Whatever you say, Lexi. But it's a remarkable co-incidence that Iain appeared to get a whole lot brighter after your interview.' She lifted her hand and gave Lexi a wink. 'But if you say you know nothing, that's fine with me.'

The waitress came over and placed the bill on the table and Carrie had it in a flash. She waved it at Lexi. 'But it'll cost you!'

Lexi grabbed the bill and swallowed the big lump of cake in her throat. Everything was still so new with Iain. She didn't want to tell Carrie that in between flights to here, there and everywhere she'd either been sleeping at Iain's or he'd been sleeping at her place.

And if carrot cake was the price of Carrie's silence, that was good enough for her.

Lexi knocked on the door of Leo's office. She was trying to put all thoughts of the last time she'd been in here out of her mind. The thought of ending up with Iain lying on top of her made her blush. She only hoped the colour she felt flooding her cheeks would not be obvious to Leo.

'Come in,' came the deep voice behind the door.

She opened it. Leo was sitting behind his desk with the phone cradled between his shoulder and face, while he scribbled furiously in front of him. He gestured to Lexi to come in and sit down in front of his desk.

She gave him a wide smile and settled into the comfortable chair. Leo had a smile on his face, and it was so nice to see.

There had been so many changes in him over the last few weeks—all to do with his engagement to Lizzie Birch, the head nurse at the Hunter Clinic. Leo had always been good at his job but his personal life and his relationship with his brother had always seemed rocky. It was so nice to see him with a genuine, permanent smile on his face.

He put down the phone. 'Sorry about that, Lexi.' He shuffled some papers on his desk until he found what he was looking for. A printout of the accounts and charitable donations that Lexi had sent him. He stood up. 'That's quite a pile you've sent me.' He looked around his desk. There was barely any of rich wood surface visible. 'What do you say we go through to the conference room and spread these out?' He smiled. 'Lizzie left us some doughnuts for the meeting.'

Lexi stood back up. 'Perfect. You get the doughnuts, I'll get the coffee.'

She walked through to the conference room and left her papers on the desk, then crossed the corridor to the kitchen and loaded the pods into the machine. Perfect cappuccinos in two minutes flat.

She could hear voices as she approached the conference room. Its doors were wide open. Her steps slowed as she recognised Ethan's voice.

She hesitated. She was reluctant to go and interrupt them, even though she was supposed to be having a meeting with Leo right now. Tension seemed to emanate from both of them as soon as they were in the same room.

Leo sounded happier today. She could hear his deep

voice easily. 'I wanted to let you know that Lizzie and I have set a date.'

'What? That's great. Congratulations, Leo. When is it?' Lexi felt relieved. Ethan did sound happy for his brother. Maybe things had eased between them?

'It's the last Saturday in April at Claridge's.'

'Wow. You don't hang about. Something else you want to tell me, brother?'

'What? No. Not yet, anyway.' There was a little edge to his tone. As if there was a smile on his face as he was saying the words.

'And are we going to have to remortgage the clinic to pay for it?'

Leo let out a laugh. 'No, that's all under control.' His voice went a little quieter. 'It was Lizzie's dream to get married there and I plan on giving her exactly what she wants.'

There was a little pause then Ethan replied, 'Making Lizzie happy is exactly what you should do.'

The edge of the cups had heated up and Lexi shifted her fingers to try and avoid being burnt. Maybe it was safe to go in now? She stepped closer to the door.

'So—I wanted to ask you a question.' Her foot stopped mid-air. Maybe not.

'What is it?'

She was close enough now to see both men. Ethan was leaning heavily on the table—still not using the walking stick that he should. Leo was sitting opposite him, his hand pulling at the edge of his ear. The way he did when he was uncomfortable.

'I wanted to ask you to be my best man.' The words came out in a rush.

There was a pause. A heavy silence in the air.

Just say yes, Lexi willed Ethan. She shifted her fingers on the cups again. *Say yes before I burn myself.*

'I don't think so, Leo.' Ethan's voice was low, so low Lexi couldn't believe he'd just said those words. She must have misheard.

'Why not?' She cringed. She could hear the tension in Leo's voice, no matter how he tried to hide it.

'I just don't think it's a good idea. Ask Declan or Edward—you've known them for a long time. They'd do a better job than me.'

Lexi could almost hear the long intake of breath from Leo. She could only imagine how hurt he felt right now. Even if he wasn't showing it.

From this angle she could see him paste a smile on his face. 'You never were very good at speeches, were you, Ethan?'

'Rubbish. Whether you wrote them for me or not.'

It was an easy let-off. Even though he was obviously hurt, Leo had decided not to enter into a spat with his brother. His voice went a little lower. 'I just thought I should ask you first. You were the one to tell me to get my act together and sort out things with Lizzie.'

'That's because I'm the smart one in this family—and don't you forget it.'

Ethan had turned and headed towards the door. The conversation was clearly over.

'Sorry, Lexi, didn't see you there.'

She pasted a fake smile on her face. 'You'd better not have eaten my doughnut, Ethan Hunter. You could be in big trouble.'

He winked. 'Why break the habit of a lifetime?'

Lexi walked into the room and put the cups on the table. 'Sorry I took so long, Leo.' She didn't want to let on that she'd heard any of the previous conversation. It seemed wrong to hear private business between the brothers. It made her uncomfortable.

Leo grabbed a cup and took a drink, pushing the plate with the doughnuts on it towards her. 'Go on, dive in.' He looked down at the papers spread in front of him and gave a sad kind of smile. 'The income of the clinic has skyrocketed since you got here, Lexi. We're going to be able to support Olivia Fairchild's charity much more than I originally thought. I want you to know you are worth your weight in gold.'

Lexi bit into the doughnut, blowing her calorie count for the whole day. It was as if the whole conversation before hadn't happened. However hurt Leo must currently be feeling, he wasn't showing it.

But Leo was good at that. He'd switched from personal to professional mode in an instant.

It was up to her to do the same. No matter how hard she found it.

She pulled out the spreadsheet she was looking for. 'I'm glad you're happy, Leo. There's just a couple of other things we have to discuss.' She laid them out on the table and opened a laptop, which had Iain's interview loaded and ready to be released.

Leo's eyes focused on the first shot. Iain in his dark suit, white shirt and red tie, standing in front of the Hunter Clinic sign with his arms folded across his chest. He let out a laugh. 'Lexi Robbins. How did you manage to get that shot?'

She raised her eyebrows and tapped her nose. 'I have my ways. But I'll never tell.'

Leo leaned back in his chair as he watched, shaking his head in wonder as the video finished. 'Wow, Lexi.

You've done a fantastic job.' He glanced outside. 'I'd better hire a new receptionist. Our phones are going to ring off the hook.'

She nodded. 'I think you'd better.'

'It goes out tonight?'

'Yes.'

'Does Iain know? He's very private. I'm surprised he agreed to shoot it.'

She gathered up her papers, a knowing smile on her face. 'Let me handle Iain. I am the PR person after all.'

Leo nodded and gave her an appreciative smile. 'You certainly are.'

Iain was deep in surgery. He was grafting skin taken from the thigh onto a patient's cheek. His registrar was driving him crazy with all the questions she was asking.

'But why did you select the thigh area?'

He took a deep breath under his mask. 'We looked at the other traditional areas. The skin on her arms was too freckly, the skin on her buttocks wasn't suitable to transfer to her face. The skin on her thigh was the best option.'

The registrar let out a little sigh. 'It just seems so odd. Most people are more conscious about skin cancers these days—particularly on the face. Why didn't she see about it sooner?'

'And why didn't you read the case notes?' Iain snapped.

There was silence in the theatre. He could sense the rest of the staff cringing but he was tired of this lazy registrar with her enquiring mind. She asked thousands of questions without once looking for the answers herself.

And what's worse was that this patient had seen her

doctor. She'd seen several doctors, several times, none of whom had referred her to get a biopsy until it was too late. Her cancer could still be treated, but if she'd been referred the first time she'd worried about the pale brown mark on her face, the surgery she would have needed would have been minimal. A tiny scar. Rather than extensive surgery into the surrounding tissues that required a skin graft. And if the registrar had bothered to do her job she would have known all that.

He gritted his teeth. He was getting to the most important part. He'd just separated the epidermis and part of the dermis layer ready to transfer to the face. His first surgical steps had been to remove the cancer thoroughly, ensuring margins wide enough to capture all the cells but small enough to allow the best outcome for the patient. Stitching the graft into place required steady hands, tiny stitches and intense concentration.

Concentration had never been a problem for Iain before. But then again he'd never been in a relationship with Lexi Robbins before.

And something was bothering him. Even though he'd almost been upfront and honest with her, something wasn't right with Lexi.

She was busy doing her job and flying around the world, drumming up publicity for the clinic and the charities. He'd taken her back to Frank's twice and she'd enjoyed it just as much as the first time.

But something was still wrong. He could sense it. He could *feel* it.

But it had been so long since he'd felt something, he couldn't rely on his instincts.

It didn't matter that he did his best to try and build Lexi's confidence. It didn't matter that she seemed happy at work and happy in his company. There was still just *something*.

And he didn't know what.

But what made matters worse was that he had no idea why this bothered him so much. Lexi was getting under his skin. He'd told her right from the start that he didn't think he had anything to offer her. But even as he'd said the words he'd felt conflicted. He'd wanted to give her an out. A way to walk away with no commitment. But he wasn't that type of guy. And Lexi wasn't that type of woman.

He snapped his attention back to his work. What was wrong with him? He never lost focus.

Twittering. The registrar was twittering in his ear again. He honestly couldn't stand it.

He turned to face her. 'What is it exactly that you don't understand now? Because right now I'm busy. Right now I'm trying my hardest to make sure I line up the skin edges perfectly to give the best possible outcome for this patient. If I make a mess of this, she'll be left with permanent scarring on her face. If I do it well, after a few months the scars will fade and although they won't be invisible they won't be very noticeable to the average person. So what do you suggest I do? Should I allow myself to be distracted by you? To answer every question that you should have researched before you set foot in my theatre? Or should I just ignore you and get on with the job?'

Even beneath the mask he could see her mouth was hanging open. He waited for a noise, a loud clearing of the throat from the anaesthetist or the theatre sister. That was the general sign from them that it was time for him to wind it back in.

But no. There was nothing. They were obviously as fed up with the registrar as he was. She started to speak—to splutter behind her mask. 'But I'm here to—'

'No.' Iain held up the needle and suture that was in his hand. He shook his head. 'Just no.' He pointed towards the door and after a few seconds she stormed out in a huff.

There was nothing ominous about the silence that fell in the theatre. He could almost hear the collective sigh of relief.

Most of the time he was criticised for his directness. Today wasn't going to be one of those days.

He gave a smile as he looked over at the theatre sister. 'Now, where were we?'

She gave an almost approving nod. 'We were about to make Mrs Abbott look beautiful again, Iain. So let's get on with it.'

With the theatre quiet, he finished within an hour. He nodded at the theatre sister. 'The notes I write will be pretty extensive. I want to take these stitches out myself. I also want the dressing left in place until tomorrow and I want to be there when it comes off. I think Mrs Abbott will be a bit shocked and I want a bit of time to reassure her.'

'No problem, Iain. I'll pass that on to the ward staff. What's wrong with you these days?' She gave him a teasing smile. 'I thought you were returning to form earlier, but it seems someone has affected your bedside manner.' She was in her late fifties and had worked with Iain for the past two years. She was one of the few who could get away with saying that.

He peeled off his mask, gown and gloves, ignoring her last statement. 'I'm also going to write up some notes about moisturiser and massage for Mrs Abbott's post-op recovery treatment. Can you give me five minutes?'

But the theatre sister wasn't finished with Iain. She brushed past him, peeling off her own mask with a big smile on her face. 'So, are you going to tell me her name?'

On one hand he was amused, but this kind of light-hearted banter wasn't normal for Iain in Theatre. He knew that they called him the grizzly bear behind his back.

'I've no idea what you're talking about.' He smiled. Then leaned over as he started to rescrub his hands. 'And if I catch you speculating about me you'll get a whiff of anaesthetic gas,' he added wickedly.

'I think after all these years I'm probably immune. But do your worst, Iain. I'll find out.' She tapped the side of her nose. 'I always do.'

Iain finished washing and walked through to the changing rooms, dumping his scrubs and pulling his suit out of the locker. He was due back at Harley Street within an hour.

Was he really worried about anyone finding out about him and Lexi?

He wasn't sure. It wasn't a position he'd been in before. And he hadn't even discussed it with Lexi. He wasn't sure how she would feel about other people knowing about their relationship. It wouldn't make much difference to the staff at Kate's—most of them didn't know Lexi well. But the staff at the Hunter Clinic? That could be different. He would have to talk to her about it.

His pager went off as he fastened his tie. He frowned

as he glanced at the number. His secretary rarely paged him unless it was an emergency. Carol Kennedy, the television presenter he'd performed surgery on a few weeks ago. Everything had been going so well. Lexi had even interviewed her again as she'd recovered. Carol wanted to use the film to show people what she'd been through and that there was light at the end of the tunnel.

Iain headed over to the nearest phone. If something was wrong with Carol he wanted to deal with it straight away. He never left his patients waiting. Never.

CHAPTER TEN

LEXI LOOKED AT her phone for the third time. *Need to talk to you later.*

What did that mean? Her stomach had been churning ever since Iain had sent the message late that afternoon. She'd tried to call him back but he hadn't been answering his phone and his grim secretary had only told her that there was an emergency with a patient.

It was after eight now. Surely he would be home by now? She rang the doorbell and let her stomach do some flip-flops while she waited for an answer.

Iain answered the door. He hadn't had time to change out of his suit. He looked tired, but smiled when he saw her.

'Hey, Lexi, I was just about to call you.'

She felt a little surge of relief. 'What happened?'

He held open the door and gestured for her to come inside.

Lexi stepped into his house. 'Is it someone I know?'

He nodded. 'It's Carol Kennedy. She had some haemorrhaging. I had to take her back to Theatre.'

'Oh, no. What happened?' She walked through to the kitchen and started emptying the bag on the kitchen table.

Iain gave a rueful smile as he picked up the crusty loaf she'd just unpacked. 'One of these. Or something similar.' He shook his head. 'She'd been warned about what to eat but thought she was doing better and could manage something she enjoyed. Unfortunately her throat wasn't completely healed.'

Lexi stared at the bread in his hand. 'Wow. I never knew a crusty loaf could cause damage to a throat.'

'Not normally. But after delicate throat surgery you have to be careful what you eat.' He picked up the cheese, pickle and cold ham she'd set on the table. 'Are we having a picnic tonight?'

Lexi smiled. 'I can't really cook. I try—but there's a real danger of food poisoning. So I decided not to even try.' She held up her hands. 'I don't want you to start getting false expectations about me.'

He crossed the room and put his hands on her hips. 'Oh, I've no false expectations about you, Lexi. You meet every single one of my expectations.'

'I do, do I?' She raised herself up on her toes and wound her hands around his neck. There it was. The picture still sitting on the window ledge. How could she have expected anything different? Of course the picture of Bonnie would still be there. There were pictures of her scattered throughout the house.

So why did it make her stomach curl so much? Bonnie wasn't here any more. And there was no question she had Iain's undivided attention. So why didn't it feel as if it was enough?

His hands were working their way around to her stomach. He still hadn't mentioned her abdominal scar. She'd already told him she'd had surgery as a child, maybe he just didn't want to pry.

It was still there. It was still eating away at her. The fact that Iain would eventually want a family of his own—one she couldn't provide. This was a fling. This was a fleeting event. And she had to keep reminding herself about that. Otherwise she could end up being seriously hurt.

Iain was paying particular attention to her neck. And their feet were moving slowly but surely in the direction of the bedroom. She pushed all the other thoughts from her mind. It was time to focus on the here and now because for the next few hours Iain was hers and hers alone.

And that was just the way she liked him.

Iain's pager sounded first thing in the morning with a shriek that made Lexi sit bolt upright in bed.

Iain's hand was on the phone in seconds, dialling in the number and listening for a few minutes. It couldn't be good. The only words he muttered were expletives.

'What's wrong?'

He shook his head. 'Can you spare some time today?'

She wrinkled her brow, trying not to think about the appointments she had, the calls to return and the final edits she had to do. 'I can try. What's wrong?'

'It's Carol Kennedy.'

'Did she have a bad night? Does she have post-op complications?'

Iain blew out a stream of air. 'Of the worst kind. Someone has blabbed to the media. One of the tabloids has been on the phone to Kate's, wanting a statement.'

Lexi cringed. 'Oh, no. Carol wanted the time to break the story herself. I've nearly finished editing the interview we did together. It's great. She comes across exactly as she is in real life, a woman with compassion and concern.'

'Well, by tomorrow she will be headline news on every front page.'

'Poor Carol. That's exactly what she didn't want.' Lexi put her head into her hands. 'I wonder…'

'Wonder what?'

Lexi stood up and walked around the bed. 'I hate to ask my parents for anything but if I could speak to my father, he has a show lined up for tonight. I could speak to him about screening Carol's interview.' She couldn't stop pacing. 'My father is quite mercenary. The thought of breaking the story would probably appeal to him.'

Iain nodded. Normally he would have hated anything like this but Carol had made her wishes clear. She wanted to break things on her terms. 'Can you talk to Carol this morning? Ask her how she wants to handle things?'

Lexi nodded. 'I take it you're happy with her recovery?'

He was picking up his clothes, pulling on his trousers. 'I'll come with you.' He paused from fastening his trousers. 'You can come this morning, can't you?'

Lexi nodded. She was Head of PR at the Hunter Clinic and this could rapidly turn into a PR nightmare. Everything else would have to wait. Including another viewing of the perfect interview with Iain. She'd watched it constantly since they'd filmed it. He was perfect. Just like a film star. And as soon as he opened his mouth and that Scottish accent came out—along with the slightly shaggy hair, good looks and toned body— he was going to be a sensation. The commercial had been let loose on the media last night. Neither of them had had time to think about it then—other priorities had taken over. She reached over and grabbed her phone. Dead as a doornail.

Iain was tucking his shirt in. 'What's wrong?'

She waved the phone at him. 'Out of charge.'

He pointed to the nearby table. 'Mine's plugged in over there—use it.'

She moved across the room and plugged in her phone. It vibrated instantly and she felt as if her eyes were bugging out her skull. *Four hundred emails. Sixty messages. One hundred and thirty-two texts.* Was somebody dead?

Then a smile crept across her face as she opened the first email. Just as she'd predicted. The world at large loved Iain McKenzie. He was going to be the latest internet sensation. She could see him in the bathroom, brushing his teeth. Better not tell him now. He'd probably freak. She could save it till later.

She sat on the edge of the bed and dialled her father's number, sighing when it went straight to voicemail. 'Hi, Dad, it's Lexi. I've got a bit of news for you—and an exclusive interview. Can you give me a call back?'

She put on her clothes and washed her face, pulling her hair back in a clip. Ready in less than five minutes.

Iain smiled. 'Let's go and see what we can do to help Carol.'

Six hours later Lexi hadn't stopped. And she'd had no chance whatsoever to respond to all the emails, messages and texts. Carol was making a good recovery following her op the day before and had given approval for her interview to be used on Lexi's father's show that night. She'd also recorded a new segment saying how she wanted to raise awareness of the type of cancer she had, and to say that her hand had been forced by the media to reveal her diagnosis before she'd wished to. It was skilfully done. Lexi's father had jumped all over the story, delighted to have the breaking news.

But even though she'd essentially done him a favour, he'd hardly even acknowledged the part that Lexi had played. It was nothing new to her. The thing that astonished her was that she still felt a tiny modicum of hurt about her father's actions. Or lack of them. Still, she had enough on her plate right now.

As for Iain McKenzie—internet sensation—she was so glad the interview had gone out the day before. If the Hunter Clinic was going to hit the news it was better to do it on her own terms. In a matter of minutes the footage of the hunky Scotsman had gone viral—just like she'd suspected it would. The phones at the clinic were currently ringing off the hook.

It seemed like she wasn't the only one who found Iain attractive. The rest of the female population were inclined the same way.

Needless to say, Iain hadn't been impressed. When they got back to the Hunter Clinic the amount of couriers with deliveries had staggered them all. Agencies looking to represent him had sent champagne and designer suits. Department stores wanting to use him for their advertising campaigns had sent their entire men's ranges. Aftershaves, flowers, bottles of whisky, ties, shirts and mountains of underwear were all waiting for him in his over-stuffed office.

Iain looked as if he might explode, but Lexi smiled.

This was exactly what she'd expected. Fabulous publicity for the clinic and its attached charities.

And as a plus point the bookings had soared.

Now, if only she could get him into a kilt…

CHAPTER ELEVEN

THE SILVER ENVELOPE was lying on her desk, the courier logo across the top. She picked it up and stared at it. Who on earth was this from?

'When did this arrive?' She walked out of her office towards Rose, one of the secretaries.

Rose looked up and gave her a wary smile. 'About an hour ago. I signed for it. Is something wrong?'

Lexi shook her head. 'I don't think so.' She tore open the envelope and pulled the thick invitation out, letting out a little yelp when she realised what it was.

'Me? Me?' She couldn't believe it.

Rose jumped to her feet. 'Lexi? Lexi? Is something wrong?'

'What? Oh, no. Everything is wonderful!' She gave a little spin, waving the invitation above her head. 'I've been nominated for a PR award; one of the biggest awards in PR!' She let out an excited squeal, 'I can't believe it. I've dreamed about this since I was at university. Every year we used to study the people who'd been nominated. I can't believe I'm one of them.'

The secretary gave a smile. 'Well, congratulations. That's fabulous news. For you, and for the clinic. Do you want me to let Leo know? He'll be thrilled for you.'

'What? Oh, yes. Thanks very much.' She kept the invitation close to her chest lest someone try to snatch it away from her. It was hers. It was really hers.

She couldn't wipe the smile from her face. It felt too good.

Finally, recognition for the job that she loved. Recognition that someone, somewhere thought she was doing a good job. There were hundreds of nominations for the PR award every year, only a few making it to the final cut. A panel had studied her work closely after the nomination. Thank goodness she hadn't known about that beforehand, it would have made her break out in a cold sweat.

She walked down the corridor, heading towards Iain's office. He was the first person she wanted to tell. Was that weird? The other people she really wanted to know were her parents. But she didn't want to have to tell them herself. She didn't want to give them the ability to shrug off her news as if it was meaningless.

If she kept quiet long enough, the press would eventually break the story. Maybe her parents would pay more attention then? Was it wrong to know that her parents would be more likely to celebrate her success if it brought them good promo?

She shook the thought from her head.

'What are you looking so happy about?' Iain had crept up behind her, placed his hands on her hips and was escorting her into his office, shutting the door with his foot.

'This!' Lexi spun around, waving the silver envelope.

Iain smiled, leaned against the door and folded his arms. 'Okay, you got me. What is it?'

She couldn't help it. She started jumping up and

down on the spot. Even wearing stilettos she couldn't contain her excitement. 'It's such a big a nomination. I can't believe I got it. I can't believe I got nominated. I don't care about winning. Just getting nominated is so, so fabulous!'

'You finalled? Really? That's brilliant! I knew you would!'

He bent down and kissed her thoroughly. His kisses took her breath away. The feel of his hands on her body made her forget everything else—including the fact they were in the clinic.

Well, not quite everything. In the currently messy recesses of her mind a little alarm bell had gone off.

She pulled back. 'You don't seem surprised.'

'Maybe I believe in you. Maybe I value the work that you do. Maybe I think the world should know how good you are. Look at the fabulous job you did with Carol Kennedy. Everyone is talking about her. Everyone is talking about the warning signs of cancer.'

She felt a little warmth spread through her chest. 'It was you, wasn't it? You nominated me for this award?'

It was an incredible feeling. A swelling of pride. Something she rarely experienced in this life—not with the parents she had.

It made her feel special. It made her feel worthy. All things she'd spent this life striving for. And in a few short weeks Iain had made that happen for her. There was no getting away from the fact that she could happily spend the rest of her life like this. Happily spend the rest of her life with Iain—if only he didn't want kids so badly.

He touched her face. 'Of course I nominated you for the award. I've seen the hours you put in. I've seen the changes you've made in the last few months. The number of celebrity clients has gone through the roof. You know they're not my favourite kind, but if they help the clinic, and help with the charity work we can do, I can live with that.' He pulled her even closer. '*You* did this work, Lexi. *You* did. I just nominated you for the award. The panel scrutinised the work that you've done. They found it worthy to give you a place as a finalist. You should be proud of yourself. The work you've done here is amazing.'

The silver envelope was still trapped between them, against the hard planes of his chest and the firm curves of her breasts. She looked down at it and smiled. 'I think this is all a ploy.'

'A ploy?' Iain arched his eyebrows.

'Definitely. You must know this invitation is for two people. You're trying to trick me into going out in public with you.' It was risky. It was more than risky. They hadn't let anyone at work know about their relationship. Everything had been kept tightly under wraps. This would blow things out of the water.

She felt her heart flutter in her chest. Beating much faster than it should. Didn't they have a special name for this? AF? Didn't this normally require medical treatment? Just as well she was in a doctor's arms.

She was pretending to breathe normally. Pretending that this was an everyday question. Pretending that she didn't feel sick asking it.

She could see Iain thinking. She could almost hear his brain ticking. Trying to decide what to tell her. Did he want to let her down gently? Because, frankly, that would kill her.

But just when she thought he was going to break

her heart, he leaned forward and gave her a kiss. It was lighter than before, a little more formal.

'It would be my pleasure to be your date. I think you'll knock them out.'

She tried not to let the hiss of relief from her lungs be audible. Her smile was back, pasted from one ear to the other. 'So,' she said as she wound her hands around his neck, 'what are my chances of getting you in a kilt?'

Lexi looked in the mirror and tried not to let her hand tremble as she took the large rollers from her hair. It fell in loose curls, just the way she'd wanted. Everything should be perfect.

But inside her chest her heart was pitter-pattering the fast beat of nerves. This wasn't about Iain. This wasn't about the award ceremony. This was about being *her*.

She shrugged the satin robe from her shoulders, immediately averting her eyes from the full-length mirror in front of her.

Her breasts were perfect. There was no denying the fantastic job her plastic surgeon had done. But although she liked them, she was still naturally shy about her body shape. She wasn't the kind of girl who'd ever go topless on a beach. She stepped into her pink satin underwear and fastened her bra around her back. There. Now she looked up.

Her hand rested on her stomach. The line of her panties didn't quite hide the scar on her abdomen. The scar that Iain had never asked about.

Just that thought sent the hairs on the back of her neck standing on end. It was inevitable. At some point he would ask and at some point she would tell him. And that time was creeping closer with every day.

Within a few seconds she'd pulled her dress over her head. Better, much better. Now her body was covered. It was almost as if she'd pulled on her suit of armour.

The dress enhanced her shape, covered all the parts of her she wanted covered. And let her move past the things she didn't want to think about.

She sat down in the chair and fastened her jewel-encrusted sandals. She could almost see the headlines. The Lexi Robbins who appeared in the press was so different from the Lexi Robbins who stared at her in the mirror.

These last few weeks had been easier. She was little more relaxed. A little more confident. She fastened her earrings. Iain. He was the difference here.

He never failed to compliment her. He never failed to tell her how good he thought she looked.

She looked up again. She liked the pale pink and silver dress. Not too much cleavage, not too much leg. She was comfortable in it. Some people might call her a princess in it.

Too bad that wasn't how she felt.

She fixed a smile on her face. There. That was better.

Iain would be here soon. Her stomach gave a little flip. She pushed the nerves away and finished her make-up with some rose-coloured lipstick. It wasn't dark enough, she would need a second coat. That could wait until Iain was here.

She flicked the switch on the radio and tuned in to some classic tunes. Anything to distract her right now. Anything to take her mind off the sea of cameras that would be waiting for her in the next hour.

Iain would be right next to her. And with him there, everything would be all right—wouldn't it?

* * *

Iain knocked on her door, the London wind whistling about his knees. This wind was for amateurs. If he was in Edinburgh right now the wind would have his kilt dancing somewhere around his ears. It had been a long time since he'd taken his kilt out of its carrier. A very long time. He used to love wearing his kilt on special occasions. Then again, he used to love going out— something he rarely did in London.

Lexi opened the door and let out a squeal. 'You did it! You wore the kilt!'

Her face was a picture. For a second he was transfixed by the sparkle in her eyes and broadest of smiles.

Until he became distracted by the floaty pale pink chiffon of her dress. A sleeveless dress with broad straps and a cross-over bodice, scattered with silver sequins that skimmed down across her hips. Her waist was accentuated by a pale pink ribbon cinched around it, giving her a perfect hourglass shape. The dress skimmed her knees. There was nothing revealing about it. Nothing to attract undue attention. But the way it clung to her body and accentuated her curves was attention-grabbing enough for Iain. That, along with how the dress rippled in the wind, made her look like a butterfly, waiting to be captured.

She'd left her blonde hair in loose curls over her shoulders, there was a light tan on her skin, and her feet were encased in red-soled silver sparkling shoes. She'd never looked so beautiful.

'Wow, Lexi. Just wow. You don't need to win the award tonight. No one will be able to take their eyes off you.'

She waved her hand and picked up her evening purse.

'Sure they won't. They'll be more interested in the free food and free bar.' She paused in front of the mirror and applied some more pink lipstick, giving him a cheeky wink. 'I, on the other hand, will spend the whole night wondering if you're a true Scotsman or not.'

'Wanna find out now?'

'Naughty.' She batted his hands away, picking up the silver invitation and tucking it into her bag.

His hands caught her around the waist. There was no way he was leaving here without a kiss. He bent forward and nibbled at her neck, catching the aroma of her trademark perfume. It sent his pulse racing. What kind of underwear did she have on under that beautiful dress?

'So, Lexi. Make me pass out with shock at the price of that dress. You look stunning.'

'This?' She shook her head. 'I bought it on the high street. I'm sure the fashion press will have plenty to say about that tomorrow.' She lifted her leg and extended her sparkling shoe towards him. 'These, however, would probably make me remortgage my house.'

'Really? Shoes?' He stared for a few moments. Sure, they were pretty. And they matched the dress. But crazy money—on shoes?

He shook his head and watched as she fastened some glittering earrings on her lobes. 'Are you ready?'

She took one last glance in the mirror then picked up her bag. Her hands were trembling slightly. Lexi Robbins was nervous. He couldn't believe it. She looked a million dollars and her work spoke for itself. Just about every newspaper in the country had covered Carol Kennedy's story after her interview had appeared on Lexi's father's show.

Carol had shown great courage, though not without

a tear or two. She'd let the cameraman film her drains being removed, the initial scars. The post-op complications. Every time she spoke there was a tiny waver in her voice that was overcome by her courage and the message that she wanted to share with others. It was media gold and everyone knew it.

The only thing that had irked Iain had been the glossing over of Lexi's role. Her name had appeared in the credits of her father's show, but very little had been said about the work she had done. That was part of the reason he'd nominated her for the award. He wanted the world to know about the sterling work that she had done.

And that was without mentioning the current waiting list of clients he'd had since his interview for the Hunter Clinic had exploded all over the media. If it had been anyone but Lexi, he might have been annoyed to be in the public eye. But it would only be for a few weeks then they would move on to someone else. Or so he hoped.

The flashlights exploded as they stepped from the car outside the prestigious London hotel. For the first time in his life Iain could hear people shouting his name, vying for his attention. And he didn't like it. He didn't like it one little bit.

'Dr Sexy! Look over here first!'

It didn't help that the hotel had laid a red carpet outside and set up sponsorship banners for photographers. Iain kept his arm tightly around Lexi's waist and tried to steer her directly inside.

'Lexi, are you dating Iain McKenzie? Is that why you did the interview?'

'Lexi, where's the dress from?'

'Dr McKenzie, what's your relationship with Lexi Robbins?'

He grimaced. Ignorant journalist. He was a surgeon. He was Mr McKenzie, not Dr. And he couldn't even begin to say what his intentions towards Lexi were—because he didn't know himself.

The hotel was stunning and after the first glass of champagne Lexi's nerves seemed to settle. She moved into professional PR mode, working the room, circulating and talking to everyone, without letting Iain leave her side.

After around half an hour he felt Lexi stiffen. He didn't even need to ask why. Her mother and father had entered the room to a round of applause. They moved through the crowd effortlessly. And after a few minutes' fascination he quickly came to the realisation that they were their own biggest fans.

They barely even glanced at their beautiful daughter and Iain could feel the fire surge in his belly.

Lexi was pretending not to notice. She was smiling and talking politely to those around her, even though it was blindingly obvious to the whole room that her parents hadn't even taken the time to acknowledge her.

She pressed her hand on Iain's arm. 'You'll need to excuse me a minute, Iain, I need to check my make-up.' He could see unshed tears hiding behind her eyes. She needed a little time out. A little space to collect herself.

'No problem,' he muttered, watching her cross the room in her fluttering dress. As soon as she was out of sight he walked directly over to the bar, where her father was ordering champagne.

He held out his hand. 'Steve Robbins? I'm Iain McKenzie. I'm here with your daughter tonight.'

Lexi's father frowned then switched into false mode

and shook Iain's hand. He could tell the man wasn't the least bit interested, but Iain hadn't even started yet.

Lexi's mother sidled up to the bar in a blue silk sheath dress, her eyes watching her own reflection in the mirror behind the bar.

'I nominated Lexi for the award this evening. She's done some really fantastic work at the Hunter Clinic.'

Penelope Crosby lifted her eyebrows. He could tell it was because the conversation wasn't directly focused on her. What a sad woman. But she couldn't deter him.

'Lexi has raised over a hundred thousand pounds in the last few weeks for the charity work of the clinic.'

'Charity work, huh?' Lexi's father shook his head. 'More likely lining the pockets of you and your colleagues.'

Iain stilled the fire in his belly. 'I don't need anyone else to line my pockets. I probably earn more money than you do,' he shot back, without the slightest hint of embarrassment. 'I think you should appreciate the wonderful job that your daughter does. She gave you that breakthrough a few weeks ago with *my* patient Carol Kennedy. None of that filming would have taken place if I hadn't agreed to it. And the only reason Carol spoke to Lexi was because Lexi was genuinely concerned about her and showed her some compassion.' He took a drink from his whisky sitting on the bar. 'A trait that obviously doesn't run in the family.'

Lexi's mother looked horrified. She'd spent her life with people fawning over her and obviously wasn't used to be spoken to like that.

Iain finished his whisky. 'Tell me, Mr Robbins, exactly how much of a rating boost did that interview give your flagging show? And have you thanked your daughter for it yet?'

Lexi's father's face started to turn beetroot. 'How dare you?'

'Oh, I dare.'

'Who do you think you are?'

'I think I'm the person who knows your daughter is beautiful, inside and out.' He replaced his glass on the bar. 'I'm the person who thinks she works hard and deserves recognition for the job that she does. That's who I think I am.'

The beetroot colour was settling on Lexi's father's face. It was turning to an embarrassed dark glow.

'It's such a pity that Lexi still looks for your approval.' He paused, there was so much more he could say here. But the truth was it really wasn't his business. He'd probably already overstepped the mark.

It was time to leave her parents' company. Lexi's mother had stopped being horrified and was back to checking her reflection in the mirror behind the bar again. And as beautiful as her reflection was, she had nothing on Lexi.

She didn't have Lexi's heart. Or Lexi's soul. She didn't have any of the compassion or humility that Lexi showed. She was so self-centred. Iain couldn't bear to in her company a second longer.

He watched as Lexi came out of the ladies and gave her a wave. He didn't want her to come over here. To listen to the indifference of her parents. He gave them a quick glance. 'I just want you to know that I'm proud of Lexi, even if you aren't.'

But no matter what he thought, Lexi was on her way over, with a tilt to her chin that proved she was ready.

She walked over, sliding her hand into his and smiling as he gave it a squeeze. She angled her cheek as her father gave her a kiss. 'Congratulations on your nomination, Lexi.' His eyes shot to Iain. 'You know that we are proud of you.' Her mother hadn't moved from the bar, almost as if she was waiting for her cue.

And there it was. 'Lexi, darling, you look wonderful!' She stepped over from the bar with her arms in the air, her blue sheath-style dress barely allowing her to move. Her arms closed around her daughter's neck just as there was the flash of a camera.

Iain cringed. It was obvious she'd orchestrated the whole thing. Lexi was spun around and positioned between her parents just as one of the photographers from a national magazine appeared. 'Oh, perfect!' the photographer shouted. 'I don't know who is more beautiful, mother or daughter!'

It was pretty obvious to Iain, but he waited a few moments as the photographer positioned them all exactly as he wanted them and snapped away. Lexi's mother spent most of the time throwing back her head and laughing—obviously the way she wanted to be captured on film. When the photographer nodded that he was finished, Lexi slid out from under her parents' grasp and took a few steps back to Iain.

He bent to give her a kiss. Raspberries. She tasted of raspberries. 'Let's go and mingle,' he said to her, guiding her away from her parents. She didn't even glance in their direction. They'd moved on to speak to another TV personality with barely a few words to their daughter. And he could tell from the tension in her body and the sheen in her eyes that she hadn't quite collected herself yet.

He glanced at his watch and scoped out the bar on the other side of the room. 'How about a little cocktail before they announce the awards?'

She jerked to attention. 'Is it that time already?' She looked stunned, almost as if she'd forgotten why she was there. He loved that about her.

They made their way to the bar and Iain grabbed the cocktail menu. 'What's your favourite? Vodka? Rum? Whisky?'

She wrinkled her nose. 'Whisky cocktail? Yuck.' Her eyes ran down the menu. 'I'll have a raspberry daiquiri.'

He smiled. 'I should have guessed. You taste of raspberries already.'

She smiled and ran her tongue along her lips. Boy, just that tiny action could drive him crazy. He gave their order at the bar and waited while the bartender mixed the frozen cocktails. Then they stood quietly for the next half-hour, his arm around her waist as they drank their cocktails.

Then the lights in the room dimmed and the compère appeared on the stage, giving a short presentation about the awards and past recipients. The PR award was one of the first to be announced. One by one the nominees appeared on screen, along with a presentation about their work. Then Lexi's face appeared on the screen ahead of them.

She flinched. 'Oh, no. I don't like my face in high definition.' She burrowed her face into his shoulder. 'It shows all the blemishes.'

Iain took a deep breath. There it was again. The fact that Lexi didn't see what he did. On the screen ahead of him he saw a beautiful fresh-faced woman. Long eyelashes around clear blue eyes, luscious pink lips and long blonde curls. She could out-supermodel her mother any day of the week.

He slipped his finger underneath her chin and tilted her head up towards his. 'Trust me, Lexi, there are no blemishes.' He kissed her again, tasting the raspberries still on her lips and pulling her closer to him.

Clapping broke out around them and they both broke apart.

'Is it over?' Lexi asked, her hands pressed against his chest. She started to clap, even though he knew neither of them had heard the announcement of the winner. A face flashed up on the screen of one of the male nominees who worked for a newly opened fashion chain. They watched as he walked up on stage in his sharp suit and gave his acceptance speech.

Iain squeezed Lexi around her waist, his fingers catching the chiffon material and silver sequins beneath his hands. 'You were robbed,' he whispered in her ear.

She shook her head firmly. 'No, I wasn't. He's done a good job. He deserves it.' She kept clapping until he left the stage. 'I feel lucky to be nominated. I never thought I was going to win anyway, so I'm not disappointed.'

He could tell she meant it. Her generous spirit was still evident, showing grace in defeat. 'Well, I'm disappointed for you. I thought you deserved to win.'

She stood on tiptoe and kissed his cheek. 'Thank you, Iain. That's the nicest thing anyone's said to me all night.' She squeezed his hand. 'What do you say we get out of here?'

She had that gleam in her eyes. The ones that could send a sweep of sensation down to his toes, igniting all the parts of his body it needed to.

'Let's go now.' Even he could recognise how husky his voice sounded. He only had one thing on his mind.

'Give me five minutes to visit the ladies before we go.' And before he could even answer she'd swept away and ducked into the nearest ladies room. All he could see was the flutter of her pale pink dress around her legs.

It was more than he needed.

CHAPTER TWELVE

LEXI STOOD IN front of the mirror and re-applied her rose-coloured lipstick. Her face was flushed. But it was excitement. Excitement over what would happen next with Iain.

He'd been fabulous with her tonight. Supporting her with her parents and keeping her close during the award announcements. But she wasn't disappointed at all about not winning.

Truth was, she already felt as if she'd won because Iain had nominated her and brought her here tonight.

She took one final glance in the mirror. The dress he'd admired so much was nice. Much nicer than some of the dresses tonight that were ten times the price. It just went to show that pricier wasn't always better.

She gave a little smile then walked back outside to meet Iain.

Her eyes swept the room. He was only a few feet away, talking to some man in a dark suit.

A voice breathed in her ear, 'Well, what do we have here?'

Her stomach turned over, thankfully not all over her dress. A blast from the past. And one she certainly didn't welcome.

She spun round in her sparkling shoes. 'Jack, what an unpleasant surprise.'

Jack Parker was standing in front of her, his arm around a buxom blonde who looked as if she was being strangled by her bright blue dress. How on earth she'd managed to contain her oversized breasts in a dress two sizes too small was anybody's guess. His tie was askew and his hair rumpled. What a surprise—Jack Parker was drunk.

He leaned forward and she got the whiff of alcohol on his breath. Any closer and he could anaesthetise her.

'I saw you up on the screen. Close up doesn't do you much good, does it?'

She took a deep breath. 'I could say the same about you, Jack,' she shot back.

He raised one eyebrow. What had she ever found attractive about this guy?

Her stomach was churning. He was saying out loud the thoughts that had sprung into her mind the second she'd seen her face on the screen. Jack Parker was still inside her head. Still circulating little horrible thoughts. It made her angry. It made her angry that she was still allowing him to influence her thoughts, and have a little bit of control over her life.

She ran her eyes up and down his rumpled suit. 'Did you pick that one straight up out of the garden after I dumped it there?'

His eyes narrowed. He wasn't used to Lexi standing up for herself. He wasn't used to it at all. She'd always found a way to try and avoid any arguments with him. Had spent most of her time trying to placate him. More fool her.

And for a time it had seemed his greatest pleasure was to make her cry. Well, not tonight.

Jack's drunken girlfriend swayed and turned to him. 'What's she talking about, baby? I thought you dumped her?'

Her hand rested on his chest. There was something vaguely familiar about her. Lexi's eyes dropped to her obviously over-implanted breasts. Of course, she was a glamour model. But her breasts stood out like sore thumbs. Lexi could tell just by looking that they were obviously too large for her slim frame. And her implants had been placed over her chest muscles instead of under, causing obvious ridge marks at the tops of breasts. Oh, dear. Even Lexi could tell this woman would need reconstructive surgery at some point. Had Jack made her do that?

She could feel the fire building in her belly. On any other day if she'd seen Jack Parker she would have ducked and hidden. She didn't like conflict. She didn't like attention being on herself. It didn't matter that she'd picked up the courage to throw him out. Even one glance of Jack brought back the overwhelming surge of not being good enough. It brought back the seeds of doubt and the memories of his cruel words and actions.

She looked across the room. She wasn't panicking—she was just looking for some reassurance. Iain was still in conversation with another man just a few feet away. He obviously hadn't realised anything was wrong.

These last few weeks with Iain had given her some new-found confidence. She felt appreciated. She felt respected. She felt…loved?

Something she'd never felt before. Either with Jack

or her parents. Her aunt was the only person who'd ever shown her love.

It was a startling realisation. It almost made her feel giddy.

Jack was wrinkling his nose at her, mumbling under his breath. She couldn't stand him. She couldn't stand to be in the same place as him. Even now he treated her with disdain. How dared he?

She straightened her shoulders, gave a smile to his girlfriend and extended her hand. 'Pleasure to meet you. I'm Lexi Robbins. Jack's never had any manners and that's obviously not changed.' As she took the action she was aware of Jack's eyes on her bust. Even though she was perfectly happy with her figure, it could clearly never compete with his new girlfriend's. And she'd never want to. She couldn't imagine the health problems the woman was likely to have in the future.

The blonde's eyes widened as she took the hand in front of her and gave it a limp shake. Jack was spluttering over his drink but Lexi ignored him.

'Brandy,' she slurred.

Brandy. It figured.

'And just so we're clear, you're wrong,' Lexi continued. 'I dumped Jack. In fact, I threw his clothes out of our flat and changed the locks. That's because he's a weasel. You'd do well to remember that.'

The colour started to rise in Jack's face. 'Rubbish, Lexi. That's rubbish. You were too boring for me.' He glanced back at Brandy, obviously desperate to save face. 'In more ways than one. And, obviously, not pretty enough.' He pulled Brandy closer to him. Was that to reassure her? Or to stop himself from swaying?

'Get a life, Jack,' Lexi sighed, and gave a shake of her head. 'You're not worth it. Not for a second.'

She spun on her heel and walked back into the ladies. She didn't want to let him have a minute more of her time. She didn't want all the little self-doubts to find their way into her mind and thoughts again. She stood for a second in front of the mirror, taking a few deep breaths.

She wanted to get of here. She needed to get out of here. She needed to find Iain and stick to their original plan. The original plan that made her knees quiver and her heart race.

The door banged behind her and before she could even lift her head to look at who had entered she was grabbed roughly from behind. There was no time to think. No time to act.

She was pushed against the wall, the cold tiles pressing against her back. Jack had one hand on her shoulder, the other around her throat.

She tried to move her arms, her hands, but his full weight was on her. He leaned forward. 'Who do you think you are? Don't you dare speak to me like that.'

She turned her head away, trying to avert the smell of alcohol that was coming from his breath.

'Look at me!' he growled.

She closed her eyes tightly and shook her head. 'Get off me, Jack. This is a public restroom, any minute now someone will walk in and see what you're doing.'

He snarled. 'Who's going to stop me?' He lifted one hand and waved it around, laughing as she took the opportunity to try and escape his grasp. 'There's no one here but you and me.'

He pressed his hand back to her body, this time

reaching up and squeezing her breast. 'You should be thanking me. Thanking me for telling you to get some shape.' He gave another little laugh. 'But you'll never compare to Brandy.'

She winced under his grasp. Jack had never been physical with her in the past, but the amount of alcohol he'd consumed—along with his bad temper—made her glad things had never been like this.

She opened her eyes and looked him straight in the eye. She didn't even notice the door open in the background. She was too focused on her task.

Fight or flight. The surge of adrenaline powered through her body.

'That's just it Jack, I don't want to be anything like Brandy.' She leaned towards him, ignoring the stench of alcohol. 'But you're right. It's just you and me.'

She lifted her knee and hammered it straight into his groin. His reaction was instant. He released her and crumpled to the floor, clutching at his groin.

She stepped over him in her fluttering dress. 'Don't you ever put a hand on me again.'

There was a movement beside her. A dark flash of something. It took her a few seconds to register that Iain had appeared.

And she didn't recognise the expression on his face. She'd never seen Iain angry before.

He lifted Jack clean off the floor and slammed him against the white tiles where he'd just held Lexi. If she'd thought Jack had been snarling at her before, he'd had nothing on Iain. The steam was practically coming out of his ears.

'Don't you dare touch Lexi ever again.' His eyes

flicked to Lexi. 'Are you okay? Do you want to press charges?'

She shook her head. She just wanted to get out of there.

Jack had shrunk back against the tiles. He wasn't so brave when confronted by a six-foot-four angry Scotsman.

Iain spun him round, grabbing him by the collar of his shirt and the back of his trousers. Jack's feet were skimming the floor as Iain thrust him towards the door. A woman opened it and walked in, letting out a little shriek when she saw the two men in the ladies. Wordlessly she held the door open as Iain escorted Jack from the building.

He was quietly efficient about it, stopping only once to pull out his card and hand it to an astonished Brandy. 'Chronic back pain?'

She nodded in a stunned silence.

'Come and see me some time and we'll chat about what's best for you.'

Jack was strangely silent. Any time his steps seemed to hesitate Iain just lifted him clean off the floor to help him on his way. They reached the outer door and Iain ejected him down the steps.

Lexi cringed as he tumbled down them into a puddle outside. Iain stood next to her and slid his arm around her waist. He pointed at Jack. 'I'm warning you, Jack. I don't want you within fifty feet of Lexi.'

He turned and steered her down the street, away from the event and towards the footpath to the Thames. She could see his hand still shaking slightly. She knew it was with rage. But she wasn't scared around Iain. He was a big man, who could probably intimidate anyone in his vicinity. But the rage would never be aimed at her. She felt secure with him beside her. She felt safe around Iain. But that wasn't all she felt and that's what was bothering her.

His arms swept around her as he laid her coat across her shoulders. She hadn't even realised he'd picked up her coat for her. She pulled it around her and slid her arms into the sleeves. March was cold in London, it wouldn't do to be without her coat.

Iain pulled her closer as they walked along in silence. Her brain was whirring with a million thoughts that she just couldn't even begin to compute.

Even though she'd tried her very best, the tiny little seeds of doubt were creeping into her brain. Seeds that Jack had initially planted and which had sprouted and grown. She'd thought she'd dealt with those. She'd thought she'd doused them with the weedkiller they deserved.

But seeing Jack again had brought them all flooding back, no matter how hard she tried. Except this time the thoughts weren't about Jack. This time the seeds of doubt were all about her and Iain.

It was ridiculous. Iain had only ever treated her with respect. He'd never mocked her body—quite the opposite, in fact. He'd never let her think she wasn't good enough.

So why were thoughts like that circulating in her brain?

Why would Iain be interested in someone like her? She wasn't a supermodel. She was clever but not a genius. She'd done a good job with the publicity and charitable donations for the clinic.

A horrible startling realisation crept over her. Maybe

he was just trying to keep her sweet? Trying to make sure the Hunter Clinic was known around the world?

No. Iain would never be like that.

He'd almost fought against the attraction between them. And he'd been more than supportive regarding her parents and her surgery.

So why was a whole host of doubts creeping into her head?

She leaned against him a little as they walked down the path to the Thames. It was beautiful at this time of night. The path next to the dark river twinkled with little lights leading towards the brightly lit Tower Bridge. If you wanted to find a romantic location in London at night, you really couldn't do better.

It was cold enough to still see their breath in the air. Cold enough to have an excuse to snuggle closer.

But Lexi felt changed from before. The feelings of uncertainty were making her feel differently.

There was no getting away from it. She'd fallen hard for Iain. Hard and fast. She'd shared things with him in a way she'd never shared with anyone at all.

And he'd shared with her too.

Only not enough.

A wave of cold air swept over her body, sending a little shiver across her skin.

That was it. That was what was wrong.

She turned and looked at his profile as they walked along the path. She could almost sense he was in as much turmoil as she was. They weren't talking. They were simply holding each other and walking. But at some point they were going to reach the crescendo of what was happening between them. Reach the tipping point.

Her velvet coat wasn't giving her any warmth right now. The cold feeling wouldn't leave her.

Iain had told her about his wife. He'd told her about his babies. It must have truly broken his heart. But there was more. There was more that he hadn't told her.

And if they really had a chance at a relationship, she had to know what it was.

It was haunting them. It was a dark stormcloud permanently hanging over their heads. Because no matter how charming, how happy Iain seemed to be, the only time the shadows really disappeared from his eyes was when they were making love.

And it wasn't enough. It wasn't enough for her any more.

Her stomach twisted. Iain still didn't know. He still didn't know about the fact she'd had a hysterectomy and couldn't have children. He'd accepted her story about being injured by a horse as a young girl and had never questioned her scarring.

This was a man who had wanted a family. A family that she couldn't give him.

Maybe his past experience would have put him off. Maybe he would tell her that he could never go through that again. It was a possibility. But it was one they had never discussed.

She had to get things out in the open. *They* had to get things out in the open.

She wanted honesty from him. She wanted full disclosure. No matter what it was.

Iain McKenzie had rapidly turned into her dream man. But his constant reassurance and support was about to backfire. Her new-found confidence made her realise what she wanted in this life.

She didn't want to be a bystander. She didn't want to be known as someone's daughter. She wanted to be loved for who she was. She didn't want things to be hidden from her. And she didn't want to have to hide anything from him.

And while she didn't mind the photos of Bonnie in Iain's house, she didn't know what they meant for them. Would Iain ever lose the shadows in his eyes? It was a miserable, selfish thought but she couldn't compete with a ghost. If Bonnie still had the biggest part of his heart then Lexi shouldn't be here. She couldn't allow herself to be second best. No matter how cruel it might seem. She deserved better.

If this relationship had any chance at all, it was time to take the big step.

She stopped walking. 'Iain, we need to talk.'

He turned to face her immediately and she sensed him hesitate as he drew in a deep breath.

Had he heard the tremble in her voice? Or was he noticing the sheen in her eyes?

Then, before she had a chance to say anything, his arms swept her in and his lips descended on hers.

It was as if all the rage and pent-up frustration was being translated into his passion for her. His arms cradled her, but his lips devoured her. Their teeth clashed as his tongue slid into her mouth. There was no mistaking how he felt about her.

And there was no mistaking how she felt about him.

He pulled back, breathless, his arms gently releasing their grip on her waist. In this dim light his dark chocolate eyes looked almost black. Darker than the bottom of his soul.

He'd blindsided her with that kiss. For a second all

her rational thoughts had vanished, as had the sinking feeling in her heart.

They stood together next to the Thames, their warm breath visible in the cold air as her rapid heartbeat quietened to a mild canter.

She had to stay focused.

She had to think of the future.

Hers. And Iain's. She needed more than his passion. She needed more than his protectiveness.

She needed his heart and his soul.

His hands rested on her hips. 'Lexi, I'm sorry about my behaviour. When I saw him touching you like that— assaulting you—I saw red. It just descended all around me. I couldn't wait to get my hands on him. I couldn't wait to get him away from you. I didn't want him near you.'

There was tension in his words—as if he'd just taken himself back to the moment again. He thought she was angry. He thought she wanted to talk to him about the incident with Jack.

'I was filled with rage. I wanted to punch him senseless.'

She lifted her hand and put it on his chest. 'And I might have let you.'

He shook his head. 'But I never behave like that.' He squeezed his eyes shut for a moment then gave her a sorry smile. 'But, with hindsight, you seemed to have got the better of him yourself.'

She nodded. 'But that doesn't mean I didn't appreciate the help.' This wasn't the conversation she wanted to have. She didn't want to waste a second of her life talking about Jack Parker.

She could tell Iain was nervous. Maybe he was worried about how he'd manhandled Jack in front of her. But Jack Parker and his welfare was the last thing on her mind right now.

He knew something was wrong. Even though his hands were on her hips, he couldn't look her in the eye. They were fixed over her shoulder on Tower Bridge.

'I need to ask you something, Iain.'

'What is it?' His eyes had met hers now. He looked worried. For the first time since she'd known him he looked afraid. What did Iain have to be scared of?

Maybe she should start slowly.

'I need to ask you why. Why do you think you felt like that?'

Confusion swept his face. 'Why do you think? Because he touched you, because he assaulted you. He should never have laid a hand on you.'

She breathed in slowly through her nose. 'And you didn't like that?' She was trying to be controlled. She was trying to be measured. Iain meant the world to her and she was going to have to be strong to do this.

'What about us?'

He stiffened, his shoulders pushing back and down, his body arching away from her. 'What do you mean, "What about us?"'

She ran her tongue along her lips. All of a sudden her mouth was instantly dry. She could do with some of the wine she'd refused at the award ceremony. She knew exactly what she was doing. Even if Iain didn't.

'Where do you think we are going, Iain?'

He shook his head. 'I don't understand. Where did this come from?' He reached up and touched her cheek. 'You know how I feel about you.'

She held her breath, trying not to turn her head towards his cheek. She had to stay strong.

'I care about you, Lexi. You know I do.'

Care.

A gentle word. A quiet word. A word without passion and without soul. Nothing like the passion he'd just shown her. Her heart could break in two right now.

Her gaze swept down to the wet street. Black, totally black. Just like the sensations that were coursing through her body.

'Care. It's an interesting choice of word.' Even she could hear how detached her voice sounded. How disappointed.

He wasn't looking at her again. She understood. He *couldn't* look at her. He couldn't give her any more. Put him on the spot and he just shut down.

This was pointless. She wanted more than Iain could ever offer her. It was time to walk away.

This was a disaster. This whole night had been a disaster and it was nothing to do with Lexi not winning the award.

She deserved better than him. He should have watched her more closely—kept an eye on her. Jack Parker would never have got his hands on her then. He shuddered to think what could have happened in there.

He hadn't been able to protect her. Just like he hadn't been able to protect his wife.

But now Lexi was asking him difficult questions. It would be so much easier to shrug them off and just continue as before. Their relationship was developing slowly. But he still couldn't be honest with her. He wasn't ready.

But her trembling lips were breaking his resolve—no matter how hard she was trying to hide them.

'I don't care about you, Iain.'

His head shot around to face her. 'What?'

She shook her head firmly as a single tear trailed down her cheek. She lifted her hand and pressed it against her chestbone. 'I love you. I didn't want to. I *don't* want to. But I can't help how I feel.' She looked at him with her big blue eyes. 'But I know you don't feel the same, Iain. I can tell. I can *feel* it.'

He opened his mouth to speak but she lifted her hand to stop him.

'Don't. Don't make this any harder than it already is. You can't share with me—not really. There are permanent shadows around your eyes. The only time they vanish is when we make love. And it's not enough, Iain. It's not enough for me. I can't compete with a ghost.'

'What?' Her words resounded around his head. 'You think you're competing with Bonnie? Why on earth would you think that?'

'Because you won't let me in.' Her answer came back straight away. 'I need more. I want more. I want you to love me like I love you. We all have secrets, Iain. Things that we don't share with anyone but the people we love.'

His eyes fixed on the black flowing water, rushing and tumbling past them. This was it. It was time to tell Lexi the truth. They had no future together. But she had to know it was because of him—not because of her. And not because of a ghost.

'I don't deserve you, Lexi. I don't deserve anyone. All I do is hurt the people I love.'

Her brow wrinkled. 'This *is* about Bonnie, isn't it? Why on earth would you say that? You've told me about

Bonnie, and about your children. That was a tragedy. A horrible thing to happen to anyone. But it was bad luck. Horrible, horrible bad luck. But why does that mean we can't have a chance?'

Her words were swimming through his head. Juggling back and forth with the blackness and feelings of guilt. The horrible weight of responsibility.

It was almost as if someone had pushed a little button, flicked a switch somewhere inside him. He couldn't think about the 'right' words to say.

He couldn't think at all. He had to get this over with. Once Lexi knew the truth she would happily walk away.

'*Because it was my fault!*' he yelled.

The words echoed through the inky black night, carrying along the dark path and beyond.

Lexi flinched backwards, shock stamped all across her face.

There was silence. Iain couldn't speak, he was surrounded by the steamy breath that he'd just shot out and his heart was pounding in his chest.

He said it. He'd got it out there. But instead of feeling the weight of relief he might have, he just wanted to crumple down into a ball. He'd lost his wife and children because of his selfish behaviour. Instead of protecting his family, he'd destroyed them completely. No wonder he had problems sleeping at night.

Lexi looked stunned. Her hand touched his sleeve. Her voice was quiet, almost whispering. 'How? How can it be your fault? Your wife died during childbirth.'

He squeezed his eyes shut. 'It's my fault because Bonnie had wanted to give up IVF. We'd already had two attempts and she was done. She'd had enough.' He opened his eyes again to face Lexi, pointing his finger at his chest. 'It's my fault because I persuaded her to give it one last go. We still had viable embryos. I wanted to give them a chance. I didn't stop and think about the effects on Bonnie—mentally and physically. I was so fixated on getting a family. I thought with my love and support we would be fine.'

It was like scraping an iron claw down her back, digging it deep into her delicate flesh. He had no idea how much those words hurt. She didn't believe it had been Iain's fault for a second. But he'd just revealed how fixated he was on a family. A family she could never provide. Yet another reason to leave.

'Are you honestly telling me that Bonnie was unhappy being pregnant?'

'What? Of course not. She was delighted. She was over the moon to fall pregnant. And when we found out she was having twins it made everything she'd ever gone through seem worthwhile.'

'So how does that make it your fault, Iain? Bonnie could have said no. She could have refused to be implanted again.'

'But she did, Lexi. I persuaded her. *I did.*' Even though he'd got the words out there, his frustration was still building in his chest. His voice was rising. 'If I had left Bonnie alone she would still be here. If I hadn't pushed for the final round of IVF Bonnie wouldn't have died. She'd still be alive. Still here to breathe. Still here to do the things she loved with the people she loved. Instead, I see her every night in my dreams. I see the panic on her face as she realises something is wrong, something is very wrong. I watch the monitors around her as she starts to bleed out and her blood pressure plummets. Amidst the panic in the room I hear her whisper to save the babies as she squeezes my hand. She believed in me, Lexi. She trusted me to save our children.'

He leaned against the barrier to the Thames, putting his head in his hands. His legs were shaking. He was back in that brightly lit room again. Filled with more doctors and midwives than he'd ever imagined. Every time he turned he was in someone's way. Watching the life drain out of his beloved wife, and watching the faces of the staff as they eventually delivered two still white babies.

'I don't deserve you, Lexi. I don't deserve *anyone*.' The words hissed out of his mouth.

He waited a moment then straightened up. Most of the anger had dissipated from his body, along with most of his energy. He stared at the black water. His shoulders sagged. He couldn't peel his eyes away from the dark, churning water. It matched his mood. 'You've no idea. To hear the words of the doctor telling you that he's so sorry about your wife and your children.' He turned to face her, to look into her blue eyes and catch the flutter of her sparkling dress in the cold breeze. His heart squeezed in his chest.

Lexi. His beautiful little butterfly. The first person he'd connected with in years. The first person he'd loved in years.

Words couldn't begin to describe the rage he'd felt when he'd seen Jack with his hands on Lexi. He hadn't been able to control himself. The red mist had just descended.

She was his. His. And he couldn't bear the thought of someone hurting her.

But what right did he have to defend her, a woman who could clearly defend herself?

And more importantly, what right did he have to expose her to his failings? He couldn't protect the woman he loved. Life had already proved that.

He couldn't do to her what he'd done to Bonnie. Lexi was the one bright thing in his life right now. He had to let her go. He couldn't drag her down with him.

Lexi was the equivalent of a shooting star. He wanted her to reach for the moon and be free to fly. She deserved someone who could love her wholeheartedly and give her the attention she deserved. In his eyes she was more beautiful than she could ever imagine. Just her smile was enough for him. The smile that reached straight up from her heart and made her eyes sparkle.

But her eyes weren't sparkling right now. Tears were marring her pretty face, tears of sadness and pity—pity he didn't deserve.

He inhaled deeply. She had to understand this wasn't about her at all. This was all about the encompassing guilt and grief that still filled him.

'You've no idea what it's like for the doctor to ask you if you had decided on names for your children.'

It was almost as if she could read his mind. She laid the palms of her hands on his chest. He felt his chest wall move against her. She knew. Lexi felt real empathy for people. It was the reason they reacted so well to her. Right now, she *knew*.

She knew how desperate he felt about naming his children without Bonnie. They'd had some provisional names but hadn't agreed on any. To name them without her—to spend the rest of his life wondering if Bonnie would have agreed with his choices—had felt like the final nail on the single oak and two white matching coffins.

'What did you call your children?'

She'd stayed exactly where she was. Touching him. Not running away in revulsion at his actions.

'Isla and Ross.' All he could see right now were the three red poppies etched on the grave.

Lexi nodded slowly. 'They are beautiful names. I'm sure that Bonnie would have loved them.' She looked up at him. 'I can't believe you've felt like this for the last few years. I can't believe you've not spoken to anyone about this. It was not your fault, Iain. It wasn't.' She stepped back and put some distance between them. 'I didn't know Bonnie but she wouldn't have blamed you for this. She wouldn't have wanted you to be crippled by guilt. Bonnie loved you, Iain—she loved you. She wouldn't have wanted this for you.' She held her arms out. 'She couldn't possibly.'

And there she was, holding her arms open towards him. And after all that she'd said tonight, it was like an unspoken invitation. One that he just couldn't take.

No matter how much he wanted to.

He stepped towards her. 'It's late. Let me walk you home.'

They stood under the streetlight and he could see the fleeting look in her eyes. The one that realised, no matter what he'd just revealed, there was no way forward for them. There was no noise. No sound. Just a drip of tears down her face.

He couldn't do it. He couldn't look at her. Otherwise he might cry too. Cry over the woman he'd already lost, and the woman he was about to lose.

'I can't offer you anything, Lexi. I've got nothing to give.'

He started to walk along the river path, giving her

no option but to follow him or be left standing herself in the middle of the night. His gran would have killed him over his lack of manners. But right now he couldn't even think straight.

Her heels caught up with him and then slowed as she stopped herself from walking alongside him, deliberately leaving herself walking a few steps behind. Maybe it was better this way?

The streets of London had never seemed so long or so bleak. Every step seemed to go nowhere. All the streets looked the same. Her footsteps never wavered behind him. She didn't try to touch him or talk to him again.

What must she think of him? A thought flashed through his mind. If she quit right now, Leo would kill him.

Lexi was doing a spectacular job at the clinic. And work was the one thing that gave her confidence in her abilities. Maybe he should quit? Maybe he should just leave to let Lexi get on with her life and meet someone new.

The pain in his stomach was so sudden it almost stopped him dead. Lexi with someone else. Was that really what he wanted? And if that was really what he wanted, why did he want to be sick here and now?

All of a sudden her door loomed in front of him. He heard her fumble for her key and slot it into the lock. He couldn't even look at her.

She wasn't his. He couldn't hurt her any more. He had to get away. He caught one last whiff of her heady perfume, the one that had driven him nuts for weeks.

'I'm sorry,' he whispered as he walked away.

CHAPTER THIRTEEN

THE BIRDS WERE even earlier than usual, their singing
causing thumps around her brain. She put her head
under the pillow. But after a few minutes it hadn't
helped.

Last night she'd cried herself to sleep after drinking
two glasses of wine. She was bundled up in the fleeciest
pyjamas she owned. March was still cold in London.
She couldn't bear to wear one of the satin nightdresses
she'd been wearing when she'd shared her bed with Iain.
Even though they'd offered no warmth at all, she hadn't
needed it. She'd had Iain to cuddle up to.

Her stomach turned over. Iain. The look in his eyes
last night. At one point she'd thought if she'd touched
him, her big, burly, handsome Scotsman might crumble.

Her heart ached for him. Now it was all out there.
Now she knew everything. And it was all her fault.

Why had she pushed him? What had it achieved?

She'd pushed him for information she could have
lived without knowing. He blamed himself. He'd spent
the last few years blaming himself.

What must that feel like? What must it feel like to
wake up every day feeling responsible for the deaths
of your wife and children? No wonder he'd never man-

aged to have another relationship. No wonder he'd told her he couldn't sleep at night.

Her stomach twisted again. There it was. His scent on her pillows. She was never going to be close enough to him to smell that again. She was never going to hold his hand. Feel his lips on hers. Feel his hands on her body.

She thumped her fist into the pillow. How could she work with him every day after all this? Some days he spent at Kate's. But at some point every day he would be in the clinic. In her work space. Just waiting for an unsuspecting moment when they would run into one another.

Maybe she should find another job? She clenched her eyes tightly shut. She loved her job. More than loved it. It was one of the things she was most proud of. Her nomination for the award had just been the icing on the cake. Did she really want to leave the job she loved? Or could she really face having to see Iain on a daily basis? From what she knew of him, it would hurt him just as much as it hurt her.

She wrapped her hands around her stomach. Maybe this wasn't emotional pain, maybe this was real pain. It certainly felt that way.

The alarm sounded next to her head and she flung her pillow at it as she swung her legs out of bed. Normally she jumped out of the bed in the morning, anxious to get to work. This definitely wasn't going to be one of those days.

The sight that greeted her in the mirror wasn't a good one. Her skin was so pale it was almost translucent, the dark circles under her eyes made her look ten years older. Smudges all over her face revealed that the last thing she'd been thinking about last night had been re-moving her make-up. Her hair was a tangled mess. She picked up a lock and dropped it again. She didn't have a single hair product that could remedy this.

She switched on the shower. She wanted to wash everything away. All the questions she'd asked. All the things she'd been told. Every look of hurt and pain on Iain's face.

He hadn't even said goodbye last night. She'd just watched him walk back along the street with his head down.

She stepped into the shower. 'Owwww!' It was scalding. She stood in the corner of the cubicle and braved her hand underneath the flow to turn the dial. A few seconds later she stepped under the torrent of water, turning her face up to meet its blast.

Wash it all away. Wash it all away.

Seven gallons of conditioner and a tube of facial scrub later she stepped out. She pulled a sombre black suit from her cupboard, looked at it for a few minutes then flung it aside.

She reached in again, this time finding a form-fitting emerald-green dress. It was power dressing. And the last thing she felt like doing today.

She looked in the mirror again as she sat down to dry her hair. Her make-up lay across the dressing-table. She lifted her chin and looked again, determination flooding through her.

If this was the end and if she was going out, she was going out fighting.

This will be a good day. She kept repeating the words in her head like a mantra as she walked along the street.

It stopped her from bursting into tears. She was going to have to get used to this. There was no getting away from it, she was going to have to see Iain every day at work whether it broke her heart or not.

The first time was always the hardest. And she was absolutely determined no one would see her cry. She was a professional.

She did her best to sweep though the reception area of the clinic as quickly as possible. 'Hi, Lexi,' Mel, one of the receptionists on duty, called. 'I'm so sorry about last night.'

Her stiletto heels stopped abruptly. She spun round, trying to stop her mouth from gaping open. 'What?'

Mel stood up and walked over towards her, a quizzical expression on her face. 'The awards, of course. We all thought you should have won.'

The panic subsided. She could breathe again. Just as well really, because a few other staff had emerged and were all looking at her.

She pasted a smile on her face. 'Oh, thanks for that. I was just happy to be there.'

Fiona, another receptionist, stood up from behind the desk and picked up a tabloid newspaper. 'You made the headlines.'

Lexi felt her blood run cold. She moved over to the desk and looked at the front page. 'Iain McKenzie's secret love—Lexi Robbins'. She let out a strangled gasp. 'What?'

Both receptionists laughed. 'It's a great picture, isn't it?' Mel gave her a sideways glance. 'You do look like a couple, by the way. And how on earth did you get our Scotsman into a kilt? He looks good enough to eat.'

'He phoned in this morning,' said Fiona. 'Something's came up. Asked me to cancel his appointments this morning. He's going to be stuck at the Lighthouse Hospital all day.'

Her mouth dried instantly. She couldn't speak as her eyes scanned the article. 'Can I keep this?' she asked, trying not to crumple the paper beneath her grasp.

'Sure, I'll buy another one.'

'Thanks.' Her feet flew down the corridor until she reached her office and slammed the door behind her. No! This was the last thing she wanted.

In a way she felt a sense of relief. Iain wouldn't be here today. She wouldn't need to see him. She wouldn't need to face him. Maybe he hadn't even seen the paper—after all, she hadn't until she'd come to work this morning.

She sat behind her desk. The first thing that caught her attention was the picture.

It was in full colour, showing off Lexi's dress and Iain's kilt in all their glory. But the thing that had obviously captured the photographer's interest was the look that was passing between them. It was there for the whole world to see.

They were both smiling, looking straight into each other's eyes. Neither of them was looking at the camera. Iain's hand was wrapped around her waist and with his other he was holding her hand—right in front of her stomach.

And with a look like that between them...

She put her head on the desk and groaned. This would be a disaster. She started to read.

Internet sensation Dr Iain McKenzie attended the Dakota Jefferson Awards last night with Lexi Rob-

*bins, daughter of supermodel Penelope Crosby
and chat show host Steve Robbins. Speculation
was rising last night regarding their relationship.*

*It was apparent they only had eyes for each
other as they spent most of the evening together
and sneaked off early after the awards. Lexi was
dressed in an as yet unidentified stylish designer
dress, with Iain in a black and white kilt, revealing more of his now famous physique.*

*Lexi and Iain work together at the Hunter
Clinic in Harley Street and she was nominated
for one of the PR awards. But maybe this is her
biggest PR coup of all?*

*Lexi launched the commercial featuring Iain
McKenzie just a few days ago and it currently has
over nineteen million views on the internet. Not
much is known about Iain McKenzie, a thirty-
five-year-old reconstructive plastic surgeon from
Edinburgh. He was widowed following the death
of his wife Bonnie three years ago.*

*Maybe Lexi Robbins has caught the biggest
catch of all?*

Could this really be any worse? Wait until Iain saw
it, it made her sound as if she'd deliberately set out to
catch him—all for the sake of publicity. Too bad her
heart only functioned around Iain and not her brain.
She couldn't have planned this if she'd tried.

The corners of her mouth turned up as she noticed a
little picture down in the bottom corner of the piece. The
one with her mother, her father and herself. Penelope
would go ballistic. Of all the people in the world she'd
expect to push her off the front page, Lexi would never

be one. For the first time that day a tiny little surge of pleasure crept through her. It was childish, and she'd never say the words out loud, but just imagining the look on her mother's face this morning would be pleasure enough. It would make up for almost being completely ignored last night.

The moment passed. And the feeling of dread returned.

What would this mean for Iain? She was cringing just thinking about it. She knew exactly how invasive the media could be. It was a miracle that they'd never found out about her hysterectomy. What if they dug into Iain's background and found out about the death of his children? That would be awful.

There was a knock on the door, followed by some muffled sounds as someone struggled with the handle. Then a burst of rainbow colours entered the room.

It was the biggest display of flowers Lexi had ever seen. Absolutely beautiful. Red, pink, yellow and orange roses, carnations and tulips, white freesias, purple and white irises and masses of greenery. In between it all were silver strands, just like the sequins on her dress last night. It was like a veritable explosion of colour.

Carrie struggled to get them through the door and slid them across the desk towards Lexi, who was already on her feet. Her heart was thudding in her chest. She worked in PR and had seen massive bouquets before, but nothing like this.

'Wow, Lexi, aren't they gorgeous?' She handed over a card in a silver envelope. 'Hopefully this will make you feel a bit better.'

'What do you mean?' She stood with the card in her hand. Who would have sent her something like this?

Her heart started thudding against her chest wall. It couldn't be—could it? Would Iain really make a gesture this big? No one at the clinic was supposed to know they were seeing each other. As far as everyone at work was concerned, Iain had gone along to the award ceremony because he'd nominated her. Nothing else. Until that picture in the newspaper this morning.

'I never got a chance to talk to you this morning, but you looked kinda sad. Are you upset about not winning last night?'

Lexi was startled by Carrie's question. Not winning was the last thing on her mind this morning. She hadn't even given it a second thought.

She shook her head firmly. 'No, not at all.'

'Then what is it?' Carrie walked around the desk and touched the tabloid at the corner of it. 'Is it this?'

She pointed to the photo of Iain and Lexi, holding hands and looking at each other as if no one else in the world existed.

It was automatic. The welling of tears in her eyes. She pulled the silver envelope apart and took out the card.

Next time it will be yours!
Love from Leo and your colleagues at the Hunter Clinic.
We're so proud you're part of our team. x

Iain. It wasn't from Iain. This wasn't some fairy story with a happy ending. A few tears escaped and slid down her cheeks.

Carrie walked behind her, reading the card over her

shoulder. 'Oh, that's so nice, isn't it? Lexi? Don't be upset.'

She wrapped her arms around her friend and gave her a hug. There it was. The first tiny sign of life. The smallest little bump in her friend's abdomen.

She made a dive for the tissues on her desk to wipe her face and nose.

'I'm fine, Carrie. Really I am. It's just a lovely gesture.' She straightened up and touched the petal of one of the pink roses. 'And the flowers smell gorgeous.'

Carrie nodded. From the expression on her face it was clear that she knew something else was wrong but she was wise enough not to pry any further.

She pointed towards the office door. 'I've just made some coffee. I'll bring you some and then I'll shut the door, shall I? Give you some privacy to get on with your work.' The phones were ringing loudly outside. 'We've got about a hundred messages for you this morning, and just as many for Iain. Why don't I filter them and leave you both the ones that are appropriate?' She gave a little smile. 'I'm assuming that you two don't want to advertise baked beans on TV?'

Lexi let out a laugh. 'Really?'

Carrie nodded. 'Oh, yes. Some of the messages will make your hair curl!' She counted off on her fingers. 'Dating companies, condom adverts, bra adverts, and a few very slimy offers of dates.'

Lexi let a shiver go down her spine. 'Oh, no, thanks. Yes, Carrie, filter away. I'd be very grateful.'

A few minutes later a strong coffee appeared on her desk followed by the sound of her door closing quietly. Carrie really was a good friend.

She scrolled through her emails, deleting many as

she went along. Interview request after interview request. Some from very dubious sources. A few from journalists about her charity work. She swithered. Did they really want to know about the charity work or were they just looking at a way to get access to her private life and Iain? She knew exactly how some journalists worked.

She flagged a few and decided to talk to Leo about them. After all, this was his clinic and although she was Head of PR, they needed to agree their plans.

The next few emails made her eyes boggle. Men. Inviting her on dates. And that was just the polite ones. The others were enough to turn her lukewarm curls into tight spirals.

After that there was a whole host of congratulatory emails and a few invites to give lectures to university students on PR. One was from her own university and she replied instantly. Finally, she flagged the ones that were real work. There were a number of issues with the charities that would have to be dealt with promptly, so she put her head down and gave them her immediate attention.

A knock at the door startled her. She gave a sigh. It would probably be another member of staff coming to offer sympathy. It wasn't that she wasn't grateful, but they'd been popping in all morning and she still had a ton of work to get done.

She held her breath. Maybe if she didn't answer they would think she wasn't in. It wasn't exactly perfect behaviour, but it would get her work done more quickly.

The knock sounded again. Mr or Mrs Persistence was not going to be put off. The door opened and she tried to duck behind the flowers. She really didn't want to talk to anyone right now.

'Lexi?'

Her head shot back around the mountain of flowers. 'Iain?' Her reaction was automatic, she stood up. She wanted to cringe. He must have seen the papers. He was probably in here to complain.

It was all she could do not to drink in the sight of him. He wasn't supposed to be here all day, so she wasn't prepared. She hadn't gone over in her head what she would say to him about last night. How to apologise for pushing him for an answer he obviously wasn't ready to give.

Her eyes narrowed. 'Iain? Why have you got scrubs on?'

He stepped into the room and closed the door behind him. 'Because I didn't have time to get changed.'

She drew in a deep breath. Iain, in navy blue scrubs revealing tanned, muscled arms and the thin material brushing against his big thighs. His hair looked as if he had just released it from a theatre cap and run his fingers through it. There was a dark shadow along his chin and a few dark shadows around his eyes. He'd obviously slept as little as she had.

'Why didn't you have time to get changed?' she asked, trying not to wonder if this question was a smoking gun. Did he want her fired over all the publicity—all the assumptions the press had made?

He walked towards her. She couldn't read his face at all. All she could see was fatigue. But there was something else. Something she didn't expect at all.

There was sparkle in his eyes.

'I've been at the Lighthouse since six a.m. Emergency surgery on a child in a road accident. The NHS surgeons needed a hand as things were more complicated than they expected and their own plastic surgeon was at the burns unit with another child.'

She nodded. It might be slightly unusual but because of the reciprocal relationship between the clinic and the two hospitals, on rare occasions they were asked to help out.

'So what's the big rush that you couldn't get changed?' She walked around the desk, her steps hesitant as she made her way towards him. 'Iain, is this about the newspapers? I'm so sorry about that. I've prepared a press release.' She lifted a piece of paper from her desk. 'I was just going to double-check with Leo before I put it out. Have you been harassed this morning?'

His brow wrinkled and he sat down in the chair opposite her with a sigh. 'Lexi, what are you talking about?'

She nodded at the tabloid on her desk.

He picked it up and started to read. Then something unexpected happened. Iain McKenzie flung back his head and laughed. The loudest laugh she'd ever heard from him.

'I bet your mother loved this,' he said, waving the paper at her.

Her heart jumped. He wasn't angry. He wasn't angry at all. Maybe he wasn't here to tear a strip off her after all.

She sat down in the chair next to him. 'Funnily enough, I haven't heard from her this morning.'

He raised his eyebrows. 'Now, there's a surprise.'

Her stomach was churning. Iain reached over and grabbed her lukewarm coffee, finishing it in one gulp.

She closed her eyes. He was too close. And she had no idea what was happening right now. 'I'm sorry, Iain.'

'You're sorry? Sorry about what?'

She took a deep breath and opened her eyes. 'I'm sorry about last night.' She indicated the paper. 'I'm sorry about that. I'm sorry about filming the advert and getting you so much unwanted attention.' She took another breath. 'And most of all I'm sorry about pushing you to tell me something you weren't ready to.'

Iain sat silent for a few minutes. 'I knew it, you're officially crazy.'

'What?' She couldn't believe it. What on earth was going on?

He stood up and pointed at the flowers. 'Tell me one thing. Should I be worried? Is someone else about to steal you away?'

She couldn't answer. She was flabbergasted. He walked around the monster bouquet and knelt in front of her.

He stared up at her with his big brown eyes. 'Because I want you to know, Lexi Robbins, I'll fight to the death for you,' he whispered.

This time her breath caught in her throat. 'They're from Leo,' she said hoarsely, 'and the rest of the staff at the clinic.'

'You don't know how glad I am to hear that. Lexi, honey, you have nothing to be sorry for. Not a single thing.' He reached out and took her hand.

'Wh-what do you mean?' Her voice was trembling. Her hands were trembling too.

Iain looked different this morning. And that didn't include the scrubs. He looked as if the weight of the world had been lifted off his shoulders. There wasn't a brooding black cloud hanging over him. There was sadness in his eyes, but it was different. It was focused entirely on *her*. Not on someone else.

His hand closed firmly around hers. 'I mean that I'm the one who should be sorry. And I'm the one who should be thanking you.'

She shook her head. 'I don't get it. What's happened?'

'I don't get it either. But I know who got me here.' He stood up, pulling her into his arms.

'From the first second I met you, no, from the first second I smelled you, you started to wake me up. You started to make me *feel* again.'

She didn't know what to say. This was so unexpected. And she was scared. He was touching her, holding her. But after last night she couldn't believe it was true.

'Iain, what's going on here?'

He lifted his hand and ran a gentle finger down her cheek. 'It's you, Lexi Robbins. This is all about you.'

Her hand reached up and covered his. She was still trembling, she couldn't help it. Had she fallen asleep at her desk? Was she in the middle of a dream? This really couldn't be happening.

Iain's warm breath was on her skin. She could smell his scent with every breath she took. 'Lexi, you're the bravest woman I've ever met. Even with the parents you have—and the bad experience of Jack Parker— you have never given up on love. Last night, when you weren't afraid to tell me you wanted more. You *deserve* more. I realised exactly what I could lose if I couldn't stop being afraid.'

She shook her head. 'You're not afraid of things, Iain. You're just not ready.'

He smiled. 'I thought I wasn't ready. But my body...' he pointed at his chest '...and heart were telling me something different.' He ran his fingers down her arms and put his hands back at her waist. 'Last night helped me gain some perspective. I finally said the words out loud. I've waited a long time for that.'

She couldn't help it. No matter how confused she was feeling right now, she couldn't stay away. She wound her arms around his neck and held him close. Their breathing unified. Up and down at the same time. They stayed like that for a few minutes.

If only time could just stop here. If only she could stay in this moment for ever. This could be perfect.

But it wasn't. It couldn't be.

Iain was having an epiphany in his life. He had hopes and dreams. And she was about to dash some of them because she'd been so focused on him telling her the truth that she hadn't done it herself.

She pulled back a little and touched his cheek just below his dark eyes. This was where she wanted to stay. This was who she wanted to stay with. He was smiling at her now. Capturing her heart the way he'd captured the heart of all the women watching the advertisement. Iain could do that to you, with just one look.

'I'm so glad you finally said those words,' she whispered. 'You would have been a wonderful father.' Would he hear the sadness in her tone? Would he understand when she told him she didn't want to steal that opportunity from him?

But Iain looked happy, his skin was brighter and his eyes positively shining. His voice lowered, taking on a quiet tone. 'Bonnie loved me, Lexi. I can say that with pride. And I loved her. We *both* wanted that family together.'

This was it. This was where everything she wanted fell apart.

'She wouldn't have wanted this for me. She would have wanted me to move on.' His eyes lowered to meet hers. 'She would have wanted me to be happy. Happy with you.'

She took a step back, out of his embrace. Her head was starting to swim. She'd never been the type to go weak at the knees, but right now she felt as if she was about to take a swan dive. She thumped down into the chair behind her.

'Don't, Iain. Don't do this.' She closed her eyes tightly.

'What's wrong? What do you mean?' He knelt down in front of her again. His face still had that exuberant look about it. He was still caught up in the moment. Thinking that they could both have their happy-ever-after. 'Do you know what I dreamed about last night, Lexi?'

He didn't give her a chance to answer.

'You. I dreamed about you. It's not the first time and it won't be the last. But now I can go to sleep knowing that I won't be haunted by nightmares. Now I know that when I close my eyes it's going to be good memories and a happy future.'

She bit her lip. She had to stop him. She had to stop him now. Before he said that those dreams were filled with their children dancing beside them.

She lifted her hand. 'Stop, Iain. Just stop.'

He pulled back a little. 'What's wrong?'

Tears started to flow down her cheeks. 'I don't want

you to tell me the next part. I'm not the woman for you. We're not going to sail off into the sunset with a family around us.'

'Lexi? Lexi, what's wrong?' He leaned forward and put his hands on her shoulders. 'Why are you crying? What is it?'

She lifted one of his hands off her shoulder and pressed it to her stomach, her hand over his. 'I can't give you your dream, Iain. I can't give you the family that you want.'

She started to sob. Now she'd started crying she didn't know how to stop.

'Lexi?' His voice had deepened but he didn't sound angry, he sounded concerned.

She fumbled for her bag and pulled out a dog-eared photograph and pushed it towards him. He picked it up and squinted at it, before placing it on her lap.

'It's you. With a baby. You look so young. What are you telling me?' The concern was laced all through his voice.

She sniffed. 'I told you that my Aunt Josephine looked after me for a while?'

He nodded.

'She is the wisest woman I've ever known. When I had my accident I was only twelve. Horses can do a lot of damage to a young body.'

He nodded seriously but said nothing, letting her continue.

She tried to brush away some of her tears. 'I had a hysterectomy, Iain. I had a hysterectomy when I was twelve. I'm never going to be able to give you the children that you want.'

She pointed to the photo. 'This is my life. This is

how I will get my family. My aunt knew straight away what she was doing when she took me to that orphanage. She was showing me that there were children who needed love. Children who needed families. Children all over the world who could benefit from being adopted.' She met his eyes. 'That's the only way I can get the family I want.'

His face broke into a smile. 'And why is that so awful? Why is that something to cry about?'

'Because it's not your only option.' The words shot out of her mouth. She didn't mean them to sound bitter. But it was the thing that was front and foremost in her mind.

He touched her face again, brushing away her tears. 'The option that I want is you.'

Her voice still trembled. 'But you deserve so much more.' Her eyes were heavy with tears and although she was scared to look at him she had to.

He stood over her, looking at her with his deep chocolate eyes with sincerity radiating from them. 'What I hope I deserve—if you're willing to forgive me—is you. You—Lexi Robbins—are the most important person to me in the world right now.'

His voice was so sincere, so solid that she took in a shuddery breath. She'd thought he would want a family too much to stay with her. 'But—'

He put his finger across her lips. 'But nothing. I watched you at the Tower. You will make some lucky children a fabulous mother. And I really hope above everything that I can make a good dad. You've got years' worth of contacts with your orphanage in China. I have contacts with the orphanage I'm going back to in Romania this summer. If there is a way to make this happen,

Lexi, we will.' He wound her hair around his fingers, cradling her head in his hands. 'And if for some reason it doesn't, then I'll still be the happiest man alive, growing old with the woman I love.'

Lexi's eyes widened. Her whole body was starting to shake. 'Iain?'

He knelt down on one knee in front of her, pulling a pale blue box from his scrubs pocket. 'I've been an idiot. I've had the most wonderful, bravest woman that I know right in front of me for the last six weeks. And it's about time I shouted to the world how proud I am of her. Lexi Robbins, will you do me the honour of being my wife?' He shifted on his knees as he held the box out towards her. 'In sickness and in health, for better or worse, for richer or poorer?'

He flipped open the box. A beautiful high-set single heart-shaped diamond.

She was shaking as he gave her a smile, a wink and continued. He nodded to the dog-eared photo sitting on the desk. 'I promise to love you even if you don't use frizz-prevention products on your hair.'

She drew in a mock sharp breath as her face broke into a smile at his cheeky comment.

'I promise to love you when you tell kids scary stories at the Tower of London.' He pulled the ring from the box and started to slide it onto her finger. 'I promise to love you when you get soaked in the rain and your running mascara makes your face like a panda's. And I promise to love you and tell you how gorgeous you are every time you get a little sad.'

Her heart was going to burst. Iain did things in his style—and that's what she loved most about him.

She stared at the beautiful ring on her finger. She couldn't have picked anything more perfect herself.

He winked at her again. 'You could take your mother's eye out with that.'

'I certainly could.' She stood up, reaching for his hand and pulling him up with her. She gave him her gravest look. 'I have some conditions, Iain.'

He straightened his shoulders, but the amused look on his face didn't change. He was happy. He was truly happy right now, and it just radiated from him. His warmth was spreading to her. Skimming across her skin and wrapping her up in his happy glow. A lifetime of feeling like this? She'd be a fool not to say yes.

She'd be a fool not to say yes to the man she loved with her whole heart.

Although she'd known for a long time she couldn't have children naturally, here was a man who was—come what may—willing to take that journey with her. She would love to be a mother, just as much as he would love to be a father. But no matter where that journey led, they would take it together.

She reached up to touch his shaggy hair. 'You have to promise me never to cut your hair. I love it.'

He nodded solemnly. 'I do.'

She nearly let out a laugh at his response. 'Are you practising?' she whispered. He nodded.

'You have to promise me that when we get married it will be a tiny wedding. No publicity. No newspapers and…' she rolled her eyes '…definitely not my parents. Your parents, absolutely.'

His eyebrows lifted. 'I do.'

She bent down and ran her hand up the length of his thin navy scrubs. She could see him arch his back, his body responding instantly to her touch. 'You have to promise me you'll wear a kilt.'

'Aha…' He hesitated.

She quirked her head at him. She'd been expecting the 'I do' response.

'In that case…' His hands came down to her hips, pulling her up close against him. Letting her see exactly what she did to him. 'You have to promise to wear your gorgeous dress from last night. I've never seen anyone look so lovely, and that's just what I want my bride to wear. Like a beautiful butterfly.'

She wrapped her arms around his neck. 'I think I can do that.' Her blue eyes were fixed on his. She didn't want to wait. She didn't want to wait a second to marry her gruff Scotsman. 'Marylebone Registry Office?'

Iain smiled. The small registry office was obviously exactly what he had in mind. 'Random strangers from the street?'

'Sounds perfect to me.' And then he picked her up and twirled her round. Her left hand was on his shoulder and the sunlight caught her enormous ring, causing a beautiful rainbow of sparkles to reflect all around them.

He smiled when he saw them. 'Guess who just got to the end of the rainbow,' he whispered, as he set her down and kissed her like he'd never kissed her before.

* * * * *

LET'S TALK
Romance

For exclusive extracts, competitions
and special offers, find us online:

 facebook.com/millsandboon

@millsandboonuk

@millsandboon

Or get in touch on 0844 844 1351*

For all the latest titles coming soon, visit
millsandboon.co.uk/nextmonth

0141 306 3232